The Quest of Eight

Part Three:

The Flight of the Wedgamaroon

Richard Reda

Richard Reda

ISBN: 0985414006
ISBN-13: 978-0985414009

Dedication

This book is dedicated to our first eight grandchildren:

Summer

Lochen

Solveig

Sean

Natalie

Stella

Quinn

Liam

ACKNOWLEDGMENTS

A special thanks to my wife, Karren for her editing and support, and to my daughter, Jill Fox, for her editing. And a special thanks to my son Jack and my grandson Quinn for the suggestion for the title

Cover art: Mike Reda and Richard Reda

i

Chapter one

A very long time ago in a land far away, there once was a young explorer. As a boy he had been very inquisitive. For as long as he could remember, he had always wondered what was beyond the horizon. When he was old enough, he decided to leave his home and explore the world outside of his village. He began his journey with the best of intentions: to learn what was to be learned; to discover new lands, to cross uncharted seas, to encounter new and different peoples, and to enrich his life. As with many of life's adventures, things did not go as planned. This young explorer had no family to speak of, and few, if any, close friends. He had no recollection of his parents, having lost them both at an early age. He had been raised by his elderly uncle, and spent more of his youth taking care of the old man, rather than being taken care of.

Shortly after his uncle passed away, he decided there was nothing left at home to hold him back. Early one morning, he left. There was no fanfare, no pronouncements and no farewells. No one missed his presence, and no one took notice when he stopped sending letters back to the select few to whom he had written. His absence was swallowed up in the passage of time, and he soon became little more than a distant memory among those who once knew him. He really didn't care. He continued his explorations, moving farther and farther from his roots. His travels stretched from one year into the next. Before long, he had lost complete track of time. In the land of his home, old friends fell in love, got married and started families. Seasons changed; children became adults; village elders passed their leadership to the next generation. His name and everything about him eventually was forgotten.

Being a young man at the start of his journey, he was no different than other young men. He didn't necessarily think he was invincible; but he just never considered that something bad might happen to him. Consequently, he often took foolish risks and careless chances. He ventured into areas wiser travelers would normally avoid. But in trade-off, he witnessed many wondrous sights: the twin suns rising over cavernous ice fields in the northernmost reaches of his world; rocky spires carved by the winds and rains that soared so high they seemed to touch the sky; canyons that filled the horizon as far as the eye could see and so deep that the rivers at the bottom looked like strands of thread; snow capped mountains that broke through the clouds; exotic beaches covered with mystical rainbow sand – depending on the time of day, they would change colors from bright white to a golden yellow, into a sparkling pink, then a vibrant purple and finally to black.

On one occasion he had set up camp on a vast plain. He saw a herd of striped ghazal that was so large it took three days for the entire herd to pass him. Previously, these animals had been only myths he had heard about as a boy. Covered with a shimmering gray pelt lined with jagged streaks of silver, they looked like flashes of lightening as they crossed the plains before his eyes. He was so mesmerized by them that he walked straight into the middle of the herd as it stampeded on its own journey. Not a single animal touched him as they swarmed past.

On another occasion he attempted to take refuge from a storm inside a nearby cave only to encounter a nest of viper bats. The small opening to the cave led to a large cavern, which was home to over a thousand of these creatures. On this occasion, he elected not to try his luck standing in the middle and barely escaped before they attacked him.

He crafted a raft out of fallen tree trunks and weathered vines, and set sail on a mighty river. After braving treacherous currents, raging rapids and an unexpected waterfall, he was swept out to sea. Unprepared for the dangers of the oceans, he nearly perished from lack of food and water and from attacks by several different predatory sea creatures. His small vessel was torn apart in a storm and, yet, he was washed from the sea like Jonah emerging from the belly of the whale onto a distant shore along the edge of a thick tropical jungle.

In this jungle paradise he found an abundance of fruits and nuts and a supply of fresh water, but he also found himself to be considered a tasty morsel by several nasty carnivores. He quickly discovered that his youthful foolishness could very well cost him his life. He learned how to fashion weapons to protect himself and traps to snare food. As the months turned into years, he saw places and animals that far exceeded his wildest imagination.

He taught himself a myriad of skills; more than just in making weapons. He learned which plants were harmful and which ones had healing properties. He learned how to make potions and poisons. He found that the needles from a calamus plant could be used with the silk strands from a Tussah spider to do very fine stitching, which he needed to make leak proof water bags and to suture the many cuts and gashes he accumulated.

Early in his journeys he encountered several different villages and larger communities, but regardless of their size, they were all much like his own. In this new land to which he had been washed ashore, however, he began to discover people who were very different. The first of such civilizations he came upon was a village of faeries. He discovered them quite by accident one evening when he was walking along the shore. At first he thought they were a colony of dragonflies. He crept closer to study them, not wanting to frighten them off. He was stunned when he got close enough to see what they really were. He made the mistake of trying to keep his presence a secret from them – not out of any desire to harm them, but only to keep himself from harm and to observe them more closely.

The faeries, however, mistook his caution for conspiracy and cast a spell on him. They had some recent encounters with other residents of the forests that had made them suspicious of strangers. They elected not to take any chances when this very large stranger was discovered – apparently spying on them. Several of them darted at him, chasing him back up the shore. He covered his head as they buzzed and swooped. Tiny flashes of bright green light stung him several times. He was much larger than anything the faeries had seen before, and it took a while before their spell finally took effect.

The spell they cast temporarily paralyzed him. He started to stagger along the beach, unable to control his muscles. He knew he was in trouble, but there was nothing he could do. He stopped and turned to swat at them, but his arms flapped uselessly in the air until his legs gave out and he dropped to the sand. When the spell took full effect, he was completely motionless, but still fully alert. In this state several of them hovered over his prostrate body as extremely fine glittering dust fell from their wings, covering him. He later learned this was faerie dust. This dust enabled them to carry him through the air deep into the forest, far from their village, where they left him until the spell wore off.

Hours passed before they eventually deposited him in the dark of night under a thicket. In spite of his fear, he was unable to stay awake, and fell in and out of sleep during the night until the first sun rose and lightened his surroundings. When the first rays of the morning sun broke through the trees, he was still unable to move anything at all. He couldn't even move his eyes. All he could see, as far as his peripheral vision would allow, were treetops and bits of sky poking through.

For nearly a day, he lay flat on his back, unable to move, speak, or do anything to protect himself. Several small and unusual animals approached him and began to scratch at the ground around him and sniff at him. His inability to react made his fear become nearly unbearable. The faeries were not altogether cruel, though. The spell that paralyzed him also warded off any potential predators. The young explorer, however, didn't know that.

When the spell finally faded and he was able to move, it was very dark. The first clue he had that the spell was fading was when he could blink his eyes. Then he was able to turn his head. Eventually his limbs were loosened and he was able to turn over and slowly climb to his feet. His first steps were erratic, but soon, he got his feet underneath him and his walking became steadier. As soon as he was able, he started running.

He began to run through the dense forest, even though he didn't know where he was going. He tripped over roots and fallen limbs, scrambling to his feet and continuing on. Branches whipped his face and pulled at his clothes. Rational thought had given way to his fear. He ran until he was exhausted. Nearly delirious and completely lost, his panic replaced his judgment. He no longer exercised any caution whatsoever and crashed blindly through the forest.

At some point, as the dawn was finally breaking, he sat down on a log to get control of himself. After a few minutes, just as he was overcoming his fears, he heard a noise in the brush to his left. His hearing became instantly alert and he jumped to his feet. He scanned the forest for any sign of movement, and then he heard a twig snap and saw a branch move off to his far right. He jerked in that direction and thought about running. But in which direction he wondered. In an effort not to make the same mistake he made with the faeries, he called out, announcing his presence, shouting that he came in peace and meant no harm to anyone. His voice cracked with the dryness in his throat and the fear he still felt. He stood up even straighter and waved his arms.

His words, though, were foreign, and his meaning was not in the least understood. Instead of being taken as a plea for peace, his shouting sounded more like the roar of an angry animal, and his size, which was considerable larger than the forest creatures that now circled him, was intimidating. They had also suffered various spells and hexes at the hands of the faeries. Like the faeries, they were not taking any chances. This stranger in their land was viewed as a very serious threat.

The first shots that struck his body felt like the stings of small insects. The explorer didn't even know he was being attacked until the barrage increased. He looked for the source of the stinging and realized he was being pelted with small stones. He jerked his head up and yelled again, pleading for whoever was shooting to stop; and then an arrow whizzed past his ear. He needed no further warning and ran off in the opposite direction. He ran right into another barrage of small stones. He stopped short and changed direction, at first heading back towards the way he had come. Recalling his encounter with the faeries, he stopped again, only long enough to turn around and run the other way.

The stones continued to strike him, stinging more and more. As he ran, the images of his recent flight flashed through his mind. He kept his head down to avoid roots and fallen limbs, and, at the same time, stole glances upward to avoid the branches whipping his face. More arrows flew by his head; more branches cut his face; more roots tripped him up. Sweat and blood filled his eyes and he could no longer see where he was going. He just kept running. This, of course, was the intent of the forest creatures.

They had purposely missed him with their arrows, although not by much. The stones that they fired from their slingshots were meant only to sting, not to do any serious harm. They had no intention of harming him; only of driving him out of their forest. They thought he might be enchanted and were afraid he'd hex them, but they were fighting to protect their home. He tripped over roots, scraping his hands and knees; but the attack continued. With every shot that drove him further and further away, their courage and daring increased. They advanced on him relentlessly.

The explorer could not understand why his appeals went unanswered. Every time he slowed down the attack escalated. Every time he fell, he pulled himself up and wiped his face and continued running. He looked back over his shoulder to see if he could spot his attackers and try to convince them he meant no harm. However, in doing so, he slammed into a large tree. Pain shot through his shoulder and across his chest.

Pushing himself away from the tree he dove through a cluster of large palm fronds.

As soon as he did this, the ground beneath his feet disappeared. He had burst through the vegetation, run off the edge of a cliff, and was plummeting down into a narrow but swiftly running river. He looked down in horror at the ground that was racing up at him and tried to shift his body towards the tiny band of water. He waved his arms uselessly as he dropped over fifty feet. Much to his surprise, he avoided the rocks and shoals on either side of the river, and hit it nearly in the center.

The river was deep enough to slow his fall, but not so deep as to break it completely. He broke the surface angled slightly to his back, and he sliced the water like a knife. His feet struck the bottom with a bone-crunching jar. His head snapped as he hit the sand and as the shock wave ran from bottom to top. His last thought was how cold the water was, that it must flow from the snow of a nearby mountain. The shock of the water and his fall turned his world black and he partially lost consciousness.

His body bobbed to the surface and he was caught up in the current. Because of the way he landed, he initially floated face up. He got tangled in other debris being carried down the river. As he was tossed and turned by the current and the eddies, he turned over, and his subconscious forced him to cling to whatever he could grasp, keeping his head above water. Eventually, the river broadened and his limp body washed up on a bed of sand. More than ten years after he first left his home, and untold thousands of miles away, this short and rather perilous part of his journey had come to an end, and the door to another had just opened.

In his semi-consciousness he dreamt as he was carried down the river. In his dreams he was gently rocked back and forth by the tides of the sea as the suns climbed higher in the sky and warmed the soft white sand that had become his resting place. He dreamt that the light vanished and was replaced by darkness. He dreamt that he was poked and prodded by unseen objects- shadowy figures that grunted and snorted. With the growing darkness his dreams darkened.

He dreamt he was bitten by something. Needles of pain spread through one of his arms as he was dragged from his resting place. He dreamt that he floated out of his body and looked down at himself. The shadows raged above his form, growling and howling in a fierce battle. He dreamt of strange looking creatures with large heads, bristling hair and small beady eyes. In the center of their faces were upturned snouts, wide mouths and large fangs rising up from their lower jaws. He couldn't recall ever seeing anything quite like them before. There was a coldness that crept through his body when these images appeared. He was frightened and tried to force his dreams to something else. He dreamt of a flash of light followed by the return of darkness, but this time, the darkness was welcoming and the light had warmed him.

He finally awoke from the dream. When he did, he raised his head and looked around. He found himself in a comfortable bed in a large room with windows all around. A lightweight fabric covered the windows, diffusing and softening the light from outside. A warm breeze was blowing through them and the sun warmed the air. Everything in the room was white, or a very pale yellow. In spite of the brightness, though, the colors were not glaringly bright, but soft and warm.

His first thought was that he had died and that this must be heaven or some other place where he would await his final judgment. His head dropped back on the pillow on which it had been resting. He closed his eyes, but didn't fall back to sleep. After a while he sensed a presence in the room. His eyes slowly opened and focused on the form. He became certain he had died and was in some kind of heaven when an apparition appeared before him. It was a small delicate woman with beautiful long white hair that nearly disappeared into the gossamer white veils she wore. The light seemed to dance around her and she floated on air as she glided towards him.

He sat up in his bed, pushing up against the headboard, and rubbed his eyes. When the fog cleared from his mind and he could see more clearly, he realized that she walked, just like anyone else and the light that surrounded her was merely the sun's reflection behind her. Still, he believed her to be an angel. She moved closer to the bed and placed a tray with food and water on a stand next to him.

"Where am I?" he managed to ask.

His voice was raw and the sounds came out more like a croak. He barely recognized his own voice. His lips were dry and cracked and his tongue stuck to the roof of his mouth. It felt like they were coated with sand.

"You're safe," the angel answered.

He noticed, though, that she hadn't really answered his question. Instead, she took a cloth from the tray and patted it across his forehead. Then she offered him the glass of water. He was at first wary, put on guard by her evasiveness. But then he realized that he didn't care, and took the glass from her hand.

"Am I alive?" he asked, after he nearly drained the glass.

"Yes, of course," she said as she laughed. "You're in my home. You have been asleep for three days, and you're probably confused and hungry, but you're quite alive, and, as I said, safe."

Her voice was very soothing. He was still uncertain; maybe he really was dead and she was just too kind to tell him the truth.

"Three days?" he said as he fell back on the bed and again rubbed his eyes. "No wonder I had such strange dreams. I kept seeing these pig-like creatures – shadows, really. And they were poking me with sticks."

"The Rebbercands," she said, smiling.

"The what?" he asked, sitting up again and clearing his throat. "You mean those things – those...people were real?"

"The Rebbercands," she repeated, smiling. "Yes, they are very real. They are the people who live in this land – outside these walls. They're relatively harmless, but they're also a bit simple-minded. They don't trust strangers or anything that disrupts their routines. In fact, they are often frightened of anything different or out of the ordinary; and your arrival was certainly different and out of the ordinary."

He was mesmerized by her voice. It was soft and melodic to the point of being nearly hypnotizing. His early anxiety, when he first thought he was dead, had evaporated with her words. He felt completely relaxed and at ease. He looked down and saw that he still had the glass in his hand, but it was full. He was certain he had nearly emptied it, but couldn't remember her refilling it.

"I'm sorry," he said. "Who are you and how did I get here?"

She smiled warmly, taking the glass from his hand, placing it back on the tray, and said, "My name is Meri Hocto, and I brought you here."

He watched as she placed the glass back on the tray, and noticed that there was no pitcher. When her words registered, he looked at her a bit skeptically. Even in his weakened state, he was more than twice her size. He could see that she was a young woman, in spite of her long white hair, but there was no way she could have lifted and carried him.

Seeing the disbelief in his eyes, she explained, "I'm an Enchantress."

When she saw that he still didn't understand, she elaborated, "I could sense your arrival, especially once the Rebbercands discovered you. You see, when they are disturbed, they emit very strong and distinctive auras, which I also picked up. I don't often interact with them, since, like you, I am very different from them. But we have a somewhat peaceful... arrangement. My home is very secure and is unseen by them. They know I'm here, but the spell in which I've enveloped this place makes it invisible to them. Anyway, they were quite disturbed by your presence. As I said, they don't deal well with change. Who knows what they might have eventually done with you – probably something not very pleasant. So I cast a small spell and transported you here. It was all quite simple."

Her voice was lilting and she ended her explanation with a slight laugh. She said all this as if everything she described was so ordinary that it really needed no explanation. He was staring at her with his mouth open.

"I'm sorry. After, 'I'm an Enchantress' I sort of lost you."

He was wondering if he was still dreaming or if he had been captured by an escapee from a lunatic asylum — or maybe he was the lunatic. His anxiety was returning quickly. It was her turn to look skeptically at him.

"But, you're a sorcerer," she stated, again, so matter-of-factly, as if this was common knowledge, that he was beginning to wonder if maybe the both of them were insane. "Surely you've encountered other Enchantresses."

"I'm a what?" he asked, pressing himself back against the end of the bed, now believing she was completely mad and he was probably in danger. She looked at him patiently.

"You're a sorcerer," she repeated. "Perhaps the misadventure that brought you here has affected your memory, but I can clearly sense your powers. Did you get a bump on your head? I'm sure I checked, but perhaps I missed it."

"Whoa, lady," he started to climb out of the bed as she reached for his head, and back up against the wall.

He staggered slightly, holding one arm out in front of him motioning her to stop whatever it was she was doing. She watched him in surprise, her arm still outstretched in her failed attempt to feel his head for some indication of a concussion.

He stammered, "I don't know who you are or what you think. I don't know what's going on here, but I have no idea what you're talking about. My name is Ena Ray and I'm just an explorer."

His eyes darted around the room, looking for escape routes. She continued to smile gently at him, beginning to understand that he either had no recollection of his powers, or was actually unaware of them.

"Please, sit down. I didn't mean to upset you," she said as she patted the bed from which he had just bolted.

Her words and her gentle tone of voice seemed so contrary to what she was saying to him that, instead of calming him, only agitated him further. He moved quickly to the nearest doorway, then stopped and immediately turned and headed for a different opening. At each entryway he was confronted with the same image outside of the room– dense forest with no discernable path. He looked and felt like a rat trapped in a maze, unable to make up his mind, his thoughts paralyzed by fear, his eyes darting back and forth wildly.

Meri watched him closely as he struggled, and then swept her hand across the air in his direction. He immediately stopped walking, looked to the nearest chair and sat down. It was as if this had been what he was searching for all along. Visibly relaxed, he took a deep breath and raised his head to look at her.

"Where am I, really," he pleaded. Her spell had calmed his body, but his mind was still confused.

"You're safe," she said emphatically. "I mean you no harm. You will <u>not</u> be harmed by anyone or anything while you are here. I promise you. I'm sorry to have caused you any distress. It is obvious that there are some things you don't know."

She was speaking slowly, her voice still low and soothing. She let him absorb what she had said, remaining in her seat on the edge of his bed, while he sat on the other side of the room in his chair.

"Let's start again – from the beginning," she continued. "Why don't I go first and tell you about me. You can ask me anything you like. Then you can tell me all about you. And we'll see if we can decide what to do from there. Does that sound all right?"

He took a deep breath and nodded yes.

"Well," she said as she pondered where exactly to start. "As you already know, I'm Meri Hocto, and I'm an Enchantress."

She slowly and precisely told him about where she came from; the history of Enchantresses; their ability to cast spells, create potions, generate visions, and the like; and others, such as sorcerers and faeries who had similar abilities. He nodded when she talked about faeries, having recently encountered them. He was completely unaware that as she spoke, she had been casting a spell on him. It wasn't intentional on her part and it wasn't the traditional kinds of spells that Enchantresses cast, but he had never met anyone with whom he felt so at ease, so welcome. Though she spoke for over an hour, the time flew by. He asked a few questions, but for the most part, let her talk uninterrupted.

When she finished, he began his own story. He told her all about himself, his home, the uncle who had raised him, and his journeys over the last several years. She already knew all of this, but she let him talk. She knew it was therapeutic and, more than that, it would help prepare him for the revelations she would be making about his true character and abilities. She could tell from his own revelations that these were unknown to him and that the powers he had were not only unknown, but undeveloped. He talked for several hours, sharing his journeys and discoveries along with his dreams and fears.

"So what's this stuff about me being a sorcerer?" he asked when he had finished his story.

She thought a minute about how to answer his question. There was no other way but directly, she finally decided.

"I told you that Enchantresses have a number of special powers."

She held out her hand and created a small ball of fire balanced on her palm. She swept her other hand over the fire and it turned into a dove and flew away. She pointed at the chair he had been sitting in and with a motion of her finger, slid the chair easily closer to her. He grabbed the sides with both hands and held tightly.

"Those were a couple of simple tricks, just to convince you," she told him. "Another of our powers is that of second sight. We are able to conjure this second sight with the aid of a special room – I can show you later, if you like. Or we can conjure the second sight within our own mental imaging. We can see the past and some of the future. Those visions are not always clear and not usually in any particular order. By that I mean we may not be able to distinguish which visions have already happened from those yet to be.

"Of course, if I have a vision of you as an old man, I can tell the difference, but our visions are more impressions rather than pictures. I suppose it's more accurate to say we understand or know these things, sometimes, instead of see them. We can also recognize these powers in others. I see these powers in you. I also see, now, that these powers have been dormant and undeveloped, and until now, unknown to you. I know much of this is confusing right now, but it will become clear in time."

She was silent for a few minutes while he took the time to accept what she was saying.

"I can teach you what you will need to know, but the question you must ask yourself is, do you want to develop these powers? Before you answer, I must tell you that if you awaken this force, you will find it to be very powerful. With power comes responsibility. There are consequences for everything. One more thing you must know, since I have already seen it. If you decide to awaken your power, you will betray me and use it against me."

At first he wasn't sure he heard her correctly; then he thought she was toying with him. As she sat there just watching him, the smile on his face faded, and he realized she was serious.

"How can you know that?" he asked. "Do you mean that I have no control? No free will to choose? I don't understand."

"Of course you have free will," she answered. "But we are all responsible for the choices we make. Your free will to choose starts with this choice now. And your free will exists every time you choose to use your powers, as well as in how you use them."

"But if I know that betraying you is a possibility – and that's all I believe it is right now – the possibility that I would betray you - I can't believe that it's a certainty - then I could also choose not to betray you. I would never let that happen," he said. "You saved my life; you gave me food and shelter. How could I ever betray you or anyone else who would show me such kindness?"

She had no answer for him. She could only remain silent.

"All right, then," he continued when she wouldn't speak, "How am I supposed to betray you? And when?"

She sighed and sat even more erectly than before. She looked directly into his eyes. Hers were filled with a sadness he hadn't seen or expected.

"That I can't see," she answered, "only that you will."

He was slightly indignant at her conviction. How could she think that of him? He had never betrayed anyone – ever. He thought back to his youth – to the most difficult and depressing times of his childhood. He never betrayed anyone; what made her think he would repay her with treachery?

"If that's the case, then why would you even train me?" he asked defiantly.

She met his gaze evenly and said, "Because that is why you were brought to me, and the decision to betray me is yours to make."

"What about your free will? What about that, then? If you know I'm going to betray you, why would you train me?"

"My knowledge is meant to be shared," she answered. "I cannot deny that knowledge to anyone, nor can I, in the exercise of my free will, deny or prohibit that same choice for anyone else. You and you alone are responsible for the choices you make. And you must live with those choices."

He thought about this for a few seconds and answered, "All right, then. If the decision to betray you is mine to make then I just won't make it. If it's mine to make then your vision could be wrong. Couldn't it? Didn't you say that they aren't always clear?"

She lowered her head and looked down at her hands, folded in her lap.

"Yes," she said. "The vision could be wrong," even though she knew it was not.

He sensed the lie in her words, but realized that any further effort to convince her that she was wrong would be futile.

"Then, yes. I want to learn everything you can teach me. And I'll show you that your vision is wrong. I will never betray you," he nearly shouted.

She raised her head and looked him in the eyes again.

"Get some rest," she told him. "We will begin in the morning."

With that, she stood up, swept her arm across the room, and the sunlight, which had poured through the windows unchanged the entire time, disappeared and was replaced by the night sky. And Meri Hocto disappeared with it.

Chapter two

Over the next few weeks, as Ena Ray regained his strength, Meri met with him and explained what it meant to be a sorcerer. He had expected to immediately begin to learn how to cast spells and mix potions, but that was not the case. He was becoming impatient, and it was hard to hide this impatience from her.

"It's important for you to understand what your abilities mean and the responsibility that comes with them," she told him. "Without this perspective, you will be nothing more than a carnival act – a cheap magician. You have a responsibility to use your powers wisely. You must never use them to manipulate others, especially for your own self-interests. You must never use your powers for self gain and never for harm."

"What if I'm being attacked?" he asked. "Couldn't I use a spell then? Couldn't I defend myself? Wouldn't that be for self-gain? And wouldn't it be possible that a spell could cause harm?"

"Those are all good questions," she replied. "Of course you could defend yourself – and, yes, even if it meant harming your attacker," she said. Anticipating his next question, she added, "But you must always use the least amount of power or the correct amount and type of power to protect yourself or to resolve the situation. More than that is a misuse of your abilities."

"How can I know the difference?" he demanded. "Will my powers tell me when someone else feels pain, and how much pain?"

"That's what I'm teaching you now," she answered, "and why we haven't yet begun to learn any spells. It's even more important that you learn the context in which your powers are to be used. Without that, you have no way to understand their potential abuse."

He knew she was right, but he felt like she had trapped him. She seemed to have an answer for everything. In all his journeys he never had any constraints on what he did or where he went. He was beginning to feel her rules were too confining. He spent a few minutes to clear his mind and refocus. She was right, he finally concluded, and forced himself to accept. Be patient, he admonished himself.

Eventually the philosophic lessons ended, and she began to teach him some simple spells. His first efforts were not completely successful. In fact, they were not even remotely successful. Sometimes the spell was not strong enough and nothing would happen, and other times he would overcompensate, and the spell would be too strong. She taught him first how to move inanimate objects. They started with a rock about the size of a coconut. She placed it on a table and showed him how to raise it up and move it to another location. After several tries, he moved it up from the table and then it immediately dropped back down, breaking the table into splinters. After several more tries, when he lifted it off the table it shot to the ceiling, broke through and disappeared into the sky.

"I'll never be able to get this right, and this is simple stuff," he shouted in frustration. "I can't even move a stupid rock right. We've been at this for days and the best I can do is fling it through the roof. Maybe we should have started with something that wouldn't do so much damage – like a feather."

"Don't despair," she said to him calmly, "it's just like when you learned to walk when you were a baby. That didn't happen overnight, did it?"

"I don't know," he answered sharply, "I was a baby. Remember?"

She thought a minute and then spun her forefinger in a circle pointed at his forehead. His eyes rolled back in his head and he rocked back on his heels, suspended as if by invisible strings. She had brought forth his own memories, deeply buried in his subconscious, of what it was like when he was learning to walk. In a few seconds his head dropped, he regained his stance, and his eyes returned to normal.

"Wow," he said, "That was...amazing. I remember everything." He was surprised at the clarity of the recollection. "You're right. I fell down all the time, but I kept getting back up. It's a wonder I learned to walk at all."

As quickly as his wonder had risen, it was replaced by a feeling of resentment.

"I thought you said not to ever manipulate anyone," he said, trying to keep his tone light, but the undercurrent was unmistakable. "What? It's not all right for me to learn how to do that, but it's all right for you?"

"I didn't manipulate you at all," she answered patiently. "I merely enabled you to remember something that you already knew. You just didn't know how to summon that particular memory."

He was not convinced. "I don't see the difference."

"The difference is that I did nothing to alter or influence your memory. All I did was to bring that memory, unchanged, to the surface. Furthermore, I did this only to help you, and not for any reason that would advantage me. Although, I suppose you could argue that by bringing your memories to the forefront will lessen your impatience with me."

Her last comment was meant to be in jest, but he took it as a personal affront. He felt she was subtly chastising him for not being able to learn as fast as she preferred. He was not satisfied with her answer or her comment, but he didn't discuss it any further. And by not discussing it further, his resentment took hold deep within his subconscious and began, slowly at first, to fester.

Meri, sensing that he did not understand or agree with her answer, attempted to clarify it further to help him grasp the difference.

"That's all right," he cut her off. "I get what you're saying. Let's just keep going with the spells."

She knew that it was not all right and that it was this instance when the seed of his betrayal had been planted. Deep in his heart, he knew, too, though he would not have been ready to admit it to her or himself.

Several more weeks passed, and Ena Ray's abilities began to show improvement. And the amount of improvement was growing at a faster and faster rate, as well. He had stopped breaking windows and furniture, and his movements of objects became fluid and nearly effortless. There hadn't been any further confrontations about the speed with which Ena Ray was learning, the lessons Meri was giving him on the ethics of how he used his power, or the issue of manipulating people. His progress had diffused those situations. During most of this time, the seed of resentment that had been planted earlier remained dormant, and the friendship that had developed between them began to evolve from a teacher-student relationship to one more of peers.

As the earlier disagreement between them faded into the past, Ena Ray noticed two things that piqued his curiosity. The first was that she recently had been absent. At first it was for a single day, here or there. Lately, though her absences had lengthened. The second was he began to notice that Meri often wore a large pendant around her neck. She didn't have it all the time, and he couldn't recall when he first saw her wearing it. He began to keep track of when she when and how long she was gone, as well as whether or not she wore the pendant when she was absent. At first he didn't see any particular pattern to either. Then one afternoon, when she was gone and he was left on his own, he had been wandering around the estate, and came upon a room he hadn't seen before.

It was not very large, but it was completely round with a domed ceiling. In the center was a pedestal with the pendant resting on a silken pad. He looked around the room. There were no furnishings and nothing on the walls. He turned back to the pedestal and walked up to it to look more closely at the pendant. The stone was very large, as he had initially noticed. It was held in an unusual band that had odd markings on the outer edge. The band seemed to be divided into separate sections. Each section had distinct markings. He had seen the pendant before, but hadn't focused on the band around it. What he also hadn't seen before was what looked like a flaw deep inside the stone. It was some kind of cloudy fracture nearly in the center. As he bent in closer he was startled when the cloud moved and the fracture flashed like a miniature lightning bolt.

He started to reach for it when he heard Meri's voice behind him.

"You can go into any room in this citadel," she said in a voice that was kind, but stern. "Any room at all, but this one - unless I am with you."

He pulled his hand back and slowly turned to face her. A wave of guilt flushed over him. He hadn't done anything wrong, but he felt as if he had invaded her privacy. The feeling grated on him.

"I'm sorry," he said, "I didn't mean to pry. What is this room?"

"It is my Sanctorum. I think I mentioned it to you your first day here, but it never seemed to come up again. Every Enchantress has one. Some are bigger; some are smaller, but the design is basically the same. It is where we are able to receive our visions more clearly than when we conjure mental images alone. But they are very private places. Others are allowed in only by invitation."

He was smart enough to know a rejection when he heard it. He hadn't been invited and was not welcome in this room. He tried to mask his disappointment and more – his irritation. He knew he would never be invited into this room.

"I'm sorry. I didn't mean to intrude. Actually, I...ah...my attention was caught when I saw this pendant. I've noticed you wearing it sometimes during our lessons."

Without asking her permission, and in a subtle act of defiance, he reached out and touched the stone with the tip of his finger. He saw a slight shift in the color, but it happened so fast, he thought he might have imagined it. He didn't imagine the tingling sensation that ran through his fingers and up his arm.

"The stone in that pendant is an amplifier of sorts," she answered his unasked question. "It serves to connect the Enchantresses with one another and facilitates our communications. It's also a conduit to the memories of past Enchantresses."

He sensed she was being purposely vague, which only increased his curiosity and his mistrust. But for the time being, didn't pursue the matter. It was clear that the pendant and, more specifically, the stone were the source of her power, or at least some of her power. He thought about asking her about the stone and the markings on the band, but decided against it. He slowly looked around the room and touched the stone once more, looking more closely to see if the color shifted again. It did, and he once more felt the tingling sensation in his hand. He slowly strolled to the doorway, looking around the room once more. He was leaving, but he didn't want to give her the satisfaction of doing so immediately. She smiled patiently at him, playing along with his game, not saying any more, but, instead, waiting for him to leave.

Neither of them said any more about his visit to her Sanctorum, and his lessons continued. A few weeks later when she told him she would be gone for a few days, he snuck back to the same place in the citadel, but couldn't find the room. He was positive he had gone to the exact same place, but it was nowhere to be found. He wasn't sure how she did it, he concluded, but she had moved the room. Either that or she had cast a spell on it, hiding it from his view. That made him more determined than ever to find the room and the stone, and even more determined that she was hiding something from him.

When she returned, he mentioned nothing about the hidden Sanctorum, and she didn't raise it either. They both acted as if nothing had changed, although she knew he had been searching for it. Instead, he asked her if there was a library where he could study the spells she had taught him to better understand them. Yes, there was, and she showed him the way. The room was enormous. He began to wonder exactly how big her citadel was. There were rows and rows of cabinets, filled with books, rolls of parchment and cases with odd artifacts. He began to spend as much of his free time there as possible, and for the time being, forgot about the Sanctorum and the pendant. He also began to teach himself spells that Meri hadn't revealed to him. After several weeks, he discovered quite by accident an ancient book that explained how to break or bypass spells cast by others. It also included entire sections on potions, with which he began to experiment.

Once he had committed this information to memory, and was certain he could perform the spells, he began to study how to re-cast spells that he had just learned to break, and to do so without leaving any trace that the original spell had been broken. He was planning on breaking the spell Meri had cast to keep her secret. To do so he knew he would also have to know how to re-cast it so she would never know what he had done. It took him longer to learn this skill than he had anticipated, and once he learned it he had no way of knowing how well he could perform it. There was no way he could practice. After some debate with himself, he decided he would just have to trust in his skills. Armed with this information and his determination, he renewed his search for the Sanctorum.

Six weeks later, he found it.

The first time he broke in, he didn't touch anything. In fact, he didn't even enter the room. He wanted to make sure that his restoration of the spell he had broken would be undetected by Meri. However, the fact that she never said anything didn't mean she hadn't known what he did. He wondered if she was just playing with him or if he had really been successful. Several more weeks went by without comment from her, so he did it again.

This time he entered the room, but again, didn't touch anything. He just looked around and studied the room more closely. He also studied the pendant, keeping his hands clasped behind his back. In addition to the cloud that moved in the center, and the flicker of light behind the tiny cloud, he saw that the stone gradually would change color. He knew now that he hadn't imagined it. Sometimes the changes were slight and other times the changes were more significant. He was unable to detect any pattern.

His second visit to her Sanctorum passed without comment, and he became bolder and bolder. Every time Meri announced that she would be gone for a few days, Ena Ray found his way to the Sanctorum where he studied the room and the stone. He started to keep track of the changes he witnessed. He wondered if the changes in the stone were in any way connected to Meri's absences. When Meri returned he began to ask her where she went. Initially she was vague about her comings and goings, and he did not force the issue. He remained persistent but not intrusive. Gradually she began to share bits and pieces with him.

There had been a long war between the faeries and the forest creatures, she explained to him. No one was certain as to its origins. Every time it seems as if a peace was being reached something would happen to disrupt those efforts – food supplies would be stolen or tainted, fires would be started, or, worst of all, little ones from both villages disappeared. It had raged so fiercely that nearby groups of people were moving away in order to avoid being drawn into it. Some had found a castle on top of a very high and very inaccessible mountain. The mountain was made of a purplish granite that had mystical powers of its own. Others, the Sea Sprites, had taken refuge in a giant bubble deep beneath the surface of the sea.

As she describe the conflict, it was hard for him to feel any sympathy. He didn't really care about either of these peoples. In fact, he more often enjoyed hearing about their plight. He recalled the spell the faeries had cast on him. It had taken him quite some time to stop having nightmares about that incident. His bitterness about this experience was still deep and strong. If they were wiped from the face of the earth, he'd be happy.

He felt the same way about the forest creatures. Although he hadn't seen them, the way Meri described them, he was certain that was who had shot at him and forced him over the edge of that cliff. All he had done was to ask them for help. Instead, they terrorized him. For all he cared, they could go the way of the faeries, too. In fact, if they wiped each other out, he would be just fine.

He didn't know anything about the people on the mountain or the sea sprites, but he assumed they were no better or different from the faeries or the forest creatures. It wouldn't bother him at all if they, too, were exterminated. The more Meri talked about them and her efforts to help them, the more he became enraged. A darkness settled around him that Meri didn't sense until later.

When he was able to put aside his own reactions to her stories, he began to focus on Meri's reactions, her moods, and her emotions during her various absences. He began to piece together the connection between her feelings and the changes in the stone. The more antagonistic or violent the events she was involved in, the more her powers were needed to cast spells. As this activity increased, the motions and the colors of the stone changed. It was just as he suspected. The stone was the source of her power, or at least amplified her power. She didn't need to wear it all the time, it seemed. He concluded that she wore it in this room and elsewhere in the citadel, as if it served to recharge her energy.

The next time he snuck into the Sanctorum, he gathered his courage and reached out a tentative hand to touch the stone. He felt a slight sting and heard a faint crackle. It was very similar to the reaction to static electricity. Reflexively, he jerked his hand back and gave a slight jump. He gave a nervous laugh and told himself to get a grip. He had touched it before in Meri's sight, and had felt that tingle. This time, though, it was much stronger. Meri had obviously cast a spell on the stone. He stepped back to the stone and boldly thrust his hand forward to grab it tightly. The jolt that passed through his body immediately paralyzed all his muscles. His jaw clamped shut almost biting through his tongue. He was powerless to let go.

He felt shock waves pulsate through him; his eyes rolled back in his head; the pain deep in his bones was excruciating. Just when he thought he was going to die, the pain subsided. He was able catch his breath, and, just as he was about to release the stone, the walls of the Sanctorum came alive with bursts of light and a montage of visions. His muscles began to relax. His heart rate slowed back down to normal and his brain told him not to release the stone – at least not yet.

The images that raced across the walls and the dome of the Sanctorum were in no apparent order and didn't seem to even connect with one another. He saw flashes of himself from years earlier, wandering across some long forgotten wasteland. That image dissolved into a completely different place and time, replaced with one of a tremendous battle. The scene was utter chaos. His head spun right to left and back again; then up to the ceiling, trying to take in the information crashing all about him. Before he could make any sense of one image, others appeared. In some instances the visions were superimposed over one another, and in other instances they completely blotted out and replaced the ones that preceded, like large paint splotches bleeding into and obscuring one another.

Images of thousands of Rebbercands flooded the walls. Ena recognized them from the shadows he had seen before being brought here by Meri, and from her description of them. A stranger appeared with them, as if leading them in battle. Flashes of light blurred over them. He saw himself on a hilltop waving his arms as if he was conducting an orchestra, but he could hear no music. An enormous black cloud raced around the room and flashes of lightning burst across the wall. What he was unaware of at the time was that this same cloud began to form not far from his location. This particular image he was seeing was happening at the exact same moment that it appeared on the walls.

The sounds were deafening, causing him to hear only a tremendous roaring. It was more than just the thunder from the storm. Scattered through the roaring he heard individual voices. He couldn't understand what they were saying. Some of it almost sounded as if the words were being spoken backwards. He saw hideous looking creatures that appeared to be living in caves. He saw a circle – a band of light like a halo floating in the air that could barely cut through a darkness that was oppressing. It glided through someone's outstretched hand and then shrunk to a small pinpoint of light. He saw a small group of people standing across an enormous chasm, all looking in his direction, and then a sudden blackness that covered everything.

In addition to the visions, Ena Ray began to sense emotional changes. He experienced surges of anger and hatred followed almost in the blink of an eye with extreme feelings of confidence and optimism. He was excited, then remorseful, then envious and resentful, then elated. Finally, he felt extremely frightened, as if he was a tiny rabbit about to be set upon by a giant hawk. The fear was unshakable. When he could stand it no longer, he forced himself to pull his hand away from the stone. In a fraction of a second, the walls and the dome went blank and the silence was nearly as deafening as the noise had been.

He sank to the floor, exhausted. Sweat was pouring from his body. He knew he had to get out of the Sanctorum. Even though Meri wasn't expected back for several more days, he needed to use the time to recompose himself and to try to understand what he had seen. As he stood up on wobbly legs and staggered to the exit, he caught a murky reflection of himself in the shiny stone near the entryway leading into the

Sanctorum. He stopped and turned back to look again. It wasn't a clear reflection, but he could see enough to notice that his black hair had turned white – not just part of it; all of it.

A wave of panic washed over him. He would have no explanation for this. Meri would know instantly that he had been in the Sanctorum and could easily conclude from there that he had also handled her pendant. This must have been part of the spell she had cast on the stone. She'll claim this as a betrayal and will gloat over her prediction, he thought. His fear froze him in place. He turned back into the Sanctorum and then spun around.

"You can't go back in there," he said aloud, admonishing himself. "Are you mad? What are you going to do? This can't happen."

He was immobile. All he could think about was being discovered. He couldn't decide which way to go or what to do. The muscles in his back and neck were rigid and aching.

"Get control," he shouted to himself.

He forced the panic down. He took long, slow breaths to regain control. There's got to be a potion or a spell that can change it back, he thought to himself. With that he headed to the library.

He spent the next several hours searching the ancient books and scrolls until he finally found what he was looking for. It was a potion; one that seemed relatively simple. It called for only a few ingredients, which were common and readily available. It also called for three drops of his blood. A small enough sacrifice, he thought. He read and re-read it several times to ensure he understood the precise ingredients and proportions.

He quickly gathered the ingredients and carefully read the instructions yet again. He wanted to be absolutely sure he understood the exact amounts and the specific items. Even the slightest deviation could have disastrous results. In learning one of his first potions, he had incorrectly added a spadix root instead of a spanex root. The plants were almost identical; it was an easy mistake to make. However, he did not exactly achieve his goal of being able to breathe underwater. The potion turned him blue, much to Meri's amusement and his embarrassment.

He had everything right and began to mix the ingredients. The last item to be added was the three drops of his blood. He grabbed a knife and held it to his thumb over the bowl with the other items. He made a quick, short slice; felt a sharp pain; and then squeezed the cut. Three drops fell into the bowl. His shock nearly froze him, and his panic immediately returned, sucking the breath from his lungs.

The blood was not red. It was black; as black as night; black as tar – no; it was more like soot. There was no glistening, no light reflected, no sparkle as he had seen any other time his blood had been shed. The three drops were a flat, lifeless black. They looked more like three black holes than drops of blood. He looked at the cut in his thumb. Had something on the knife caused the change? No, the blood seeping from his wound was just as black. He looked back at the three drops. They had vanished and the other ingredients withered and turned to dust, turning the same dull black as the spots of blood.

This was not part of the instructions. This was not supposed to happen. He had expected the potion to be a fluid he would drink. The instructions said to swallow the potion. All that was in the bottom of the bowl was a black dust. How could he swallow dust? Had something gone wrong? He decided to mix another potion. He gathered the same ingredients and this time he cut a different finger. The blood was the same, dead black, and the effect on the ingredients was the same: it turned them to black dust.

"NO!" he screamed.

What was he doing wrong? It took every ounce of strength he had to force himself to calm down and carefully go over the formula one more time. With painstaking meticulousness he repeated the steps. After this third attempt the results were the same. He had to conclude that he had done everything right and this was how it was intended to come out. With great uncertainty, he scooped up the black dust and swallowed it. Instantly the inside of his mouth became incredibly dry. It was nearly impossible for him to swallow. The dust caught in his throat. It felt like coarse sand as it burned and sank into his stomach. He coughed and choked, but managed to keep the potion down. He could feel a change of some kind working its way into his blood stream. When he began to feel a tingling sensation in his scalp, he ran to find a mirror.

The white in his hair began to fade. It turned back to black, but something was different. It was not quite the same radiant black it had been before. It seemed dull to him. He wasn't sure, though, if he was imagining the difference or if it was real. He pulled the hair in different directions, baring parts of his scalp. The color had completely covered the white, but there was no shine, no...life – that was it. There was no life to it.

He decided there was nothing more he could do. He went to clean up the two earlier attempts and saw that the dust had eaten into the bowls. Nothing was left in either bowl, other than the cracks and charring at the bottom. He wondered what this potion was or would be doing to him.

"What have I done," he wailed. "If she only hadn't been such a...a...witch about that room. None of this would have happened. This is all her fault."

His shouts echoed through the rooms and halls. He looked down at the bowls, and he slowly came to the realization that there was nothing more he could do. However, he had to hide the evidence of his actions.

He wrapped the bowls in a cloth and hid them in his room. He had no other way to dispose of them – at least not until Meri gave him another lesson in potions. Then he would purposely include the wrong ingredients and pass off these damaged bowls as the results of a failed lesson.

In the next four days, before Meri returned, Ena Ray debated about returning to the Sanctorum. Even the incident with his hair and blood was not enough to dissuade him. He knew, however, that he wouldn't have time to counteract any additional side effects before Meri came back, but his curiosity was as addictive as a narcotic. He returned to the room, sometimes several times in a single day, but he couldn't summon the courage to go in. Or maybe it was a survival instinct that convinced him not to enter. He couldn't decide. In either case, he came close, but didn't go in.

Instead, he diverted his attention by spending more time in the library, trying to find out why his blood had turned black. He opened the earlier cuts to see if anything had changed, and was in agony each time to discover that it had not. He searched in vain for an antidote. He couldn't even find any references to what would cause this to happen in the first place, not to mention how to correct it.

During this time, he kept looking at his hair. It was still black, as it had been before the change; but it was the same dull black that seemed to have resulted from the potion. By now, though, he wasn't sure if it really looked different, or if it only seemed that way because he knew it was different – or thought it was different. He was driving himself crazy. He was constantly worried that Meri would see the change instantly and would discover that he had disobeyed her instructions not to go into the Sanctorum and not to touch the pendant.

Maybe he could lie to her. He could deny ever going in the Sanctorum and just tell her he had been experimenting with potions and one had gone wrong. He dismissed this plan, though. He knew she would ask to know exactly what ingredients he had used and what he was trying to create. His lie would be exposed immediately.

Maybe he should just confess before she even asked. What would happen then? Would she punish him? What could she do? She certainly wouldn't send him to his room. He wasn't a child. She could banish him from the citadel. Where would he go? Would she return him to the Rebbercands? No, he thought. She's not a cruel person. She wouldn't do anything to harm him.

The anxiety was eating away at him. He could feel the knots forming in his stomach. He found himself grinding his teeth. The punishment he was putting himself through was far worse than any she could or would inflict.

And then she returned.

He tried to assume an air of normality, except he couldn't recall or even imagine what that was anymore. Unable to decide between lying to her and confessing, he did neither. He greeted her cheerfully. Not too cheerfully, he told himself – she'd suspect something. He asked her how her travels went. Don't ask too much, he told himself. That wouldn't be normal. He was trying hard to remember how he reacted and what they talked about when she returned from other absences.

"Are you all right?" she asked.

"Yes. I'm all right," he said a little too defensively. "Of course I am. Why wouldn't I be all right?"

Shut up, he told himself. The more you say, the more you risk exposing what you did. If she figures it out, just deal with it then.

"Something looks different," she said as she walked up to him.

She looked him in the eyes, studying him closely. He forced himself not to turn away from her gaze. He began to perspire. He could feel the drops of sweat forming on his forehead and upper lip. He fought the urge to wipe them away and just stared back at her.

"I'm not sure exactly what," she said, "but something's different."

His resolve was starting to crumble. She knows, she knows, she knows. The words rumbled through his head, nearly blocking out all other sounds. He was on the verge of spilling everything and just asking for her forgiveness. But then she reached her hand up to the side of his face. He struggled not to pull away from her and gave her a nervous smile. His mouth clamped shut. Before he could open up to her she spoke again.

"You're shaking," she said with a look of concern. "I know what's different," she announced.

"What?" he asked apprehensively, his voice a dry whisper.

"You're thinner. You look sick. I think you have some kind of virus. I'll mix a potion for you and you'll be right back to normal," she said as she left the room.

Chapter three

A few days later, just as the next lesson was about to begin, Meri asked Ena Ray if he would mind postponing the lesson. She said that she had something else planned. There was someone she wanted him to meet.

"He's another student of mine, and very much like you," she said. "I've known him since he was a child. His powers aren't as natural as yours, though, and, in truth, it wasn't evident that he had any until just recently."

"Another student?" Ena Ray asked.

He wasn't sure how he felt about this. He was surprised that his initial reaction was to be somewhat jealous. He dismissed that feeling as being petty. Why should he think he was the only person in Meri's life?

"Of course. I mean, it's your decision. Who is he, and where has he been?"

"Well," she said, wondering how much she should share.

After a few seconds debate with herself, she decided to tell him all that she knew. She didn't want him to form opinions based on her accounting, but rather on his own interaction. At the same time, she wanted his first impression to be at least neutral if not positive, instead of negative. The newcomer's appearance could be...what, she wondered. Off-putting? He was, after all, somewhat out of the ordinary.

"His name is Tebaga," she began. "His mother was a Rebbercand, but his father was not. It seems that no one really knew who," or what, she thought, but didn't say, "his father was or where he came from, but it was evident almost from the time of Tebaga's birth that his father had not been a Rebbercand."

"So what does he look like?" Ena Ray asked with a nervous laugh. "My limited recollection of them was that they weren't all that attractive to begin with. Is this person a gargoyle or something? You're making it sound like he's really hideous."

"His appearance can be somewhat of a shock," admitted Meri. "I don't want you to judge him by that, though. His community has already done that."

"Oh, no. I wouldn't do that," he quickly answered. "I mean, I've seen a lot of strange looking people and I've been misjudged myself. I hope that you don't think I'd treat him badly just because of the way he looks."

"No," she said. "I didn't think you would. I've never believed that of you. But I wanted to prepare you rather than surprise you."

He thought about that for a minute and then decided she was being honest with him.

"Thanks. I'll keep that in mind. So tell me more about him. You said the villagers had already pre-judged him. What did they do?"

It was evident from the time he was born that he was different. No matter how much his mother's family or the other villagers persisted, she would not reveal who his father had been. Once he was born, it no longer really mattered. Tebaga bore some similarities to the Rebbercands, such as the bristling hair and the narrow, deep- set eyes, but his face, especially his chin, was more pointed. He didn't have the upturned snout-like nose of the Rebbercands, nor did he have the large teeth protruding from his lower jaw.

He had small sharp teeth in what initially appeared to be a small mouth – until it opened. His jaw was hinged much like a snake's and he had a row of very narrow, needle sharp teeth that appeared within days of his birth. Unlike the Rebbercands, his body was not short and stocky. Instead, he was tall and on the thin side. His arms were longer than normal, but his legs were short almost to the point of looking out of proportion to his body. There was also a small stub much like a tail at the end of his spine.

Because the Rebbercands had difficulty dealing with anything that was too far out of their ordinary standards, the arrival of a child with no father, and especially one that looked like Tebaga, created a high level of controversy and became a source of conflict. Many of the Rebbercands wanted to exile him and some even wanted to do him harm. Others were more accepting, or at least professed to be. Even though their hearts were not really in it, they argued that their people needed to be more inclusive of those who looked different or came from a different world.

"This disagreement raged for years as Tebaga grew up," Meri continued to explain. "He has often been the target of pranks and practical jokes ever since he was a small child. As he got older the pranks became more like hazing and then like threats."

A small section of the Rebbercand population took up his defense and became more aggressive in challenging those who wanted him gone.

Those in opposition stated that he would never be accepted and they would have nothing to do with him or his mother. She no longer fit in, and he never would. The community became divided and that division was yet another change in their lives that they were not equipped to deal with. Families and friends took issue with one another and broke apart. Eventually some of them resorted to violence. At first the violence was directed towards property: windows were broken, walls were written on, and small fires were started. Then things got even worse. They started demonstrating and even attacking one another. And then the violence began to be directed to the source of their conflict. Tebaga was attacked one evening by a mob that covered their faces. His supporters retaliated and the violence escalated.

"I had lived among, and yet separate from the Rebbercands for a very long time," she said. "Since they were a relatively peaceful people and the land in which they lived was idyllic, I thought this was the perfect place for me to live, study and teach. I didn't avoid them, but I interacted with them only on extremely rare occasions. I knew my presence was a change that was difficult for them to deal with. I never let them know of my powers, because I believed their awareness, or their knowledge of my abilities would influence even further how they lived. This would go against everything I believe about my powers. So I lived on the edge of their community, and purposely limited my involvement with them. Now, however, that community was on the verge of permanently damaging itself and doing harm to innocent bystanders. And the life of an innocent child was at risk."

In a rare intervention, she froze time, moved Tebaga into a safe and sequestered area of her home, and cast a spell on the Rebbercands. They would remember Tebaga, but would have no recollection of her at all. They would not be able to recall any details of when or how he left them or the disruption his presence had caused. She thought about moving to a different location, but decided against it. Separating him from everyone and everything he knew would be unfair to him.

Instead, she created multiple dimensions to her home to give it the appearance to anyone inside that it was a vast estate. In reality, it was folded in on itself and was completely contained inside a large tree in the center of the Rebbercand village. She opened a mystical portal between the area in which Tebaga lived and the rest of the village. It could only be found and accessed by the few childhood friends he had. Over time these friends had stopped coming. Meri extended the spell to cover them and to keep her location secret. It was soon after that when Meri discovered Tebaga's deeply hidden mystical abilities. She had begun to teach him how to grow and use those abilities when Ena Ray had arrived.

"And that's the student I would like you to meet," she said as she finished.

"How is what you did to the Rebbercands not manipulating them?" he asked.

Her entire account of Tebaga went uncommented on. Instead, Ena Ray had focused on the ethical issue on which she had cautioned him – the manipulation of other people for your own end. She was a bit taken aback by what seemed to be the more important matter to him. He had disregarded the plight of a child and was more concerned about what he viewed as conflicting guidance on the use of his powers.

"First, the spell I cast was not for my personal gain," she answered calmly and confidently. She had been expecting him to raise this matter, but not for it to be his first concern.

"Second, I did nothing to affect their decisions to fight or not to fight, to agree or not agree, or to act or not act. I only removed the source of their disagreement. Tebaga could just as easily have left on his own. The actions, reactions or inaction of the Rebbercands would be the same. There was no manipulation."

"But you changed their memories," he challenged her.

"Their memories were not changed at all. Everything they experienced or knew is still contained in their memories. I did nothing to eradicate them, only to minimize their importance and impact. Further, the only things that are not clear to them are my presence, which had no impact on their ability to decide for themselves, and when and how Tebaga was taken from their midst, which also had no impact on their ability to decide things."

"What about Tebaga?" he continued. He knew better than to try to debate with her, but he felt frustrated by what he viewed as her being hypocritical. "He didn't get to decide whether to leave or not. You just moved him."

"He is free to return any time he likes. I've never closed the portal. In fact, he initially returned often to see his friends — the few who were able to accept him as he was. They decided on their own to reduce and then to discontinue their contact."

Ena Ray was silent. He was unable to see the distinction she was making and yet couldn't explain it to himself, either. He decided to let it go.

"Well, where is he?" he finally asked.

She studied him for a few seconds before answering. She met his eyes and could see the resentment growing. She struggled trying to understand what she could do to steer him down another path from the one on which he was headed. I can only open doors, she thought to herself. He has to decide for himself which ones to enter.

"I can see that you're not satisfied with my answer," she tried one more time. "What can I do to make it clearer to you?"

"You've made it perfectly clear," he said dismissively. "Don't worry about it. I understand. So, where is he?"

"He's in the atrium," she answered, resigned to the fact that she didn't and wouldn't get through to him. "Why don't you go introduce yourself? I will be gone for a few days, and I'm sure you will enjoy his company."

Ena Ray turned to look out the window and saw the strange looking person practicing a levitation spell with the fountain. He turned back to say something to Meri, but she had vanished. He wasn't sure if she walked out of the room or just cast one of her many spells and disappeared.

"I hate it when she does that," he said to himself. "Why can't she just leave like a normal person?"

As soon as he said it, he laughed. What's normal, he wondered. He turned back and watched the odd looking young man, studying him for a few seconds before he walked out to the atrium and spoke. It was the stranger he had seen in his vision in the Sanctorum. That vision had only been fleeting, but he was sure it was the same person. He tried to remember the context in which this vision appeared, but his entire experience had been so chaotic, that he quickly discarded the idea of trying to make any sense of it.

Ena Ray's appearance surprised Tebaga and his concentration on lifting the small fountain faltered. The fountain dropped to the ground and the bowl cracked. Water splashed across the floor, and Tebaga only watched as it soaked his feet.

"Oh, nuts," Tebaga said. "You distracted me." He looked at Ena Ray and then turned his attention back to the damaged fountain. "I don't know any spells for repairing things, or for cleaning up all this water. Do you?"

"No," answered Ena Ray. "I'm still playing with small rocks. I haven't tried anything as big as that."

It was a lie, and he didn't really know why he told it. He had a deep feeling that he should keep some things secret, at least for the time being. He had taught himself quite a few spells during the time he spent in the library. He hadn't shared any of those secrets with Meri. He wasn't about to share them with this stranger.

There was no need for them to introduce themselves to each other. Meri had provided the basic information to both already. The normal period of discomfort when strangers first meet quickly evaporated. They had much in common and immediately launched into comparing notes on how much they had been taught. That discussion blended easily into the topic of their mentor and how they met her. From there it went on to a wide variety of subjects, including her recent and growing absences. Neither of them knew what she was doing, or if they did, they kept it to themselves.

Over the next few days, an unusual relationship developed. They didn't exactly become friends, but they formed an unspoken alliance. It was clear that they each had plans for their future, which they were keeping well hidden, not only from each other, but from Meri as well. It was also clear that they viewed each other as a potential partner or resource in achieving their closely guarded goals.

Once Meri returned, and she repaired the damaged fountain, all of their lessons from that point forward were together. As their individual skills developed, Meri could see a significant difference. Ena Ray was clearly a much more powerful sorcerer, and more confident in his abilities. He was also much more subtle in the use of his powers, tending to avoid the spotlight. He often minimized his capabilities, even when Meri knew that he was holding back.

Tebaga on the other hand was somewhat of an exhibitionist – more flash and flurry than substance. He was certainly powerful, but not as adept as Ena Ray. She noted that Ena Ray seemed purposely to let Tebaga steal the attention; he seemed purposely to let Tebaga appear to be more powerful; he seemed purposely to let Tebaga think he was the leader. He was also adept enough that Tebaga appeared to be completely unaware of the differences in their capabilities. Ena Ray was doing to Tebaga exactly what she had cautioned him against: he was manipulating Tebaga, but not by casting spells or doing anything obvious. True to his nature, he was being very subtle and manipulating Tebaga by his own restraint.

As the days turned into weeks and then into months, their respective skills grew at a faster and faster rate. The friendly competition that developed between them was an additional factor in the escalated learning rate. Eventually, they were teaching each other and were venturing into areas that Meri would not have approved – if she had known.

One day Ena Ray asked Tebaga if he had ever gone back into the village after Meri had taken him in.

"No," he answered, almost too fast; and then he realized that Meri might have told the true version of events. He corrected himself before Ena Ray could question him. "Well, not recently, at any rate. I went back a few times at first. You know – to see the few friends I had. But that changed, and I stopped going. I've thought about going back off and on, but I decided I wasn't going to return until I was sure I had the upper hand."

"What do you mean?"

Ena Ray was sure he already knew the answer, but he wanted Tebaga to express it. He wanted Tebaga to think that what they did next was his own idea. This was almost going to be too easy, he thought.

"I don't intend to be pushed around or bullied again," he said with an undercurrent of vehemence in his voice. "I was a pariah in that village. Even those who tried to defend me didn't really care about me. I was their social conscience project. Nobody – not one of them ever cared about me. If I go back it will be on my terms, not theirs."

"Of course. I understand why you'd be…" Ena Ray paused, searching for the right word that would push Tebaga in the right direction, "afraid to go back there."

"Who said I was afraid," Tebaga answered defensively. "I wasn't afraid then and I'm not afraid now."

"I'm sorry," Ena Ray said deferentially. "I didn't mean to suggest anything. It was a poor choice of words. I never thought for a minute that you were afraid."

He let the seed he had planted take root, and stopped talking. He knew that his silence would make Tebaga believe just the opposite, especially the longer he let the silence between them continue.

"I'm not afraid," Tebaga said again a little too loudly.

"What if we went together?" offered Ena Ray after several more seconds elapsed.

"I don't need a guardian," countered Tebaga.

"Of course not. I didn't mean to imply that you did. I just thought it would be interesting for me to see where you grew up."

By now, Tebaga's anger was clouding his judgment. He had taken the bait completely. In his mind this was a dare. He was sure Ena Ray didn't believe it when he declared he wasn't afraid, and the "offer" to go with him was a statement that Ena Ray wanted to see for himself that Tebaga wasn't afraid.

"Fine," he said. "Let's go right now. The portal is still open. I don't care if you come along, assuming you're not afraid."

"I guess that would be all right," said Ena Ray, pretending to be reluctant, but ignoring the dig. "Maybe we should let Meri know what we're doing."

"I don't need her permission," Tebaga nearly shouted. "I can do what I want, whenever I want. Are you coming? Or are you going to wait for permission?"

"OK, OK. You're the boss. I'm right behind you." This was just the reaction Ena Ray expected.

Tebaga led the way to the portal. Ena Ray had passed it dozens of times a day and never realized what it was. It looked like a simple mirror. He told himself that he'd have to remember exactly where this was and what Tebaga did to open it. Just as they were about to pass through, Ena Ray stopped him.

"What now?" demanded Tebaga.

"Just a little spell so they can't see or hear us."

He spun his hand in a small circle above both their heads and whispered an incantation. They could still see and hear each other, but when Tebaga looked in the mirror, their images had vanished.

"Where did you learn that?" Tebaga asked suspiciously.

"I just picked it up along the way," Ena Ray answered, and then, to distract him, he went on, "I thought we might want to have some fun."

Tebaga's first thought was that he was lying. Meri must have taught Ena Ray how to do that, and never taught that same skill to him. But that thought was eclipsed by Ena Ray's other comment about having some fun. That was enough to draw Tebaga's attention away from the fact that Ena Ray was displaying skills far beyond his own capabilities. He smiled mischievously.

"Yeah. This just might be fun. Let's go."

With a single step they passed through the mirror, and were standing in front of a large tree in the center of a bustling village. Ena Ray looked back at the tree and only saw a large knot at the point from which they exited. He gazed up the trunk to the branches spread out in every direction. The tree was enormous, but he couldn't comprehend how Meri had her entire compound folded inside.

He turned his attention from the tree to the surrounding village. He knew from her explanation of his arrival that he must have been here, but none of it looked familiar. As the residents walked by, he could see the resemblance between the Rebbercands and Tebaga, as well as the very obvious differences. The Rebbercands all looked pretty much alike – not so much facially, but in the way they dressed, the way they walked, and in their overall appearance.

His observation moved from the passersby to the nearest structures and then to the streets, intersections and the town square. Their houses and buildings all looked alike. Everything was in neat rows. Everything was made from the same materials and was the same color and design. He quickly understood how anyone in the least bit different would stand out like a sore thumb, and would probably be just about as welcome as the plague.

As they walked along the dusty road, Tebaga leaned close to Ena Ray and whispered to him, "That guy there," he pointed, "Is named Grewt. He's sort of the leader."

"You don't have to whisper," said Ena Ray, speaking at his normal volume. "They can't hear anything we say."

"Oh, yeah. I forgot," he said, somewhat embarrassed.

The earlier feeling of mistrust that Tebaga had when Ena Ray first cast the spell that made them invisible to the Rebbercands resurfaced, but only for a few seconds. Ena Ray could see it in his reaction, so he quickly distracted him.

"Was he one of the ones who treated you badly?" he asked.

"They all treated me badly," Tebaga answered, his attention redirected to the Rebbercands. "Some were just worse than others."

He described how the Rebbercands were bound by traditions. Their entire lives were controlled by "the way things used to be." Changes only came about by necessity. They always talked about the way things used to be, but as far as Tebaga could tell, things had never changed from what they used to be. That was why they all sort of looked and acted alike.

Their current leadership quickly beat down anyone who thought, acted, or looked different.

"Beat them down?" asked Ena Ray, recalling the poking and prodding, as well as the bruises of his encounter with them. "You mean they actually hurt people?"

"No, they didn't beat them down that way. It was more of a psychological thing. They would first talk to the person. It was more like a lecture or an order. It wasn't a discussion. They didn't want any excuses; they wanted compliance. If that didn't work, the offending person would be shunned – you know – ignored like he or she didn't even exist. If that didn't bring them in line the shunning would get worse. They would lose their job, wouldn't be able to get food or clothing or anything like that. If they still didn't get the message and either change their ways or leave, then things could get physical."

"Is that what happened to you?"

"Yes, although I tried to fit in. I dressed, and acted and talked like them. It didn't do any good. No matter what I did, it was never enough. I wasn't one of them and they couldn't get over that. And they made sure I never forgot it."

Ena Ray thought about this for a minute. "Didn't anyone come to your defense? What about your mother's family?"

"Actually, yes. But not my mother's family. They were the worst of all, although there were a few who defended me. And they were the most unexpected group. There's a small, but growing faction that is even stricter about following the sacred 'sameness.' They were the ones I least expected to side with me."

"The sacred sameness?" asked Ena Ray. "Really?"

"No, that's just my word for it. But with them it's just like a religion. They believe that in order to have a completely fair and safe society, it's

46

important that everyone speaks with one voice. There's a real division between this new group of people and the older generation. They older group are all pretty narrow-minded and stuck in the past – their version of the past, which I learned wasn't exactly accurate. Their version changes, depending on what is needed to rationalize their present. This new group also values the past, but sees it differently. They encourage returning to the former days of glory, where everyone had a position and a specific role."

"Wait. You're losing me. The older group changes their own past, but the newer group doesn't?" Ena Ray asked.

"Well take women, for example. In the past, they never had leadership positions. Now they do. But the older group claims that they've always had them, when the newer group claims that's not true. The newer group admits that there are a lot of women who make good leaders or workers, but they say that shouldn't be their primary role. They're supposed to stay at home and raise their families. If they can't find a man to take care of them, then it's all right for them to find a real job."

Ena Ray was about to interject, but then decided to remain silent. He was trying to understand something that seemed to make no sense at all.

Tebaga continued, "And the kind of job, not just for those women, but for everyone, shouldn't be changed just because someone thinks they can do something else or something better. Certain people belong in a certain place. If you have a really important job, it's because you're meant to have that job. If you are just a laborer, then, that's all you're supposed to be. The older group believes that in the past everyone could move ahead depending on their skills. That's not true, and the newer group thinks that's the way it should be."

No wonder these people had never progressed much beyond grass huts, Ena Ray thought to himself.

"For some reason I could never figure out, it was members of this newer group that had less of a problem accepting me. So I voiced my agreement with the leaders of this newer group, and was made to suffer for it. I became the target of the established leadership. Some of the newer leaders tried to protect me and keep me in the village. It was that jerk, Grewt, who raised the most vocal objections. It was almost like he saw me as a threat to his leadership."

Ena Ray was taken aback by what he heard. In spite of his own issues with Meri and her teachings, he never considered her an inferior person because she was a woman. According to what Tebaga was telling him, this newer group of Rebbercands thought women were second-class, and Tebaga said he agreed with them. He wondered what Tebaga really thought of Meri. He decided not to explore this any further for the time being, storing this information for use later on. Right now, he needed to do something to further bring Tebaga under his influence. He looked around and spotted the person Tebaga had indicated was the source of his exile.

"Well," he said, "If he made your life here such a misery, then I think it's only fair that he reaps what he sows. Don't you? Watch this."

Grewt was walking across the town square with a scroll opened in front of his face. He had a rather pompous air about him that Ena Ray took offense with, even without knowing the history he had with Tebaga. A few yards ahead, a carpenter had just put down his toolbox to draw a drink of water from the well. With a slight wave of his hand at the precise moment, Ena Ray slid the toolbox into the path Grewt was taking. He tripped over it and slid, arms splayed, flat on his face into the dust. The scroll flew into the air and Ena Ray wiggled his fingers slightly. A sudden gust of wind, appearing from nowhere, caught the scroll, lifted it higher into the air and then deposited it down the well.

Grewt jumped up sputtering, dusting his pants and straightening his vest and shouting at the carpenter. At the last second, while looking for the scroll, he saw it as it disappeared down the well. He ran over, swiping at it with his hand, but missing as it dropped down the shaft and splashed into the water.

Tebaga let out a peal of laughter, covered his mouth, then looked at Ena Ray and burst out laughing again.

"Oh, this is great. It's my turn, now," he said.

He watched Grewt leaning over the rim of the well, looking at where the scroll had just landed. The carpenter turned to face him, unaware of what had just happened, and wondering why Grewt had been yelling at him. He was still holding a large ladle of water in his hand. Tebaga flipped his wrist, awkwardly but effectively, and the ladle twisted on its own motion, splashing water all over Grewt.

The two invisible sorcerers laughed heartily.

"That was good. Now watch this," said Ena Ray.

As Grewt was wiping the water from his face, the stunned carpenter was apologizing repeatedly. He had no idea what could have happened. In the middle of his explanation, Ena Ray flicked one hand, sliding the toolbox immediately behind the carpenter. Then he waved his hand, making Grewt thrust his hands forward, and shoved the carpenter over his own toolbox. The carpenter still had the stunned look on his face as he spun his arms to keep his balance, and flew backwards onto the ground with a thud.

"Oops," said Ena Ray, "I probably shouldn't have done that. It might be considered a little inappropriate manipulation. Meri wouldn't approve."

Tebaga jerked his head in Ena Ray's direction. The look on his face was one of shock at having been caught doing something wrong. When he saw the crooked smile on Ena Ray's face, he laughed, "I don't know. That's an interesting philosophical issue. I think he would have pushed the carpenter over on his own. Maybe we need to explore this further."

And the two laughed even harder.

They spent the next few hours playing similar pranks on the unsuspecting Rebbercands before they returned to the portal. After they departed for the night, Ena Ray reflected on their excursion. Oh, yes, he thought, this has some real possibilities.

Chapter four

Meri returned two days later. She offered no explanation or any information about her absence. She resumed the lessons as if she had never left at all, announcing, "I think we'll study spells that can make you invisible to anyone around you."

She was looking at Ena Ray as she said this. He kept a straight face as he returned her gaze, but he was keenly aware that she knew exactly what he had done. Tebaga was just as certain that she knew what had gone on. A feeling of uneasiness rose up inside of him. And his uneasiness was made worse by the fact that she never looked at him when she made her announcement. He shifted his gaze from her to Ena Ray and back. He wasn't sure what was going on, but he knew something was. For now he dismissed his doubts, but not easily. He forced himself to concentrate on learning as much as he could and vowed to watch Ena Ray closely.

A week or so later Meri was once more inexplicably absent. The two students took advantage of this opportunity to practice their "new" skill of invisibility, once more walking through the village playing simple pranks on the Rebbercands. As one of these pranks was unfolding, Tebaga brought up Meri's comment about the invisibility lesson.

"I have no idea what she was doing," Ena Ray told him.

He recalled Tebaga's comments during their first excursion into the village, when he was talking about the views of the more extremist members of the village. He remembered thinking at the time that Tebaga had told him that he didn't really agree with their views, but voiced them to fit in. He thought he'd see how true that was and decided to play on what he was certain were Tebaga's feelings about women. He needed to convince him that Meri was just like all the rest, and not to be trusted.

"When she taught me that spell, she led me to believe you already knew it." He knew not to become too defensive about the matter. It would only raise Tebaga's suspicions further. He needed to drive a wedge between Tebaga and Meri. "I'll admit, she didn't come right out and say that. It was just the way she seemed to make sure she and I were alone when she showed it to me. I just thought she had already taught it to you." He could see Tebaga thinking this over.

"Apparently I was wrong," Ena Ray continued. "I'm really sorry. I probably should have pointed that out to her when she announced that would be the next lesson, but she gave me such a stare, I thought she was trying to tell me to keep it secret. I don't understand her sometimes."

That was enough, he thought. He had started to tip the scales of suspicion ever so slightly towards Meri. Tebaga might not be completely convinced, but he now at least had doubts. Ena Ray would work on that in due course. In the mean time, he decided it would be to his advantage to share another spell he had developed.

"Hey, do you know how to duplicate someone's voice?" he asked Tebaga.

He knew that Tebaga already knew how to do this, but wanted to make him believe that he had a skill that Ena Ray lacked. Ena had learned this long ago, but had never used it. Until going into the village, he hadn't had the opportunity or the interest in using it. He was glad he had never let Tebaga know he had this skill.

"Yes, I know how to do that," answered Tebaga.

"Really," Ena Ray said, acting surprised. "I wonder why she didn't teach me that. Show me how," he asked.

Tebaga failed to ask or even wonder why Ena Ray would bring this up in the first place, if he didn't know how to do it. He was blinded by the fact that he seemed to know something his classmate didn't. They spent a few minutes going over the spell and Ena Ray made a halfhearted attempt, purposely doing it poorly. Tebaga corrected him and they both spent the day making it appear that various villagers were saying things that they would never actually say, causing all sorts of trouble and embarrassing situations. For Ena Ray, this was child's play, but Tebaga was easily amused and took pleasure in causing his former persecutors a certain degree of torment. Everything was starting to fall into place. A plan was beginning to form in Ena Ray's mind.

Eventually, every time they left Meri's hidden sanctuary and entered the village, they immediately set about causing chaos among the Rebbercands. Over time the pranks became much more devious, complicated, and destructive. Tebaga would take any chance he could to outdo Ena Ray. At the same time, Ena Ray tried to focus the pranks on the older group of Rebbercands, making them look as if they were being played by the younger ones, to help divide two groups further apart. They were spending more time in the village, since Meri's absences were becoming more frequent and getting longer each time.

It was during one such absence that Ena Ray declared that he was getting bored with the simple practical jokes. He asked Tebaga if he had ever played chaturanga. Tebaga said that he had heard of the game, but didn't know much about it.

"It's very interesting," Ena Ray said casually. "It's a game of strategy. I learned it when I was a child living with my uncle. There are usually two sides. There can be more, but the basic game can be played with two. Each side has a token or a flag – any object will do: something of no real value – just a symbol of some kind. They also have a set of pieces or players. Depending on the level of the game, these players are craftsmen or soldiers; something of that nature. The number of players is not really important, except that each side should start off with the same. These pieces have different skills and can do different things. Those skills all have to be agreed upon by the players at the beginning of the game, so they start off even. Then the object of the game is to use these pieces to steal the other team's token."

Tebaga was not particularly skilled at strategies, but he was very competitive.

"What sort of skills," he asked.

Ena Ray explained. There were five categories of pieces. The lowest and least skilled were the Broons. These were usually used to set up traps or serve as bait. In a traditional game, there were usually far more Broons than any other piece. They were the most expendable. The next level of skill was the Hrocs. They were usually used for creating diversions. They could be very valuable, but their use was limited. Above them were the Skopos. They were more devious and could be used for diversions or attacks, or served as spies. They were among the most versatile of the pieces. Next were the Cleffyds. They were the key guardians of the token. They had some limited magical powers, and were the most difficult to trick. They could also direct the movements of the Broons. The most powerful piece was the Gynan. There was only one, and this was usually the leader of the team.

He went on to explain some simple strategies and how each piece would factor in and be used. The game, he explained, often used trickery and deceit to fool the opponent and make his token vulnerable. Knowing that Tebaga was not much of a strategist, he made the game sound as simple as possible. Having merely fundamental knowledge of the game would be sufficient for his purposes.

"Do you have this game?" asked Tebaga when Ena Ray had finished his explanation.

"No," answered Ena Ray. "I had a set as a boy that was carved from Elisian granite. It was very nice and very expensive, but I wasn't able to take it with me when I left home. I haven't seen one since."

"Then why did you bother to explain this game to me?" asked Tebaga, clearly frustrated by the discussion.

He had struggled to listen and understand the concepts and was irritated that it had been for nothing. He wondered if Ena Ray was gloating over the fact that he knew how to play this game.

Ena Ray smiled slyly, "Because I thought it might be fun to use the Rebbercands as our game pieces."

Tebaga was so surprised by this answer that it took a few seconds for him to fully understand. His resentment immediately dissolved, as he pondered the possibilities. When the idea finally sunk in, he started to laugh.

"Oh," he said, "but won't Meri be upset with us? This sounds like 'manipulation.'"

To Ena Ray's surprise, he said the word imitating her voice in an exaggerated manner and wiggling his fingers in the air like he was casting a spell. The seed of resentment he had planted had grown much more than he had anticipated.

"Probably," he answered. "But I don't intend to tell her." He let the implication hang there for a moment, and then went on. "And besides, we're not going to hurt anyone and it's not going to be permanent. It's just for fun."

When Tebaga didn't respond immediately, he added, "But if you're too worried…"

"I'm not afraid," snapped Tebaga, not realizing Ena Ray had said nothing about being afraid.

At that moment Ena Ray knew his trap had already sprung and that Tebaga had no clue the trap had even been set. He's been captured, thought Ena Ray, and he doesn't even know he's been hunted.

"Good," he said quickly, before Tebaga could find any other reason not to proceed. "Since I'm more familiar with the game, I'll let you choose your players first. In fact, I'll offer to take that Grewt person as my Gynan. If he's as stupid as you've indicated, then that should give you a slight advantage."

Tebaga wasn't sure if Ena Ray was being sincere or not. He was finding it harder and harder to tell. Whatever, he thought. It's just a game. He'd play it once, just to appease Ena Ray, and then blow off any later suggestions on the basis that he didn't really like the game.

"OK," he said. "Then I'll take Rumblehead as my Gynan. He's the one who first took me in."

"Oh, yes," said Ena Ray, "I remember you mentioning him. A good choice."

They started identifying their players, alternating between one another, and indicating what roles each player would have. Then they identified the token to be protected. They cast spells on their respective teams and set about playing. Tebaga was making several extremely bad plays, making it almost impossible for Ena Ray to let him win. At one point Ena Ray had to call a stop. With a wave of his hand he froze everyone and everything in the village, forgetting that this was a skill Meri had not yet taught them.

"How did you do that?" Tebaga asked as he looked around in a circle at the village.

Ena Ray quickly covered up, "Uh, it's a fairly simple spell. I really don't recall when I learned to do this. I suppose it was one of the early ones Meri taught me before she had us taking lessons together. It had to be. You mean she didn't show you? She probably just forgot about you."

He took advantage of this unexpected opportunity to widen the wedge between Meri and Tebaga.

"I'll show it to you when we get back to the citadel – just act as if you don't know how to do it if Meri should decide to teach it to you someday." He let the implications of this sink in before he continued.

"Anyway, the reason I stopped everything is I wanted to explain a strategy here and show you how to better use your players."

Tebaga seemed to be considering the apparent slight from Meri. He tried to push it from his mind and get re-engaged in the game, but it wouldn't go completely away. Ena Ray was speaking to him, but he was barely listening: something about the better use of his Hrocs. He couldn't wait for this stupid game to end.

When the explanation was over, Ena Ray removed the spell he had cast. The game resumed and shortly thereafter Ena Ray won. Tebaga wasn't surprised, but it added to the foul mood that had developed with the discovery that Ena Ray had been shown yet another spell that Meri hadn't seen fit to share with him.

Ena Ray could see that Tebaga was more upset about the frozen time spell than he was letting on. I need to be more careful about what I do in front of him, he admonished himself. He couldn't think of any other way to explain how he had been teaching himself spells and potions. He also needed to get Tebaga's mind back on this game. It was essential to his plans that Tebaga become more adept at playing it. He was afraid that

Tebaga would be so discouraged that he'd reject any further suggestions to play.

"Look," he said, "I was at an unfair advantage. I've played this game before, although I have to admit, you picked it up much faster than I did." He lied.

"Really?" asked Tebaga. "I didn't think I picked it up at all."

"You're being much too modest. You nearly had me on more than one occasion. That's another one of the strategies – not to let your opponent know how close he is to defeating you. I think that's the only reason I won. I thought I was pretty good at this, but you've caught on much faster than I did."

Ena Ray continued with the false flattery, trying to invent things that would convince Tebaga he was better than he actually was.

"Let's try another one," he suggested. "Just a short one this time."

Tebaga wasn't particularly interested in playing any more, but his competitive nature made it difficult for him to accept defeat so easily. Reluctantly he agreed. This time Ena Ray made a number of deliberate errors, always disguising them. In the end he had made enough that Tebaga won – barely.

"Ha!" he said at the end of the game, "I knew you were holding out on me. I played for more than a year before I won my first game. You are a natural strategist. I think you let me win some of those earlier skirmishes just to set me up at the end."

The fact that he had not only won, but that in doing so Grewt ended up on his face in the mud added to Tebaga's elation. Maybe this wasn't such a bad game after all. Maybe he was better at it than he thought. He certainly enjoyed this more than the simple pranks they had been playing previously.

"What happens now?" he asked Ena Ray. "Won't they all remember being used as pieces in this game, especially Grewt? He's all covered in mud. Surely he's going to be able to recall how that happened."

"No, " Ena Ray answered. "Don't you remember? The spell we cast on them makes them think this was a dream, that is, if they can recall any of it at all. It's all going to be a blur and will quickly evaporate the more they try to think about it. As for your friend Grewt, he'll just think he tripped over something again."

This time when Meri returned and resumed the lessons, she made no subtle references to their activities in the village. In fact, she made no references at all. Ena Ray was certain she knew they had done something, even if she couldn't tell exactly what it was. He wondered why she didn't make some smart remark. By not doing so, he was even more suspicious. He studied her closely to see if he could detect any sign that she knew and was holding back. But nothing revealed itself.

Instead, she looked a bit distracted. Maybe she's too focused on whatever is going on that takes her away for so long, he thought. She would never speak of her absences or what caused them. Lately, though, she was beginning to look tired and stressed whenever she returned. Ena Ray wondered if whatever was taking her away from her citadel was also affecting her powers – maybe straining them. If her powers are related to the pendant, then, he concluded, he should see some indication in the stone itself.

To confirm this suspicion, the next time she left, he made some excuse to Tebaga, and secretly returned to the Sanctorum to look at the pendant and the stone. This time the stone was a deep red and the cloud inside was nearly black. The flashes were more visible and more frequent. He thought about touching it. He reached out and as he did so, it flashed and crackled. He snatched his hand back, thinking it might be better to leave it this time.

Whatever is going on, he thought, must be really big. If the reactions in this stone are any indication, she's consumed with it.

He thought some more about the fact that she didn't say anything about their trips into the village. He recalled that she looked tired; more than normal – and she was thinner. Then he realized that on those times when she was back in the citadel, she was spending less and less time with Tebaga and him on lessons, and more time by herself.

"She needs more time to restore her powers," he said out loud.

She's too distracted to focus on what we're doing, he concluded. It's affected her ability to see us or to see what we're doing. How can I use that, he asked himself. He decided to see how much he could push her.

One afternoon when Tebaga was otherwise engaged in his studies Ena Ray cornered Meri. It was evident that she was preparing to leave again and was trying to prepare herself.

"I don't want to overstep my bounds," he said, which quickly alerted her to the fact that this was exactly what he wanted to do.

"Why don't you ever talk about what you do when you leave?"

"It's a private matter, and really nothing that concerns you," she answered, trying to cut the conversation short.

"OK, I can understand that it may be private, but I disagree that it doesn't concern me – us. The fact is that you're not here. Tebaga and I have been left with a lot of time on our hands. Of course, we've been using that time wisely – studying in the library."

He was gambling that she wouldn't challenge this blatant lie. If she was as distracted as he thought she was, she wouldn't know for certain that it was a lie; she could only guess.

"But you're supposed to be our teacher," he continued when she didn't take the bait. "How can we learn from you if you're not here? That's not really fair to us, now, is it?"

"I've already told you, it's a private matter," she said. She was getting irritated with him.

"I respect that," he said. "I mean if you're seeing someone – some kind of lover or something..."

He knew this was not the reason for her absence. Since the lie about studying didn't evoke a reaction from her, he thought a jab about her love life might be enough to push her. Her glare at him told him he may have cracked her façade.

"I am not seeing a lover, not that it would be any business of yours if I were," she snapped.

"I didn't think so," he cut her off, trying to further irritate her. "I mean, it's not like you couldn't have a lover, but I guessed it was something else. But don't you see? All I can do is guess. You wouldn't believe what Tebaga thinks."

He threw that last comment in to stir things up.

"I don't care what Tebaga thinks," she nearly shouted. "I don't care what you think for that matter."

"Look," he said, again cutting her off. "You don't have to explain. You're right. If you want to date the Rebbercand village idiot, that's your choice. And you're also right that it doesn't matter if Tebaga thinks you've abandoned him, just like his family and friends have..."

He was hoping his comment about Tebaga would be like a dagger, and he was right.

"I'm fighting a war," she shouted.

He hadn't expected that.

"A war?" he asked. "With whom? Where?"

"I'm fighting a war with a league of sorcerers - Kelpies who have violated the laws that bind us all," she said. "The planets are almost in perfect alignment, and their powers are increasing. My colleagues had tried to talk some sense into them, but that didn't work. We now have to resort to more drastic measures."

"Like what," he asked. This was a side of Meri that he had never seen or even imagined.

"That's not something you need to know," she answered somewhat curtly. "You'll be safe here, and you won't be abandoned. I promise, but that's all I can say. I have to go now."

He was too stunned to stop her, even if he had been able to. He tossed this around in his mind for several hours, finally deciding that this was Meri's secret to share, not his. For the time being, he would keep it from Tebaga. If she later revealed it and let it be known that she had already shared it with him, he'd take his chances. It was better for now to keep Tebaga in the dark. He wondered if these Kelpies were in some of the images that appeared on the walls of Meri's Sanctorum. He had made a number of clandestine visits, still trying to unravel the mysteries of the visions — especially those dark clouds that seemed to be getting more and more dominant each time.

At the same time he was contemplating a way to make use of Meri's revelation, he also knew he had to continue to get Tebaga into the village to play their game. It was important to his overall plan that Tebaga become more adept at the game. Meri's bombshell helped things along, but it was merely one piece in his puzzle.

Tebaga was, in fact, getting better at the game, but Ena Ray still had to make intentional errors to allow him to win. Every once in a while Ena Ray would edge him out for a victory, but only on rare occasions and only by narrow margins. He had to make sure Tebaga didn't suspect his victories were false, and, at the same time, he needed to keep Tebaga's interest in playing and winning. He was getting closer and closer to the level at which Ena Ray needed him.

The games were becoming more physical and the players were being used in more violent ways. They would often gang up on opponent players, knocking them down and once in a while even throwing a punch or two. On more than one occasion, a player ended up with a bloody nose or a bruise. Tebaga didn't seem to be put off by this. In reality, it seemed like the violence made it even more enjoyable to him. He started initiating it without any suggestion or provocation by Ena Ray. On a few occasions Ena Ray had to stop things before they went too far. He taught Tebaga a spell that would make the players believe that any injuries they received were the result of some other accident, of which their memory was a bit vague.

As Tebaga became more familiar with the game's strategies and more confident in his abilities, Ena Ray decided to introduce a few changes. Instead of trying to obtain the opponent's token, he suggested the prize be something in possession of neither team and that they compete to obtain it. At first Tebaga was reluctant to change the goal.

"Now that I've learned to play your game, and beat you at it most times," he complained, "you want to change the rules."

"Oh, no," answered Ena Ray, "the rules stay the same. It's just the target that's different – something we both try to get. The leader of the Rebbercands - the one that Grewt guy is always toadying to - what's his name?"

"Argun," answered Tebaga.

"Yes, Argun. That's the one – kind of a pompous little guy. I've seen him in the village with some kind of medallion around his neck. He doesn't wear it all the time. Do you know what I'm talking about?"

He had chosen something similar to Meri's amulet. He would use these games as practice sessions for his real assault.

"Yes, that's his Crest of Authority. He wears that whenever he meets with the village Directorate. That's the group that sets out all the rules and regulations all the villagers have to follow. The Directorate also serves as the judge on any allegations of violations of the hundreds of rules. When Argun wears that Crest, there's a Directorate meeting in session and he's in charge. Why do you ask?"

"Where is it when he's not wearing it?"

"He keeps it on this bust in a special room in his home. I was only there once, but I can't imagine he keeps it any place else. That would be a change, and I've told you how much they don't like change. You still haven't explained why you want to know."

"I think it would be a real challenge for our teams to compete in an effort to take the Crest from Argun's home, display it to the other team and then return it without him knowing about it. And since you already know where it is, you have an advantage."

"Are you crazy?" Tebaga shouted. "He's got that thing in a well protected area in the center of his home when it's not dangling from his neck. It would almost be easier to take it off his body in the middle of a meeting of the Directorate."

"Now that would be a real challenge, wouldn't it?" Ena Ray smiled slyly at Tebaga, waiting for him to take the bait. He could see Tebaga thinking this over, and let the silence hang between them.

"How would this work?" Tebaga finally asked, and Ena Ray knew then the next part of his trap had been sprung.

"We would start from equal distances from the target and on opposite sides of the village. Since you know where he keeps it, I get to pick my starting point. Part of the strategy would be not only to trick or deceive Argun, but to block the other team's advances."

This added a new dimension to the game. It also provided a chance for Ena Ray to experiment with more spells he had been learning on his own. He planned to cast spells over Tebaga's team as well as his own. He had already learned how to read their thoughts – the ones implanted by Tebaga as he moved his players about. Now he would learn how to make counter moves with his own team as he made slight alterations to the moves Tebaga was making.

But he didn't plan to stop there. He wanted to manipulate Tebaga's thoughts, too. He wasn't powerful enough to control Tebaga, but he believed he was powerful enough to plant ideas in his head. Ena Ray would focus on thwarting Tebaga's team's efforts, and then on taking his time at making his own attack on the target. When the game began, it worked even better than he had hoped. After hours of maneuvers and counter-maneuvers, Ena Ray swept in and grabbed the prize only seconds before Tebaga was able to. He not only showed off the captured Crest, he put it around his own neck and imitated Argun, issuing commands and judgments.

At first Tebaga just laughed at the mockery of their unwitting target, but soon he viewed Ena Ray's behavior as gloating directed at him – rubbing his victory in Tebaga's nose. And soon the gloating became irritating; Tebaga could feel his anger building until, finally, he demanded a rematch.

Ena Ray didn't answer the challenge immediately, which further infuriated Tebaga. Tebaga was barely able to contain himself. That's right, Ena Ray thought, keep that fire burning while I fan the flames. He played with Tebaga's anger a bit more, before agreeing. In the rematch, he won again, by just a few steps. This time, though, he had to wait for Tebaga to get closer before snatching the victory from him. Tebaga could see that victory just beyond his grasp. He had won all those other times; why was he being beaten now? He demanded another rematch. And he lost again. When Ena Ray claimed that he had enough for one day and returned to the citadel, Tebaga was nearly blind with rage.

When they returned to the citadel, Ena Ray played the gallant winner, offering to serve Tebaga some refreshments.

"Please," he said. "Since I was the victor today – all three times," he added to further tighten the noose, "let me serve you."

Tebaga was unaware that Ena Ray had slipped a potion into his drink. The spell would only last long enough to suit Ena Ray's purposes. That night Tebaga couldn't sleep. He told himself it was only a game and he shouldn't be so upset, but he couldn't calm himself. The potion was having its effect. The next day Tebaga found Ena Ray reading in the library.

"I want another rematch," he demanded.

Ena Ray slowly looked up from his scroll.

"Oh, not today, if it's all right with you," he answered, turning back to the scroll. "There's something I wanted to go over before Meri returns."

He had told Tebaga that Meri would be gone for several days, when in fact, he was certain she was due back sooner rather than later. In Tebaga's mind, they had plenty of time to be on their own and to play their game as often as they liked. Ena Ray knew that his claim to want to go over some reading before Meri returned would be seen by Tebaga as just another attempt to gloat over yesterday's victories, and to avoid giving Tebaga the opportunity to beat him.

"She won't be back for several more days. You'll have plenty of time. I want another chance to beat you," Tebaga shot back.

Ena Ray slowly looked up from the scroll, and stared at Tebaga, purposely not answering immediately and giving him more time to get angry.

"Well. I suppose if you really want to," he finally said. And with that they returned to the village.

As the game began, Tebaga started with the same strategies he always used. He's so predictable, thought Ena Ray. He began to deploy his players to form a counter attack, but then Tebaga became completely unpredictable. Before Ena Ray could unfold his own game plan, Tebaga's team attacked Argun as he was returning from a Directorate meeting. He was wearing the Crest around his neck, returning home. Tebaga used a group of six or seven Broons to assault him and knock him down. They started kicking Argun and throwing punches until he could no longer raise his arms in defense. The attack was over in a matter of minutes. One of them reached down and yanked the Crest from his neck.

Several of the other players, who were in reality other members of the village, stood guard watching the mayhem. Tebaga stood in their midst with his arms folded. The Broons slowly and arrogantly walked off, leaving Argun in the dirt, bloody and beaten, and carried the Crest back to where Tebaga was standing, just a few yards away. Tebaga placed the Crest around his neck and turned to Ena Ray with a smile on his face.

"You never said we had to wait for the target to be in Argun's home."

Ena Ray watched Tebaga for a few seconds too shocked to speak. He looked from his opponent to Argun lying semi-conscious in the dirt, bleeding. He finally shifted his gaze back to Tebaga, thinking, I may have underestimated you after all. There is a devious streak in you after all. Forewarned is forearmed. I won't make that mistake again.

"That's right," he finally said. "I didn't. Well played, my friend. Well played. What do you say we make it even more interesting?"

Tebaga laughed as he strutted around admiring the Crest hanging around his neck, "Ah, now that I've beaten you, you want to make it _more_ interesting?" He looked up at Ena Ray with a sly smile on his face. "How do you plan to do that?"

Ena Ray smiled back and said, "Let's give them weapons."

Chapter five

Tebaga's euphoria at beating Ena Ray evaporated instantly. He stared at him, uncertain if he fully understood what he heard. He waited for him to explain himself. When nothing more was forthcoming, he opened his mouth to speak.

"Weapons?" he asked. "What do you mean? What kind of weapons?"

"Yes, weapons. All kinds of weapons," Ena Ray answered.

Tebaga thought about this for a minute. His initial reaction to this idea was to reject it. How could such violence be part of a game? Ena Ray didn't interrupt his thoughts. He knew Tebaga would yield to the idea eventually, especially in light of his team's attack on Argun in the last game.

"Like what?" Tebaga finally asked.

Ena Ray noted that he hadn't raised any concerns about the potential harm that may result from the use of weapons; only about what kind of weapons.

"You know, of course, that this game is based on the concept of war, and that the players are different levels of warriors," Ena Ray began. "It only makes sense that these warriors are armed, don't you think?"

He felt certain that Tebaga had never made the connection, but the time for belittling him was over. He now needed to be persuasive.

"Broons are the front line warriors, which is why there are so many of them. They would be only lightly armed; and with something that doesn't require much skill in using. I believe clubs would be adequate for them. The Hrocs are the second line of attack. Some of this attack is still hand to hand, but some if it can be accomplished at a distance. And, as you know, they are normally used for diversionary measures. I would think that they should be armed with spears. Skopos are more long distance fighters. They are used to soften enemy lines and as such, they need to be more fluid in their movements. I would say that their weapon of choice would be the bow and arrow. Cleddyfs are probably the most brutal warriors. They are certainly the most treacherous. They're the slashers and hackers, and should be armed with the two-headed axe. That way they can do damage coming and going. Finally, the Gynans are the most strategic warriors. Let's arm them with cross bows – very accurate, very stealthy and very lethal – and daggers, just for good measure."

Tebaga was taken aback more than just a little. He hadn't been prepared for this much. He had never known the Rebbercands to use weapons before. They certainly had axes and other such tools, but they were used only for cutting wood or making buildings and furniture. To his knowledge the Rebbercands had never used a weapon against another person. They could be brutal at times, but nothing more than punching or kicking. He didn't think they would even know how to use them in this manner. He wasn't sure how he felt about this whole development.

"Well," he finally found his voice and asked, "How many of them would have to have these weapons?"

Ena Ray leaned in close to Tebaga and smiled.

"All of them."

"All of them?" Tebaga repeated. "All of them? I don't understand. Why would we need to arm all of them?"

Ena Ray continued to smile, but his smile wasn't warm.

"To defend themselves," he answered, "why else? I think that everyone should have a weapon. That would only be fair, don't you think?"

"Everyone? But surely, you mean we would only need to arm those who are involved in the game," said Tebaga, trying to introduce some level of control, and beginning to worry that this might be getting out of hand.

"Of course not," Ena Ray responded immediately. "Everyone needs to be able to defend themselves. Besides, those arrows and spears don't know who is playing the game and who isn't." When he sensed that Tebaga wasn't completely convinced, he added, "You weren't so concerned when your team roughed up Argun. Shouldn't he have been able to defend himself? As I recall there were, what? Six or seven Broons attacking him? Don't you think if he had a dagger with him that it might have leveled the playing field just a little?"

"Yes. But..."

He started to say everyone involved had been part of the game, until he realized that Argun hadn't been a player. He had been an innocent bystander. He wasn't even the target. It was that cursed Crest he was wearing. Tebaga was now trapped by his own actions. Little did he know that it was a trap of Ena Ray's setting.

"I suppose you're right," he finally admitted. "They need to defend themselves. But what if they get hurt?" he asked feebly.

"We can patch up their cuts and bruises, just like we have with the bloody noses and the bumps they've gotten in the past," Ena Ray responded, dismissing this argument with a wave of his hand.

"But weapons are lethal. People could get more than just some bloody noses and bumps. What happens if someone gets killed?"

"We can just cast another spell," Ena Ray lied.

He well knew there was no spell to bring someone back from the dead. Tebaga wasn't sure about that last part, but he was close to the point where he was hearing only what he wanted to hear. Ena Ray knew he needed only a slight push in the right direction. Giving in to Ena Ray, he reached for the Crest.

"I suppose I should get this back to Argun before he knows it's gone."

And now for the last part of his plan, thought Ena Ray, he seized on the matter of the Crest. He had expected that he would have to raise it himself, but Tebaga handed it to him on a silver platter.

"I have a better idea," said Ena Ray. "Keep it."

"What?" asked Tebaga, looking up in surprise.

"Yes. Keep it. I see no reason for us to remain invisible to our teams, or to anyone else for that matter. We've become powerful sorcerers. What do we have to fear? Once we're done playing, the spells we cast will make them forget all about us. What's the point in hiding from them anymore?"

He moved closer to Tebaga and put an arm around his shoulder.

"We can cast any spell we like. We can make the whole village forget everything," he continued. "Even the past. As far as they would be concerned, you were always in charge. And with you wearing that Crest, they'll know you for the leader you truly are."

"But what about your team? If they see this Crest, won't they refuse to attack? How will that work?"

"I'll make them see something else. Whenever they see that Crest on you – only during the game, of course – they'll see their worst enemy."

Since Tebaga had caved in to Ena Ray's suggestion, he convinced himself that it would be fun in spite of his misgivings. He also convinced himself that all the destruction could be undone with the wave of a hand.

"Okay," he said, forcing a smile on his face. "But if I'm wearing the Crest, what will the target be – and don't say me," he joked half-heartedly.

Ena Ray laughed unconvincingly, "Of course it won't be you. I wouldn't do that to my friend. Let me think a minute. I'll come up with something good – something that won't put you or me in harm's way."

He had known all along what the target would be, but he had to make it look like this was a spur-of-the-moment idea. He walked a few steps away from Tebaga pretending to think. Then he turned back with a look of recognition.

"I know," he announced.

Rubbing his hands together, feigning a heightened level of excitement, he went on.

"It's perfect. I should have thought of this earlier. Ohhh, yes. You're going to love it."

"What?" demanded Tebaga, slowly beginning to share Ena Ray's excitement.

"Do you know that statue in the main hall of the citadel," he asked.

He was referring to an image of a sea horse on a large wave, carrying a rider on its back. It was a statue intricately carved from a rare stone and had been given as a gift to Meri by a Sea Sprite a long time ago. The stone was a milky white and with an unusual iridescent sheen. The statue stood about six inches high and was on display in an alcove in the main hall. The sea horse was on the crest of the wave. The rider was a woman in gossamer veils with flowing hair and a starfish tiara.

"Meri's statue?" asked Tebaga incredulously. "Inside the citadel?"

"We both know the secret to the portal," cut in Ena Ray, "so it will be even, and the fact that the only way into the citadel, at least for the Rebbercands, is through the portal, that will make it much more of a challenge."

"We can't take them into the citadel. What if Meri finds out? What if...?"

"She's not going to find out," Ena Ray cut him off. "She hasn't discovered all our trips to the village or the games we've been playing. How is she going to find out about this?"

"But what if she comes back right in the middle?"

"We won't start until right after she leaves. You know as well as I do that she's been gone more and more lately. And every time she's gone it's longer than the last time. You're not backing out on me now, are you?"

Things had gone too far for Tebaga to back away now. He reluctantly agreed, and the planning for the game began. It wasn't long before Meri once more departed and Ena Ray's strategy was put to the test.

The sides had been drawn up well before the date of the game, and this time it seemed as if nearly the entire village was included. Tebaga had never seen so many weapons at one time. He was powerless to stop it all, or to even temper it. Part of him didn't really want to. He knew it was too late for him to have second thoughts. He forced any misgivings behind him and committed himself fully to the game.

As the Rebbercands on both sides were armed, many of them had no idea how to use what had been handed to them. Several were shot with arrows accidentally as volleys were released into large crowds. The careless swinging of two headed axes resulted in more than one severe injury. Before too many were injured prior to the start of the game, Ena Ray and Tebaga cast spells so that each player became an expert with the weapon assigned. As a result, not only did their skill levels change, but their demeanors did as well. They seemed to personify a sense of brutality and remorselessness.

As this transformation evolved, the sky above the village slowly darkened. Ena Ray looked up. The clouds from his vision were forming. For a second he was uncertain about what he was planning, but the more he stared at the clouds, the more he was filled with confidence. He wasn't sure if he was drawing energy from the impending storm, or if the storm was a reflection of his growing might.

At the onset of the game, Tebaga's forces were marshaled far to the east of the tree that hid the citadel, and Ena Ray's were to the west. When the designated time to declare the start arrived, both commanders were on hilltops overlooking the initial deployment. As the battle evolved, they would change positions, but this was where they began.

Ena Ray could see his opponent off in the distance, casting the same kind of spells on his players as he was. He smiled to himself at the image of Tebaga, waving his arms. He looked like a conductor at the head of an orchestra. This thought made him freeze for a second. That image was familiar. And then he realized he must look the same. It stuck him that this was the image of himself he saw on the walls of the Sanctorum when he last held the stone and pendant. He faltered for only an instant wondering what other parts of his vision might appear. He looked back up at the black clouds that had nearly filled the sky.

He thought about his visions and recalled seeing stone likenesses of several Rebbercands. He looked back to Tebaga's army. Those likenesses had appeared as soldiers. Casting one more glance back at the clouds, he returned his stare to a small group of the opposing forces furthest away from Tebaga and he focused his thoughts on them. A rumble of thunder split the air, followed by a slight flash. His first thought was that this was wrong. Lightning always came first. He looked at the group and at first thought they looked the same. Then he realized they had been turned to stone. By now Tebaga had begun to move his forces forward and no one noticed the small team that was left behind.

Interesting, he thought, a wicked smile creeping across his face. I'll have to remember that. And then he refocused his thoughts on the task immediately at hand.

The initial plan of attack for both players was the same. They advanced their Broons on one another, neither side making a straight path for the portal. Hundreds of them came at each other wielding their clubs. Tebaga hadn't realized the number of players that had been included. He still thought of them as players, although this had gone far beyond a game. They attacked each other with fervor. He was appalled by the sights and sounds of the violence, but when Ena Ray's Broons began to drive forward, overwhelming Tebaga's team, he overcame any hesitation he might have had. He advanced the Hrocs, ruthlessly directing them by first throwing their spears, and then giving chase when Ena Ray's Broons began to retreat. He was relentless, showing the fleeing Rebbercands no mercy.

Tebaga discovered an instant too late that the retreat of Ena Ray's Broons was only a deception. His Hrocs were drawn into a trap and caught in a cross fire between Ena Ray's Hrocs and his Skopos. The Skopos were deadly accurate and Tebaga's Hrocs were soon on the run. Seeing the shift in the battle and in the strength of his position, Tebaga moved from the hilltop to better direct the main force of his attack. He reassembled his remaining Broons and Hrocs and launched a counter attack, reinforcing them with his Skopos, and at the same time, cordoning off the portal to the citadel. At the same time he sent his Clyddfs straight to the tree itself.

On the opposite hillside Ena Ray watched as he guided his fighters, setting traps within traps, drawing Tebaga's men into one deception after another. As he divided Tebaga's soldiers, isolated them and cut them down, he noticed a team of Clyddfs begin striking the tree with their axes. They weren't using any finesse to enter the portal; they were hacking at the tree itself.

"What's he doing?" Ena Ray exclaimed out loud.

The tree, which hid the entire citadel, was a giant Sabine. It was nearly five feet across at the trunk and its limbs stretched out nearly twenty feet in each direction, stretching more than sixty feet into the air. It was the centerpiece of the village. Although it had been created by Meri to disguise her sanctuary, in the minds of the Rebbercands it had been there for centuries. But it wasn't real, and now Tebaga's Clyddfs were hacking at it.

Tebaga had forsaken all efforts or even perceptions of stealth and strategy. He was using brute force to gain entrance to the citadel and defeat Ena Ray at his own game, just as he had in taking the Crest from Argun. He was, however, unaware of the consequences, and Ena Ray was furious with himself for not having anticipated such a move.

"The fool," shouted Ena Ray.

As his anger rose, he was oblivious to the increased intensity of the blackened sky. The rumble of thunder was deeper and more prolonged. Lightning flashes flickered high above them, as yet undirected.

The object had been to use each other's army to gain access to the portal, not to destroy it. He redirected all of his warriors towards Tebaga's Clyddfs. He needed to stop them from cutting down the tree. He moved every available fighter to the village center, but they were met with a shower of arrows from several Skopos that Tebaga had held in reserve. These were supplemented with a small band of Clyddfs and a larger unit of Skopos that Tebaga had also held in reserve. In addition to these fighters, Tebaga had established a mystical force field that shielded the ones cutting the tree.

He is better at this game than he has let on, thought Ena Ray. He wondered who had been fooling whom all this time. He also realized that he was no longer able to control Tebaga's fighters. His spell over them was being blocked, and he was unable to penetrate the force field. He realized too late that Tebaga had become much more powerful than he had been led to believe. He had to quickly change his strategy.

He pulled back his fighters. Unlike before, this time none of Tebaga's soldiers gave chase. That was all right. Ena Ray needed to regroup. He scoured the battlefield for any wounded warriors. He cast a spell on all he could find, repairing their wounds and rebuilding their strength. He cast another spell and rearmed the Broons with swords to replace their clubs, and gave them shields to protect themselves.

He then changed the spears of the Hrocs to maces – spiked metal balls attached to a wooden handle by a length of chain. These would do much more damage than the spears. He also gave them all shields. He waved his hand again and made the shields impervious to any weapon. Then he assembled his newly reconstituted force and had them stand ready, with his Gynans; his lead Gynan, Grewt was at their head. In a fit of rage he watched a unit of Tebaga's Hrocs make a feint towards Ena Ray's flank, cutting away at the units he had recently revitalized. He turned away, thinking there was nothing to do now, but let Tebaga destroy the tree and open the gates of the citadel. He missed the flash from the sky that turned the entire attacking unit to stone. The storm was beginning to act independently of his direction; interpreting his will.

Tebaga saw what Ena Ray had done with his army, and while his Clyddfs continued to attack the tree, he moved his remaining Broons into formation. He, too, converted their clubs to swords, and reinforced their numbers with squadrons of Hrocs, arming them with the same weapons Ena Ray had given his fighters. They were set into formation behind more Clyddfs ready to attack as soon as the citadel was breached.

Tebaga's Clyddfs were attacking the tree in a systematic manner. Instead of chopping at the sides to make the tree fall, they had cut a large vertical slice in the center. They were cutting into the heart of the tree, carving an opening. The gouge went from about a foot above the ground and upward nearly six feet. As they continued to drive their axes into the trunk, the opening began to look like the iris of a cat's eye – narrow at the top and bottom, and widening closer to the center.

The fighting among the other warriors had diminished as both sides regrouped for the invasion of the citadel. The opening was now nearly two feet wide and almost as deep. The next blow of an axe struck the tree's heart and a streak of light burst forth, nearly blinding those closest to it. A second strike at the heart released another explosion of white and a rush of wind that threw the Clyddfs back. The tree had been breached; the portal was open.

The ground surrounding the trunk began to shake. The vibrations were rippling outward in circles from the center of the tree. As Tebaga and Ena Ray looked on from their respective positions, they watched the tree slowly split open on its own. The shock waves actually pushed nearby buildings away and the Rebbercands scurried to avoid being crushed. Everything was being pushed away as the circle around the tree expanded. The split in the trunk cracked upward, opening wider and wider. Light shot outward and upward as the tree divided itself and peeled away. The light was so bright it diminished the imposing black sky above. Ena Ray's uncontrolled fury at what Tebaga was doing was having a direct impact on the power of the storm. By now, hundreds of Rebbercands, from both sides of the conflict were frozen stone statues.

Every person, every animal, every plant and every building was pushed back farther and farther or buried underneath in an ever-widening circle as the tree split and the citadel began to emerge. Each room in the citadel unfolded as the spell was broken. Those nearest covered their ears as the ripping and crashing sounds became deafening. They shielded their eyes as the light intensified. They ran in fear as the mystical home that had been concealed from them for years grew and grew. Those that didn't run were trapped beneath.

Finally it was done. The building was immense. It dwarfed the entire village of the Rebbercands, spanning more than a hundred feet in every direction. There were domes and spires, towers and ramparts. It rose over a hundred feet into the sky and was made of a glistening white marble with veins of gold running through. The tree itself was nowhere to be seen. Trunk, branches, limbs and leaves had all disappeared. All that surrounded the palace was a film of dust as it settled to the ground. Everyone watching was silent. Even the thunderous storm was quiet.

Ena Ray and Tebaga were stunned. They had lived inside for months – or had it been years? Neither could really recall. Time inside the citadel had no relevance to the outside world. But neither of them had understood the enormity of the home in which they had lived. Their respective warriors looked to their leaders, unsure of what to do next. Both sorcerers reacted in the same instant, directing the invasion as their respective goals dictated.

Tebaga's soldiers advanced through an opening on the eastern side of the citadel, as Ena Ray's swarmed through a western gate. Both armies wandered through a labyrinth of halls and rooms. Tebaga finally ran to the front pushing aside his warriors. He scanned the halls and rooms, trying to recall the layout of the building. Finally he led the way to the main hall and to the alcove that held the statue.

Ena Ray waved his hand and his soldiers divided, creating an opening to the front. The statue had been a ruse. The real target was in the Sanctorum. He didn't need to rush. He had learned the way and knew that Tebaga would be otherwise occupied. Besides, he needed to wait for the last piece of his plan to fall into place.

As the two armies infiltrated the citadel, they eventually encountered one another. Still in battle mode, they began to attack each other. Fighting in the corridors spilled into adjacent larger rooms, each of which was destroyed in turn. Both armies became savage and frenzied; uncontrollable, they smashed windows, crushed ceramic artwork, ripped apart books and scrolls, and shattered furniture. Their leaders had each gone off in their own direction seeking their own prize, leaving the warriors unchecked. The fighting soon filled nearly every room in the palace. Outside, the storm had once more begun to rage.

Ignoring the carnage behind him, Tebaga rushed into the main hall and spotted the statue in the alcove. He had beaten Ena Ray to the target. He strutted like a peacock over to the image and swept it up in his hand. Holding it high in the air, he shouted, "Ena Ray, where are you? I've captured the statue. I'm the victor."

"What have you done?" the voice behind him demanded.

Tebaga spun around to see Meri. The grin from his face was immediately replaced with a look of shock. His voice froze in his throat as he slowly lowered the hand holding the statue. He looked around the room guiltily, his head jerking from right to left, looking for an ally of any kind, only to find himself alone. The remnants of his army stood silently in the doorways leading to the main hall, staring from him to Meri and back.

"Answer me," she shouted. "What have you done?"

"You're not supposed to be here," he answered feebly.

He began to cower as the rage in her eyes bore through him.

"You're not supposed to be here," he repeated in a near whisper.

"I have lived here in peace for nearly two centuries, and in a matter of minutes you have destroyed all that I hold precious."

She was moving slowly towards him, her words like a growl through her tightly clenched teeth.

"I took you in when no one would have you; I shared my home and my knowledge; and this is how you repay my kindness?"

She raised her hand high in the air and cast a spell as she brought it down slowly. The air around him became thick and hard to breathe. The light that emanated from the walls of the palace dimmed.

"I banish you. Your appearance will reflect your soul – a soul no one shall see. I banish you to the core of the earth, to be buried behind a mask so no one will have to look on you. I banish you to a chamber within a chamber, so that no one can rescue you. I cast you out and bind you over forever such that no one but another Enchantress may set you free."

The energy from her spell moved like rippling water toward him, and with a flash of pale red light, Tebaga was gone. She then turned to the army still looking on, crammed into each of the entryways to the main hall. Raising her hand again, she cast a second spell.

"And you who followed this dark sorcerer, I banish forever. You will have no home. You will have no honor. You will wander the land finding no solace, setting no roots, having nothing of your own. All who look upon you will see you as the pariahs you are. You will have no friends or allies."

The light flashed a deeper red this time, and the Rebbercands of Tebaga's army vanished. Meri looked around at the destruction and knew there was more to be dealt with. She had to confront her prediction of betrayal, and headed for the Sanctorum.

Ena Ray was waiting for her. He had known when she was due back and had timed his arrival in the Sanctorum to coincide with her return. As soon as she was in the citadel, it was safe for him to take possession of the pendant. He placed it around his neck, with the stone centered over his heart. He could feel the power of the stone entering his body. At that instant he knew the fury of the storm was his to command.

Meri entered the Sanctorum and saw him standing in her private, sacred room. The pendant was strung around his neck.

"As I predicted, you have betrayed me," she said to him. The rage had left her momentarily. Now she was only filled with sadness. "I just hadn't seen the extent of your betrayal and the additional damage you would do. I had underestimated your lack of conscience, your lack of remorse, and your treachery."

"You're wrong," he answered. "I have no intention of betraying you. I only want the power that you have kept from me."

In spite of all he had done, in Ena Ray's mind he did not see his actions as a betrayal. Deep in his heart he still entertained the hope that they would be peers; that they would remain friends. His arrogance had blinded him to the truth of his actions.

"No," said Meri, "I am not wrong. Your presence here is a betrayal. The exploitation of Tebaga, of the Rebbercands, and of your own powers is a betrayal. You cannot be trusted. You are as bad as the Kelpies I have fought – no; you are worse."

"That's not true," he shouted at her in anger. "It's you who betrayed me. You kept from me the full extent of my power. You denied me what was mine. You treated me like a child instead of the equal I am."

The sky above the citadel was filled with storm clouds. Ena Ray looked up at them, and then slowly lowered his gaze to Meri. He said nothing but his threat was clear: yield to me or become a image of stone. Without taking her eyes off of him, she snapped her fingers skyward and the motion of the storm froze in place.

"That is how you would prove your friendship?" she demanded. "With a display of power and your pathetic threats? You have shown no respect for your abilities and have disgraced yourself. I can no longer protect you."

With that she thrust her arm forward. His body felt like it was encased in ice – immovable. All he could do was watch. Waves of energy billowed out from her outstretched hand, distorting the air in expanding circles. The wave moved towards him and then engulfed him. He was powerless to stop it or to counteract it. She slowly stepped towards him.

"I banish you. You will be a bodiless form that will betray no one ever again. I banish you to a faraway place and as cold as your heart where no one will find you."

She looked into his eyes and for a moment her heart softened.

"I cast you out and bind you over such that only when the planets are once again aligned and the power of the pendant is once again in your possession can you be freed."

A burst of lightning appeared from the center of the wave directly at him. It struck the center of the pendant, just over his heart. The blast tore the stone apart, sending pieces in several directions. The band around the stone flew upward, spinning in the air as the pieces of the stone itself scattered. Ena Ray could feel himself thrown back by the blast against the wall of the Sanctorum. As he fell backwards, his eyes focused on the band as it drifted above his head.

His last image was his fingers slowly closing around the spinning band as his body seemed to dissolve. All the sounds around him, including his own screams, blended together into a single roar. The room stretched as if it was being pulled at the top and bottom and then twisted. And then everything went black – and cold.

With the flash of light, Ena Ray was gone and the black clouds overhead evaporated into the evening sky. All this time, soldiers from Ena Ray's army had been gathering in the entryways to the Sanctorum awaiting instructions. All but one. Before Meri could turn around Ena Ray's Gynan, Grewt, let loose a shot from his cross bow. It struck her deep in the center of her back, throwing her to the ground. She fought to raise herself up and face him. With a flick of her hand and with a gasping breath she cast her final spell.

"I banish you and your kind to the underworld. Your image shall be cast to reflect your souls."

In a flash of green light, Grewt and the rest of Ena Ray's army were turned into gargoyles and driven deep underground. As soon as the spell was cast, Meri, the citadel and the entire Rebbercand village disappeared in a giant haze of blue smoke.

Chapter six

The pieces from the shattered stone from Meri's pendant scattered hundreds of miles away from the site of her citadel. It had broken into four pieces. One piece was picked up by various animals and carried even farther away, often being dropped from one remote location to another. One piece landed in the ocean and sank to the bottom. It was swallowed by a fish and traveled thousands of miles. Another was lost, mixed with rubble, buried in sand, and finally encased in ice in a far off place. The fourth piece – the center of the stone - was picked up by a Blue Falcon who found it in a jungle and flew for days with it clutched in his talon. It spotted a smaller bird fluttering several hundred feet below him, and not having eaten for some time, the Falcon dropped the stone and went after the prey.

The stone fell through the trees, bounced off several branches, ricocheted off a large rock and tumbled through the dirt and underbrush into the shadow of a fallen tree trunk. It remained there undisturbed for more than four hundred years. During that time the tree trunk rotted and collapsed, covering the stone. Wind and rain further covered the stone in mud and other debris and then uncovered it hundreds of times in those four centuries. A stream developed over the top of it, and over time the water eroded the layers of dirt above it. Eventually, the current washed it further along. Along the way, it became lodged in a niche in a piece of granite in a bend in the stream's bed.

One summer day, a forest creature was hunting in the woods near this stream. It was a hot day and he had been searching for several hours. When he came upon the stream, he bent down to take a drink. A flicker of light caught his eye. At first he thought it was the sun reflecting on the water's surface, but the sparkle came from near the bottom. The stone's color was nearly the same as the sand and granite in which it was resting. He reached into the water and waved the sand away. As he did so, he spotted a glistening stone. It seemed to change color slightly and flashed in the sunlight. When he reached in further to pick it up, he felt a slight tingling or vibration. It was so subtle and lasted for such a short time, that he thought he must have imagined it.

He put the stone in a pouch on his belt and forgot about it until several weeks later. When he was digging around in the pouch looking for something else, he felt the stone, which had shifted into a corner under several other items of interest that had been gathered along the way. The forest creature removed the stone and examined it. At first he was inclined to toss it way, but something made him reconsider. He decided he liked it and that it was a gift from above. Throwing it away would probably offend the spirits who had delivered it to him. Studying it closely, he saw that the stone appeared to have been broken from something larger, and had an unusual shape and a very distinctive coloring. He had never seen anything quite like it before. It was a triskelion. He thought it would make a nice adornment, but he wasn't sure what to do with it. Hanging it from a necklace of some sort wasn't practical. He then decided to put it in an armband.

He fashioned a band from leather, engraving a series of symbols that had come to him in his dreams. In the center of these symbols, he cut out a place of honor for the stone. The band had rawhide strings on the ends to allow him to tie the band around his arm. The stone seemed to change color depending on what the forest creature was thinking or doing. Most of the time, it appeared to almost glow. He wore it proudly until he was killed in a battle. On that day, the glowing ceased. The armband was taken from his body by the invader who had attacked him – an unusual looking person with a snout-like nose, bristling hair and tusks jutting up from his lower jaw.

More than a hundred years passed. The armband with the stone was passed from one generation to the next by the invaders, but not handed from father to son. It was fought over and went to the victor. All this time the stone was a flat dull color. The fights had been over the intricately designed armband, rather than the stone imbedded in the side. These invaders had no real home, but settled in a place only long enough to build houses and erect monuments, and then they would leave. Eventually they returned to the same land of the forest creatures that their ancestors had visited over a century earlier. This time, however, they were not as successful as they had been previously. This time the forest creatures were not taken by surprise. This time the forest creatures drove the invaders back to the sea.

After the battle, one of the forest creatures found an armband with an unusual looking stone in it that had been worn by one of the fallen invaders. He untied it from the invader's arm, cleaned it off, and kept it for himself. The stone seemed to glow almost immediately. As he grew older and had children of his own, he passed the armband down, as did his descendants, from one to the next. Centuries passed and the leather band became worn and frayed. The rawhide strings had been replaced several times over, but the symbols remained as clear as the day they had been engraved. During an attack by an Eremites Bear, the bear's claw struck the armband. The leather protected the arm of the forest creature, and kept him from losing it, but the stone was knocked loose and was lost in the dirt.

About a month later a wanderer entered the lodge of the forest creatures. Normally suspicious of strangers, they sensed that this one was different. He was an alchemist, he told them, searching for knowledge. They welcomed him into their homes and he lived with them for many years. During the course of his stay, he noticed the old, worn armband with the distinctive engraving, and offered to repair it. As soon as he touched the opening where the stone had been, he could sense the power of the missing piece. He asked what had happened to it, and was told how it was lost, but no one could be sure exactly where.

He knew he would not likely be able to find it, but he also knew that something that powerful wouldn't remain lost forever, and shouldn't fall into the wrong hands. Placing his thumb over the setting he whispered an incantation. Miles away, under leaves and dirt, the triskelion slowly shrunk in size, becoming nearly invisible. Satisfied that he had hidden the stone as well as he could, he then returned his attention to the band and in repairing it.

He revitalized and hardened the leather giving it the strength of metal. He sealed the open ends to make the band a solid circle, discarding the rawhide strings. Then he duplicated and reversed the band, and inserted it inside the original one, giving the entire object mystical qualities. By turning the inner band and aligning the strange markings that now appeared both inside and outside, the size of the band would change to fit any wearer.

When he gave it back to the forest creature, he was asked why the band needed to be able to change its size. The alchemist smiled at him and only said that the time would come when this might be necessary. Offering no further explanation, he retired for the night. The next morning he had disappeared as mysteriously as he had appeared.

The tradition of passing the armband from one generation to the next continued for centuries until a time when the forest creatures were again invaded by strangers. The Dozer who now had possession of it was a mighty leader. He was readying a party of hunters to meet these strangers. They had been discovered cutting down trees in the forest and wanted to trade with the forest creatures. Their offer had been rejected, but they continued to cut the trees. Two other groups had met with the strangers, but had not returned.

This Dozer was taking another group of forest creatures to force the strangers from the forest and to learn what had become of others who had gone before him. As he was leaving, a young boy ran up to him, asking to come along. The boy idolized this Dozor, who had been a mentor to him, especially since the boy's great grandfather had disappeared soon after first speaking with these same strangers. He stopped the boy and told him maybe next time.

As he talked to the boy, a dark cloud passed overhead. The Dozer took this as a bad omen. He told the boy to return to the village and turned to continue to his meeting with the strangers. As an afterthought he called the boy back to him. He then removed the armband and placed it on the boy's arm. The boy's idol and mentor never returned, and the young boy eventually became a Dozer himself, wearing the armband he had been given.

Just about the same time that the Alchemist was living among the forest creatures, deep in another part of the forest, a Skiouros monkey was rooting around for nesting materials. These animals were excellent at building nests high in the trees, and were also notorious pack rats. Digging in the dirt, she came across a tiny, odd looking stone, brightly colored and cut in the shape of a triskelion. She picked it up and added to her hoard of materials. Skiouros monkeys are nomadic creatures and after a short period of time, the herd gathered what items they could carry and moved off. The stone went with them.

Over time and after many similar moves, the stone was left behind and again covered in leaves and twigs. One day a tremendous storm struck the area and the leaves, twigs and stone were washed into a gulley and from there into a larger stream. Stuck to the underside of a large leaf, the stone was carried miles and miles down this stream to a large pool. As the leaf floated to the bank carried by the movement of the water, the stone fell off, dropped to the bottom and nestled between some pebbles.

One day a young faerie was having some fun chasing a dragonfly. The faerie and the dragonfly soared high into the sky and then swooped downward towards the pool of water. By chance the sunlight filtering through the trees and shrubs along the edge of the pool reflected off the stone and attracted the attention of the faerie. She broke off from her chase and fluttered over the surface of the water searching for the source of the reflection. She flew back and forth over the stream looking for the sparkling object that had caught her eye.

Just as she was about to give up, thinking it had been her imagination, she discovered it. She plunged into the water, avoided the nearby fish that was about to gobble it up, snapped up the stone and flew home. Being enchanted creatures themselves, she was oblivious to the tingling electrical feeling of the stone. When she got home, she showed her treasure to her grandfather, who fashioned a necklace for her from which the stone hung. This pendant became her most valued possession. It was passed from mother to daughter for the next several centuries.

One day the young faerie princess who now wore the stone on the pendant was riding a grasshopper. In her excitement, she was carried deep into the forest where she was thrown off and soon discovered she was lost. There she met and was rescued by the young Dozer who wore the armband his long lost mentor had given him. The developed a friendship in spite of the centuries of conflict between their two peoples. Not long after this friendship was established, they took part in an incredible adventure. At one point in this adventure, they discovered that the stone from the faerie's pendant fit perfectly in a space in the forest creature's armband. But it wasn't until they gave the armband to an

Enchantress that the true powers of the tiny stone were unleashed. This all happened more than a thousand years after Meri's spell shattered the original stone and sent Ena Ray to the Crystal Citadel and Tebaga to his secluded prison.

Since the Alchemist had redesigned the armband, by shifting the inner band the size of the band could be adjusted. It was expanded from the size of the forest creature's arm to fit the Enchantress, who wore the band around her head like a crown. At one point, though, the stone had to be removed from the armband and given to the faerie to release some demons. It was much larger now than it had been when the faerie wore it as a necklace, but that couldn't be helped. In the center of the stone was the substance that caused the flashes of light that had been seen so many times over the centuries. It was called Nostrumite, and had an unusual affect on other materials. When the faerie dropped the stone on a statue made of Lambentite, the stone shattered and the demon trapped in the Lambentite was released.

The faerie was horrified by the shattering of the stone and was certain that it had been lost forever. But she was not aware of all of the powers of this stone. Even before the demon was released from the Lambentite, the particles of the stone rose into the air and came together again in their original form. The only evidence that the stone had shattered were very thin lines – almost like a spider's web – throughout the stone. The band was now back on the Enchantress' head with the stone centered in between the original engravings. When the band was worn with the stone centered on her forehead, it served almost as a third eye – an eye that enabled her to see beyond the walls of her Sanctorum.

After the release of the demon, Stella offered to return the stone to Summer. She declined. It belonged with the band. Stella then offered to return it and the armband to Sean, but he knew she could make better use of it. She had insisted, since it had been a gift to him from someone he so greatly admired. He still refused, telling her that the real treasures from his mentor were his memories, not a simple band with a stone in it.

She was wearing that band only a few weeks later as she viewed some disturbing images in her Sanctorum.

She had hoped that her last encounter with the Rebbercands would be the last time she'd ever see them, but it didn't appear that would be the case. The visions that raced across the walls and ceiling of her Sanctorum were filled with these vicious creatures. She knew that the visions that materialized on the walls before her often blurred past events with the future, so it was hard to tell if what she was seeing had already happened or was yet to come. She also knew that her visions would not manifest themselves unless there was an imminent threat. Consequently, she believed that the Rebbercands were up to no good once again, and that the strife they often caused would infringe in some way on the realm of the Sea Sprites. However, she was unable to make any sense of what she was seeing. In spite of that, the thought of another encounter with them was making her stomach knot.

There were hundreds of them and they were in some kind of underground cavern. Was this just a memory of the past, or were they back underground? She didn't see any Trepans in her visions – the society that lived underground which the Rebbercands forced to dig mines. If she had, she would have felt confident that what she was seeing was nothing new. The fact that they were absent from these visions only added to the confusion. She knew she hadn't seen more than a small portion of the tunnels underground during her time with the Trepans, but still the caverns that were appearing now looked quite different.

She also saw tidal waves crashing over villages, but she couldn't tell where. These images often blended or overlapped the other images, making it more difficult to get a clear idea of where they were occurring. The water itself was also obliterating any indications of their locations. She saw intermittent images of a large dark cavern, but couldn't tell where it was, or what significance it had. Throughout all of this, she had no visions whatsoever of Princess Natalie, but she had an overwhelming sense that she was in danger. It was all so frustrating.

As she scanned the images, every time the impression of the large dark cavern appeared, she felt like the air was being sucked out of her room. She had never experienced such a physical reaction to any other single image. There was something very ominous about this part of the vision. She cleared her mind and concentrated only on the cavern. Slowly the other images faded away and the underground area came to the forefront. Gradually the projection filled the walls and ceiling of her Sanctorum. It was almost as if she was in the cavern herself. It was hard to see, since everything was so dark. Then she felt another physical reaction to the image. The air became cold and dank. Goose pimples formed on her arms and she struggled to maintain her focus.

When her eyes adjusted to the low light, she could better see the shape of the cave. She turned around completely taking in the view that filled every part of her room. The cavern was a near perfect circle about twenty or thirty feet in diameter. The walls curved up into the domed ceiling nearly forty feet above. There were a number of shadows that appeared at various intervals along the base of the wall that looked like passages to separate exits or tunnels. She couldn't see more than a few inches into the passageways.

"This looks like a Sanctorum," Stella muttered; a chill running through her body. "How odd. But it doesn't have the same feel to it."

In the center of the cavern she could barely make out some kind of object. It appeared to be a large rectangular shape, raised on some kind of pedestal, and it was generating a pulsing glow. The clarity of the image faded in and out. This seemed to be the only source of light in the cave. Stella concentrated harder. The stone in the band around her head began to change color, but she was unable to see it.

The box-like image was blurred at first, but then started to get clearer. It seemed to be man-made rather than natural. The edges were too uniform. As it grew and filled her field of vision, she was able to make out some strange markings on the surface of what looked like a container of some kind – maybe even a sarcophagus; she wasn't sure. At the same time, the stone in her headband had turned a bright red and began emitting rays of light.

Stella took a few steps towards the image of the box. Suddenly a shock wave blasted forth from the container and threw her up into the air and halfway across her room. She landed jarringly on her bottom and slid quickly across the rest of the floor until she slammed into the wall on the opposite side of the Sanctorum. The images on the walls all disappeared instantly as well as the cold, dank air.

Right at that moment, Princess Natalie walked in. She stepped through the doorway, having just missed the shockwave and its affect on Stella. There was no trace of the images on the walls or the cold that had accompanied them.

"Oh, good," she said to Stella, looking at the blank walls and the Enchantress on the floor, "I'm glad to see that you're not busy. There was something I wanted to ask you."

Stunned, Stella looked up at Natalie and, readjusting her headband asked, "What? What do you mean I'm not busy?"

"Well," she answered, "you're just sitting there relaxing on the floor, doing nothing. I simply assumed you're not busy."

Then she looked around the room. It was completely empty and there were no images or other projections on the walls or ceiling. Everything was quiet. It was not like Stella to sit idly in the Sanctorum.

"Why exactly are you sitting on the floor?" Natalie asked.

"I'm NOT sitting on the floor," Stella responded a bit indignantly, still sitting on the floor where she had landed.

Natalie was taken back a bit by Stella's insistence.

"Uh, you're on the floor, and you're sitting. I'm not sure how you would describe it, but to me, you're – I don't know - sitting on the floor?"

Stella got up and brushed herself off. She was a bit shaken by her experience and uncertain as to what would cause it. She wanted to get to the bottom of it all, and couldn't shake a feeling a growing irritability.

"That's not what I meant. I know I was sitting on the floor, but I wasn't – oh, never mind. What do you want?" she snapped.

Natalie raised her eyebrows at Stella's brusque response. In spite of their very close relationship, Stella had always addressed Natalie as Princess or your Highness. Something was apparently distracting her. Maybe she's spending too much time in this room, she thought to herself. I need to take her out more often.

"I was on the north side of the island," she said, deciding to leave the discussion about getting out more often for a later time. "We have received notices from some of our outposts in that direction of minor tremors – nothing really serious; just unusual. I was fairly certain that the Trepans had finished their repairs along the shoreline to the north and had moved on much further inland. I was wondering if you could conjure any images that might tell us if something was going on that we should know about."

As Stella walked from the far side of the Sanctorum towards Natalie, the Princess noticed a small flicker of light from the stone in Stella's headband. The center appeared to be slowly fading from a glowing white and the tips of the three arms were fading from a bright red. The stone seemed to be changing color and returning to its normal golden brown hue. Something had happened. That explained why Stella was on the floor, and probably why she was being so cranky. She decided not to ask. She knew that Stella would tell her in her own time.

Although it was not like Stella to keep secrets from Natalie, she usually preferred to have as much information as possible. As an Enchantress, she was relied upon to help protect the Sea Sprites, and most importantly, her Princess. To do so, she had to be sure that what she was seeing in her visions was not only real, but something that hadn't already happened.

Right now, she didn't know what to warn Natalie about. As disturbing as she felt her vision had been, she couldn't explain the source of that disturbance.

She smoothed her clothing and brushed a strand of hair from her face. She took a deep breath and seemed to regain her composure. The feeling of irritability slowly evaporated. She realized she had been rude earlier and that Natalie had let it pass. She had a moment of shame, but then answered.

"Of course, your Highness. In fact I was just scanning some very unusual images. I haven't been able to make much sense of what I've recently seen, but I received no images of Trepans, so I would assume your scouts are correct. There is no indication that they are in this area any longer. As to the tremors, nothing in my visions revealed anything about tremors. If I had a little more information, I might be able to narrow in on something more helpful."

Stella hesitated about mentioning the tidal waves. She knew these often followed tremors, but since she couldn't tell if the visions were new or past occurrences, she didn't want to raise concerns falsely. And without any indications of tremors, she had nothing tangible to connect to the tidal waves. She didn't like to be so unresponsive, but she really had nothing much of which she could make any sense.

Natalie could tell there was more that Stella wasn't sharing. While she appreciated Stella's desire to provide accurate information and not to raise any false alarms, sometimes she thought Stella was a little too cautious. She kept looking at her, waiting for the Enchantress to continue. Nothing was forthcoming.

"All right," she finally said when she could wait no longer, "out with it."

"What do you mean?" asked Stella. "Out with what?"

"You know what. There's something more that you're hiding."

"Hiding? I'm not <u>hiding</u> anything," she said a bit defensively.

"I know you too well. When you start repeating my questions, I know you're holding something back. Maybe you're not exactly 'hiding' anything, but there's more you're not telling me. OK – I understand that you have seen something and you're not certain what it is or what it means. I won't hold that against you. I won't accuse you of raising any false alarms. But I need to know. Now give it up!"

"Repeating your question?" asked Stella.

"Yes. Just like that."

Stella let her shoulders slump slightly as she let out a sigh and rolled her eyes. "Sometimes you can get really pushy, you know?"

Natalie just smiled. She had opened the door. Stella would finally start talking, and now she probably wouldn't be able to get Stella to shut up. Oh, well!

Stella straightened herself up and began to describe what she had seen in her vision. Natalie listened patiently as Stella went into nearly excruciating detail about the images of the Rebbercands, the tidal waves and the cavern that looked like a Sanctorum, the odd box or container in the center, and finishing with the jolt that had sent her across the room where Natalie found her. When she was done Natalie remained silent as she thought about all of this.

"OK. Let's start at the beginning. Couldn't the visions of the Rebbercands just be memories of our recent battle with them, instead of a projection of something yet to come?" she finally asked. "There have been no recent reports about them, from anywhere. There's no reason for you to start seeing them now, is there?"

"Yes," Stella answered, "that's completely possible, and no, there's nothing I've come across that would prompt those visions now."

"But?" asked Natalie.

"But everything about them is different."

"Different how?

"Well, for example, the leaders, or what appeared to be the leaders, were not the same. I saw no images of B'nair or any of the others we last encountered."

"I wouldn't think so," interjected Natalie. "B'nair fell into the river of lava. I would hope we wouldn't be seeing him again."

"Yes, but that only leads me to believe the visions are not of past events. Otherwise I think it's reasonable to assume he would appear in them, simply because he was such a dominant figure. But he's <u>not</u> there, and these people all looked – I don't know – different. Maybe more organized – more militaristic. I don't know. I can't explain it any other way. And I didn't see any Trepans. If these visions were just resurfacing memories, then I'd expect to see Trepans, or if not them at least some of our friends. I didn't see either."

"All right. The Rebbercands are probably new visions." She rolled her eyes and said sarcastically, "Something to look forward to. Tell me more about the tidal waves. Could you tell where or when they were occurring?"

"No, I'm sorry. The only thing I can say is that they were nothing like what we've experienced before. They were very powerful. So I have to assume that they haven't happened, either. Anything that big or that destructive would be in our histories someplace."

Then, as an afterthought, she added, "But there also seemed to be something blocking it. I can't be positive, and I only came to this conclusion through the images of how the wave seemed to divide and splash. I'm not describing it clearly, I know, but it just looked like it hit something; that it was somehow diverted or blocked."

"Like what; a rock or a wall? Buildings maybe?"

"No; none of that. I couldn't see whatever it was that broke the wave."

"You couldn't see because something was in the way, or was the vision distorted?" Natalie persisted.

"No," Stella repeated. "I mean there was nothing there for me to see. The vision was clear enough. Whatever the wave hit wasn't visible."

"Could it have been some kind of force field?"

"I suppose," Stella answered, but didn't sound convinced.

"Then that's a good thing, isn't it? It means someone is going to be alerted and try to redirect it – apparently successfully, if your vision is accurate."

Natalie could see that Stella was still not so optimistic.

"What about that last vision? The cave with the box in the middle – what do you think that was? You said it looked like a Sanctorum. Why?"

"Because of the precise way it was shaped. It looked pretty much like mine, except bigger- much bigger. It wasn't like any of the others I've been to or seen, but I'm certain that's what it was. The one odd thing about it was that there were several entryways into it. Normally they only have one or two. I suppose big ones may have three, but I think that's rare. I couldn't see more than a few inches into them. I suppose it's possible they could be something else."

"And the box?"

"That one was a real puzzle. At first I thought it was some kind of rock formation or a large slab of broken stone, but when I got a better view, it was clear that it was made by someone's hand. There were also some kinds of markings on the outside, although I couldn't read them."

"How could you tell all this, if the cave was dark?"

"The container or box or cube, whatever it was, seemed to be generating a kind of glow or an aura of some kind. Maybe it was the stone itself. I couldn't tell what the exact source was, but it didn't look like the light was coming from inside the box. As I concentrated on the thing and the image became clearer, that's when I received some kind of jolt. I've never felt anything like that before."

"Did you have any warning it was coming?"

"I didn't think so at the time, but looking back, I did get a kind of tingling sensation the first time I saw it. I didn't make the connection until just now."

Natalie thought some more, and then asked Stella, "Did you know that the stone in your headband had changed color?"

"No. There was a flash of light just before I was thrown to the floor. I thought it came from the image on the wall. Maybe what I saw was a reflection from the stone."

Natalie was as puzzled as Stella. "Weird," was all she could say.

They stood there in silence for a while considering the possibilities. Neither one had any answers or knew what else there was to discuss or ask. Finally, Natalie moved to leave.

"I think I'll go back to the north shore of the island tomorrow afternoon. I'll check reports from the other outposts first, though. Nothing's going to fall off into the sea, is it?" she asked half joking, trying to lighten Stella's mood.

"One never knows, does one?" she answered sarcastically.

As Natalie was about to leave, Stella cleared her throat and asked, "You're not planning on leaving the island, are you?"

Natalie stopped short. "I wasn't planning on it. Why? Is there something else you're not telling me?"

Stella thought. What did she know? Nothing. She hadn't seen any images that included Natalie; she had no specific flashes or other impressions that involved her. She had no reason to believe Natalie was in danger. Nothing, except an unsettling feeling deep inside her. That wasn't enough to base a decision on.

"No," she finally answered. "I just wondered. That's all."

Natalie stared at her a few seconds before leaving. After she walked out, Stella decided to go to the Archives to see if she could find any reference to those markings she saw on the block in the cave, and, with any luck, maybe decipher them.

Chapter seven

While Stella was pouring over old scrolls in the Archives, the evil forces to which she had been alerted were hard at work. Far to the north of her island was a small army of Rebbercands. They were deep underground in the channels Stella had seen but could not locate, and they were on a specific mission. They were led by a ruthless individual named Bacham. Bacham had taken a group of select individuals from a much larger force that was several hundred miles north and to the west of where he was now. That force was waiting for his small team to complete its work and before they could move on to their own target. In addition to being the leader of this elite squad, Bacham was also B'nair's replacement as the leader of the Rebbercands.

Bacham had operated for several years in B'nair's shadow, resenting every minute of it. Their leadership styles had been very different. B'nair had been slick and oily, ingratiating his way to the top. He usually had a smile on his face, though it was clear to anyone who met him that his smile went no deeper than the surface. He was calculating and deceiving.

He was smarmy and sneaky. He was also long gone, having disappeared into a river of molten lava, and Bacham felt this hadn't happened soon enough.

Bacham on the other hand was cold, calculating and merciless. He never smiled and his stare created instant fear in those who encountered it. And those who had the misfortune of disagreeing or disappointing him, usually only did so once. He tolerated no mistakes, no faltering, and absolutely no disloyalty. His anger was quick and lethal. If B'nair had not met his end in the burning magma deep underground, Bacham would have found a way of disposing of him on his own.

One other difference between them was that Bacham also had in his possession, a piece of the stone from Meri's pendant.

The history of this piece of stone was not unlike that of the one that Stella had in the headband she wore. Except, that is, this one was found by a gargoyle more than a century before. He never fully understood the power it contained – as much as gargoyles can fully understand anything. He was content to be entertained by the slight electrical charges the stone emitted and the shifting colors, both of which occurred for reasons that were a mystery to him.

Very much like the armband that had been fought over and won by generations of Rebbercands, this stone was the target of envy and murder, which was common among the gargoyles, and passed from one generation to the next. The passage was not from parent to child, though, but from vanquished to victor, and the passage was one of treachery, deceit and blood.

As the lives of the gargoyles moved along their own path, so did the lives of the Rebbercands who suffered the curse of Meri Hocto. Over the centuries that passed from the time of Tebaga's banishment, the Rebbercands' memories of him and his role in their disbursement twisted and turned as much as their nomadic lives had twisted and turned. After a while, the Rebbercands themselves began to twist and turn, disagreeing on where and how to live. Without roots, their society foundered. Their history became blurred and conflicted.

Many of the descendants of the original families clung to their recollections of the past. However, eventually a separatist movement emerged, with a growing group dedicating themselves to the memory of a vaguely remembered hero named Tebaga. In their distorted lore he became a martyr and Meri became the witch that placed a curse on him, taking away the greatest leader in Rebbercand history.

This falsehood grew over time and became an obsession among the Rebbercands. Like the original families, the members of this separatist group were equally bound to past traditions, but as time moved on, these traditions more and more became redefined to meet the personal needs and selfishness of the leaders. Deviation from the directions and mandates of these leaders was tolerated less and less. Dissidents were no longer shunned; they were often exiled or secretly executed. As a result, the Rebbercands had become an army of fanatics and Bacham had become their current ruler.

As a young boy, Bacham had been a member of an exploratory party that ventured into a distant forest. They had been searching for their next home – the place his people would live for the next few years until they would move on. While on this exploratory party he had come across a large boulder that seemed to be blocking the entrance to a cave. He could see that the boulder had been moved to open the entryway and closed again several times. The Rebbercands had never lived below ground, and Bacham had no real desire to change that pattern, but the stone and the cave piqued his curiosity. He was certain that someone lived behind the boulder and they may have something worth taking. He volunteered and stayed behind as the raiding party went on ahead. They continued to search out an appropriate new home, and he remained hidden in the nearby vegetation to watch the rock.

He found a place secluded enough to keep out of sight, but still be able to see the boulder and the cave behind it. He watched for the next three days. As darkness fell on the third day, he thought that maybe he had been on a fool's errand, and that the blocked cave amounted to nothing. But about two hours after sunset, he saw the boulder move. The movement was slight at first – just a crack; and then the crack widened enough to allow two creatures to come out. They poked their heads around the edge of the rock as stealthily as they could, looking furtively from side to side. When they believed that they were unobserved, they exited the cave and quickly pushed the rock back in place.

They were gargoyles. He had never seen creatures like these before, but he had heard about them from other, older Rebbercands who had traveled more widely than he. They were hideous, but he was not frightened or put off by their appearance. He felt an odd kinship with them that he couldn't explain.

He followed them as they crept through the forest. The light of the half moon seemed to glisten on their skin, making it easier for him to see them, although there were times they seemed to disappear. They looked like they were foraging for something, but at first he couldn't tell what. They had rooted around in the bushes and scurried over to a nearby stream where they perched along the side. He soon learned that they had fashion short spears from fallen branches and were seeking fish in the stream.

Eventually, they had collected several fish and then made their way back to the rock. Bacham had followed them during their expedition, keeping hidden in the brush. When he saw that they were returning to their lair, he debated about making contact. He had waited three days to find out what was behind that rock. He was afraid they would disappear into some underground hideout, and he'd lose them indefinitely. He had to make his move, so he decided to present himself to the strange creatures. He stepped out from behind a large tree, raised his hands and called out.

"Don't be frightened. I mean you no harm," he announced.

However, the large double bladed axe that he carried in a sling on his back, still visible and easily accessible, as well as his militaristic appearance did not instill either of the gargoyles with confidence. They were suspicious creatures by nature, barely trusting each other. In addition to not being trusting, they were not particularly smart. Instead of running away, or escaping inside the cave, they murmured something to each other and turned back towards Bacham. In spite of the fact that Bacham was more than twice their size and that he clearly was well armed, they dropped the fish and with their simple wooden spears, attacked him.

One picked up a handful of stones to add to the short stick that he snatched from the ground. Without any other communication between them one gargoyle began throwing the stones. As soon as he began to get pelted, Bacham reacted defensively. Not wanting purposely to harm them, he pulled the axe from its sling and used the blade as a shield, deflecting the stones. The gargoyles were not inexperienced warriors and used their same hunting tactics in their attack. Unfortunately for them, Bacham was a more adept fighter and strategist. He saw through their attack plan and knew that a peaceful discussion was quickly becoming out of the question. He kept shouting that he meant no harm and came in peace, but they persisted in their attack. His training and experience took over and he brought down his axe methodically and surgically. In very short order, the attack was over, and the community of gargoyles had two fewer members.

He stood over the bodies and decided that other night predators would soon pick up the scent of blood and would adequately dispose of them. There was nothing more here for him to do. He looked back at the boulder blocking the entryway to whatever was behind it, and gave up on his thoughts of exploring the cave. Even if he were able to establish a peaceful encounter with whoever else lived on the other side of that stone, once they learned of what he had done to these two, any alliance or other interaction he might have had would come to an abrupt halt.

Furthermore, without knowing what was behind the boulder, he knew it was foolish to try to gain entry on his own.

He was frustrated by the fact that he was unable to make peaceful contact, even though he knew that wherever his people went, peace was never long lived. He tore a piece of clothing from one of the victims to wipe the blood from his axe. He did this as he was about to leave and catch up with his squad when the moonlight glanced off an object lying on the body of one of the gargoyles. He saw something flicker in the light. He moved back to where he saw the reflections, and straddling the body, he bent closer to look down at the item. It appeared to be some kind of stone, cradled in a webbing and hung by a thin strap around the neck of one of the gargoyles.

"Hunh," mumbled Bacham dismissively, "some childish trinket."

And he started to walk away, thinking nothing more of it. As he did, he looked over his shoulder, first up at the night sky, and then down at the two bodies, giving one more glace at the destruction he was leaving behind. Out of the corner of his eye he saw something. He was certain that the stone flashed. Something deep in the recesses of his mind told him to go back. He hesitated a moment, then turned and went back to the body.

He looked more closely at the stone and was startled to see a small flash of light appear. The stone was a golden brown with a murkiness near the point. It was somewhat triangular in shape. The bottom edge was smooth with a finished cut, but the other two sides were jagged. It was as if it had been broken off from a larger piece. The flashing and the cloudiness in the coloring were more pronounced at the tip of the two broken sides. He dropped the piece of cloth to the ground and then reached down and pulled the necklace free. As soon as the stone was in his hand, he felt the electrical charge tingling against his skin. This was no ordinary stone.

He stood there motionless for several seconds, studying the talisman, feeling the slight tingle in his hand. He closed his fist around the stone, squeezing it tightly. The charge intensified making his back arch and his head jerk skyward. Every muscle in his body tensed, his eyes closed, his teeth clenched tightly, and he stopped breathing. The large axe fell from his other hand, slipping easily from his fingers.

Flashes of color flew across his eyelids and dream-like visions raced through his mind. Behind the colors he saw a strange looking creature surrounded by Rebbercands. He was unmistakably their leader. There was another stranger surrounded by a smaller group of Rebbercands, but the image of this person was not as distinctive. Both images dissolved into what looked like a crypt hidden deep in an enormous cavern. He also saw a nearly blinding flash of white light immediately followed by a complete and total blackness. At the same time it felt as if his body had plunged into a sea of ice.

He opened his hand, releasing his grip on the stone. The intense cold and blackness vanished, and he dropped to his knees, the strength gone from his legs. He let his breath out in a gush and sucked in fresh air to his lungs, which were now burning. He could make no sense of what he had seen or experienced, but he knew that this stone had some kind of powers. His first thought was to tell the current leader of the Rebbercands, B'nair, about this find. But, then his innate greed and ambition killed that thought.

B'nair would keep the stone and the power for himself, Bacham considered. He will not always be strong. He will not always be our leader. Bacham had been in the group that was challenging B'nair's leadership. Why should he turn over something that would further his hold on the Rebbercand leadership? He decided to keep the discovery of the stone and everything about it to himself. At least until the time was right.

He wiped the sweat from his brow, grabbed the handle of his axe, and struggled to his feet. He placed the axe back in the sling on his back and once more looked around the forest and then back to the carnage at his feet. He pocketed the stone and staggered away from the grizzly scene, breaking into an easy jog, heading off in the direction his team had gone three days before.

Over the next few years, he kept the events of that night and the secret of the stone to himself. He didn't even share any of this with his closest friends. In rare moments of complete solitude he would grasp the stone tightly, hoping for additional, different insights, but the experiences were always the same. His body would become painfully rigid and then an overwhelming coldness would encompass him. His visions were also always the same – the two strangers, the Rebbercands, the flashes of color followed by a blinding white light and then a crushing blackness. He needed to learn more.

He believed the stone had some kind of connection to their long absent leader, Tebaga, and the other sorcerer, Ena Ray, both of whom had been destroyed by the witch, Meri Hocto. He had no explanation for this belief, though. Nothing in the physical sensations or the visions would cause him to make such a connection, but deep inside he had an unshakable conviction that all of this was interrelated. He was certain that the strangers in the visions were Tebaga and Ena Ray. That sensation was reinforced each time he held the stone tightly. There had to be a way to find out more, but his efforts were frustrated.

One afternoon he had been conducting reconnaissance in a distance marsh. It was another assignment from B'nair meant to be punishment. He knew his people would never settle here, no matter for how short a period of time. It was much too inhospitable, even for them. Most of the plants were poisonous. There were all sorts of deadly creatures. Even the insects were unbearable, many of them carrying disease or toxins. It was also extremely hot and humid and there was little, if any, solid ground. Who would want to spend any more time here than was needed to just pass through?

The twin suns were at their zenith. There were no clouds to filter their intense light and heat. There had been no shade to be found for miles. He could hardly wait until he could return to the encampment and his party of searchers could leave this area completely. He finally came upon a small mound of dirt – one of the rare tiny islands in this hellhole - with a large tree. He checked to make sure that the tree presented no dangers. When he was certain it was safe, he decided to sit down for a few minutes to rest. He looked all around him to ensure that he was alone. When he was convinced that no one was near, he removed the stone from his pocket and rolled it around in his fingers, admiring the coloring.

It was once again an unusual shade of golden brown. Sometimes he could see the colors churning beneath the surface, turning from golden to a reddish brown and sometimes there were reflections of light flashes. He would turn the stone over and over, examining it from every direction, but he could never see the source of the flashes. It was as if they were occurring someplace else, and only a sort of echo of light coursed through the stone. It was as if the source of the light came from the part from which this piece had broken. The flashes started there and then reflected in this piece. He wondered if there were more such pieces.

As he was once again studying it, turning it in his fingers, it slipped from his hand and tumbled down the mound towards a pool of water. He watched in horror as it bounced along the ground, struck a root and flew up into the air. It was headed right for that pond of fetid, scum-covered water.

"NO!" he shouted, jumping up and chasing after it.

He scrambled as fast as he could, slipping and skidding in the loose dirt to get his footing. He had to be careful not to fall into the water, but he knew that if the stone sunk, it would be lost forever. He would not reach in after it. One of his men had reached into a similar pond only two days ago, and lost his entire hand to some kind of reptile hidden beneath the surface. He couldn't tell how deep the water was that his stone was rolling towards because of the thick layer of gray-green scum on the surface, but it wouldn't matter. Unless he could see it clearly, he wouldn't risk putting his hand in. He clambered after the stone, but could see he wouldn't be able to catch it. Once it hit that root, it bounced into the air. It was starting its drop downward, and he could see that it was already too far over the edge of the water.

Bacham watched in utter dismay as the stone landed with a plop. But instead of sinking in the murky liquid, it had fallen onto a large leaf that was just under the coating on the water. The stone landed flat on the leaf and separated it from the scum. The rippling of the water cleared an area around the leaf, and it spun first to the left, and then back to the right. It spun back and forth, finally coming to a stop as if it was pointing at something. A wave of relief washed over Bacham as he rushed to the edge of the water, bent down and reached for the stone.

He stopped his hand in midair, just inches over the stone and the leaf, and then quickly pulled his hand back. Remembering the earlier encounter with a water inhabitant, he wasn't going to risk losing his hand. He pulled a long knife from a sheath on his belt and carefully drew the leaf towards him. When it was against the land, he picked up the edge with his other hand and pulled it gently from the water onto the land.

Just as he did so, a large Heladerma snake shot up, snapping at him. In a split second, he jumped backwards out of the snake's range and brought the knife down sharply, spearing the snake through its head and pinning it into the sand beneath the water. It had come within inches of taking a large piece out of him. Bacham held him in place with the knife stuck through its head. The snake's body writhed and splashed for several seconds before becoming still.

Bacham waited a few more minutes before removing the knife and pushing the dead snake back into the water, where, he hoped, it would satisfy or at least occupy the attention of whatever else was in there. He also hoped it had no relatives that would be seeking revenge. He hadn't realized he had been holding his breath. He relaxed and allowed his breathing to return to normal.

Then he flicked the surface of the water with his knife, clearing away the layer of scum.   When nothing else jumped up, he put the leaf with the stone back on the surface of the water and turned it so the point of the stone was facing towards him. The leaf spun around and then back and forth until the stone was pointing in the same direction as it had previously. He had never seen this happen before. He looked closely at the water to make sure nothing above or below the surface was making the leaf move.   He placed it in the water and turned it in different directions three more times.

Regardless of which way he started or how far away from the end position, the stone always returned to point in the same direction. He wasn't sure what this meant, but it convinced him even more that this stone had some very special properties. He was determined to discover them. He was also convinced that this stone was in some way connected to Tebaga and the witch, Meri Hocto, who had cursed him.

From that point forward, any time he could influence where the Rebbercands moved or invaded or searched, he led them in the direction toward which the stone pointed. Sometimes he was successful, but all too often he met with resistance. Not surprising, the greatest resistance came from B'nair, who seemed to have his own set of priorities that he was keeping to himself. Bacham resisted sharing the secret of the stone with B'nair. He knew B'nair would take the stone from him and use it for his own purposes. So, instead, he held his tongue and followed orders.

He endured this for many years, until one day things changed. He was assigned to take part in the construction of a giant statue to celebrate one of the Rebbercands' great leaders: Reng'n. He had argued with B'nair that this project was foolish, but was overruled. Because of his opposition, he was given menial assignments, and was kept out of the operation and any aspects of the construction. Once more this was intended as punishment. Little did he know at the time that this would save him.

The statue was being built with a substance that was mined deep underground.   B'nair had personally taken charge of the mining, overseeing the units that enslaved the Trepans, who actually did the digging, as well as managing the mining operations. Then disaster struck. Somehow the statue cracked open releasing a giant demon, which flew down the mine shaft. Even more demons were released by some magical power. The Trepans revolted and the demons attacked. As a result, nearly all of the Rebbercands overseeing the mining were killed, including B'nair.

Only one of the Rebbercand guards escaped, a cutter named Sapin. She was hysterical when the rescue party found her. She claimed that an army of rebels had attacked. There had been no evidence of any such attack. All the arrows that had been found belonged to the Rebbercands. Sapin had claimed that the attacking force had greatly outnumbered the Rebbercands and had superior weapons. Again, there was no evidence of any of this. She made no reference at all to the demons that had actually been the source of the slaughter.

Sapin had a reputation for being a tremendous liar, but in this instance there were no survivors to determine if her account was truthful or not. The fact that she had survived, and that she had no recollection of the demons, led many to believe she had fled and hidden in cowardice instead of remaining to fight. She was saved from execution only because she had managed to capture one of the rebel Trepans during her so-called escape.

Afterwards, no one could verify that B'nair had been killed, but he was never found. The only fact that had been determined as true was that nearly two dozen demons had destroyed the Rebbercands in the cave – except, of course for Sapin, for some unexplained reason. Afterwards they had come out of the mine to terrorize the Rebbercands in the village, forcing an end to the construction and a departure from this home sooner than anticipated. The screeches of those demons still haunted Bacham. The disappearance of the former leader, on the other hand, had created an opportunity for Bacham. He had opposed B'nair's folly in building the statue; he had opposed B'nair's decisions as leader; he had opposed

B'nair's less than stringent adherence to the ways of the past. Now he would no longer have to oppose B'nair. Now he would be the leader.

For many years leading up to the moment when Bacham became leader of the Rebbercands, he had taken every opportunity to move his people in the direction indicated by the stone. Sometimes his excursions had been prohibited, but other times he had been given a free hand under the guise of searching for a more suitable homeland. With each move he searched for information that would explain the past and the power of the stone he kept hidden. At every opportunity he also interrogated any civilizations he came across. Often these interrogations were cruel and involved various methods of torture. He was relentless and ruthless in his pursuit of information. Whenever he came upon vast libraries of information, he would interrogate the guardians of these libraries, searching for records, folklore, myths or anything that would expand his knowledge. After absorbing all that he considered important, he would destroy everything.

Of course, the information he had obtained through torture was almost always invented to satisfy what his victims believed he wanted to hear. As a result more often than not, it was totally inaccurate. Over time he had assembled a few pieces of fact and many more pieces of myth or fiction. He was getting a clearer, although not necessarily accurate, picture of the past. From what he learned, he believed that an ancient leader and sorcerer named Tebaga had battled with a powerful witch named Meri. She had imprisoned another sorcerer named Ena Ray, who Tebaga was trying to rescue. He had been a leader of an army of Rebbercands and had managed to slay the terrible witch after a long and bloody fight.

She had used all sorts of magical powers, but Tebaga's strength of character had shielded him. The battle ended with him overcoming all obstacles and defeating her, although he was unable to save Ena Ray. She had been driven over the edge of a cliff to the rocks below where she died a slow and horrible death. He had tried to save her and was nearly pulled over the edge himself. He had grasped the edge of her robe to keep her from falling, but her attempts to destroy him, even at the risk of her own life, had forced him to lose his grip. As she fell, she cast a final spell, burying him deep inside a mountain.

Bacham was so convinced of this distorted recounting of the actual history, that anyone who he interrogated in his quest for answers, who provided him with any true accounts, was tortured over a long period of time and then disposed of mercilessly. He could not be deterred from his own self-defined history. He became obsessed with finding this ancient leader, who all accounts indicated was still alive, and trapped beneath a mountain. Finding Tebaga became Bacham's primary life mission. He used every resource at his disposal to this aim.

Part of the myth surrounding the imprisonment of Tebaga indicated that the spell that locked him away could only be broken by a powerful Enchantress. Bacham had heard of such a person who, with her friends, had defeated a powerful ally of the Rebbercands: the sorcerer named Ena Ray who Tebaga was unable to free. Bacham was enraged that once again an attempt to overcome the curse of the witch had been foiled, and another brave Rebbercand ally was suffering. He believed that this Enchantress and her army were responsible for the overthrow of the Rebbercand dynasty, the imprisonment of Tebaga and his loyal servant, Ena Ray. He began to formulate a plan to crush this Enchantress and her evil associates, to free Tebaga and to rescue Ena Ray.

Over the years as he developed this plan, he had kept it to himself, waiting for the right time and enough information to put it into play. By the time B'nair was leading the excavation teams below ground, and the construction of the icon to the Great Reng'n, Bacham had pillaged enough libraries that he believed he had discovered the location where Tebaga was being held. The legends of it being protected by a spell were probably true. It would be difficult not only to get there, but to penetrate the defenses as well.

After the attack by the Trepans, he had interrogated the captured rebel personally, and quite intensely. Before he died, the prisoner revealed that a small band of strangers had aided the Trepan rebels in their attack on the Rebbercands. He was certain that an Enchantress had been one of the strangers, and had been influential in the release of the demons. He had also told Bacham where this Enchantress lived.

Bacham shared this with no one. He gave orders that the Trepan's body was to be dropped into the river of lava to destroy any evidence of the interrogation. He then returned to the surface where he announced his own appointment as the Rebbercand leader. He directed all but a select few to gather up what belongings had not been destroyed and to move to a new settlement. He announced that he would be sending a unit of elite soldiers to the island location where Tebaga was imprisoned, explaining where it was and how they would get there.

One Rebbercand voiced an objection, an ambitious rival named Hubkah.

"But that's far out to sea and once there, it's at the base of an active volcano," he complained. "You put us in further danger by sending us there. And where will you be while the rest of us are so perilously exposed?"

Bacham approached Hubkah with the same stoic face he presented to everything and everyone, betraying nothing. His pace was neither threatening nor submissive, but when he was only a few steps away, in mid-stride and in a single motion, he removed his double headed axe from the sling on his back and swung it with lightning speed. As Hubkah's head rolled down the hill, Bacham asked if there were any other objections. Not a word was spoken.

He identified a small group to stay behind and accompany him, and he put Sapin in charge of moving the rest of the Rebbercands to the island mountain.

"I'm sure I can trust that you will accomplish this simple task without losing anyone," he said to her dryly. "You are to set sail immediately, and then keep the warriors there until I arrive. You are to do nothing else. Is that understood?"

She swallowed loudly, bowed her head and told him she would not fail.

"See that you don't," he responded, as he turned away and led his small band back into the mines.

When the Rebbercands had begun extracting the minerals for the construction of the statue to Reng'n, Bacham had been given the task of mapping out the passages. This was meant by B'nair to be a punishment for Bacham's frequent confrontations. It turned out for Bacham that it wasn't a punishment after all. He traveled through the many underground passageways and caverns, and knew them quite well. The Trepan prisoner he had interrogated after the revolt had identified the location of the Enchantress and the island on which she lived. As soon as he heard this, he recalled a seldom-used passageway that was not far from there. He also knew that less than a hundred miles to the north of that island and a few miles to the east were the ruins of an ancient city deep beneath the floor of the sea. He needed no map to lead him to this location. That was where he headed with his small team.

It took nearly a day to reach this city. He had force marched his soldiers the entire way. He had chosen them well. No one voiced a complaint or asked to rest. They all knew better than to present anything but full compliance with his demands. He had them exchange their double headed axes for large sledge hammers, and told them that they would be an instrument of revenge on those who had attacked their comrades and killed their former leader. He hadn't told them that they would also become part of a larger sacrifice and would not be making the return trip with him.

When they finally arrived at the site of the ruins, they saw a large open area several hundred feet long. A very long time ago it had been a library and center of learning and arts. There was an enormous domed roof that was supported by two long rows of tall pillars. When the structure had been built, it had been carved out of the rock, rather than constructed. Even the pillars had been carved from the existing stone. They formed two parallel lines of high, wide, elegantly engraved arches. The stone work that covered the walls, the pillars and the ceiling had all been hand carved by hundreds of talented artisans, and it was extremely detailed and beautiful. The artistry and the history were lost on Bacham and his soldiers. Their purpose there was destruction.

He convinced them that this arena was still in use and was a meeting place for the enemies of the Rebbercands. Whether they knew this was a lie or not, no one challenged him. He ordered them to destroy the pillars, which were the most beautiful part of the structure, since that would demoralize and strike fear into the hearts of their enemy. He told them that they would be rewarded and celebrated for their task. He told them he was going back up the passageway to stand guard and defend them against anyone who might come to try to stop them. He had lied about everything, believing it was justified for the greater good of his plan.

They began to pound their enormous hammers against the pillars: one soldier for each pillar. They were lined up in the same parallel lines as the pillars; each of them standing back to back along the inside area of the pillars. They struck at the bases, driving the pillars outward from the center. Bacham left them to their work, but did not go back up the passageway as he had claimed he would. Instead, he headed to a secret trail that wound back towards the shore and the surface. He needed to be well away before the pillars collapsed. When they did, not only would the stone from the ceiling fall, but hundreds of thousands of gallons of water from the sea above would come crashing down as well. It was a shame that so many good soldiers would be buried alive, but Bacham reasoned that it couldn't be helped. It was all part of his plan.

Chapter eight

It was the pounding of the sledgehammers against the pillars that the northern outposts had reported as minor tremors. Except it didn't seem like the tremors were minor, to those who were stationed in this outpost. The small station was in a bubble on the ocean floor, similar to the bubble in which the Sea Sprites had lived for centuries. It was nestled on a bed of more than ten feet of sand, which covered thirty feet of rock and shale. The shale was comprised of several interlocking layers and sat on top of hundreds of feet of limestone. Several centuries ago, Trepans had discovered this limestone deposit and began carving a town center into it. It was meant to be a place of learning – a place to celebrate the arts.

They had used their best artisans, designers and architects. They had created a large room, keeping the ceiling intact and supported by two long lines of intricately carved pillars. Throughout the construction, they had used the project itself as a learning tool; teaching the younger artisans and builders the trades of their ancestors. They had also carefully calculated the weight of the stone and seawater above the pillars and as they carved away the limestone around these pillars, they had carefully calculated the necessary thickness of each pillar and the precise distance between each one of them.

It had been an engineering marvel. The designs were exquisite. The balance and symmetry were perfect. It had lasted hundreds of years and had been treasured by those who designed and built it as well as the many generations that followed. And now the entire project was being destroyed by a small group who neither valued, nor understood, the beauty and grandeur they were defacing.

With each blow of the sledgehammers, the vibrations traveled up each pillar, through the shale and sand, and shook the bubble outpost that sat hundreds of feet above. At first the hammer blows were random, which is what made the lookouts in the outpost think that they were natural minor earthquakes. As the team of Rebbercands continued, they fell into a rhythm with one another, and each hammer fell against each pillar in perfect unison. That convinced the observers differently.

"That's not a natural tremor," announced Virginia, the Dryad who was in charge of the outpost and whose senses immediately went on high alert. "Something very bad is happening. We need to find out what and where this is going on."

The reverberations shook the tiny bubble each time the hammers struck the pillars. The Sea Sprites knew the shaking was coming from beneath them, but had no idea how far, who was doing it or exactly where it was taking place. They only knew that their station was feeling the effects. Virginia sent a messenger back to the main island to report to Princess Natalie. The vibrations were quickly becoming more regular and more severe. She could see that the pounding was taking its toll on their bubble, and she was certain that whatever was going to happen would do so before the messenger would even reach the island. She needed to take action before disaster struck.

She decided to send two scouts out to see if they could locate the source of the tremors. The scouts had been gone for only a few minutes when the ground beneath the bubble began to shift. The sand was moving in swirls, sinking in some places and placing uneven stress on the wall of the bubble. Virginia realized she had to act sooner that she had planned, and couldn't wait for her scouts to return. She thought about sending someone after them, since there was no other way to call them back, but she was afraid of putting anyone else in danger. She had experienced earthquakes before, and was well aware of their unpredictability and the extent of devastation they could cause. The scouts would have to fend for themselves for the time being. Right now she had to focus on everyone else.

She sounded the alarm and called for an immediate evacuation. In addition to the ground shifting, each tremor was shaking the bubble to its foundation. It would come apart in a very short time. The seals at the base were already weakening. It wouldn't hold for much longer, unless the vibrations stopped. There was no indication that this would happen.

"Where should we go?" asked a frightened young Sprite.

"Head back to the island, but try to get to the surface. Don't go by sea; try to get to the land," Virginia shouted over the rumbling sound that was creeping up from beneath their feet. "And hurry," she added. "Move like your life depended on it."

She made sure everyone had evacuated the outpost and told her trusted assistant to take the lead and make sure everyone got as far away as possible.

"Where are you going?" asked the assistant.

"I have to see if I can get those two scouts back. They don't know we're evacuating, and I'm responsible for their safety."

The assistant was getting more worried than she had been before. She tried to talk Virginia out of going after the scouts.

"But you have no idea where they are," she argued. "If these tremors worsen, there's no telling where the ground will cave in. You could be lost as easily as them."

"What if it was you that I had sent out? Would you want me to leave you behind?" Virginia asked. "Do your job."

The assistant didn't answer. She only nodded, and turned away to lead the evacuees to the surface and back to the island.

Meanwhile, not too far below them, the team of Rebbercands was making rapid progress in its task. Small cracks began to appear near the base of the columns where the repeated hammering had been focused. It was as if they were all chopping at trees. Swing after swing brought the giant hammer-heads crashing into the exact same spot. Eventually the limestone began to become pulverized and turn to powder, creating large indentations. Small gaps at the point of contact became larger gaps. Pieces started to break off and fall in chunks from areas above the softened stone.

The Rebbercands were grinning widely. One of them shouted to pick up the pace, and the swinging of the hammers increased in tempo. As the cracks widened, another one shouted that this was just like chopping trees in that forest they had invaded not too long ago. The swinging continued as this comment slowly began to sink in. Yes, they all agreed: this was just like chopping trees. The hammering echoed off the walls and ceiling as the impact of their actions began to dawn on some of them. The repercussions of their efforts started to become clear, but the dawning was as slow as the dawning of the sun.

Finally, one of them stopped swinging his hammer. He looked up the towering column at the ceiling it supported. Those closest to him soon stopped swinging their hammers to look at him and then to see what he was looking at. Further down the line, the pounding continued in an unbroken rhythm.

"What is it, Gallen?" one of them asked, wiping the sweat from his brow. "What do you see? What's up there?"

"I was thinking of those trees we cut down," Gallen answered.

He knew something wasn't right, but he couldn't quite make the connection. He kept staring at the tops of the columns and the structure they supported. Then his eyes slowly traced the length of the columns to the bottom where his men were pounding. He looked at the space around him. Bit by bit the pieces were coming together.

"Remember what happened when we cut through?" Gallen finally asked.

"Yeah, they came crashing down like thunder," his comrade replied with a chuckle. "What else would they do?"

"Exactly," said Gallen, turning to his partner. "Where do you think these columns are going to fall when we break through? Do you think they're just going to float away? And what do you think is going to happen to all that rock up there? That rock up there that these columns we're knocking down are holding up?"

Not being very bright, the others nearby also stopped hammering and looked up at the ceiling pondering his question.

"I don't know," his partner answered. "I suppose they'll fall down. And I guess we'll...move out of the way?"

Gallen shifted his stare from the ceiling to the Rebbercand who had answered him, wondering when he, too, would put the pieces of the puzzle together.

"And where do you think we'll be standing when that happens, you fool?" he finally asked when it was apparent that those puzzle pieces might never get put together.

The others who had been staring at the ceiling slowly lowered their heads and looked at each other. One by one it began to dawn on them where the columns would be falling, where all the debris was going to land and where they were not going to find any shelter. However, their realization came too late.

The hammering further down the line of columns had been unrelenting while the realizations of this small group were finally taking shape. The columns at both ends of the row had cracked through and began to give way. They separated from the bases where the beating hammers had chipped away. And then they broke free from the ceiling, slid past the fractured bases, crashed into the floor, and slowly toppled into open spaces along the sides of the hall. The increased weight and the sudden shift caused the columns next to them to collapse, and from that point forward it was like a line of dominos. Large chunks of falling limestone came rocketing downward burying the Rebbercands from the outside inward. Too late, the others realized their imminent fate and began to panic.

Only Gallen understood that they had been betrayed and were doomed. He alone understood the futility of trying to escape. There was no place to go. The cave in was happening on both sides of them, trapping them in the center. He watched as each of the columns quickly collapsed and the ceiling above caved in under the pressure of the water above it. He watched a shelf more than three hundred feet long and nearly a hundred feet wide drop like a trap door opening the way for hundreds of thousands of gallons of seawater. His last thoughts were of how beautiful the engravings in the stone had been, but these thoughts were quickly obliterated by his knowledge of the deceitful treachery of Bacham.

As the ceiling of the hall buckled and the sea rushed into the giant opening, the scouts Virginia had sent out were almost immediately above the fissure. They saw the sand of the ocean's floor instantly disappear and they were both sucked into the opening and dragged down into the cavern. They never knew what happened. Virginia had been too far away to call them back to safety, but not far enough to avoid the suction. She, too, was pulled into the devastation and swallowed in the abyss. She had seen the scouts disappear, and knew then what was happening. The bubble that had been their outpost was unseated from its foundation and instantly crushed, as it slid into the opening with the water, sand and shale. Her assistant and the rest of the Sprites fleeing the scene struggled with all their might to fight the nearly overpowering rush of millions of gallons of water. The assistant directed the escape, urging everyone on; staying at the end of the line to make sure they all got out. Nine of them made it to safety. The assistant and two others did not.

On the surface of the sea, the immense opening and shift of ground pulled the tide away from the shore into the opening. Water raced away from the land, far out to sea crashing into the newly created hole. Water from the opposite side of the opening swelled up, generating towering waves. The water continued to pull away from the shore all the way down the coast and far beyond the island of the Sea Sprites. And then it reversed course.

- - - - - - - - - - - - - - - - - *** - - - - - - - - - - - - - - - - - -

Sean had spent several weeks with Quinn in the Ice Kingdom, and, as interesting as it had been, he just couldn't get used to the cold. It might have been the sudden temperature change from the lava fields they had unexpectedly left to their equally unexpected arrival in the north, but he didn't think so. Even with all the extra clothing Quinn had provided, he couldn't get warm enough. He finally decided that it was time for him to return home.

He declined the offer to use the transporter stone that had brought him here. After his trip to the stars with Lochen and his sudden extraction in the middle of a fight with B'nair, he was convinced he had had enough of transporter stones. He preferred more traditional transportation, like walking. The thought of solid ground under his feet comforted him. Quinn had also offered to take the quicker route back by water, but Sean told him as much as he hated transporter stones, he hated water more.

"Thanks, but no thanks," he said. "I'll stick to the slow but steady method that has served me well so far."

Quinn hated to see his friend leave. Still trying to be the accommodating host, he insisted on escorting Sean, at least until they reached the land between the Ice Kingdom and the Venomous Swamp. Even though that was a much longer way, it would get him beyond the Ice Kingdom and closer to terrain he was more familiar with.

"At that point you could bypass the Swamp and follow the forest and jungle to the west and make your way home. If you decide to go through the Swamp, though, maybe you'll have more luck than I did in finding Liam."

"Isn't there water in the Swamp?" asked Sean, already knowing the answer.

"Oh, yeah," answered Quinn, "I forgot about that."

"As much as I wouldn't mind seeing Liam, he's going to have to come and visit me. Either that, or drain all that water out of his Swamp – and all those other nasty things, too."

Having exhausted all the other options, it appeared that they would be traveling more or less on foot. When the time came, Quinn began to attach Rover and Kelsey to his sled and pack it with supplies.

"I'm not getting on that thing, either," said Sean. "You can ride it, if you like, and I'll just walk along side."

Quinn laughed. "You're going to have fun trying to walk up some of the mountains were going to have to cross."

"I'll cross that bridge when I get there," Sean grumbled.

"I don't think we'll be crossing any bridges," said Quinn. "We don't really need them, you see. The water around here is frozen, and you can just walk across."

"It's just an expression," said Sean, rolling his eyes. "But you said the magic word: walk. That's just what I plan to do."

Sean watched as Quinn piled all sorts of odd things on the sled. He thought about asking, but considered that it would only delay his departure. Once the sled was filled with provisions, Quinn set out warm clothing for Sean. There were several layers of woven shirts and pants as well as fur covered jackets and leggings. Living in a hotter climate in the forest, Sean was not used to so much clothing. It seemed to take forever to get dressed, especially since he had to ask several times what something was and how he was supposed to put it on. By the time he was fully clothed, he could barely move. In addition to the number of layers, many of the garments had belonged to Quinn and were much too large for Sean. He had rolled the cuffs on his shirts and pants up so much that they further hindered his movement. The hood over his head kept flopping over his eyes making it difficult for him to see.

He tried walking normally, but that didn't work. He then tried a sort of hopping motion, but kept falling over and getting up was a real chore that left him worn out from the exertion. In the end, he was able to master an odd sort of shuffling maneuver. Using this method, he slowly waddled out the main entry to the frigid summer air. The sudden shock of the drop in temperature took Sean's breath away.

"Wow," he gasped. "That air is really something."

"Yeah," shouted Quinn, surveying the horizon. "It's really warmed up."

Sean had to twist his entire body in Quinn's direction to look at him. He reached up with his finger tips and pulled the muffler from the front of his face and lifted the hood up over his eyes. He was nearly speechless when an even colder blast of arctic air filled his lungs. The air was so sharp it nearly burned when he breathed in. He was positive he could feel frost forming on his eyebrows and eyelashes.

"Warm?" he coughed and sputtered. "You're joking, right?" He pulled the muffler back up and lowered the hood.

"No," answered Quinn, smiling broadly and taking a deep breath. "It's got to be up to nearly ten thermals by now."

"Ten thermals?" asked Sean, once again lowering the muffler and raising the hood. "What's that? Like - freezing?"

"Oh, no," Quinn laughed. "Freezing is thirty thermals. It's not that warm out here, yet. Maybe by midday it's possible it could warm a little more, but probably not. It would have to be a real heat wave to get up to freezing."

What did I do to deserve this, Sean asked himself. He was waddling, hopping, shuffling to keep up with Quinn.

"So, how long will it take us to get to a place that's not covered with snow?" he asked a little bit breathlessly.

"If we keep having this kind of really good weather, it should take about a week to ten days." Quinn answered.

"A week to ten days? Good weather?" Sean asked in disbelief.

He wasn't sure he could keep walking – or doing whatever it may be called – like this for a week to ten days. And this was supposed to be summer. He couldn't imagine what it would be like in winter. He knew it was dark almost all the time in the winter. The thought of it being this cold and dark all day long sent yet another shiver of cold up his spine.

"What happens if the weather gets bad?" he asked, nearly shouting through the muffler; not wanting to even imagine worse weather.

"We may have to hold up in a cave or a tent and wait it out. Then it's anybody's guess as to how long it will take to get to southern edge of the Ice Kingdom."

Sean just rolled his eyes again. Wait it out? In a cave? Wonderful. He was about to ask how long waiting it out would take, but then thought it might be better if he didn't know.

"Shouldn't we have waited until morning and get an early start?" he asked, glancing up at the sky to see the twin suns directly above them.

Quinn laughed. "It doesn't matter. This is summertime. The suns never set."

After about an hour of tripping over his overlong clothes, falling over and struggling to get up, and further exhausting himself by trying to catch up and to keep up, Sean acquiesced and got on the sled. He expected to have to stand on the back with Quinn, but instead, Quinn had him sit nestled in with the supplies. It was much better than he thought it would be and even somewhat warmer, and certainly much more comfortable, but he couldn't force himself to admit it to Quinn. It didn't matter, though, since Quinn already knew.

Rover and Kelsey seemed to thrive in the open air and appeared to be tireless. They ran with ease, even pulling the weight of the sled, its cargo and its passengers. In fact they seemed to be impatient when Quinn had to stop the sled to get Sean situated.

"Don't they get tired?" asked Sean, marveling at their stamina.

"Eventually they will. They'll let me know when that happens, trust me. They'll start whining like little babies. But once we get going, the sled pretty much just slides along. It will really sail when we cross over ice, but it gets a bit harder going uphill. When that happens, we'll get off and help push."

In spite of the cold and being encumbered by more clothes than he had ever owned in his entire life, Sean was enjoying himself. The minute patches of his face that peeked out from between his muffler and his hood had gotten numb from the icy breeze that blew at him, but even that wasn't so bad. Quinn had smeared some smelly, greasy stuff on his face. He told him it would keep him from getting frost bitten, whatever that was. They were racing across a seemingly limitless expanse of ice and snow, but he was amazed that the scenery was far from boring. In fact, it was beautiful. Sean could understand why Quinn loved it here so much. If only it weren't so cold. They passed immense mountains, vast glaciers, several inland ice ponds, and herds of hundreds of Arctic

Tarandus. These were graceful antelope-like animals, but not quite as big. They also had some pretty mean looking fangs.

As they passed one such herd, Sean remarked that he didn't see any trees or plants and asked what exactly did the Tarandus eat?

"Each other, mostly," Quinn answered. "There's moss in several places on the sides of the mountains they can get at, but if that's not around, they eat each other."

Sean stared in wonder. At first he wasn't sure whether or not Quinn was joking with him. He looked back at the herd off in the distance, and then he saw some of them instantly turn on one of the other herd members that had stepped into a small chink in the ice. It appeared to have injured one of its legs and was limping. Within a few short steps it was savaged by those around it and was gone in an instant. They had devoured it completely. Only a few bones remained. The only other sign that remained was the patch of blood in the snow. Sean was glad that Quinn was steering the sled in a slightly different direction.

"Can your dogs go any faster?" he mumbled as he watched their sled move slowly away from the herd.

After several hours, just as Quinn had predicted, Kelsey and Rover began whining. They kept up the pace they had been running the entire day, but they began looking back at Quinn with really pitiful faces. When he didn't immediately respond, they started barking and whimpering, and then let out a few short howls.

"See what I told you?" asked Quinn. "They want me to find a place to stop for a rest. And we haven't even gone that far!"

"Why don't they stop running, then?" asked Sean. "I mean, it's not like they have to ask you for permission, is it?"

"They know better. Even though they're tired, they know that this may not be a safe place to stop. They're looking at me to decide. They won't stop until I've checked things out and tell them it's all right."

Quinn gave a careful scan in all directions, and then noticed a small rock formation ahead and off to the right. There was no sign that it was a cave; instead it seemed simply to be a large outcropping that was flat on one side – worn away by the ice and wind. He aimed the sled in that direction and slowed it down as they approached the rock. Before stopping, he ran the sled in a wide circle around it before coming to a stop on the side opposite the direction of the wind. There he brought the sled to a stop and climbed off. He uncovered Sean and told him he could get up now.

"Were you looking for a good spot or something?" Sean asked about the circling of the rock.

"I just had to make sure someone or something else wasn't using this rock as a shelter. Things around here don't usually like to share their shelters – or their food. It looks pretty safe, though. We can set up our tent next to the rock, away from the wind, and in a few minutes, we'll be as snug as ice slugs."

Ice slugs, thought Sean. How wonderful. The image left him feeling a bit creepy, and far from snug.

It only took Quinn a few minutes to pull the necessary items from the sled and to set up the tent. It was an old fashioned tepee. Sean remembered that his ancestors used to live in similar structures. Quinn used parts of the sled as the poles and wrapped several skins around them, leaving an opening in the top. He spread more skins on the ground near the edges of the tepee, and lit a small fire from some branches he had tucked away in the supplies on the sled. He was right. In a very short time, the inside of the tent was warm and cozy. The fire was in the center, and the smoke rose out the opening in the top.

"Aren't you going to let Kelsey and Rover come into the tent?" Sean asked. "I know it's not very big, but wouldn't they be warmer?"

"They're not a lot of fun to sleep with," said Quinn. "They hog the bed and always take all the blankets."

He started laughing at the reaction from Sean, who was staring at him wide-eyed, holding tightly to the skins that were covering their bedding.

"I'm only joking." said Quinn. "Don't worry about them. They'll each dig a hole in the snow, cover themselves up and be as warm as we are. Besides, they need to stand guard. You never can tell what may come along in the night. They'll hear it long before we will. Try to get some sleep. We'll get an early start tomorrow."

Night, thought Sean as he lay flat on his back staring up at the light coming through the hole in the top of the tent. Something might come along in the night? This isn't night. It was as bright as midday. How can anyone sleep with all this light? And who can get warm sleeping in snow? He wasn't sure how much of what Quinn was telling him was true and what was a joke. He was about to comment, to see how much Quinn was messing with him and how much was really true. But when he turned to ask, he saw that Quinn was sound asleep.

He rolled back and looked up at the opening in the tepee again. Unable to sleep, and not believing that the dogs were sleeping in the snow, Sean lifted the blankets and quietly crept to the tent opening. He pulled the flap aside just a few inches and stuck his head out. It was still incredibly bright. He had to shield his eyes as he looked out in front of him.

Not far from the sled he saw two mounds under the snow. Nothing was moving. He cleared his throat, and Kelsey and Rover both popped their heads up at the sound. When they saw who it was, Kelsey whined and Rover gave a short yip. Then they wiggled their heads, burying them once again under the snow. He crawled back to his makeshift bed and thought, as he yawned widely, I'd never be able to sleep in the snow like that. And

I'll never be able to fall asleep in all this light. He had barely finished the sentence when his eyelids dropped like lead weights and he was out.

True to his word, Quinn quickly dismantled the tent, repacked the sled and continued early the next morning. During their travels, whenever he spotted any dried out bones or some piece of driftwood that somehow managed to get frozen in the ice who knew where, and then get pushed across miles of ice by a glacier, he would stop to pick it up.

"It's hard to find firewood around here," he announced. "You have to grab it whenever you see it."

They had been lucky with the weather and were making very good time, although to Sean, the differences in the scenery were impossible to tell, and everything looked the same. As far as he could tell, they hadn't gone far at all. On their third day, they were slowly making their way up a long hill. Rover and Kelsey were pulling the sled and Sean and Quinn were pushing from behind. When they finally reached the crest they stopped to rest. As they were catching their breath, Sean scanned the horizon, looked up at the sky and immediately lost his balance. He sat down hard. Barely able to tell the difference between the sky and the land, he had lost his sense of equilibrium, and became very dizzy.

"Whoa. Take it easy," said Quinn as he grabbed Sean's arm. "That's what we call white out up here," he explained. "It usually happens just before a storm, where the sky is filled with flat white clouds and they're the same color as the snow on the ground. That's when you have to just hunker down and wait it out. That is, if you don't fall down first. Take a few minutes and you'll get your balance back. It doesn't last long. Just try not to look too high into the horizon."

"Why am I so dizzy?" asked Sean, trying to stand up again with his eyes squeezed shut. "I can close my eyes and still know which way is up. Maybe I could just walk with my eyes closed. Wouldn't that be better?"

"Uh, I don't think so; because if you close your eyes you might fall into a crevasse or run into a pack of wolves or Tarandus that are tired of eating each other, or a whole bunch of other things – none of which are really good. And if you keep your eyes opened too much, staring at the sky, they'll deceive you. You won't be able to tell up from down; you'll get real dizzy; and you'll fall over. If that happens, you might freeze, and then for sure you'll be eaten by wolves, narwhals, Tarandus, or even rabbits - kind of like a Sean-cicle."

Quinn sat down next to Sean. As they were talking, Kelsey jumped up and became fully alert. She was immediately followed by Rover. Both dogs were looking in the same direction and began to emit a low threatening growl. Quinn and Sean stood up and looked in the same direction the dogs were facing. Sean reached out and held on to Quinn's arm, steadying himself with one hand and shielding his eyes with the other.

"What is it?" asked Sean, still holding on to Quinn and pointing with his free hand to a small black blur off in the distance.

"I don't know," said Quinn. "Whatever it is, it's traveling alone." After a few seconds, he added, "and it seems to be making music."

The sound was very far off and faded in and out with the winds. As the image got closer, the sound became steadier. Whoever it was, he or she was playing a narwhal bone horn. Quinn recognized the sound. The player was hitting a few off notes, but as the tune was repeated, the performance improved.

"Shouldn't we go down to meet whoever it is?" asked Sean.

"No," answered Quinn. "Just because he or she is playing music doesn't mean it's friendly. Let's wait a little while longer. At least until we can tell who or what it is."

Their past experiences with certain mystical forces had left them a bit on the suspicious side. They sat on a nearby mound and watched as the stranger approached. Kelsey and Rover stopped growling, but kept their guard up. They took a few steps forward and then lowered themselves to the ground keeping sharp eyes on the figure, waiting for him or her to get closer.

Chapter nine

Bacham had raced through the hidden passageway, reaching the surface and a safe distance from the shore just in time. He had studied the tunnels extensively in planning this operation. One wrong turn and he would have been as doomed as those he had left behind. He could hear the crashing of the columns and the ceiling as they gave way to the tremendous weight of water that filled the cavern. He moved to a point on a cliff overlooking the sea and saw in the distance the area that had caved in. It was like a shadowy line in the water. The cavern cave-in had started the suction effect, but the water would also be rushing in to fill all the passageways and other underground canyons and similar openings. He had managed to create a mini-earthquake under the sea. The first part of his plan had been a success.

There was no time to be wasted. He had arranged for another small squadron to meet him near the cliff's edge. Once he located them, he led them on a quick march further down the shore. He was racing to get to the island of the Sea Sprites, which was about a mile further south. His plan required him to reach the island in fifteen minutes or less. If his calculations were right, the depression in the ocean floor, which was at this moment rapidly pulling the tide away from the coast, would create a large wave effect. After the water flowing away from the shore crashed into the water from further out to sea, it would begin to sweep back the way it had come, followed quickly by the rest of the sea. This time, though, it would not just be a returning tide; it would be an enormous raging wave. That wave would be heading directly towards the Sea Sprites' island.

His calculations had, in fact been right, if not underestimated – grossly underestimated. The collapse of the ceiling in the underground cavern had started a chain reaction, causing a similar collapse of a much larger coastal shelf for several miles along a fault line that ran parallel to the shore. The collapse along this fault line resulted in an effect much greater than the mini-earthquake and subsequent flooding he had anticipated. The returning wave was growing into a wall of water that continuously increased in size, power, and speed as it made its way back to the shore.

On the island of the Sea Sprites, Stella had returned to the Sanctorum after consulting several ancient prophecies in the palace library. She was still trying to make sense of the images she had seen previously when an overwhelming sense of panic and alarm struck her. She had no sooner entered the Sanctorum than she was struck with a crystal clear vision of a Dryad named Virginia. Stella froze in the center of her room and the images on the walls around her took on an unusual clarity. They became the visions Virginia was seeing herself at the very instant she rushed after the scouts.

Stella could feel the hammering that Virginia had felt. The reverberations rose from her feet to her head, increasing in intensity. She sensed the same panic that Virginia was feeling. She could see Virginia directing the evacuation of the outpost. She saw the structural integrity of the bubble over their outpost begin to diminish. She heard the thunderous roar as the pillars and ceiling collapsed. She felt the pull of the water all around her as she was drawn unstoppably into the cavern. She sensed the same resignation as she stopped fighting the inevitable and gave herself over to the sudden blackness. Stella's heart felt like it was empty. She was overwhelmed with grief.

When Princess Natalie entered the Sanctorum she found Stella collapsed on the floor with tears in her eyes.

"What's happened?" she asked, dropping down to put her arms around Stella. "Please, tell me. What's wrong?"

"Six of us have been lost," Stella answered in a halting voice, tears streaming down her cheeks. "And more are in danger."

She bolted to her feet and grabbed Natalie's arms. She wiped the tears from her eyes and cleared her throat, trying to regain her composure.

"You are in danger," she shouted. "There is a giant force of water approaching. You must not go near it. Promise me. You must leave. Now!"

Stella was frantic, even though she had not formed any specific images of the Princess being in danger. As much as she tried to make sense of it, she couldn't shake the sense of impending disaster. She assumed the source of this was the oncoming flood of water. That was the only logical conclusion. Natalie tried to steady her Enchantress.

"I will make no such promises," she replied, standing firmly. "I will not abandon my people. Tell me what's happening. What is the source of the danger? What can we do together to protect our people?"

Stella reached up to touch the stone in her headband. She was desperate to ensure the safety of the Princess.

"I can shield the island," she declared. "I can cast a spell to divert the threat. But the faeries and forest creatures near the shore will be in jeopardy. They won't be able to stop this. They must be warned."

Stella was trying to think of any way she could to get Natalie off the island without it appearing that she was trying to have her hide from the oncoming danger. She knew she would have to convince Natalie that the Sea Sprites were not in danger, and that she would have to be the one to save the faeries and forest creatures.

"I'll send emissaries," Natalie told her. "Tell me what danger they face so my representatives can sufficiently convince them. I can't leave now. I must stay here with you to protect the Sprites."

"No," insisted Stella. "I can shield our people. The faeries and forest creatures will not listen to your emissaries. They are both stubborn and sometimes prideful people. They will have to debate any information from emissaries. The words must come from you, otherwise they will not listen. The mass of water that is coming at us will crush their villages and bury them under the sea. Nothing they can do will stop it or save them. Only you can convince them of this. You must believe me in this. They will listen only to you."

Natalie debated her options quickly. She knew they had to act fast and she didn't have time to argue with Stella.

"Please assure me that our island will come to no harm," she finally said. " – that you will come to no harm. Promise me that. Otherwise I will not leave."

"I swear to you, your Highness, I have the power to protect the Sprites. And I will be safe as well."

She wasn't as convinced of this as she sounded, but she needed to get Natalie off the island. The wall of water that was racing in their direction was growing larger and stronger, as was the sense she had of the danger that was facing Natalie.

"All right," Natalie agreed reluctantly. "I'll go to the faeries and forest creatures myself. But once I've ensured they're moving to safety, I'll return to face this with you. Don't even try to talk me out of it. Is that clear?"

Stella knew that by then it would all be over – one way or another.

"I understand," she said, "now, please go."

"Where will you be?" Natalie shouted back to her as she ran from the Sanctorum. "I need to know where to look for you."

"At the north side of the island," Stella answered heading off in that direction, "but search for me here first."

If Natalie was able to return before the wave had passed, she wanted Natalie in the safest place on the island. That would be in the Sanctorum. Stella knew Natalie wouldn't stay there long, but at least for a little while she'd be as safe as possible. She only hoped all of this would be over before the Princess returned.

Natalie ran out of the palace and to the sheltered cove where the boats were anchored. She quickly climbed aboard her fastest ship and set sail for the mainland. She wasn't even sure whether Summer and Sean had come back, yet, from their travels. If they had not, it would be all the more difficult to convince the leaders of their people to move to a safe place. But if they had returned, they would be in danger, as well. She couldn't decide which situation she preferred more.

She had chosen the smallest and swiftest craft in her fleet to carry her across the short channel that separated her island from the edge of the forest where Sean's people lived. She sailed the tiny ship herself, directing her guards to stay behind on the island. If Stella were able to protect the Sprites, her guards would be safer left behind. She sailed straight across the channel towards the Lodge of the forest creatures. The village of the faeries was south of here and it would be easier to reach them cutting through the forest from the lodge than by going directly by sea. She was gambling that the faeries, sensing danger, would take flight. The forest creatures, however, had no such ability and would be more threatened by the anticipated flood. It made sense to go there first.

She barely made it to shore when the channel water drained away, being drawn by the larger rush of water towards the collapsing cavern and out to sea. It wouldn't be long before the channel was awash in the returning tidal wave. As the boat slid across the sandy beach, Natalie jumped out and ran headlong into the forest, leaping over fallen trees and low shrubs, ducking under branches and weaving in and out. She had been so focused on getting to the Lodge that she didn't notice the rapidly receding water, or that it had pulled her boat away from the shore with it.

She was less than a hundred yards from the edge of the Lodge when the unusual silence alerted her to some unseen danger. She didn't slow down, but started paying closer attention to the lack of noise. The forest creatures could be incredibly quiet when hunting, but their Lodge was almost always buzzing with sound. By now, she should have heard signs of activity, but there were none. In fact, there were no sounds coming from the birds and insects in the area, either. Something didn't seem quite right, but the hairs on the back of her neck rose, and seemed to be shouting to her.

By now she was on full alert. She slowed to a halt and took a few seconds to get her breathing under control. When she calmed down, she advanced slowly and stealthily, moving from cover to cover behind the trees that zigzagged along the entryway towards the Lodge. There were still no sounds she could detect coming from the Lodge. As she got closer, she got down on her hands and knees, and slowly crept forward as quietly as possible, keeping herself hidden in the low lying brush. At the very edge of the main Lodge clearing, she spotted something that made her freeze.

The huts in the Lodge were arranged in several circles around the central hut, where the Lodge leaders met. The circles were divided by a path that cut across the clearing. Two Rebbercands were sneaking from one hut to the next on the far side of the clearing, near the path. She held her breath, dropped flat to the ground and slid backwards under the nearest cluster of Banchu leaves. When she felt she was securely hidden, she eased her head up and moved some of the leaves to create tiny openings for her to see.

The Rebbercands were quietly and quickly searching each of the huts, moving from her right to her left coming toward the center of the Lodge. In spite of their size and their bulk, and the large double headed axes they were carrying, they were being extremely quiet, but thorough. They were also moving in a very disciplined and militaristic manner. This was nothing like the disorganized and unmanaged movements of the Rebbercands she had observed in her last encounter with these creatures.

A subtle change in the sunlight to her left caught the corner of her eye. Moving her head slowly to the edge of her peripheral vision, she turned towards the change. She nearly gasped when she saw four more Rebbercands, each armed with crossbows, entering the clearing from the opposite side. Two of them were checking huts on the north side of the path and the other two were covering the huts on the south side. That led her to believe that there were at least two more with the first group that she hadn't seen. Eight of them? How many more were there, she wondered. And what were they doing?

They're hunting the forest creatures, she thought, trying to trap them. She felt she should do something, but she didn't see any of the forest creatures, so she wasn't sure who to warn or what exactly she could do. As she had suspected, the first two were joined by two others who had been going through the huts blocked from her view. These four passed from her right and joined the four on her left. When they were looking away from where she was hidden, she inched her way further to her right, crawling as quietly as possible under the leaves and low branches. She reached a small opening – a slight path separating the cover she was hiding under from another cluster of vegetation.

She wanted to get as far away as possible – back to her ship, but by now the way she had come was too exposed. To move forward, she would have to cross a short open space. She gathered her courage, and just as she was about to leap to the other side, a foot came down barely six inches from her face. It was another Rebbercand. She nearly bit her tongue to keep from making a sound, ducking down as far as she could. There were too many and they were too far apart from one another for her to cast any kind of spell. If she tried, even moving as fast as she could, it would alert the others to her presence, so she squeezed herself as flat as she could and waited for the Rebbercand nearest her to move. It seemed like it took forever, but he finally entered the clearing to join the others. She then backed up the way she had come until she heard a rustling in the bushes behind her.

She turned very slowly to look behind her only to discover that she was now surrounded by them. Her heart was hammering in her chest and beads of sweat were covering her forehead. The palms of her hands were wet with sweat as well. During all of this she didn't see a single forest creature or any sign that anyone other than she and the Rebbercands were anywhere near the Lodge. Since the Rebbercands seemed to be searching for them or something else, she concluded that the forest creatures had been alerted to the presence of the Rebbercands and had left the Lodge.

Great, she thought, now what do I do? There was no way for her to head for the faeries' village. That way was blocked off, and for all she knew, they, too had already been alerted to the presence of the Rebbercands. But she couldn't stay where she was, although she curled in as tightly as she could under the bushes. It wouldn't be long before this area would be hit by the tidal wave. If Stella's visions were correct, it was possible this whole area could be under water – under a lot of water.

------------------ *** ------------------

Sean and Quinn had watched the figure as it continued its slow advance. Sean had both hands up to the sides and tops of his eyes to narrow his focus and to shield his eyes. During that time Kelsey and Rover had remained quiet, keeping careful eyes on the same image. As the music became clearer, the tune became more fluid and recognizable. The dogs cocked their heads in confusion, repeatedly looking back at their master, who was as clueless as they were. They whimpered, but stayed where they were, sifting their gaze back and forth between Quinn and the approaching stranger. Nearly an hour passed before the figure was close enough for the observers to be able to make out details.

Whoever it was, was covered from head to toe in a long dark robe with a large hood that was pulled close around the head. Only the hands were visible. It was evident that he wasn't wearing gloves, as they could be seen where they held the narwhal bone horn, covering and uncovering the holes that created the tune being played. The notes of the tune had been disbursed by the wind, but at this range were now clear.

"I think I recognize that stranger," said Sean, as he stood up, straining to get a better look at the approaching figure.

"Isn't that 'Ode to Joy' being played on the narwhal bone horn?" asked Quinn, who also got to his feet.

"Lochen?" they both shouted in unison.

At the sound, the figure stopped, looked up, raised one hand to shield his eyes from the glare of the ice and snow, and then raised the other hand to wave before continuing on. At this signal, Sean and Quinn ran towards him with Kelsey and Rover barking frantically and running ahead of them.

"Well, it's sure good to see you two," Lochen said, reaching down to scratch the muzzles of the two dogs. They were barking excitedly, wagging their tails, running around and jumping. They knocked him over with their exuberance and licked his face.

Lochen looked up and saw Sean and Quinn approaching. He gently pushed the dogs away and struggled to his feet.

"It's sure good to see you two, too," he said, staring at Sean with a puzzled look – watching him waddle uncomfortably along.

"What are you doing here?" asked Quinn.

"Aren't you freezing?" asked Sean.

"I came to find the two of you, and to answer your question, Sean, yes, actually, I'm quite cold," he answered.

As his friends finally reached him, they could see his robe was covered with a layer of frost from top to bottom, and in some places near the bottom chunks of ice actually clung to the material. His feet were covered in blocks of snow and ice. His face was red from the cold, and his hands were nearly blue.

"How did you get here?"

"Why is there ice on your clothes?"

"Did you come by yourself?"

"How long have you been traveling?"

They bombarded him with questions. All the while he stood there shivering, trying to answer until Quinn finally suggested that they set up the tent, light a small fire and open up some food supplies. Once they were settled in and Lochen had warmed up, he was better able to explain what had recently transpired.

He had discovered after their adventure with the Trepans that Quinn and Sean had not been lost to the river of lava, but had instead been transported at the last minute – last second, to be more accurate – to the Ice Kingdom. No one understood initially how that had happened, but the Alchemist had assured everyone that their two friends were safe. Princess Natalie and her Enchantress, Stella, returned to their island, while Solveig, Summer and Liam returned to the Swamp to help guide some of the tunnel reconstruction in that area. Lochen had decided to remain behind for a short while to help the Trepans and the rebel forces begin the reconstruction of their tunnels. He was interested in learning how they were able to do this as efficiently as they did.

Although it had only been slightly more than a month since Sean and Quinn had disappeared, Lochen was surprised that Sean still hadn't returned. He came to the conclusion that either the transporter stone that had carried the two of them back to the Ice Kingdom was damaged, or, more likely, that Sean was more than a bit reluctant to use this method of transportation again. So, Lochen decided it might be nice to come for a visit and then to escort Sean back to his people when he was ready to leave.

Having no aversion to using transporter stones himself, Lochen found one of suitable size and teleported himself to the Ice Kingdom. His calculations, however, had not taken into consideration some significant factors. Most importantly, the damage that had been done by the Rebbercands' abuse of the Trepans and their tunnels had misdirected the natural flow of the lava, and had eroded large areas of the ice shelf exactly in the area Lochen had projected his landing. Consequently, his transporter stone missed depositing him on solid matter and had reconstituted about twenty feet from shore, well away from any icebergs or ice slabs, and into some very cold water.

The shock of the water had been so severe, that he lost his grip on the stone. It then immediately sunk to the bottom, which was much further away from the surface than Lochen had imagined. He tried to go after it, but it was lost in the murky depths. He was able to swim to the ice shelf before hypothermia crippled him, and began to walk in the direction he just felt was correct, based on where he thought Quinn's home was and the position of the suns. There had been very little in the way of fuel or other materials to burn, and even with his sorcerer powers, he couldn't start a fire with nothing. He was able to cast a spell to extract the water from his clothing, which helped a little, but not much.

Along the way, he came across the mostly eaten carcass of a narwhal. He took what was left of the hide and lined the inside of his robe for additional warmth, and he constructed the horn from one of the bones' making the holes by digging at it with smaller pieces of bone. Although the skin from the carcass wasn't as warm as he would have liked, the additional lining had kept him from freezing. And, he was certain that the music would convince anyone who heard it that he was friendly and that the notes he missed as he learned how to play it might possibly be discordant enough to ward off any potential predators.

"How long have you been traveling and how did you know which way to go?" asked Quinn.

"Since the suns don't completely set at this time of year I can only estimate my travel time by their locations at different positions on the horizon. But, I would venture a guess that it has been just over four days since I landed in the water. As to the direction, I just tracked the progress of the twin suns across the sky and since I knew approximately where I put ashore, I estimated the direction. I also recall your descriptions of your home, and included that information in my estimations, although I admit, that part was more of a guess than I am normally comfortable with in making such computations. Apparently it is safe to conclude that my assumptions were more or less accurate."

Quinn stared at him in wonderment. "But if you had been off by only one degree, you could have missed us by a mile."

"Actually," answered Lochen, "if I had been off by one full degree, at this distance I would have missed you by more than five miles."

Lochen looked at both of them, took in the supplies on the sled, and said, "It looks like I'm too late for a visit, but, judging from the supplies on the sled it appears that I'm just in time to join Sean on his return home. So – when do we leave?"

Sean and Quinn were speechless for a few seconds. They looked at Lochen, then turned to each other and then broke out laughing.

"You've been walking for four days in this climate," said Quinn. "We can start after you've rested."

"Oh," answered Lochen, somewhat puzzled. "I'm not sure I need to rest, but if you'd like to wait a while, that's fine."

Quinn didn't know what to say, except, "Well, all right, then. Let's get things repacked and loaded on the sled, and we can head out."

It took them a few short minutes to dismantle and store the tent. Quinn found some additional clothing that he gave to Lochen, explaining that the narwhal hide really didn't smell too good, and was likely to attract unwanted predators, in spite of whatever tunes he played on the horn. Lochen acquiesced and admitted that the new clothing was much more comfortable, and, in fact, a bit more pleasant smelling.

Lochen and Sean alternated taking turns riding on the sled. Whoever wasn't sitting stood on the back with Quinn while he steered. The dogs didn't seem to notice the additional weight. If they did, it was not evident in the speed they maintained while pulling it. With three of them, pushing the sled up hill was a little easier, and they made fairly good time. Fortune was with them on the weather front as well, since the rest of the day was sunny and clear with just a slight wind. After a few hours the dogs started whining again, and Quinn announced that they would stop for a longer break.

When the break was over and everyone had a full meal – the first really full meal Lochen had had in the last four days, and the first that was hot – they started off again. The sky was getting slightly overcast, but there were no signs of storms – at least not yet. The clouds had darkened sufficiently so that the effects of the white-out were no longer a threat. As they traveled, Quinn talked about the scenery and the various animals that lived in this Kingdom. He explained which ones they really needed to avoid. Lochen mentioned that he had seen a large herd of some kind of animal he had never seen before.

"Those were probably Tarandus" Quinn explained after Lochen described what they looked like.

"Yeah," piped in Sean. "They're pretty nasty. They eat each other. Can you believe that? I even saw them doing that."

A few hours later about a half mile off to their right Lochen spotted the remains of three or four animals that appeared to have fallen prey to something larger. The corpses were lumped together next to a large mound.

"Those look like Tarandus bodies," said Quinn, "although you don't usually see that many dead ones all in one place, especially ones that still have that much flesh on their bones. When they attack one another, there's usually nothing left except for their hooves, horns and fangs. They get picked clean, and pretty quickly."

"That's incredible," said Lochen. "Could we stop for a minute? I'd like to get a closer look. I've never had the chance to study these animals before, and this might be my only opportunity. I'll be quick. I promise."

Quinn scanned the horizon and didn't see the rest of the herd or any other predators.

"Sure, I suppose," he said, and started to turn the sled in that direction.

"That's not necessary," said Lochen. "We needn't change our course. Just stop here and I'll run over. It's not that far."

Quinn debated for a second. Not seeing any danger anywhere on the horizon, he didn't see any harm in letting Lochen go off on his own.

"All right," he said. "But don't take too long. And if you see anything moving – anything at all – get back here fast."

"Yes, of course," Lochen answered, half paying attention, his interest already riveted on the animal remains. "Thank you. I won't be but a moment."

Quinn turned the sled towards the mound against which the carcasses had fallen and came to a stop about half way there, letting Lochen go off to explore. Even though he didn't see anything even remotely dangerous, this didn't feel right. He kept the sled pointed towards the mound in case he needed to get to Lochen quickly. Sean, sensing Quinn's uncertainty, got out of the sled and got his sling shot out from underneath the layers of clothing. He found his pouch with the stones for the sling and made sure they were easy to get to. They watched as Lochen awkwardly ran over to the carcasses.

Lochen moved as briskly as he could with all his additional clothing impeding him slightly. He was excited about the chance to see these interesting animals up close. He was so focused on the remains, that he was oblivious to everything else in the surroundings. He crunched his way across the snow in breathless anticipation, making mental notes of the images of the Tarandus. He failed to notice the large mound of snow behind them move slightly.

When he finally reached the bodies, he crouched down for a closer examination. He wished he had something to write with so he could record his observations. Unfortunately, he didn't, so he would have to commit them to memory. He could see the forms of four bodies. The shapes were essentially the same, so he concluded that they were all the same animals.

He saw the sixteen hooves of different but similar sizes, indicating that the animals were all about the same age and size. He counted eight fangs, noting their lengths and how sharp they were. He tugged on one of them to see how secured it was to the rest of the skull. Not enough tissue had been eaten away to be able to remove the fang. He studied the bodies and could see that although they had been ravaged by some kind of ferocious beast – and it appeared from the bite marks that it was only one - there was quite a bit of meat still on them.

That's odd, he thought to himself. Most animals would not leave this much meat behind. He estimated there was several days' food still here. Perhaps the attacker had been frightened off – by either the rest of the Tarandus herd, or maybe even by the three travelers and their two dogs.

Wouldn't that be amusing, he thought. He scanned the horizon for any signs of other predators. There was nothing to be seen. He examined the eight horns, which were obviously used in defense against attacks. He reached down to move one of the bodies to get a better look at the head of one of the others. When he did so, he noticed a large black object that had been uncovered by his actions.

I wonder what that is, he said to himself. He bent closer to get a better look at it. He still couldn't identify what it was; so much of it was still buried under the snow. He reached out to touch it. It was cold and wet, but not at all frozen. That's odd, he thought and he squeezed it. That was when he noticed the two large red eyes on either side of the black object pop open and glare at him.

"Oops," he said.

He pulled his hand back from what he realized was the nose of a large animal. He slowly stood up and began to back away when his foot caught on a piece of one of the carcasses, and he sat down hard. The animal behind the red eyes and black nose shook the snow off its head and slowly rose up. It seemed to keep rising for a very long time. The beast was enormous, towering over Lochen. It bared its teeth and uttered a low growl, as it lowered its head and moved it closer. Its nose was now only inches away from Lochen's face; its fangs glistened; its growl sending reverberations throughout Lochen's body.

Sean spotted the beast first and quickly loaded his slingshot. He moved a few steps forward to improve his angle. As he pulled back to fire, he shouted for Lochen to drop to the ground. Just as he let the stone loose, Quinn saw what he was doing. He reached out to deflect Sean's arm and throw the shot off, but he was too last and was only able to shout, "NOOOO!"

Lochen turned back to Quinn and Sean just in time to see the stone rocketing towards the animal, whose eyes were glued on him. He jumped up at the last minute, blocking the target. The stone struck him soundly on the side of his head. Everything went black as he fell to the ground. The animal stepped forward, lowered its massive, growling head and sniffed the unconscious sorcerer.

Chapter ten

After helping free the Trepans from the Rebbercands, Liam had volunteered to help them reconstruct their tunnels and return the underworld to the balance that had previously existed. A team had offered to go with him to the Swamp and start there. That way they could conduct some of the necessary reconstructions and assist Liam with his improvements. Life in the Venomous Swamp had been perilous enough as it was. The additional poisons that were introduced to the water and land by the damage directed by the Rebbercands had reversed much of the work he had done to make the Swamp more hospitable. Besides that, those poisons were driving the animals and reptiles out of the Swamp, and some of these creatures presented a real danger to other areas. The balance of nature in the lands outside of the Swamp was now being threatened.

Solveig knew that Lochen would soon be off on another adventure, but was confident that life in her mountain castle could carry on without her for a little while longer. Since she, too, was interested in making the Swamp a less threatening place, she agreed to help him. She had wanted to visit Liam earlier, but had been discouraged by all the hazards. Now she would have the perfect guide to keep her safe.

Summer, on the other hand, was fascinated by all the poisonous creatures, toxic plants, and lethal waterways. She was also fascinated with how Liam had adapted to his environment and lived quite comfortably. She marveled at the interesting inventions he created to survive and get around in his world. She agreed to help out, too, but was hoping for something a bit more adventurous. She had never left her own village until she met Sean. By now she had traveled more than anyone else in her family or her village. She loved it and was becoming a bit of an adrenalin junkie.

The three of them had spent the weeks after the attack on the Rebbercands exploring the tunnels and caverns with the Trepans. The small group that had accompanied the trio to the Swamp focused their effort to redirect fresh water, construct walls and diversions for lava flow, and build vents to the surface for releasing steams and gases. The work went much faster than normal thanks to the magical powers Solveig and Summer brought to the effort. They all learned a great deal from one another in the process.

Once the reconstruction under the Swamp had been completed, the Trepans thanked everyone for their help, and went off to another project. Liam, Solveig and Summer returned to the surface to spend some time finishing the project of mapping and charting each of the areas of the Swamp that Liam had started before being called away. They were on one of Liam's specially constructed vehicles heading towards the eastern part of the Swamp. This one could float like a boat through the rivers and streams, drive up on land over rocks and sand, and even fly short spans a few feet above the ground. This was one of his newer creations, and he was especially proud of it. He had named it the *West Wind*. It was larger than some of his earlier constructions, and made more solidly so that it could navigate larger bodies of water. This was its maiden voyage, and he was very happy with how well it handled.

"How do you come up with these things?" asked Summer.

She was fluttering near his shoulder watching him at the controls. He had his right hand on a lever that steered the craft. With his left hand he was pulling on a rope that adjusted a large sail, and both feet were pedaling to keep the thing moving. He was doing this effortlessly, all at the same time while he was watching where they were going and still keeping an eye out for danger. He had a telescope mounted on a stand to the right of his head and would periodically sneak peeks through it.

"I don't know," he said. "They just come to me. When I run into a problem or a special situation, I just think of how to solve it, and the rest just happens."

"Why did you name it the *West Wind*?" asked Solveig, who was standing at the bow of the ship enjoying the breeze.

"Because that's the direction the wind usually comes from. I'm hoping that one day I can sail her out to the Cerulean Sea to give her a real test. Oh, and one more thing. This is the first one that I built that can fly. I know it can't fly very far – just a few feet or so, but when it does, it's like being the wind itself."

He looked over his shoulder at Summer, who was lazily flapping her wings, listening to him.

"I suppose that sounds silly to you," he said. "I mean, since you can fly. Being able to rise up just a couple feet in the air for just a few seconds is probably ridiculous to you."

"Not at all," she answered, spinning around in front of him so she could face him. "I know exactly how you feel. It's exciting. Can we give it a try?"

"Right now? You don't have to ask me twice," he said with a grin. "Hold on Solveig. I have to admit. I don't know what to expect."

They were rolling across a sandy expanse. He made a slight turn to his left, and they headed towards a narrow gorge. He was pedaling faster and faster. As they neared the gorge, he moved his right hand from the rudder to a lever near his seat. With a quick pull a pair of arms sprung out on each side of the vehicle, the front bounced upward and they were flying. They didn't go far, but, then, they didn't have to. The craft flew over the gorge and landed gently on the opposite side – about 15 feet across.

Solveig was grinning widely. "That was fun. Let's do it again!"

"Why not?" said Liam.

He picked up speed again, steering for another rise in the ground to give the ship some lift. As soon as he found one, he gave the lever another pull, which tilted the arms slightly, and the craft nosed up into the air. It rose more than ten feet up, and then glided through the air for about thirty feet, before bouncing back down.

Since Summer could fly, this was not such a big deal, except for the fact that this big boat – wagon – whatever it was – had been able to leave the ground at all. She did have to admit, though, there were times she took her ability to fly for granted. She could understand Liam's excitement about being able to soar in the wind. She shot up into the air and whirled around the top of the main mast, her hair flowing in the wind behind her. She was happy for her friends to be able to experience this.

She then zoomed down towards Solveig, who was standing at the bow, grinning like a schoolgirl. Her hair was whipping around her, across her eyes and blinding her. As they sailed across the open plains, she tied her hair in braids to keep it from blocking her view. They were headed towards the southeastern area of the Swamp.

"I set out sensors around this area some time ago, but I didn't get to complete the charting and the final adjustments," he shouted up to them.

While much of the Swamp was damp and covered with thick marshland and dense vegetation, this area was more sandy and barren. That did not make it less dangerous. There were large pockets of quicksand and areas infested with sand vipers. As they entered the more opens spaces the terrain began to look more like a desert than a swamp. Liam had retracted the arms that lifted the ship off the ground. They rumbled back inside the hull and locked into place. Then he took one foot off a pedal and kicked a lever near the floor. When he did this, a rumbling from lower inside the hull sounded and pontoons the length of the craft sprung out and unfolded on either side.

"What are those for?" asked Solveig.

"Quicksand," he answered.

Summer and Solveig exchanged worried looks. Solveig raised a hand to her braided hair. They both silently recalled an experience some time ago that they had with quicksand and pulling Lochen free from it.

"The quicksand pools in this area are not like what you've see in the jungle," he explained, seeing the looks on their faces. "They're not the small marshy kind. These pools can be more than a hundred feet across. But you don't get sucked down, like people think. It's more like being on water, except that you can't sail across it like water. You can float for a while, but you can't really move. These pontoons will help keep us afloat and the sail, combined with the paddle wheel that I can pedal, will get us across. We just have to hope there's nothing living in those pools."

Summer and Solveig's worried looks did not improve with this tidbit of information.

"Living?" they both mouthed silently to each other. "What could live in there?"

"Sand vipers mostly," he answered. "They can get pretty big. All sorts of prey get stuck in these pools. Like I said, you don't really sink in this stuff, but you can't get any traction, so you don't go anywhere. I've seen some large animals get stuck. They wear themselves out trying to escape. The motion alerts the Sand Vipers that dinner is being served, and the victims are too tired to fight."

"How far does this desert go?" Summer asked, anxious to change the subject.

"The actual desert is about two hundred miles wide at this point, but the land after that towards the Cerulean Sea doesn't look much different – at least not right away. The animals, though, are a little bit easier to deal with. There are still some nasty ones. Trust me, but most of the ones on the other side of the desert are not poisonous. There's about another two hundred miles of land after the desert, which takes you to the sea. The stretch in the last half is where the vegetation gets interesting. It has a lot of really different trees and other plants. I've only been there a few times, but from what I recall, it's really very nice. "

About an hour later, they ran into one of the quicksand pools. Just as Liam had said, the craft floated without getting sucked down, but it slowed almost to a stop. The jerk threw Solveig up against the railing. She leaned over the side to look down at the ground, not seeing a significant difference from the sand in other areas of the desert. No wonder he wasn't able to avoid this, she thought.

"Don't lean over the side," Liam cautioned Solveig. "I know it's tempting, but if there are any Sand Vipers living down there, they can reach pretty far up. Those long red braids of yours would be a very attractive target. They wouldn't bite them off. They don't really like eating hair. They'd use them to pull you in."

She quickly pulled her head back and grabbed a braid in each hand. Summer stifled a laugh, but increased her altitude a few feet, just in case they thought they might like to try snacking on a faerie.

In the mean time Liam was shifting levers and pulling ropes. The sail filled with air again, and the paddles, once lowered into the sand, started to move. The ship seemed to grind along, picking up a little bit of speed, but the scraping of the sand was making an ear piercing screech and the grinding of the paddles in the sand was nerve wracking. Solveig covered her ears with her hands, and Summer flew up into the air to escape the noise. She soared high above the ship and made a sweeping circle.

Liam watched as Summer climbed higher into the sky. "Just keep an eye out for Blue Falcons," he shouted.

"I'm not afraid of being attacked by Blue Falcons," Summer shouted back. "I'm much faster and much smarter than they are."

"It's not the Blue Falcons I'm worried about," Liam answered. "If they're flying around, they usually end up being a meal for a Gryphus Condor. A faerie would barely be dessert, and I'm not so sure you could outrun one of those."

Summer stopped in mid-flight, took a quick look in every direction, and then decided that maybe the screeching and grinding coming from the sand wasn't so bad after all, and flew back to the ship.

"I thought you were hoping for a little adventure," laughed Solveig. "Wasn't the challenge of trying to outrun a Gryphus Condor adventurous enough for you?"

"Adventure, yes; dinner out, no," Summer shot back.

They managed to cross the small lake of quicksand without any incident, and Liam considered them lucky. Solveig had seen some movement not far off to her right, but nothing broke the surface and nothing struck the ship. She thought that maybe the size of the boat was enough to make whatever it was she saw reconsider any attack. Not long after they were out, they came to the last set of sensors at the very end of the desert. Liam climbed down from the ship and examined them to make sure they were properly calibrated. While he was doing this he noted some odd readings.

"It looks like there have been some minor tremors somewhere ahead," he said. "It's hard to tell for sure, but normally the readings out here are pretty flat. The sensors are designed more for tracking things above ground, but they'll pick up motion below ground if it's a strong enough vibration."

"What do you suppose caused it?" asked Summer.

"Could it have been our work with the Trepans?" asked Solveig.

Liam thought about it for a few seconds. He had no other explanation. "I suppose that was probably it, although these notations seem to be random at first and then more regular. And they're very weak. It doesn't look like they occurred where we were working. I'm really not sure what it means."

"I thought these hadn't been calibrated, yet," said Solveig. "Do you think that could be a factor?"

"I guess that makes sense," he said, and then thought nothing more about it. He made the final adjustments and announced, "Well, they've all been calibrated in this direction, and this is the last of them; so I guess we're done."

"What now?" asked Summer.

Before Liam could offer an opinion, Solveig piped up, "I think we need a vacation. Don't you think we deserve one?"

"What do you have in mind," asked Summer.

Solveig shifted her look from Summer to Liam and suggested, "How about we keep going and take this thing out on the Cerulean Sea? Didn't you say you wanted to take it out for a real test? What else do we have to do?"

"She," said Liam. "Not it. A boat is a she."

He, she, it, whatever," answered Summer. "You didn't answer the question. Are you stalling? Come on. I think that's a great idea. I don't have anything else to do and you don't either. Count me in."

Liam's initial reaction was reluctance. He hadn't planned on doing more than just check out the sensors, but as he tried to come up with reasons to say no, he decided that, yes, they needed a vacation, and it would be really great to take the *West Wind* out on the Sea, especially with two of his best friends. He always traveled with more than enough provisions, so that wasn't a problem. It didn't need to be a long trip – just a quick run. The more he thought, the more he was convincing himself to do it.

He smiled at the both of them and said, "Why not?"

"Yes!" Summer and Solveig shouted.

With that they were off. Liam reset the sail. The pontoons and the wings had been retracted and he made sure they were secure. Then he repositioned the wheel gears and lowered the wheels. He gave his two shipmates a smile and started pedaling. The wind quickly filled the sail and with Liam's pedaling, the ship picked up speed and was moving fast across the ground. Summer flew to the top of the main mast to serve as look out, and Solveig offered to take turns with Liam pedaling the craft. As soon as they hit the hard packed ground past the edge of the desert, the ship rocketed ahead.

The wind whipped through Summer's hair as she leaned forward, her elbows on the edge of the tiny crow's nest, her head held in her hands, and her wings tucked tightly behind her. The view was beautiful, even as it raced past her. The ground ahead was wide open. The hard packed sand was a pearly white and small palm trees and Banchus were beginning to appear; and the sky above was a brilliant blue. She looked down at Solveig who had taken over and was pedaling with ease as Liam adjusted the main sail and the jib. They were both laughing and smiling.

She was having the most fun she had had in a very long time, and was really excited about the thought of being on the open sea.

Solveig was amazed at how effortlessly she could pedal the ship. Liam was a real genius at building these things, she thought. She had seen the maze of gears and pulleys below deck one time. When she had asked why so many were needed, he explained that they all worked together to make moving the boat with the least amount of effort. She wasn't sure she understood it all, but he was right about making this thing move easily.

She looked up at the crow's nest and couldn't see anything of Summer but her long hair blowing behind her. Inspired by this vision, she reached up, loosened her braids, shook her head and let the wind blow through her hair. Her smile widened even further. She couldn't believe how exhilarating this felt. Even with the sail a few feet in front of her shielding her from the wind, a strong breeze was blowing past her.

"How fast are we going?" she shouted to Liam.

He looked at a wind gage on the back of the ship, and then glanced at the sky and then down to the rapidly passing ground.

"I don't know," he shouted back, "but if I had to guess, I'd say nearly seventy miles an hour. You know you don't have to pedal that fast. The Sea isn't going any place."

He was smiling as broadly as she was. The wind was making his shirt and pants flap. He had stowed his hat long ago.

"Are you kidding? I'd pedal faster if I could," she laughed as she threw her head back and pushed even harder against the pedals.

They alternated every once in a while and both kept up the rapid pace. The idea of a vacation on the Cerulean Sea had thrilled each of them, and the anticipation fueled their fire. They laughed for no reason at all, and couldn't stop grinning. They were still speeding along three hours later when Liam motioned for Solveig to slow down.

"Are we there," she asked. Breathing hard from the exertion.

"Not yet," Summer shouted down from the crow's nest and pointing forward. "I can see the Sea, but it's still way out there."

"Something's not right," said Liam. "Look at the ground. It's wet sand. We should have reached the Sea by now."

"Maybe it's low tide," said Summer.

Liam looked to the sky. "No. It's not the right time for low tide. In fact, the tide should be high. I'm telling you, something's not right. Look at the water line back there." He pointed to a place where the sand changed from dry to wet. "That's where the water line should be by now. Not way out there."

"I think we should keep going forward to see what we can find," said Solveig. "I don't think the answer is back here."

"OK," said Liam, "but let's take it slowly. We don't need to rush into something we're not prepared for. Summer, let us know if you see anything."

"I'll do better than that," she answered, flying up out of the crow's nest and out towards the sea. "I'll scout ahead."

In a very short time, she was racing back. Her wings were flapping frantically. Neither Liam nor Solveig had ever seen her move so fast before.

"We need to get out of here," she shouted. "Turn that thing around. Hurry! I've never seen anything like it. There's a giant wall of water heading this way. It goes on as far as I could see, and it's as high as..." she was at a loss to describe the enormity of the wall, raising her arms high above her head and flying upward to make them extend even further.

"As...as...I don't know, but it's really, really high. A lot higher than this ship."

"Can we go to the north and avoid it?" he shouted back to her.

"No," she was screaming now. "I can't see where it ends to the north and it's coming too fast. We'll never outrun it. We have to go back the way we came. Move it!"

Without wasting a second Liam turned the ship around, lowered the sail, and extended the pontoons while Solveig began pedaling again as fast as she could. Summer raced back and forth between the vacant shoreline and the ship providing updates on the progress of the wave.

"Why did you take down the sail?" asked Solveig. "And lower the pontoons. Won't that slow us down?"

"The wind is behind us," he answered without stopping. "The sail won't help. Actually, the sail will get in the way. The pontoons won't do anything right now – they don't touch the ground, so they won't add any drag, but we'll need them if the water reaches us. We need to be as stable as we can."

"It's coming pretty fast," shouted Summer on her next return. "But it also looks like it's coming at an angle."

"What do you mean," asked Liam.

"It looks higher towards the south," she said.

"That means the epicenter is miles south of here," said Liam.

"What epicenter?" asked Summer. "I thought that had to do with earthquakes, not walls of water. What do you mean?"

"That kind of effect is caused by an underwater earthquake," he told her. "Somewhere out to sea – probably not all that far – and south of here there was an earthquake. That explains the reading on my sensors. That earthquake is what caused this tidal wave."

"How far south," asked Summer in a voice approaching panic.

"I can't tell," he answered. "It depends on too many variables."

"Where's Lochen when we need him?" declared Solveig. "What's your best guess? Can you give us that?"

"If it's as long as Summer said, it could be miles – it could be anywhere from just a few miles to hundreds of miles. I just can't be sure. I'm not even close to sure. I just don't know. I'm sorry."

By now they began to hear a low rumble. The sound was coming from the rushing tidal wave. Summer could see its approach from her vantage point high above the crow's nest, as she flew up higher and back towards the oncoming wave to get a better view. She could see that where they were was near the end of an enormous curling wave. It wasn't as far north as she had originally thought, but she still didn't think they could outrun it in that direction. A different worry confronted her now. She shot back down to the ship.

"How far are we from Natalie's island?" she demanded.

Liam thought a few quick seconds and said, "I'm pretty sure it's several miles to the south."

"Several miles?" exclaimed Summer, "not more than that? Are you sure?"

"It might even be closer," he said in between his running around securing things on the deck of the ship. "It's hard to tell. When we left the desert we turned in a southerly direction. Why? What difference does it make?"

"We need to turn south," shouted Summer, without explanation. The panic in her voice was rising.

By now, the thunderous roar of the rushing water was much clearer and closer. Liam ran to the back of the ship and could see the top of it.

"South?" he shouted back to her. "Are you nuts? We'd be headed right into the path of that thing. We're going to be lucky to avoid it as it is."

"My family," Summer nearly screamed.

She couldn't say anything more. She realized that the wave was not going to be stopped or diminished be Natalie's island, and would crush her tiny village. The feelings of helplessness she had when that cursed storm had turned them all to stone resurfaced. It was all happening again. They were in danger and she was nowhere around.

"There's nothing we can do to save them," Solveig called to her, afraid she would just take off. She peeked over her shoulder and could see the wave growing larger behind them. Liam had moved the jib around so that it could take in as much wind as possible. She was pedaling with all her might trying to put more distance between them and the wave.

"Solveig, are you holding out all right?" Liam asked. She had been going strong even before they had to reverse course. "Let me know if you need a break."

"I'm all right. I'll let you know if I get too tired."

She knew how awful this was for Summer. She could hear the anxiety in Summer's and Liam's voices. If her family was in danger, then so were the Sea Sprites and the forest creatures. After all they had been through together, she only hoped that her friends were safe.

The tide that extended to the north of the wave was now rushing over the shore. Summer looked to her right to see it crashing through the sand dunes and through the trees. This wasn't even part of the wall that was still off shore. It was just the trailing edge, and it was flooding the coast, gushing past the normal high tide line and streaming into the forest. It wasn't just rushing past the trees; it was either uprooting them or snapping them in half. She had never seen so much force and destruction before.

"Pedal faster," Summer shouted as she watched the mountain of water continue towards them.

All she could do was shout encouragement. The thought of floating in the air above the two of them without being able to help was killing her. She looked down at Solveig who was hunched over the gears and controls. Her face was beet red with the exertion; sweat was pouring down her body, but she was pumping her legs furiously. There was no magic in Solveig's arsenal that would get them out of here, and her own faerie dust was useless in this situation.

"Wait a minute," she said out loud to no one in particular. "Faerie dust!"

She had been hovering about twenty feet above the ship watching in shock at the impending disaster. As soon as the thought entered her mind, she swooped downward and began sprinkling faerie dust all over the ship. Some of it was blown away by the wind, so she moved closer to the ship and more towards the front, sprinkling frantically.

"What are you doing?" shouted Liam. "Stay up as high as you can. That wave is going to overrun us. Save yourself."

"Faerie dust," was about all she could shout.

"It's - too - big," panted Solveig, her breathing coming in gasps. "Never - fly!"

Summer sped past the ship and then turned around to come at it head on, flying in low. She looked like a dive-bomber as she came in over the top sprinkling another load of faerie dust on the ship. She was looking down as she passed over the stern and brought her head up at the last minute, coming nearly face to face with the towering wall of water. By now it was on a downward crash.

"Stick out those arm things," she shouted back to Liam. "Hurry! Make that thing fly."

She pulled up just in time, flipping over backwards as she turned sharply around and swooped back down towards the ship to give it one more shot of faerie dust. At the last minute, the craft began to rise slowly into the air. Liam had deployed the "wings" just in time, and the ship's natural short hop of a lift in combination with the faerie dust raised the boat high enough to stay just in front of the collapsing wall instead of just under it.

"Stop pedaling and hold on tight," Liam shouted to Solveig, who gladly stopped immediately.

She slumped over the controls, her legs feeling like rubber bands, and grasped the nearest thing that was secured tightly to the frame of the ship. Summer was launched further skyward by the blast of wind as the wave crashed on the coastline and washed over the land to the desert. Liam steered the ship, riding the crest of the wave like a surfer. They had managed to lift just enough that the water slammed into the shore underneath their ship instead of on top of it.

The water flooded inland and washed the trio and their ship almost halfway back to the desert from which they had just come before exhausting itself and slowly receding back to the sea. The ship spun around as it passed trees submerged in water, bouncing off the tops and swirling in eddies as the water was absorbed into the ground or dragged debris with it back into the sea. Large trunks and branches careened into the pontoons on the sides of the ship, shaking the boat but not breaking it.

When the water finally settled down, the shore was still under several feet of water, and the waves of the aftershock were still rocking the boat back and forth, but Liam had control of the rudder and was able to steer it. He relieved Solveig at the pedals, while she sat numbly along the bulwark. Summer floated down to join them, a look of utter defeat on her face.

"Where are you going?" asked Solveig as she watched Liam reset the sails and turn the bow of the ship to the south instead of back towards the Swamp.

"We need to get to Summer's village and to Natalie's island. We need to see what help they need."

"They're gone," said Summer. "They're all gone. Nothing could have survived that; especially not my village."

Chapter eleven

Jochen's head was throbbing. Everything was still floating through his mind, but none of it made any sense. What had he been doing? He couldn't recall exactly. Something about a large black nose. It was coming back to him. He had acted impulsively in going to inspect the...what? What had he been inspecting? Noses? That didn't seem right. And then Sean had fired his slingshot. His initial thought had been to duck down, but when he saw the look on Quinn's face, saw him waving his arms and shouting, "No," he sensed the warning was not for his safety, but for the animal's safety.

What animal? The nose animal? Oh, yes, it was that rather large, toothy animal. Sean was shooting at the nose animal, but Quinn didn't want him to do that. He remembered then. He reacted immediately by doing the only thing that came to mind. He stood up. If he had even just a split second more to think, he would have cast a spell on the projectile instead of jumping up to block it. The stone had struck with such force and so quickly, that he had no recollection of being hit at all – only the aftermath: a throbbing headache.

"Let this be a lesson to you," he said, thinking he was talking to himself. "The next time, divert the missile with a spell. Or on second thought, just duck. Or on third thought, don't go squeezing cold, wet, black objects buried in the snow. Or on fourth thought..."

"What are you talking about?" a voice called to him from the mist. "How many thoughts are you having, anyway?"

"I'm sorry," he said. "Are you in my dream? Are you an angel? I don't usually have anyone talk back to me in my dreams. Not even angels, although I don't recall ever having a dream about an angel. I could be wrong, though. After all, I would have been dreaming."

Aside from what he believed to be an imaginary dialogue, what returned him to consciousness was someone rubbing his head with a moist towel. Was this the person who had been speaking with him? Was this an angel? I've never seen an angel, he thought. I wonder what they look like. When he summoned the strength to open one eye, everything was a blur. White, pink and black images were swirling together. That's a funny looking angel, he thought. He closed the eye, took a deep breath and forced both eyes open, hoping that this would put things right.

Everything was still a blur, but not because his vision was impaired. He blinked repeatedly. No, my vision is just fine, he thought. It was because there was a mound of white fur immediately in front of his eyes. He wasn't being attended to by a moist towel. He was being licked by the animal he had taken the stone for. Unsure of what to do, he gently raised his hand to move the beast's enormous head away.

"Uh, thank you. I think," he said. "I'm quite fine now. I appreciate your attentiveness, but I really must be going."

He moved the head and tongue far enough away for it all to come into focus. At arm's length he was able to see an enormous head in front of him, with an enormous mouth and even more enormous teeth. He considered that, since those enormous teeth hadn't devoured him by now, he was relatively safe. With this in mind, he removed one hand from the head. He reached up and felt a huge knot on the side of his head where the stone had hit him.

"I'm really, really sorry," said Sean when he saw that Lochen had returned to the world of the conscious. "I thought you were in danger. Honest! I didn't expect you to jump in the way. Normally when I shoot at someone, they duck. They don't purposely try to get hit, especially in the head."

He moved closer to express his regret to Lochen. As he did so, the animal shifted its gaze from Lochen to Sean and let out a low growl.

Quinn inserted himself between the animal and Sean, serving as mediator, extending his arms and nudging Sean safely behind him.

"It's all right, wolfy," Quinn apologized. "He didn't know any better. If he did, he wouldn't have tried to...to...ah...do what he did."

"Wolfy?" asked Lochen as he struggled to sit up.

He held both sides of his head to keep the swirling to a minimum. When everything stopped spinning, he saw Quinn standing across from him and Sean somewhat hidden behind. Lochen, himself, was sitting between the front legs of a giant arctic wolf, with its massive head looming over the top of Lochen. He nearly fell over on his back as he looked up at the wolf. Even if I was standing upright, Lochen thought, this animal would still tower above me. Feeling a bit uncomfortable this close to such a fierce predator, and in spite of his natural curiosity, he thought it prudent to establish a little more space between them and started to inch his way closer to Quinn, wiggling forward on one butt cheek after the other. As he did so, he noticed a large scar along the wolf's right leg near his paw.

"Yeah," said Quinn. "That's probably not his real name, but I didn't get a chance to give him a proper one."

"You know each other, I take it," said Lochen. "I hope your introduction to one another was less painful than mine."

The wave of pain that shot through his head made him reconsider moving any more than he had to. He stopped wiggling. Quinn explained his encounter with this particular wolf not long ago and how he had helped heal its injured leg.

"But he disappeared almost right after that. I never knew if he healed all right or if something else – something worse – happened to him. I still have the shard of crystal I removed from his leg," Quinn said, pulling the piece from an inside pocket. "I kept it as a sort of good luck charm. When I first saw it I thought it was a piece of ice. But it's not. It's some kind of crystal – really sharp, too."

He had tied a rawhide strap around the top of the fragment and often wore it around his neck. He was holding it forward for Lochen to see. The wolf let out a low growl at the sight of the crystal. Quinn stuffed it back inside his shirt, out of sight from the wolf, which stopped growling as soon as it was gone. Lochen held the sides of his head as he leaned back again and looked up to see the wolf's lower jaw. The wolf looked down at Lochen and lowered his mouth to give Lochen's head a quick lick with his giant tongue.

"I've never seen a wolf this big," said Lochen. "It really is an amazing creature, although I have to admit, I'd rather be seeing it from a different angle."

"Actually, I haven't seen one that big, either," said Quinn. "He was pretty big when I met him the last time, but he's grown a lot since then."

"He's the size of an elephant," said Sean, peeking out from behind Quinn.

The wolf shifted his glance from Lochen to Sean, and Sean quickly ducked back behind Quinn. Not knowing what an elephant looked like, Quinn just nodded. Sean didn't really know what an elephant looked like, either, but he had recalled hearing about such an animal from Solveig. He assumed the animal was pretty big, since the name itself was so big.

Lochen slowly stood up. When he did, the top of his head was still below the level of the wolf's jaw. He reached a hand out to steady himself and the wolf lifted its scarred paw. Lochen reflexively held onto the offered paw until he got a closer look at the scar on the paw. He smiled up at the wolf and slowly withdrew his hand.

"Well, an elephant might be a bit of an exaggeration," he said, still smiling at the wolf, "but not by much." He said over his shoulder to Quinn, "and you say you were in a cave with this creature? And he didn't eat you?"

"I guess he wasn't hungry," said Quinn, shrugging his shoulders.

"Or you were incredibly lucky," said Lochen. "But it certainly appears that he remembers your act of kindness."

"I think you're right," answered Quinn, as he tentatively reached up and stroked the wolf's muzzle. "And judging by how much he's been watching over you since you took one in the head for him, he won't forget that you saved his life, too."

The wolf gave Quinn's hand a friendly lick and then lowered his head to give Lochen another lick. He just glared at Sean.

"Looks like Sean's the only one he's not going to invite for dinner," Quinn said with a laugh, giving Sean a friendly push. "Unless he IS dinner."

"I'm really, really sorry," repeated Sean, as the wolf gave another low growl at the mere sound of his voice.

He carefully ducked back behind Quinn, not wanting to make any quick movements. When nothing happened, he peeked around Quinn's elbow to sneak glances at the wolf, which hadn't moved from his position of guarding over Lochen. But the wolf still hadn't taken his eyes off Sean. It wasn't clear if the wolf thought Sean had shot Lochen on purpose or was aiming for him, but it was clear that it had taken a protective attitude towards the sorcerer who had put himself in the path of the stone. It was also clear that he regarded Sean as an adversary he tolerated only because of the company he was in. And it was clear that the wolf never forgot any kindness done to him, no matter how long ago that might have happened.

Sean's only sources of solace were Kelsey and Rover, who had positioned themselves behind Sean and Quinn. Although the wolf made no threatening movement towards them or their master, neither of them had grown any fonder of it since their last encounter. They both kept a safe distance and didn't do anything to attract unnecessary attention to themselves. At some level, the two dogs understood that Sean was not in good favor with the beast, and they crawled to either side of him, pushing their muzzles under his arms. Sean wasn't particularly comfortable with the dogs, but since it seemed that they were his only allies at the time, he timidly stroked their heads.

Getting impatient with being the odd man out, Sean finally asked, "So are we going to stay here forever, or are we going to get moving sometime soon?"

Lochen stepped forward uneasily, and said, "Yes, I'm fine, really. We should continue on. I think I've seen enough of the Tarandus."

"Are you sure you're all right?" asked Quinn as he watched Lochen teetering. "You've got quite a lump on your head."

"It's not that bad," inserted Sean, a bit defensively, "I've seen worse. I hardly even used my hardest shot."

Lochen and Quinn turned to look at him, but remained silent.

"What?" asked Sean.

"I'd say we're losing daylight," quipped Lochen, "but since the suns don't set, that seems somewhat ridiculous. However, I agree that we've spent far too much time here. We should press on. As long as I can ride in the sled for a little while, I should be back to my old self in short order."

"All right," said Quinn, "but we're going to take it easy."

As they regrouped and repacked, Quinn re-harnessed the dogs to the sled. Lochen climbed on top of the supplies and nestled under a pile of skins, propping his head up, while Sean climbed on the back with Quinn. When all were ready, he gave the command for the dogs to get moving. As they pulled out, they started barking. The wolf gave a short howl and began to run along with them. Kelsey and Rover, still a bit annoyed at not being the center of attention, and not enjoying the presence of the wolf, picked up the pace. Step for step, the wolf stayed with them well off to the side, but running parallel to them. Quinn pulled on the reins and turned the sled away, and the wolf turned with them.

"It seems we have an escort," said Lochen.

"That might not be a bad thing," said Quinn, as he watched the movements of the wolf. "It'll be a couple of more days before we get to the end of the Ice Kingdom and the dry area at the edge of the Swamp. That's where we'll have to leave the sled and send the dogs back. There are a lot of things that could see us as a tasty meal. Having a wolf this big tagging along with us might provide some added protection."

"Wonderful," was all Sean could say.

The sled raced across the open fields of ice and snow, and the wolf was never far away. A few hours later Quinn felt they had gone far enough and set up camp. All the way the wolf had maintained the same pace and the same distance off to one side. He would stop periodically and sniff the air, but then would immediately catch up. This time the wolf stopped when they stopped, and sat leisurely by, watching while they unpacked the sled. Once they started erecting the tent, however, the wolf ran off out of sight.

"Was it something we said?" commented Sean, sarcastically.

"I guess he's come as far as he thinks is necessary," said Lochen. "That's too bad. I was rather enjoying his company. I'll be sorry to see him go."

"Me, too," said Quinn.

Sean was wisely silent about the sudden departure of the wolf.

The late evening sky was still light. One of the suns was very low on the horizon, and the other was not far from it. The days had already started to get shorter, even though it would be another month before there would be a full sunset, and even then, only one of the suns would set. There was a golden glow across the ice and snow, and the sky was crystal clear. There was a gentle breeze blowing and there was an absolute stillness all around them. But the temperature was dropping and they needed to stay warm.

Sean and Quinn found some old carcass bones and Lochen used a little magic to light a fire and keep it burning. In a matter of minutes the inside of the tent was warm and comfortable. Quinn broke out some strips of jerky for dinner. He was skewering them onto a stake to hold over the fire to heat them up.

"Not more narwhal fat," whined Sean. "I can't believe you didn't you bring anything else to eat."

"It's narwhal jerky," countered Quinn. "Not narwhal fat. Who eats fat, anyway? Do you eat fat back home? I don't think so."

"Whatever," answered Sean. "It's just that it all tastes like feet."

Lochen laughed. "How would you know what feet taste like?"

"It's just a saying," groused Sean. "That stuff just tastes nasty; it smells bad, and it's tough as leather."

"Look around," said Quinn. "Do you see anything we can hunt? I can always make you a bowl of snow soup. Or maybe I could interest you in a bottle of our finest melted snow. It was fresh last month. Or would you like a moss sandwich? I can whip one up in about two weeks. Would that be more to your liking?"

"Can't we send out for chicken?" asked Sean.

"Sure," said Quinn. "If you can ever get Liam to tell us what it is. I'll have him deliver some right to our tent. Would that make your Highness happy?"

"Yes it would," Sean shot back. "And would you rub my bunions? I'd be so happy if you would do that for me."

As they were bantering back and forth, they heard a crunching in the snow outside the tent, but no sound of barking from the dogs. They all poked their heads out of the tent flap to see what was making the noise. They were surprised to see the wolf returning to their camp. In his jaw he was dragging a large Tarandus. He approached the opening to the tent, dropped the Tarandus just below Lochen's and Quinn's heads and then lay down a few feet away. Everyone stared at the carcass and then at the wolf, not sure what to do. Kelsey and Rover eyed the wolf suspiciously, but kept silent, burrowing deeper into the snow. Sean, who was more tired of narwhal jerky than any of them eagerly leaned forward and stuck his arm out through the tent flap to reach for the Tarandus. Just as he tried to pull it into the tent, the wolf let out a low and ominous growl and he snapped his hand away.

Sean shrunk back and tried to wedge himself into the back of the tent, as far out of sight as he could. Nobody else moved again until the wolf nudged the Tarandus with his nose in the direction of Quinn and Lochen, and then moved back away from it, lay down like a Sphinx and just looked at them expectantly.

"It seems we're being treated to a dinner of fresh meat," said Lochen. "I'd say we've been offered a gift."

Quinn opened the flap and stepped outside. He went about cutting the meat up and roasting pieces over the fire. He would toss a piece to the wolf every once in a while and it would be snapped up in mid air and nearly swallowed whole. He cut a few pieces off for Kelsey and Rover, who sniffed it, glanced silently at the wolf and then warily ate it. The wolf for the most part ignored both of them. Quinn glanced from the dogs to the wolf to Sean and back to the wolf. Then he cut a large piece for Sean and kept one eye on the wolf as he handed it over. Seeing no reaction, Sean gratefully grabbed it and dug in. When everyone had their fill, Quinn cut up the rest and wrapped it in the skin to preserve it. Then they all fell asleep for a few hours rest before heading out again.

It was nearly midday and they had been traveling for more than six hours when the wolf, which had been running several hundred yards to their right for almost the whole time, stopped suddenly. He sniffed the air and then without a sound of any kind or any look back at his traveling companions, he ran off and disappeared behind a crest of glaciers.

"What was that all about?" asked Sean.

"I don't know," said Quinn. "I was puzzled by the fact that he followed us this far. Maybe he just figured enough was enough and that we could take care of ourselves. Or maybe he has a girlfriend that he forgot about."

"I know he liked the both of you," Sean continued, "but, personally, I'm not sorry to see him go. He was giving me the creeps."

"I suppose that might be due in no small part to the fact that you tried to shoot him," said Lochen. "I know that would make me a bit on the testy side."

"I said I was sorry, Geez!" said Sean. "I thought he was going to eat you. Don't worry. It won't happen again."

They continued on uneventfully for almost another hour before the dogs started whining. They were looking from side to side instead of back at Quinn, and in between the whining they were each growling.

"Are they tired already," asked Sean. "We just took a break not too long ago. Are we going to have to walk now?"

Quinn motioned for everyone to stay quiet. He pulled the sled to a halt and hushed the dogs, and then scanned the horizon. A look of concern fell over his face. There was the faintest of sounds coming from several directions.

"What's wrong?" asked Lochen, and then, he, too, heard the odd barking as it became more distinctive. "What is that noise?"

"Ice jackals," said Quinn. "They usually travel in packs and are very ruthless hunters. We need to find a place to hide."

"Hide?" asked Sean, wildly turning his head in every direction. "Really? There's rocks and ice. And, oh, there's that slab of a mountain over there. Do you think there's some secret cave nearby? There's nothing nearby. Where are we going to hide?"

Quinn ignored him and turned the dogs and sled towards the rock wall about a mile to their left that Sean had pointed out. He drove the dogs hard, aiming right for the wall. He had heard the barking coming from in front and behind them as well as to one side. The only avenue of escape was towards the mountain. Normally Quinn would have considered the barking a trap purposely set to direct him one way or the other, but the mountain to their left was too big. The jackals would never travel over something like that.

"Lochen," he called, as they raced towards the large slab of rock, "can you blast a hole in the side of that thing?"

"A hole?" asked Lochen.

"Yeah, a hole, or a cave or some kind of opening. Can you do that?"

"Yes, of course, but that won't keep the jackals out. They'll just follow us. And since I don't know how thick it is, I may not be able to blast through it."

"I know, but it will keep us from getting surrounded by them."

As they neared the face of the cliff, Lochen waved his arm and pointed his finger. A sharp crack was followed by a small explosion, and the opening appeared just in front them. But before they could reach it, seven jackals sprung up from the snow between them and the mouth of the cave. They had buried themselves in the snow and waited for an approaching prey. It had been a trap after all. They shook the snow off their coats revealing fur that was a dirty white in color. Their hair was short and wiry – almost bristle-like. It had blended in easily with the snow. They stood there blocking off that exit, with their large mouths hanging open filled with very sharp teeth. They started moving forward, their nasty razor like claws digging into the icepack.

"They were leading us right into a trap," said Quinn. "I can't believe I fell for that. There's nothing left now but for us to try to fight them off."

He pulled the sled to a stop, untied the dogs and told them to run. Neither one did. Their hackles were raised and they were ready for a fight regardless of the fact that they were outnumbered. Quinn knew that the seven in front of them were going to soon be joined by several more from behind, and maybe even more when they least expected it. In minutes they would be surrounded, and then it would just be a matter of time.

"It's OK to shoot at these guys, Sean" shouted Quinn as he pulled a bow and some arrows from the sled.

Lochen jumped up and began hurling bolts of lightning at the herd of jackals. They were very elusive and cagey animals, avoiding the shots nimbly. Even though he wasn't hitting them, it was enough to slow down their attack and make them change direction. Sean was able to make contact with his slingshot, disabling one or two of them. He was timing his shots to Lochen's bolts of lightning and making the most of every one. The two fell into an unspoken rhythm. Then the second wave hit – from behind.

Quinn had stored only a few arrows, and knew that he would soon run out and be left with only a spear – not much good against a pack this large. Lochen was shifting from front to back, sending electrifying blasts in both directions. He was starting to wear some of the attackers down and making contact with more of his blasts. Fur was flying in several directions, but the attack continued and the distance between the jackals and their targets was shrinking. He thought about forming some kind of force field, but knew they jackals would just wait them out. This needed to be finished here and now.

Sean had run out of stones to shoot and was breaking small chunks of ice out of the ground around him with a stick, when he looked up and noticed a third siege coming from their right. Things were getting even worse. They were losing ground in their defense. Kelsey and Rover had gone after one of the attacking jackals, only to be separated from the group and led on a wild goose chase. All of Quinn's shouts after them had fallen on deaf ears. Soon they were nearly out of sight.

"Sean and Lochen, try to concentrate more of your shots on the part of the pack standing between us and the cave," shouted Quinn. "If we can eliminate that obstacle, we can at least be in a better defensive position. I'll try to keep the rest of them at bay."

Lochen started waving both arms in that direction, sending repeated blasts indiscriminately, usually hitting nothing, but at least creating somewhat of an opening. They began to inch their way forward, when the pack on their right cut off any further exit. Just as they felt they were doomed, they heard a thunderous roar and a flash of white appeared behind the pack that had just cut them off. It was the wolf.

His enormous jaws snapped and his razor sharp teeth cut through flesh and bone, as he ravaged the attacking pack. The other jackals immediately stopped their attack on the travelers and went to the aid of their brothers, jumping on top of and nipping at the ankles of the wolf.

Instead of seeking retreat in the cave, Sean, Quinn and Lochen shifted their own attack to come to the aid of the wolf. None of them had to say a word; they knew they had to help their savior. Soon the jackals had swarmed over the wolf. There had been nearly two dozen in the initial attacking party. That number had been reduced to about ten, all of which were climbing over the wolf, biting at his back, sides and legs as savagely as they could. He was inflicting severe damage on the jackals, but he was losing ground. The jackals were oblivious to the losses they were suffering, and kept up the attack.

With the focus of the jackals' attack much narrower, Lochen was more effective in the blasts he shot at them, and began picking them off one by one. Sean was out of stones and grabbed a spear from the sled. He and Quinn, disregarding their own safety, ran into the fray and singled out the assailants that were doing the greatest damage to the wolf. When the jackal's attention was diverted to the two of them, they effectively and efficiently speared the attacker and either wounded or killed it, or chased it off.

In a few short minutes, the battle was over. The four surviving jackals ran off, leaving a badly injured wolf behind. They assumed he would be left by the others and would eventually die of his wounds. They would be back to finish him off in any regard. When they returned, they would bring others with them.

Kelsey and Rover eventually returned to the scene, having finally realized they had only been following a diversion. Quinn tied them to the sled, and then, with the help of Sean and Lochen, loaded the wolf on and headed for the cave. Inside, Lochen created a fire to warm them, while Quinn took a look at the bites and cuts. Sean, in spite of his earlier fears, was stroking the wolf's head and telling him it would be all right.

"He's been badly injured," said Quinn, morosely. "Unless you have some special magic, Lochen, I don't think we can save him."

"We're not leaving him," objected Sean. "There has to be something we can do to help him. We are NOT leaving him."

"We have no thought of leaving him, Sean." Lochen assured him. "I admit, I have never ministered to a wolf before, but I do have a few tricks up my sleeve. Let's not give up hope – not just yet."

He turned to Quinn and asked, "Go through your supplies to find something that could be used as bandages as well as something to clean out the wounds. Anything. If need be, we can melt some snow, but we have to wash out the wounds."

When these had been provided, Lochen cast a spell over the wolf making him fall asleep. While the wolf was unconscious, the three cleaned the cuts, making sure there weren't any dirt or jackal parts in any of them. When they were satisfied everything was clean, lacking a needle and thread, which would have been preferable, Lochen had to cast another spell so that the cuts all closed up.

"That should hold him temporarily," said Lochen. "Suturing would have been better, but this will have to do. The spells won't last more than a few days, though. He'll still need to rest and stay motionless for that time while his own skin makes those closures permanent. He also needs to regain his strength."

"This is as good a place as any to make camp," declared Quinn. "We could use a rest ourselves anyway."

"Sounds like a good idea to me," said Sean, who hadn't stopped stroking the wolf's head. "I was getting tired of riding in a sled all day. Besides, I don't mind spending a few more days in this vacation land."

Lochen kept the wolf asleep for three days with a series of spells, except for brief periods when they gave him food and water. All during that time they kept the fire going and kept the wolf covered in layers of skins to make sure he stayed warm. After each meal, Lochen checked the wounds and determined that they seemed to be healing nicely. Finally, he allowed the last spell to wear off, letting the wolf awaken from the deep sleep naturally. When the wolf finally awoke from his long rest, he seemed to know he had been out for some time and had been carefully tended.

He staggered to his feet to survey his surroundings. He was still a bit unsteady, so he sat back down and then nuzzled each of his caregivers with his nose and gave them each a big lick, including Sean. It seemed that past grievances had been forgotten or forgiven. Sean cradled the wolf's head in his lap and stroked the fur. After another day, the wolf made it clear he needed to get out of the cave and back to his own life.

"We're about a day or so away from leaving the Ice Kingdom," Quinn told them, sharing in their reluctance to see the wolf depart. "That was as far as he would have been going anyway. It's time he left us and went back to his own pack."

The wolf seemed to sense this, too. Before they all parted company, Lochen turned to Quinn.

"Can I have that crystal you pulled from his leg?" he asked.

"Sure," said Quinn, pulling it out of his shirt and handing it over.

Lochen took the crystal from Quinn and held it in his hand. He waved his other hand over the shard, murmuring an incantation and then took the rawhide string that was attached to it and tied it around the wolf's neck.

"I've cast a spell on that crystal," he told the wolf. "It should protect you from any man or beast you may encounter."

The wolf gave him a final lick with its tongue, then turned and bounded off the way they all had come.

Chapter twelve

Stella tried to gather as much information as she could from one final vision in her Sanctorum. She knew she had little time left, but wanted to make sure she had the latest information. With Natalie leaving the island to warn the faeries and forest people, she thought the Princess would be away from the unidentified danger she had sensed earlier. However, there was still a persistent nagging feeling she couldn't ignore.

She was hoping one more attempt might uncover what was causing that feeling. Something still wasn't right, but the images of the impending flood were demanding her attention. The visions she conjured on the walls of the Sanctorum were dominated by scenes of flooding, but there was an area that was more blurred than normal.

No, she thought to herself, it's not blurred exactly. It's obscured. Something is blocking the vision from that sector.

Could this be what was nagging at her, she wondered. It must be. She couldn't think of what else would be the source. She also felt that she should know why her vision was being blocked, but couldn't focus on the reason, and that was frustrating her. Saving the island was overriding her attention to all other matters. She had a faint impression that the danger to Natalie was in some way related to the blocked vision. And she had fleeting glimpses of Summer and some kind of flying boat which was carrying Liam and Solveig. They appeared to be trying to escape from someone or something.

She wanted to expand those visions as well, but now wasn't the time. In fact, the intrusion of these visions was distracting her from the threat to Natalie. She couldn't get it clear if the tidal wave was the threat or if it was something else; and if it was something else, what was it? The tidal wave headed for the island was becoming such a dominating factor that it inserted itself into all the images that were appearing, blotting everything else from view. She made a mental note to devote her full concentration on solving the riddle of the blocked images once the crisis of the tidal wave had been addressed. As an afterthought she made another mental note to sort out why Summer, Solveig and Liam suddenly appeared in this same vision, and to try to discover where they were.

Reluctantly, she left the Sanctorum and ran out of the palace, across the grounds to the north side of the island. The wave was much closer than she had expected – and much higher. The sight of the wall rushing towards the island nearly took her breath away. The force behind the wall of water was incredible. She could see further up the shore that it had already started to break. Water was crashing into the beach. Trees were snapping like twigs as the water pounded the shore line and drove past everything in its way, flooding the entire coast. This was worse than she had imagined or envisioned.

She found a small rise near the edge of the island – a small cliff facing the oncoming wave. She looked from one end of the wave to the other where it simply blended into the horizon. This was too big and too strong for her to stop. She would have to try something else. She braced herself and spread her arms wide apart. Lowering her head slightly, she concentrated all her power into a single force. The stone in her headband flickered for a second and started to change color, unbeknownst to her. As the wave was about to hit the island, an incredible electrical field formed around the entire island, much like the giant bubble under which the Sea Sprites had lived beneath the sea. The roaring wall of water collided with the force field and splashed against it as if it were a wall of granite.

The force of the impact pushed against Stella. She was sliding back away from the edge of the cliff. She concentrated even harder and mustered all her strength to stand firm. The water continued to crash against the force field with a thunderous roar. Water shot hundreds of feet into the air, splashing in every direction around the field, over and away from the island. The wave dissipated as it broke against the bubble. The effect was to ripple down the rest of the wall, causing it to break up slowly and minimizing the power of the tidal wave as it ran further south of the island. The water came down like a heavy rainfall instead of the destructive force of the wave it had once been.

Once the wave had collapsed, Stella waved her arm in a sweeping motion over the horizon of the island. The newly created bubble diverted the torrential rain and saved the island from flooding. She couldn't stop the water from washing ashore, however. It had been all she could do to save the island. She sat down on the ground for a few minutes to gather her strength. She felt something on her upper lip and noticed that her nose was bleeding. The tidal wave had taken more of a toll on her than she had realized.

Now that the island was safe and she was able to catch her breath, she knew she couldn't take as much time as she needed. She got to her feet and went in search of the Princess's Guards. Stella found their leader and directed her to form a search and rescue party and take it to the shore across the channel to search for Natalie and anyone who needed help. She placed her thumb on the leader's forehead to establish a telepathic link, before sending them off, so she would be able to communicate with her.

"I'm going to the Sanctorum to see what images I can conjure," she told the team leader. "When I locate the exact position of the Princess, I'll transmit that image to you. Right now, I'm only assuming she went to the faerie's village, but I don't know that for certain. Your primary objective it to ensure the safety of the Princess, but if anyone else needs help, you are to do whatever you can. Now, hurry."

The guard ran off to assemble the team and make for the shore. Stella returned to the Sanctorum. She looked in each of the hallways on the way there, and in the Sanctorum when she arrived, but she could find no indication that Natalie had returned. She attempted to conjure a vision of the Princess, which normally should have been easy. A clear vision would not appear. Instead, there was still a small area that was most definitely being blocked by some kind of distortion. She was certain now that this distortion was occurring at Natalie location, but she was unable to get a distinctive picture of where that was. The images were flashing in and out, leading Stella to believe something intense was happening, but that was being hidden as well. All she could see was a blur of forest and indistinct figures. There wasn't enough to allow her to make a distinction between whether the images were in the faerie's village or the Lodge of the forest creatures. She couldn't tell where to send the guards.

She considered whether she should stay where she was or if she should make a guess and go to one village or the other. The problem was that she couldn't make a decision, and she didn't know what else to do. If Natalie was, in fact, not in danger, and had been able to evacuate the faeries and forest creatures, then she'd be returning to the island shortly. In that case, she'd be expecting to find Stella here. If Stella went after her, they could pass each other along the way, and, depending on where Natalie had gone last, they could easily miss each other. But if she wasn't safe, then the longer Stella did nothing, the worse the danger to Natalie could be. She had never felt so indecisive in her life. Her inability to conjure a precise image only added to her frustration.

She decided to trust her instincts and go after the Princess. Sitting in the Sanctorum or anywhere else on the island waiting for Natalie to show up would only drive her crazy. She tried to think like Natalie, and concluded that she would have gone to the Lodge first. It was closer, and the faerie village could be reached faster from there. Given the time that had lapsed, she should be in the faerie village by now.

She decided that was where she would send the guards, while she would go to the Lodge. She was about to head out when she was struck with an overwhelming sensation of fear. It came from nowhere and was caused by nothing she could discern. She was knocked off her feet by the shock wave that hit her like a bolt of thunder; the breath flew out of her body and her heart was pounding. Her first reaction was to curl up and hide, but she didn't know from what. She tried to shake it off. She took a deep breath and struggled to her feet, and then as quickly as it had come, it was gone.

The sensations that coursed through her mind and body only added to her confusion. When she tried to sort things out, she realized that she hadn't felt fear for herself. It was as if she was feeling someone else's fear. As ridiculous as that sounded, she had no other way to describe it.

There was no logical reason for her to think this fear was related to Natalie, but she believed it was. She paused for a second, and then ran out of the palace to the harbor to find a ship. Along the way, she sent a desperate mental message to the leader of the guards to go to the faerie village; that she was heading for the Lodge. Deep down inside, though, she feared that Natalie would be found in neither location.

- - - - - - - - - - - - - - - - - ✳✳✳ - - - - - - - - - - - - - - - - -

Liam couldn't ignore Summer's statement that everyone in her village was gone, but even if she was right, they had to go somewhere. They couldn't merely disappear. She was so distraught that he was hesitant to ask her any details to explain her comment. He tried to think more positively, in spite of what he had just experienced. It was certainly possible that her village had been flooded and that the faeries were not able to escape. But they could fly, he thought. As soon as the water started to break through the forest they would have taken to the air. That only made sense.

Regardless of what may or may not have happened to the faeries, the Sea Sprites and the forest creatures probably needed help – maybe more than the faeries. And although he hoped Summer was wrong, they needed to find out one way or the other. Even if the faeries had flown out of harm's way, they would need help reconstructing their village. He reset the sails and rode the flood waters as they slowly receded back to the sea. Solveig was exhausted, but in agreement that they needed to go help. There was no time for them to delay.

"You may be right," she said to Summer, "but then again, maybe you're not. We can't just give up. We need to get there as quickly as we can. Liam's right."

Summer was trying as hard as she could to be positive, but she couldn't convince herself. They were floating past all sorts of rubble that had been washed back and forth across the shore, and dodging hundreds of broken trees. The flooding extended far into the land. In some instances only the tops of trees were visible, but at least the waves had stabilized. Liam kept the ship out on the water and it was gaining speed. How could her village survive this kind of disaster, she wondered.

All Summer could think was that they were hurrying to hear bad news or to see some kind of disaster. She took some consolation, though, from the thought that she had such good friends who would rush to help her village without concern for their own safety. If anything could be done to help, they would do it. She knew she would do the same for them. In fact, the forest creatures and the Sea Sprites would have faced the same destructive force as the faeries. Whatever happened to her village would have happened to them as well.

"You're both right," she finally acknowledged. "We have other friends who may need help, too. Let's get going before anything worse happens."

She flew back up to the crow's nest to stand watch. Far ahead she thought she could see the wall begin to cascade. The splashing water from the crashing wave and the way the suns reflected on the surface sometimes obscured her vision, but it looked like the wall had hit something immovable and was breaking up. It looked more like a huge rainstorm now instead of a tidal wave. Maybe her village would be safe after all. She was afraid to get her hopes up.

Liam steered the ship easily from the flooded shore into the actual sea. He was following the tail of the falling wave, skimming along the wake. The speed of the water combined with the wind in the sails had the boat rocketing forward. He was pedaling, but it didn't require much effort and didn't really make them go any faster. However, he couldn't do nothing, and this gave him a sense of action.

"This isn't exactly how I envisioned my sail in the Cerulean Sea," he shouted to Solveig over the wind.

"Maybe not, but it's holding up very well. You should be proud. And I'm sure glad you made this thing so that it could fly," she answered as she moved from the bow of the ship back to where he was seated.

"Actually, what just happened gave me some ideas on how to improve on that part of the construction," he said. "I think I can make it fly even better."

Solveig laughed, "You nut. In the middle of nearly getting crushed by some monster wave, you're thinking about home improvement projects?"

Liam looked at her a little bit startled. "Well, when you put it that way, I guess it does sound a little nutty."

After a few seconds, they both looked up at the crow's nest.

"Do you think her village is gone?" Solveig asked. "Could she be right?"

Liam looked back at the still flooded shore, and then said, "Look at what happened here. If anyone had been living here, they'd all be underwater.

The only thing that might have saved her village is the fact that Natalie and Stella's island was not too far off their shore. You know that both of them would have done something – anything - to save Summer's village as well as their island. Don't you think? And don't forget about Sean's Lodge. That wasn't too far away, either. I have to believe that the people in all three villages were somehow saved. If not, the alternative is just too unthinkable."

Solveig stared ahead along the line of the wave, and could see the same thing Summer was witnessing at that same moment. The wall of water looked to be breaking up, as if it were crashing against something solid.

"Do you remember any cliffs or large rocks north of Natalie's island?" she asked.

"No," he answered. "Not that I recall. I remember Sean talking about cliffs and caves where he and Summer used to go, but I think that was in some kind of cove. That would have been somewhat sheltered from this wave, I would guess. Why?"

"Look up ahead," she told him. "See down near the horizon line? It looks like – splashing. I don't know how else to describe it."

By now the wall had hit Stella's force field. From the direction the trio was approaching, the spray from the wave hitting the shield looked like a row of geysers. Water was shooting high into the air as it came into contact with the invisible field. Water was dropping back to the surface harmlessly.

"I see it," said Liam. "It looks like the wall is breaking up. I'll bet Stella put come kind of hex on it." He laughed.

"Summer," Solveig stood up and shouted, "Do you see what we're seeing?"

Summer flew higher into the air to improve her vantage point and got a clearer picture of the destruction of the wall as it encountered Stella's force field. She could see the spray coming down like rain. As it landed on the bubble, it splashed and then cascaded down the sides in sheets, making the form of the bubble more visible. Her spirits began to lift. Maybe Stella and Natalie had worked a miracle.

Solveig had moved to the side of the ship, up against the bulwark. She was leaning over sideways, looking up at Summer, when a shockwave hit her like a punch. The impact knocked her off balance. Her feet went out from under her, and she went head over heels – over the side of the ship and into the water. Liam immediately turned the ship in the opposite direction and called to Summer.

"Solveig fell in! Do you see her?" he shouted. "I can't see where she is. I don't want to turn back and run over her."

Summer swooped down from the crow's nest and out over the water. She was criss-crossing back and forth, trying to cover as much area as she could. The residual waves were still rough and the water was murky. Solveig had sunk nearly to the bottom before bobbing back up. Her head broke the surface through a pile of debris and she gasped for air. Shaking her head, she caught sight of the boat turning around and heading back for her.

"Help," she yelled. "I'm over here."

She looked around to make sure there wasn't any more post-flood debris or creatures floating nearby, recalling some bad experiences in other bodies of water. She pushed herself away from the wreckage through which she had resurfaced and began to swim in the direction of the ship. Before long, Liam pulled the boat up alongside of her. He reached down and scooped her out of the water.

"What was that all about?" he asked. "Fine time to go for a swim," he laughed nervously.

He moved the wet hair from her face and examined her head, looking for signs of a bump or bruise. He was glad to discover that she was wet and a little shaken, but otherwise all right.

"I didn't do it on purpose," she sputtered as he found a blanket to wrap around her. "I just had this unbelievable sensation of ..."

"What?" asked Summer and Liam in unison when she didn't finish the sentence.

She looked at them with a puzzled expression, "Fear, I suppose. I don't know how else to describe it. I felt extremely afraid. I'm not sure why, and what was even odder was that it didn't feel like the fear was mine. I think I felt someone else's fear – some kind of sudden panic. Does that make any sense?"

"Maybe you bumped your head," offered Summer, as she fluttered up closer and moved a lock aside herself.

"I didn't bump my head," insisted Solveig, pulling her head away. "My head is just fine. It was something else. Something is wrong. I don't know what, exactly."

"Does it have anything to do with the tidal wave?" asked Liam. "Maybe you got the sense of fear from one of the villages about the tidal wave."

Solveig thought a minute before answering, "Sort of. I don't know. No – I don't think so. It was a different kind of sensation. This was more sudden. I know this sounds nuts, but I think we need to get to the island as fast as we can."

------------------ *** ------------------

Shortly after they saw the last of the wolf, Quinn had to untie the dogs and send them home. They had arrived at the end of the Ice Kingdom just as he had predicted, less than two days after the wolf had left them. They had reached the beginning of an open stretch of land. Much of it was still covered with snow, but there were large patches of foliage breaking through. It was clear that this was the end of the Ice Kingdom. To their right was the beginning of a forested area that ran along the western edge of the Swamp, and to their left was a large cove. Beyond the edge of the cove was the Cerulean Sea.

"We have two options at this point," Quinn announced. "We can leave the sled, put as much as we can carry into back packs and head out along the western side of the Swamp, which is the long way."

"Haven't we already had this discussion?" asked Sean. "I like walking. Walking is fine by me. I'm not in any hurry."

Quinn smiled at Sean and then winked at Lochen.

"I just thought you might have changed your mind. It would be a lot quicker for you to get home if you went by sea. All we have to do is open the kayaks I have stored on the sled, and set sail to the south. It would be as easy as walrus pie."

"Ugh!" answered Sean. "Another delicacy I couldn't get used to. No thanks. No thanks to the walrus pie and no thanks to getting into one of those floating things."

"I can always cast a spell on you to eliminate your fear of water," offered Lochen. "If that's all that's bothering you."

"It's not fear!" Sean answered, raising his voice. "And nothing is bothering me. I just don't like it, that's all. Is that so hard to understand?"

Quinn and Lochen looked at each other and responded at the same time, "Yes. It's impossibly hard to understand."

"I thought you weren't going any further than this," Sean said to Quinn in an effort to change the subject. "What does it matter to you if I walk or take a chance on drowning? You'll be back in your ice cube house."

"It's an igloo," he answered. "And originally I wasn't going any further than this. But after your last experience with the local wildlife, I'm worried that you won't make it home in one piece. I'd hate to find your bones in some jackal poop."

"Oh, really?" asked Sean. "Jackal poop? I see. I hope you know I can take care of myself, just fine, thank you very much."

Attempting to avoid an argument, Lochen interjected, "I'd certainly enjoy Quinn's company. That is, of course, if you have no objections."

His attempt was unsuccessful, as Sean answered, "I see. My company is not good enough? Are you worried about me shooting you again?"

"Of course your company is sufficient," said Lochen. "And, no, I have no concerns about being the target of another one of your missiles. It's just that I've found there has always been safety in numbers. We have all been quite ready to look out for each other in the past. Why change that?"

This seemed to calm Sean down. He mumbled a bit before agreeing to Quinn coming along, but he was still adamant about not traveling by water.

"That's fine with me," said Quinn. "We can walk; whatever you want. I just wanted to put all the options up for consideration."

He began to unload the sled and sort out the essential items they would need and would be able to carry. When he was done, he repacked everything that was being left behind and tied the sled down. If he didn't come back this way, some other traveler would be welcome to use whatever he or she needed.

"It would probably be a good idea to leave some of the arctic clothing behind," he pointed out. "I know it's still a little cold, right now, but that's going to change quickly and when it does we'll have to either carry it or leave it behind. We might as well do that now."

As cold as he was, Sean was more than happy to shed some of the layers and have a little more freedom of movement. Almost instantly, though, his teeth started chattering. Lochen was about to wave his hand over Sean's head, when Sean stopped him.

"No spells," he demanded.

"Why not?" Lochen asked. "I can easily make you more comfortable. It would just be a simple spell."

"If I let you start putting spells on me, how do I know you won't have me clucking like a chicken — whatever that is - or doing something equally goofy, just for fun?"

Lochen looked at him with a puzzled expression. "I hadn't thought of that. But the idea is quite interesting."

"Oh, yeah, like <u>now</u> I'm going to trust you," said Sean warily. "No thanks. Keep your spells to yourself. I'll just freeze."

Just as Quinn was shouldering his backpack and handing another one to Sean, Lochen stood straight up as rigid as a board, and then fell flat on his back. Quinn and Sean looked at him, unsure of what was happening. Lochen then rolled back and forth in the snow without saying a word, but with a look of shear panic on his face.

"What's he doing?" asked Sean in a low voice. "Come on, Lochen. Quit playing games. This isn't funny."

"I don't know," answered Quinn in a similar low voice. "I don't think he's playing games."

After three or four minutes of turning, twisting and rolling in the snow, Lochen slowly got to his feet. His eyes were a bit glassy. He gasped as if he had been holding his breath for some time and then coughed up water.

"Where did that come from?" asked Quinn.

"He didn't go near any water," said Sean with an edge of panic in his voice. "Where did that water come from?"

They ran over to him and grabbed each of his arms to help hold him steady. He was wide awake, but seemed to be staring ahead with an expression of fear on his face. He was pale as a ghost, and he was also soaking wet.

"Okay," said Quinn, "this is really starting to freak me out! I know you could have gotten a little wet from rolling in the snow, but not soaked like this."

When he didn't answer, Quinn shouted, patting his face gently, "Lochen! Lochen! Are you all right? Come on, buddy. Snap out of it."

He seemed to be oblivious of the wet clothing as his eyes gradually regained focus and he realized where he was. He looked at his surroundings, then to Quinn and Sean, and finally at himself.

"Something happened," he said.

"You think?" asked Sean. There was an edge of panic to his voice. "You stood up stiff as a tree, then keeled over and started rolling around in the snow. It looked like – I don't know – like maybe you were – what? – swimming? Then you stood up and spit out a bunch of water, and your clothes are soaking wet. And you only say, 'something happened?' What? Are you nuts? Of course something happened!"

He ignored Sean's tirade. Coughing to clear his throat, he added, "Something happened to Solveig…well, not exactly to Solveig. I can't explain it. I don't think she's in trouble, but she was terribly frightened by something – something unnatural. No, that's not right either. It wasn't unnatural."

"You're not making a lot of sense," said Quinn.

"When does he _ever_ make a lot of sense?" asked Sean. Lochen's loss of composure was beginning to make him very nervous. He was pacing around frantically, trying to make sense out of what he had just seen.

"I don't know any other way to explain it," said Lochen. "I think Solveig received some kind of vision, or felt something terrifying. I'm not sure exactly what, but it affected her greatly. That's what I felt and just experienced."

"That's all I need to know," said Quinn. "We need to find her. We need to do it now. Do you know where she is?"

"She was with Summer and Liam in the Swamp," said Sean. "We need to head out for the Swamp."

"No," said Lochen. "I mean, yes. They were in the Swamp, but that's not where they are now. They've left the Swamp. I'm certain of it."

"Did you see something when you went all nutty?" asked Sean.

"No," he answered. "I saw nothing. At least I can't recall seeing anything. I believe my eyes were open, but..."

"And exactly how do you know this?" interrupted Quinn. "How do you know they aren't in the Swamp any more – if you didn't see anything?"

"Salt water," said Lochen. "I had a mouth full of salt water. The water in the Swamp, although it may be fetid and even poisonous in many areas, is all fresh water, or in some areas it may be brackish where the salt water from the sea joins the fresh water from...."

"Who cares about what kind of water you spit out?" shouted Sean. "What does any of that have to do with where they are?"

"The closest salt water is in the Cerulean Sea," Lochen answered as calmly as he could. "That's where they are."

Sean, not savoring the thought of venturing out on the sea, wasn't sure he believed Lochen. How could he remember what he spit out? He needed to see for himself. He reached over and squeezed the still soaking cloth from Lochen's robe and tasted. His face puckered and he rolled his eyes.

"Poop," he said. "Salt water."

"I'm sorry," Lochen said to Sean. "If there was any other way…"

"Forget it," Sean interrupted. "It's not like you did this on purpose. You didn't, did you? This isn't some practical joke?"

The look on Lochen's face was answer enough. Quinn had already unpacked the sled while Sean had been grilling Lochen. He pulled out a dry change of clothes for Lochen, and threw them over to him. Lochen changed as quickly as he could, while Sean, resigned to returning to the water, and helped Quinn in assembling three kayaks. Quinn tied them together with rails from the sides of the sled to form a center pod with pontoons on either side. Then he used pieces of the sled's runners to make a short mast that he secured to the center kayak. He tied the skins from the sled to fashion a sail. He moved quickly and efficiently, having done this several times before. While Lochen dried off and finished changing, Sean helped move supplies from the sled into the kayaks.

When all was ready, they moved the makeshift catamaran to the water's edge. Without a word, Sean climbed into the middle one and Quinn and Lochen pushed off. As the craft slid into the water, they jumped into the ones on either side. Quinn started to pull out the oars, but Lochen stopped him.

"I know this isn't the ideal way to travel in these things, but time is of the essence. And my apologies to you, Sean."

Without any further word, Lochen waved his right hand and the sail filled to near bursting with a strong wind propelling the tiny ships into the vast sea.

Chapter thirteen

Natalie periodically poked her head up from under the leaves and branches under which she was hiding, watching as the Rebbercands went methodically from hut to hut, criss-crossing the village. She had remained hidden in the low lying brush for what seemed like an eternity, until finally, they all seemed to be moving away from her. Still, she kept as silent as she could, straining to hear any sounds that one or more of them had remained behind. She knew better than to take any chances. They were extremely sneaky and very suspicious. When she was certain that it was safe for her to move, she slowly inched her way backwards out from under the foliage.

Her legs had started to cramp, she had been scrunched down for so long. She ignored the tingling as the blood recirculated, and kept creeping away from the Lodge. When she was clear, she quietly stood up and stretched her legs, flexing the muscles repeatedly. She kept a close watch on the huts in the clearing and the Rebbercands as they continued to move in the opposite direction. She took a few steps backwards, feeling with her feet and her outstretched arm for any branches or twigs, moving one step at a time. She was holding her breath and concentrating hard on not making any sounds, while hugging the trunk of a nearby tree. Easing away from the tree and gently releasing the air in her lungs, she turned to make a dash down the nearest path to the faerie village.

As soon as she turned, she was startled to run head on into one of the Rebbercands. She let out a gasp of shock. Her back arched, the muscles nearly in a spasm as a wave of uncontrollable fear washed over her. Had he been there the whole time she wondered? He was watching her with a leering smile on his face. She quickly regained her senses and clapped her hands, no longer concerned if the other searchers heard her. A small flash of light shot out at the Rebbercand, who ducked his head to one side and raised his hand reflexively.

The flash hit his hand and immediately bounced off and dissipated, fizzling to the ground. They both watched as the tiny bolt dropped away. He was as surprised as Natalie at the ineffectiveness of her spell. Unfortunately for her, he recovered first. He took one long, quick step towards her and reached down to scoop her up in his arm, tucking her under his arm tightly into his side.

"This may be even better than I had planned," he announced to no one in particular.

He strode off through the forest, cutting away the branches in his path with a large double-headed axe he carried in his other hand. He moved back towards the Lodge and met up with the rest of his party.

"My lord," one of them said as he approached Natalie's captor, "we need to leave immediately. The wave is nearly upon us. If you wish to move on to the island to obtain your goal, we have little time."

"That won't be necessary," he answered. "It seems providence has delivered to us a prize sufficient for our purposes. Gather your men. We leave immediately. Let the wave take the island and this collection of hovels."

Natalie squirmed and screamed, kicking to try to free herself.

"Scream all you like, Princess," he told her. "No one is around to hear you but us, and we will not be helping you."

He walked quickly through the vegetation, carrying her easily under his arm. They were soon joined by nearly a dozen or more Rebbercands and they all started to run in a loose formation. She was able to turn slightly to look at her captor's face. The only other one she had seen had been B'nair. They were all so ugly, that it was hard to tell one from another. With this one, though, she could see a difference from B'nair. Unlike him, this one did not have the same oily smile. In fact his look was stern and merciless.

Once the shock of her abduction ran through her, she was filled with anger. How could she have been so careless? She thought she had been careful, but apparently not careful enough. What had they been looking for? It was obviously not the forest creatures. The other one said something about moving to the island. What did they want on the island? Or who? Why had her spell not had any effect? He had been as surprised as she was that it hadn't worked. That was puzzling. She tried to slide one arm free, but each time she did, the one carrying her would adjust and tighten his grip. By now he had moved that horrible axe into some kind of sling across his back.

"Where are you taking me?" she demanded to know.

He looked down at her before responding. She wasn't sure at first if he heard her, but the glare in his eyes escalated her fear. The question caught in her throat.

"You are going to help me find our master," he finally said to her dryly.

"I don't know what you're talking about. I don't know who you are or who your master is. You must have me confused with someone else."

Once again, he didn't respond immediately. This time, though, she was certain he heard her. He was purposely not answering her. When she believed he was just going to ignore her, he looked down at her with an icy stare.

"What you know or don't know is completely irrelevant to me; and I know exactly who you are. I don't have you confused with anyone."

They were running quickly through the forest, dodging in and out of the trees. Branches lashed against her. With her arms pinned between her captor's arm and side, she was unable to protect herself. The sky had quickly darkened and to make matters worse, out of nowhere it started raining. It was coming down in torrents, as if the skies just opened up. As the rain splashed into Natalie's face, it covered her in sheets, some falling into her mouth. Salt water, she said to herself as she gasped for breath and spit it out. She was completely stunned. Why is it raining salt water? Where was it coming from?

She tried to concentrate on this question and to force her thoughts from the fear that was rising inside her. Salt water, she repeated. It had to come from the sea – the sea that was rushing in a giant wall towards the island. Stella! Stella must have blocked the water, somehow shielding the island and changing the wall into rain.

Stella, Natalie thought, as she was being taken farther and farther away from her island. I must get a message to Stella. I must warn her. I must...what?

She was about to transmit a telepathic distress call, but then stopped. Why had they captured her, she wondered again. Was this intentional or an accident? She had to find that out before she did anything else. She didn't want to be the bait for a larger trap. She wasn't about to put anyone else in danger.

"What do you want with me?" she spoke up again.

When there was no response, she pleaded, "You must have the wrong person. You don't know who I am. What help can I be to you?"

"I've already told you. I know exactly who you are, Princess. And you are going to help release the spell on my master."

"I don't know who your master is or what spell he is under. I don't know what you want of me. I can't do anything to help."

"My master is the sorcerer Tebaga," was all he said.

Natalie was familiar with the name, but knew very little about who he was or what had become of him. She had heard the stories that had been handed down for centuries. There was so much myth intertwined with fact that she didn't know what was true and what was not.

"Then you are sadly mistaken," she argued. " Or you've been misled. I have no idea where this Tebaga is, if he exists at all. And even if I did, I wouldn't know how to help him or that I would help him if I could."

"I can assure you. He exists, and I know exactly where he is. And in spite of what you may think, you are exactly the person I need."

"Then go help him yourself," she shouted back at him. "I won't do it. In fact, if the legends are true, I <u>can't</u> help you."

She stopped herself short. She feared she had said too much already. They had captured the Sea Sprite Princess. The person they really needed, if the legends were, in fact, true, was an Enchantress. They needed Stella. She had almost put Stella in jeopardy by transmitting a distress signal to her and by blurting out to this Rebbercand that he needed an Enchantress instead of a Princess.

"I am well aware of the legends, and you're right," he snarled at her. "You, yourself, can't help me; but your Enchantress can. I am sure once she discovers you are gone, she will do everything she can to find you."

The Rebbercand said no more; declining to elaborate on whatever plans he might have. Natalie thought of what she could do to escape and at the same time keep Stella away from this person. She began to worry that Stella would begin to search for her; that she would conjure an image of her being kidnapped and try to follow. That was the worst thing she could do, but it was also the most likely thing she would do.

While these thoughts were running through Natalie's mind, Bacham was doing his own reflection. He had been careless himself when he had snuck up behind this Princess as she hid in the brush and watched her. He should have knocked her unconscious. He had let her crawl from her hiding place and confront him instead of taking her unawares. She had nearly escaped by casting that flash spell.

He had raised his hand defensively purely out of reflex, knowing that this would not have done anything to protect him from a spell. He should have been stunned at the very least, but he wasn't, and he didn't know why. He knew little about Sea Sprites, but he knew that they had very few special powers and that their spells were not very strong. The real power was with the Enchantresses that each Sea Sprite Princess was united with. Even so, her spell had been blocked. He himself had no such powers. What had happened, he wondered. Why had the charge dissolved when it struck him, and fallen uselessly to the ground?

The rain was coming down much harder and the ground was slick with mud, but they would be safe from any flooding. In a relatively short amount of time they had managed to reach a range of low hills, high enough to stave off the flooding. He drove his soldiers hard, but they were all well-conditioned. They would be able to run at this pace for a long time. That was good, since they had a long way to go. Picking up the Princess when he did had been an unexpected windfall.

His original plan had been to invade the island and take the Enchantress in the confusion created by the tidal wave. He knew this was risky. As it turned out, it was far riskier than he had anticipated. He knew the destruction of the ancient cavern would create a small tidal wave. His plan was that this tidal wave would only cause moderate flooding on the island. It would have been enough to create a sufficient level of confusion to mask his invasion.

What he hadn't counted on was the destruction of the cavern spreading to the nearby network of tunnels. When that happened, the resulting tidal wave was much greater than he had planned. His team would never have made it to the island, or, even if they did, they would not have survived the massive flooding from the much larger wave. When they had reached the village of the forest creatures and found it deserted, they initially suspected a trap.

As his men searched the village, he had grown impatient. He had seen the wall of approaching water and knew that he had less time and a much smaller window in which to act. He was certain his plans had been dashed. In desperation he had decided to attempt the abduction of the Enchantress on his own. Circling around the eastern edge of the village, his eye had been caught by movement in the underbrush. At first he believed it to be a forest creature that hadn't managed to escape. Then he saw it was someone else.

He convinced himself that it might be worth his while to delay his run to the island. Something told him that what he was seeing might be advantageous to his plans. He had watched closely as Natalie had crept back from the village perimeter and hidden under the bushes. He had never seen the Princess before, but he recognized her from the description Sapin had provided after the mining disaster.

Sapin had claimed the Trepan rebels were assisted by other creatures, and described one of them as being a Sea Sprite Princess. No one had believed her, but Bacham had not dismissed her claims so easily, in spite of her reputation for lying. He had interrogated her thoroughly and obtained detailed descriptions of each of these alleged rebel aides. Once he spotted Natalie, he recognized her as one of those Sapin had identified. It only took him scant seconds before he decided to modify his plan.

The Enchantress certainly wouldn't release the spells on Tebaga's prison voluntarily, he reasoned. Bacham had considered that some amount of persuasion – he didn't like the term torture – would be necessary, but he had to admit that it might not have been successful. Now, though, he had been presented with an alternative. This alternative would give him some leverage that he didn't have before – the kind of leverage that would make "persuasion" much easier. The Enchantress might be more inclined to help out in order to save the life of her Princess.

His thoughts of the spell that he deflected and of Natalie's Enchantress led him to think about the legends and myths surrounding Tebaga and the Enchantress who had imprisoned him – Meri Hocto. He recalled some vague reference to a pendant that the Enchantress had that may have been the source of her power. The ancient lore of the Rebbercands told of another sorcerer, one of lesser importance, who had deceived Tebaga and had stolen the Enchantress' pendant. The pendant had been destroyed. It had broken into several pieces, and those pieces had scattered to distant places.

Was it possible, he asked himself. Could the stone he now had in his possession be part of that pendant? He reached his free hand into the pocket where the piece was secured. He knew it had been special, but he hadn't realized exactly how special it might be. That would explain the mystical properties that kept pointing him in the same direction. If it was, in fact, a part of the pendant of Meri Hocto, that might explain how the spell of the Sea Sprite Princess had been deflected. His excitement at this thought began to rise. The power that was at his fingertips could be greater than he ever imagined. He had to find out.

After a while, they were near the other side of the forest. The rain was still falling, but it had slowed down a little bit. Most of it was residual drops falling from the leaves and trees they were passing under. As they reached a clearing, Bacham called for the group to stop and rest. He dropped Natalie roughly to the ground and ordered one of his warriors to tie her to a nearby tree. When that was done, he told them he wanted to be alone with his captive, and ordered them to move further away while they rested. Ensuring he was alone, he removed the stone from the inside pocket of his cloak. What should he try, he wondered.

He put the stone in one hand and with his other, he pointed at a nearby rock and concentrated on moving it. Natalie watched him in silence, wondering what he was doing. Nothing happened. He tried again, but still nothing happened. He tried several more times with the same result. He eyed her suspiciously, wondering if she was placing some kind of hex on him, preventing him from moving the rock. He moved out of her sight and tried again. The result was the same: the rock remained unmoved. Then he put the stone in the other hand and used that hand to point at the rock. Try as he might, the rock never moved.

His curiosity would not let him stop. He moved back in front of Natalie, staying several feet away from her. He called over one of the guards.

"Untie her," he ordered, "and watch her closely. If she does anything to me, club her, but DO NOT KILL HER! Is that understood?"

"Yes, my lord," answered the guard.

The guard did not really understand, but knew enough not to challenge any order given to him. He then carefully untied Natalie. When she was loose, he jumped back a step or two and stood over her with a club poised.

Natalie remained seated at the base of the tree, rubbing her arms and wrists where the ropes had cut into her skin. She looked around at her surroundings and thought about just running. She had no idea where they were or where she would go if she were able to escape. She also admitted that she would be no match for their speed. She thought about the earlier spell she had cast which was neatly deflected by the Rebbercand leader. Even if she could cast a spell that worked, the one standing next to her would strike her before she could cast one on him.

For several seconds, nothing happened. She looked from the guard to Bacham and back, watching them both closely. Then she jumped up and sharply clapped her hands at the guard standing next to her. The flash of light that flew from her hands threw him several feet into the air and up against another tree. The club he had been holding in his hand over Natalie's head came crashing down on his own head. The impact of hitting the tree and the club dropping on his head rendered him unconscious.

Even before the club landed, and in the blink of an eye, Natalie turned toward Bacham and clapped again. Another flash of light shot at him. She had moved so fast that he didn't even have time to raise his hand in defense. He was still looking at the guard by the time the second blast struck him. The flash hit him in the chest and dissolved ineffectively in a spray of sparkles to the ground.

He looked in stunned surprise at the sputtering embers of the lightning stroke as it bounced harmlessly off his chest. Before Natalie could react to her own surprise, he took two long fast steps and scooped her up again, and threw her against the tree. She struggled to get away, but he pressed his foot against her body and re-secured the ties. He had learned one thing at least. The particle of stone was a shield of some sort, he thought as he tied her tightly. It may enhance the powers of those who have such gifts, but to those who did not, like himself, it was a shield. If nothing else, it would protect him from spells. Now he knew two of its capabilities. It stood to reason that there must be more. The closest thing to a smile crept across his face. He made sure her bindings were secure and then he moved back to where he had been standing before. He looked over at the still unconscious guard and then squatted down.

He reached inside his cloak and removed the stone, holding it between his thumb and finger, staring at it closely. Even in the dim light, it had an unusual sparkle. Before he could shield it from her view, Natalie caught a glimpse of the object. At first it didn't mean anything to her, but something about the color of the stone struck her. She thought about what had happened. Twice her spells had been deflected. Both times against this particular Rebbercand, they had simply bounced off him harmlessly. However, her last spell had not been diminished when she cast it on the guard. She glanced over at him. He was still lying motionless against the tree.

It was not her own power that was the problem, she concluded. The Rebbercand leader must have some kind of shield or protection. She also reasoned that he hadn't known of this shield himself. That was why he conducted that little experiment. Her second failed spell confirmed his suspicions. She thought carefully about what happened immediately afterward. He had retied her to the tree and then removed an odd looking stone from his cloak. He was studying it, but he was also very purposely hiding it from her view. Why, she wondered. There was nothing unusual about the shape. As far as she could tell it was not very big; it appeared, in the quick glimpse she had of it, to be pointed at one end and roughly rounded at the opposite end. There was nothing remarkable about the size or shape. What about the color?

Think, she told herself. What did you just see? She closed her eyes and concentrated on the flickering image. She had seen it only for an instance. Was it gold? Yes, sort of, but it also seemed to be a reddish brown... She stopped in mid thought and her eyes popped open. It was the same stone as in Stella's headband. She had been given that stone by Sean. Or was it Summer? It was Sean; she was sure. Where had he gotten it? She racked her brain to recall the story. It had been found by one of his ancestors. He never said when or where, and he didn't know much about its origin.

Stella's powers always had been much greater than hers, but after she was given that stone, they seemed to increase more and more every day. Natalie had never made the connection between Stella's expanded powers and that stone. She thought it only enhanced her visions. Could it do even more? Could this same stone give the Rebbercand any powers? She would have to watch closely and be very careful. A Rebbercand was dangerous enough. One with mystical powers would be disastrous.

Bacham pocketed the stone and ordered everyone to continue on their journey.

"Where are we going?" demanded Natalie.

"You are not in command here, Princess.   You are not one to make demands."

"I will never help you get what you want," she shouted.

 "I don't need your help. I only need you," he said to her dismissively.

"That doesn't make any sense," she said.

She decided she needed to purposely antagonize him. If she made him angry enough, he might reveal more of his plan than he intended. She had to be careful, though. She didn't want to make him angry enough to harm her.

"You must be as stupid as you look," she said, almost grunting the words as she bounced, pinned to his side while he ran.

He ignored her comment, but she could tell he was getting irritated. He had reflexively squeezed her more tightly to his side. She needed to keep needling him to make him reveal his plan to her.

"I've already told you I don't know where this person, Bedbugger, is."

"The master's name is Tebaga," he snarled at her.

"Whatever," she persisted. "I still don't know where he is, and even if I did, I wouldn't tell you. You're obviously too stupid to find him yourself, and now you've kidnapped someone who can't help you in the least. That's beyond stupid."

He stopped short and jerked her into the air, bringing her within inches of his face. She now worried that she had gone too far in irritating him.

"I've had enough of you," he growled at her.

He dropped her to the ground and once again pressed his foot against her to keep her from escaping. She twisted and turned futilely while he pulled a cloth of some kind from his cloak. He tore a strip off and stuffed the remainder in her mouth. He took the strip and tied it around her mouth, securing the cloth, tying it tightly.

"I have had enough of your idle chatter," he snarled between clenched teeth. "I will be glad to be rid of you. I am beginning to think you might be right. I must have been stupid to take you instead of going after your Enchantress. You just happened to be handy and a better means to my end."

With those words he pulled the gag tightly. "This should stop your interminable noise."

He's going to use me to trap Stella, she realized. She had been successful in frustrating him enough to shed light on his plan – at least part of it. Why would he need Stella, she thought. He needs the powers of an Enchantress. One by one, the pieces began to fall into place. The myths of an evil sorcerer – a second one, besides Ena Ray – must be true. At least this Rebbercand thought they were true. She shuddered at the recollection of the encounter with Ena Ray. She had never felt such evil before. Could it be possible that there was another sorcerer, just as evil? Or maybe even worse?

She had to do something to disrupt these plans. She thought about sending a message to Stella, but decided that this would only play into the hands of this monster who had kidnapped her. That had to be avoided at all costs. In fact, she had to make sure any communication of any kind between her and Stella was blocked. She concentrated on this for a moment. She would have to conjure a spell to cut her off from Stella.

This would be very difficult. When Sea Sprite Princesses were very young, they were matched with an Enchantress right from the Enchantress' birth. They were soul mates, almost as if they were one person. Their lives were intertwined and interdependent upon one another. It was not only difficult to break that tie, it was painful. Stella would know it was broken the instant it happened. Natalie didn't want to cause her that amount of pain, but she knew if she didn't, Stella would ignore her own safety to come to Natalie's rescue. Nothing would stop her, and Natalie couldn't allow that.

She began the chant that put the spell into motion. Bacham looked up at the mumbling sound Natalie was making beneath her gag, wondering if the Princess was trying something new to hex him. Seeing that she was still secure and that the gag hadn't come loose, he thought, let her try. In a few seconds it was done. She felt a stabbing pain in her heart – as if she has lost a most important part of her life. Her eyes filled with tears – not because of the pain she felt, but because of the pain she was causing. Her thoughts were interrupted when Bacham stood up, and without a word, untied her. He scooped her up under his arm and strode quickly to a clearing near where they had stopped.

They had moved to the edge of a steep cliff overlooking a wide river. Ahead she could see a gathering of Yders flying overhead. Her blood ran cold. These winged reptiles were viscous predators. Many a Sea Sprite had fallen victim to them. As the Rebbercands approached the gathering, Bacham shifted Natalie under his arm. The Yders landed close to the gathering of Rebbercands. Bacham walked closer to the beasts. He stopped when they were only a few feet away. One of the Yders lowered its head and sniffed at Natalie. Its beak was big enough to eat her whole. She began shaking in fear.

"I would imagine if I turned one of these pets loose, you might change your mind about helping me," Bacham threatened. "Don't worry. You're safe," he continued, "for now. We have a long way to go. These fine creatures will carry us much of the way."

As Bacham climbed onto the back of one of them, he loosened his grip on Natalie just enough that she slid down and forward towards the creature's head. It turned its grotesque head back and snapped at Natalie, clipping some of her hair in its razor sharp jaws. Several strands fell to the ground as the beast lapped up the rest with its tongue.

"Just a little taste," said Bacham, "to let him know what kind of treat awaits him – and a little reminder for you of what you'll face if you cause any problems. Do we understand each other, Princess?"

Natalie looked at the Yder. It was running its leathery tongue across the edges of its beak, lapping up a few loose strands of hair it had missed. Its eye focused sharply on Natalie. She then turned her head up towards Bacham and nodded.

Bacham only stared at her; his eyes were flat and dead. "I thought you would see things my way."

For the time being, she thought to herself. Only for the time being. I will still do everything in my power to disrupt your plans.

The other Rebbercands each mounted one of the creatures. The Yders let out a shrill scream and began beating their leathery wings. They circled two or three times before Bacham took the lead and turned the group to the southwest. He had barely tightened his grip and Natalie felt as if she could easily slide from her captor's grasp and fall to the ground, which was growing farther and farther away. When she thought she couldn't be in a more precarious position, Bacham tossed her across the neck of the Yder on which they were mounted, like a sack of potatoes. Now he wasn't holding her at all. She was certain that she would not be allowed to fall, but that this was another attempt to frighten her. It was working.

Her arms were tied to her sides, so she was unable to hold on to anything, not that there was much to grasp. The gag in her mouth would prevent her from calling out if she felt like she was slipping, although she wasn't sure she wanted to be rescued, if she did slip. She was loosely wedged between the animal's neck and Bacham's legs. The jerky flapping of the Yder's wings made the flight extremely uncomfortable. In addition to the ropes chafing against her skin every time the creature flapped its wings, the scales that covered its body scraped against her, too.

As the Yder's and their riders fell into a loose formation, she watched as the ground sped by below her. Before they had taken off, she thought she heard one of them mention that they were heading to the Viridian Ocean. That appeared to be the case. If so, they were traveling to the far side of the forest they had been running through. She would never be found that far away. She needed to think quickly before she was lost completely. She had already blocked herself from Stella. She needed to send word to someone else. She thought of a number of the Dryads, but dismissed them. That wouldn't work. They would only report to Stella, and she'd be no better off, and Stella would again be in jeopardy.

Solveig, she thought. That might work. Solveig's powers were similar to hers, more so than her other friends or any of the Sea Sprites. Natalie could transmit a message to her and that might prevent Stella from coming after her Princess on her own. She only hoped that Solveig was in a place where she would be able to receive the message. If she was in her castle, there wouldn't be any problems, but Natalie was certain that Solveig had agreed to spend some time with Liam helping the Trepans. If she was still underground, that could make things difficult. She couldn't worry about that now. She would just have to take a chance, even though she wasn't certain whether Solveig would receive the message, and, if she did, if she'd understand it. Natalie was quickly running out of options.

She cleared her mind and then focused on the image of the Rebbercands, the Yders, the Viridian Ocean, and Solveig. She concentrated so hard that the images began to swirl in her mind's eye until they blurred into one single explosion of bright blue and green light. The explosion then immediately shrunk to a pinpoint of light and then vanished. Her head was thrown back as the message flew from her mind to its target. The shock was so powerful, a small trail of blood trickled from her nose and she felt like she was sliding off the neck of the Yder. Bacham was oblivious to what she was doing until her head jerked back. He placed a hand roughly on her back and made sure she wasn't trying to jump off.

"I don't think you want to leave right now," he said to her in a nasty voice. "It's a long way down and your landing wouldn't be altogether pleasant."

She ignored his jibe. She knew the message had been transmitted, but had no way of knowing if it had been received. The rain that was the result of Stella's diversion of the tidal wave was now a fine mist, and was quickly dying down. Even so, she was soaked to the skin which made her even more uncomfortable. As they climbed higher in the sky, the air became cooler, and she started shivering. She couldn't recall a time when she felt any worse than she did now.

As the mist settled over her, it was just strong enough to wash away the trickle of blood from her nose after the images had been sent, and before Bacham could notice. The mist was also just strong enough that Natalie did not feel the sudden rush of water that Solveig experienced when she was knocked into the Sea at the instant she received the images. And because she didn't feel the sudden rush of water, she couldn't know that it was the same salt water which Lochen was covered in, miles away on a field of snow. And she couldn't know that all this happened at the exact same time and all because of the exact same event.

Chapter fourteen

*T*he wall of water crashed into the force field Stella had created and broke up into a less destructive rainfall as it soared far over her head and fell to earth over the forest beyond the shore. She had managed to save her island, the Lodge of the forest creatures and the faerie village as well most of the area further south along the shore, although she was unaware of any of this. Once the immediate threat to the island had passed, and she had instructed the guards to head for the faerie village to locate Natalie, she ran to the harbor to find a ship to take to the forest creatures' Lodge.

By now the bulk of the wave had passed, and was cascading like rain from the island deep into the forest. Stella arrived at the harbor to discover that the tidal wave had blown most of the ships out into the channel. There were a few that managed to remain secured. She began searching for someone to sail the closest of the small ships that were still usable. She had never sailed one by herself before. Finding no one, she thought about just swimming across the channel. It wasn't that far, and she was an excellent swimmer. Before she could do so, she was struck with an intense pain. Her heart felt like it was exploding. She fell to the ground in a stupor. She didn't lose consciousness, but she felt like she was numb all over. She struggled to her feet, but was unable to stand. She felt like she was being battered about.

She felt instantly panicked, and looked around for help, but no one was nearby. Everyone had taken shelter, and the guards had already left for the faerie village. The Sea churned back and forth, but the danger of any more tidal waves or rip tides seemed to have passed. The channel was fairly calm, in spite of the continuing downpour. She got to her hands and knees in an effort to crawl into the water. She couldn't wait any longer. Between the stab of pain and her earlier worries about Natalie, she felt compelled to get to the Lodge as soon as possible.

Before she could go any further, she was wracked with another spasm of intense pain. Stella rolled over on her back and stared at the sky. What was happening to her? She could barely catch her breath. The pain spread from her heart outward throughout her body. She had never felt anything like this before, and it was terrifying her. Her first thought was that someone had hexed her or put some kind of curse on her. Her mind was reeling; it was hard to think clearly. Who would do this to her, and why? Not now, she pleaded to no one in particular. She needed to find Natalie.

She tried to relax and control her breathing, but the pain was severe and unrelenting. Each convulsion was worse than the one before. She summoned all her strength and tried again to stand. As soon as she did everything started spinning, she was struck with another seizure of incredible pain and fell to the ground. Where is everybody, she nearly shouted. She called for help, but her voice only came out in a whisper, and there was no one anywhere near to hear her. She tried to focus on Natalie, but was unable to form a solid image of her, which only increased her panic.

She twisted her body, fighting the pain, turned to her stomach and then pushed herself up to her knees. With her head hanging low, she forced herself to crawl. She knew she couldn't make it across the channel to the Lodge. She needed to get back to the palace. She needed to find help or to get to her potions. Her knees and palms scraped across the rocks, which cut into her skin. She didn't feel this at all; the pain in her chest was too great – it blocked out everything else, except for her rising panic.

She inched her way back to the palace area where she finally attracted the attention of a guard. Upon seeing her, the guard called for help as she ran to assist.

"My lady," the guard said in a voice nearly choked with distress, "What has happened? Who did this to you?"

"Has there been any word from the Princess," Stella asked, ignoring the questions the guard was asking her. "Has anyone seen her?"

"None, my lady," the guard responded. "There's been no word, nor sighting. We were not aware that she had left the island. We thought she was with you."

"No, she went to warn the forest creatures and the faeries of the tidal wave. I take it she hasn't returned."

"No, my lady," answered the guard. "There has been no sign of her. I will send a party to search for her immediately."

"Go yourself," ordered Stella. "Take an armed escort with you, and be extremely cautious. Is that clear?"

The guard was stunned by the Enchantress' words. "But I first need to get you some help. You're in obvious pain."

"No," groaned Stella. "I will be fine. Someone else can tend to me. You must leave immediately."

"Is the Princess in danger?" she asked.

"I don't know," answered Stella. "I cannot summon a vision of her, which I find troubling enough. But I have a sense of another presence – something evil."

"Let me at least stay with you until help has arrived," she said.

"No," Stella shouted. "Go now. Others will be here soon enough. Go first to the Lodge of the forest creatures. If she's not there, then try the faerie village, but hurry."

Against her better judgment, the guard left Stella in a heap on the ground, soaking wet and in extreme pain. She quickly gathered a party of well-armed searchers. She directed one of them to help Stella and then took the rest in a quick ship, heading for the opposite shore. Within minutes the guard that remained behind found Stella and brought a small rescue party. They helped her to her feet and half carried her into the palace.

"Take me to the Sanctorum," she demanded, when it was clear they were taking her to the Apothecary.

"My lady," objected the guard, "you need to rest and be attended to. We must take you to the Apothecary."

"My well-being is irrelevant," she argued. "I must locate the Princess. I cannot do that in a sick bed. Get me to my Sanctorum."

The stress in Stella's voice was enough to convince the attendant to do as she had been instructed. They carried her into the Sanctorum and left her by herself as she ordered. She tried to conjure images of Natalie, but none would come. A tremendous sense of loss filled her. She was coming to the gradual realization that her connection to her Princess had been broken. The fears she had harbored when the pain first struck her heart were now confirmed, and the vague feelings of apprehension she had experienced when the visions of the tidal wave first appeared now made sense.

She had been matched to the Princess since her birth. Without that connection she was lost. She sat heavily on the floor of the Sanctorum – bloody, bruised, soaking wet and heartbroken - and wept.

------------------ *** ------------------

Solveig couldn't seem to get dry, as much as she tried to. She had been rescued from the sea some time ago, but it was as if she was still swimming in it. Liam had found a blanket to cover her, but it soon became soaked. He tried to wring it out, but to no avail. Each time he put it back around her, it was immediately soaked through once again. Summer was at a loss as to what to do.

"It's like she's under her own private rain cloud," she said.

She reached out to touch the edge of her robe. Only the tips of her fingers that came in contact with the material immediately covered with water. The rest of her hand was dry. This was too weird, she thought. She looked at her hand and then raised her fingers to her mouth and tasted the water.

"Hey," she said, startled. "This is salt water."

"What's going on?" asked Solveig, who was getting more and more concerned. "I'm not hot, so it's not like I'm sweating. In fact, I feel a bit cold. Where is all this water coming from? And why is it salt water?"

"I can get you more blankets," offered Liam.

He wasn't sure where he'd get them. He hadn't stocked the ship for a long journey, and especially not one out on the open sea. But he couldn't think of anything else to say. He had never seen anything like this and he was beginning to panic. He couldn't imagine what it was doing to Solveig.

"I don't think it will help," Solveig told him. "But thanks for offering."

She stood up, agitated, and walked to the front of the small craft and stared ahead towards the horizon. As she took the few steps from the stern to the bow, she shrugged off the water soaked blanket from her shoulders and as the blanket dropped to the deck, the stress from her body seemed to shed as well. Summer fluttered behind her and hovered over her shoulder, just watching her.

"What are you looking for?" asked Summer after several minutes had gone by and Solveig hadn't moved.

It was a few seconds before she answered. It was as if she had just awakened from a deep sleep and wasn't exactly sure where she was or what the question was. Her eyes were a bit glassy and she seemed to be in a fog. The fear and anxiety she had been feeling just seconds before had evaporated.

"Uh," she struggled to focus, "I'm just looking at…"

She seemed confused. She staggered backwards a step or two and reached out to the bulwark to steady herself. Summer rose into the air to avoid running into her. Liam was pedaling hard at the back of the ship. He moved his head back and forth to look past the sails to see what was going on.

"What's wrong?" demanded Summer.

Almost immediately, the fog that had enveloped her seemed to clear away, and she was fully alert.

"I don't know," she said, rubbing her eyes. "I had a sudden feeling that I was being lifted high into the air. I didn't feel like I was falling, but I felt like I was really high up and there was nothing for me to hold on to. It was really weird."

She laughed nervously and bent down to pick up the blanket and pulled it closer around her. She reached up to feel her face and noticed that she had suddenly dried off. Weirder and weirder, she thought. She seemed unconcerned that only seconds before she was unable to get dry, and now that had inexplicably changed. Summer could only watch her as her own anxiety began to rise. Something was not right, but she couldn't put her finger on it. She could see what was happening, but was at a loss as to what was causing it. They needed to get to the island. They needed to see if Stella could explain or, hopefully, remedy this. She spun around and flew to the back of the ship.

"Can you make this thing go any faster?" she asked Liam.

"No," he told her. "I've got the sails stretched to the maximum and I've increased the ratio of the pedal gears as far as they'll go, and I'm pedaling as fast as I can. In fact, I'm going to need a rest pretty soon, which means we'll be slowing down, instead of speeding up." He looked past Summer towards Solveig. "I don't think she's going to be able to take over for me, and you're too short. Anything you can do with faerie dust?"

Summer thought about that for a minute before admitting that faerie dust probably wouldn't help with what they needed. If she had to raise the boat into the air a little, or if it needed lights in the dark, yes; but to make it go faster? Her faerie dust just wouldn't last long enough to make it worthwhile.

"No," she finally had to tell him. "Sorry. Maybe Solveig can do something. If she's not too...whatever. I'll ask her."

At that moment the small ship ran into some unexpected turbulence. Although the tidal wave and the aftershocks had subsided, the sea was still rough in places. The small boat was not made for such rough seas, and Liam had to slow down. Solveig simply stared straight ahead and, pointing forward, shouted, "No! Faster."

Summer flew to her side and around in front of her. Solveig's eyes were glassed over and her expression was blank.

"Are you all right?" she asked.

No response.

"Can you cast a spell or something to make the ship go faster? You know, like you just asked?"

Still no response.

Summer fluttered right in front of her face, peering deeply into Solveig's eyes. She waved her arms and shot her hands forward trying to make her blink, but still got no reaction. She seemed wide awake, but clearly her mind was off someplace else.

"Hello. Anybody home?" she fluttered right between Solveig's eyes, still getting no reaction from her.

"Something's wrong," she shouted back to Liam. "You have to come up here and see for yourself."

Liam tied off the controls and made his way to the front, thankful for the brief respite, in spite of the reason. He moved to one side and looked closely at Solveig's fixed stare; then he moved to the other side and looked again. He waved his hand up and down in front of her face. He snapped his fingers at her eyes. She didn't even blink.

"I think she might be in shock," he said. "She said she didn't hit her head when she fell overboard, but I'm not so sure. I suppose even if she didn't hit her head, maybe not enough oxygen got to her brain. I didn't think she was under water that long, though. I just don't know what to make of this."

He tried to move her over to a nearby bench to get her to sit down, but her body stiffened. She raised her arm forward again and pointed.

"No! We have to hurry. There's trouble."

Her voice was flat and lifeless. She almost sounded like a robot. Liam looked from Solveig to Summer.

"I think she's in a trance. Did you see anything to cause this? She seemed all right once she got out of the water. Did something happen after that?"

"No," said Summer. "I saw the same things you did. I'm getting really worried."

Liam felt Solveig's forehead. She was completely dry, but her skin was cold. Then he noticed that her clothing, which only a few minutes ago were soaked throughout, were now completely dry.

"This is all just too strange," Liam said to Summer. I'd give her some kind of herbal remedy, but I wouldn't know what for. I don't know what's wrong with her, and I don't want to give her something that might make her worse. This is really starting to worry me as well."

"I think we better head for shore and see if we can light a fire," said Summer. "She looks like she's very cold."

"Good idea," he said as he went back to the tiller, untied the controls, and steered the ship towards the shore.

"NO!" screeched Solveig, still pointing in the same direction. "Don't stop. We need to hurry. Don't stop," she insisted.

"OK" said Liam, immediately returning the ship to the original course. "Don't get all bent out of shape. We'll keep going."

He reset the sails and began to pedal again, pushing the ship harder than he was comfortable doing. His legs were beginning to burn. He knew he wouldn't be able to maintain this pace for very long. He needed to rest. He was also worried about pushing the ship this hard. It would be getting dark soon, and he was just as worried about what would happen then. He was a bit uncomfortable sailing his craft in its maiden voyage this far out to sea at night, but what made things worse was that the tidal wave and subsequent flooding had thrown all sorts of obstacles into the sea. Those obstacles would be invisible in the dark.

However, his misgivings about the abilities of the ship and the potential dangers in the water were far outweighed by his concern for Solveig. He looked at Summer, who could only stare back. He could see that she felt the same way. His hope now was that the ship would hold out long enough for them to get to wherever Solveig was leading them. He also hoped that their original destination of the island of the Sea Sprites was still where they were going. At this point, he was no longer sure of anything.

------------------ *** ------------------

Quinn's makeshift catamaran made up of the three small kayaks was racing across the tops of the waves. Sean had buried himself in the center shell, covering his head with anything he could find and mumbled incoherently. Quinn was seated in the opening, holding on tightly in the kayak that was on the shore side, although they had left sight of any shore whatsoever long ago. Lochen was perched sideways on the top edge of the opening of the outermost shell. Periodically, he'd hook his feet on the lip of the opening and lean out over the water to keep the craft balanced whenever a gust of wind caught the sail and raised the odd looking craft on its side.

Every once in a while, Sean would lift his head up and look at his companions. Then he'd take in the seemingly limitless vista of water in every direction, moan loudly, and duck his head back down. His moaning became louder each time the wind tipped the trio of boats on edge. Quinn's side would roll towards the water, Lochen's side would rise high into the air with Lochen stretched as far as he could over the edge as a counterbalance. Sean had to see this only once to be convinced not to look again. Each time it happened he was certain they were going to tip over. Finally, he could take no more.

"It's getting dark," he shouted. "We can't do this in the dark. Are we going to at least put into land to camp for the night?"

"No," Lochen immediately answered in a flat and lifeless voice. "We have to hurry. There's trouble."

"Then can we at least slow down?" Sean whined. "We're going to end up in the ocean and we'll probably drown or get eaten or worse."

"No," Lochen repeated in the same flat and lifeless voice. "We have to hurry. There's trouble."

The tone of Lochen's voice caught Quinn's attention. It almost sounded like Solveig. His head jerked to the left.

"Are you all right?" he asked. "You sounded kind of unusual for a minute."

Lochen slowly turned his head towards Quinn. It looked like he had been daydreaming, but then his focus sharpened.

"Yes," he said. "I'm fine. How are you?"

Quinn was a bit puzzled by the question. "Me? Uh...I'm OK. I wasn't sure you were, though."

"Really?" asked Lochen. "Why wouldn't I be all right?"

"The way you said what you said," Sean shouted, his head still buried beneath the top of the kayak. "You sounded like a freaking zombie trying to imitate Solveig, and doing a bad job. What's up with that?"

Lochen furrowed his brow. "I'm certain that I don't know what you're talking about. Quinn simply asked me if I was all right and I told him I was. That was the extent of our conversation. What was so wrong with that?"

"No," said Sean.

He pulled the cover off of his head and poked it above the top of the opening. He clutched the rim as tightly as he could, his fingers white with stress, pressing into the edge of the kayak opening. It was impossible for him to look at Lochen without taking in the enormous expanse of open sea. He gulped hard.

"That's not what I'm talking about. It's what you said before that. You know, 'No. We have to hurry. There's trouble.' That part."

The words were no sooner out of his mouth than he ducked his head back beneath the top of the opening and scrabbled at the covers to bury himself once again.

"I beg your pardon," said Lochen, clearly puzzled. "I really don't know what you're talking about."

"He's right," said Quinn. "He asked you if we were going to stop on shore to make camp and you said, 'No. We have to hurry. There's trouble.' I heard it, too. Plain as day. And he was right about you trying to sound like Solveig."

At that Lochen's eyes seemed to lose focus, his head turned towards the front of the kayak, and his voice came out in a flat monotone, "No. We have to hurry. There's trouble."

Sean popped his head out from under the covers again, looking to see if Lochen was just joking. He looked at Quinn for confirmation, and then he and Quinn both pointed at Lochen and said simultaneously, "There. You see? That's it. That's the voice."

Lochen's eyes appeared to sharpen. He turned back and looked at Sean and Quinn and saw them pointing at him.

"What?" he asked.

"Dude," shouted Quinn. "Are you playing games with us? Never mind. I know better than to ask. But, seriously, don't you know what just happened?"

Suspecting something happened about which he was unaware, Lochen asked, "No. What happened? Tell me precisely."

Both Sean and Quinn began shouting excitedly, talking over one another to the point that Lochen couldn't understand what either of them was saying. He had to interrupt them several times and have them start over. When he got them to calm down and explain, he thought a minute before responding.

"Something unusual appears to be happening," he announced.

"You think?" Sean shouted incredulously. "First you get soaking wet – for no reason at all. And if that's not weird enough, you're soaked in salt water. And now you go off on a mental trip to zombie-land and you're talking all funny, sounding sort of like Solveig, and you just _now_ think something unusual is happening? Seriously?"

Lochen only stared at him, deep in thought. He turned to look at Quinn.

"Am I nuts, or something?" asked Sean. "Don't answer that. I'm NOT nuts. I know it and you know it."

Quinn wasn't sure what to say. After giving some thought to all this, Lochen suggested that Quinn try adjusting the sail and to steer their craft towards the shore.

"Oh, thank you. I can't wait to get on solid ground. At least you haven't completely lost your marbles," said Sean, glad that they were finally going to get off the water and onto something that wouldn't shift under his feet.

"Oh," said Lochen, "we're not going to land. I'm sorry to disappoint you. This is just an experiment."

"WHAT?" cried Sean. "Is this another one of your science projects?"

"It's not exactly a science project," said Lochen. "It's more of a simple experiment to see if what I believe has happened, has, in fact, really happened. It's nothing related to science at all."

Sean just stared at him – speechless.

"Whenever you're ready," said Quinn.

"Go ahead," answered Lochen.

Quinn trimmed the sail, slowed the craft down and steered in an eastward direction, towards shore.

Within a few seconds, Lochen's eyelids dropped halfway down and in a flat but loud voice he said, "NO! Don't stop. We need to hurry. Don't stop."

Quinn returned to the original course and speed and Lochen's expression changed at the same time. Sean and Quinn stared at him, waiting for some kind of response. Lochen looked at them as if nothing had happened. He asked them what happened and had them repeat it several times in detail.

"I believe that Solveig has become some kind of conduit and whatever messages or images she is receiving, she is subconsciously sending to me, or I'm somehow picking them up independent of whether she's sending them. I can't tell at this point where the origin of these messages is. However, I believe this is more serious than I thought."

After several seconds of stunned silence, Sean asked, "Does this mean we're going to shore or not?"

"Definitely not, I would think," answered Lochen.

Sean moaned and dropped his head down below the top of the kayak.

------------------ *** ------------------

Night had fallen and the Yders were still carrying their riders. Natalie was still bound and gagged and draped over the neck of the one being led by Bacham. The air had started to feel warmer to her, in spite of the night. She had dried off and stopped shivering. She could feel and sometimes see that they passed through thin clouds, so she knew they were still high above the ground. At least she couldn't see exactly how far up they were, she thought. She also concluded that they had turned south, which was why the air felt warmer. She strained to see through the darkness to determine whether they were still over land or if they had reached the Ocean yet.

It was too dark for her to tell. She sniffed the air and could detect a distant aroma of sea air. But she couldn't tell if that aroma was coming from directly beneath her or off to the distance in a direction she couldn't determine. She squirmed slightly in her bindings just to see if she would get any reaction from her captor. Nothing. Maybe he wasn't paying attention to her any more.

She thought if they were over water, she might be able to work her way off the back of the beast she had been thrown onto and drop into the sea. It would be a long drop, but she felt she would rather take the chance. As a Sea Sprite, she had lived all her life in or near the water. She was an exceedingly powerful swimmer, even if she was tied up. The only problem would be timing. If they hadn't reached the sea yet, she could be dropping over land and she was certain she couldn't survive a fall of that kind. Depending on how high they were, even landing in water could be perilous.

She slowly wiggled one foot out of its shoe and let it drop. Bacham didn't seem to notice her movement. As soon as it was off, she listened intently to find out if she could hear it land, what it landed on, and how long it took to reach the surface. One, two, three, four, five, six, and then a very faint splash. They were over water. That was good, although she couldn't tell how deep the water was – that was not so good. It took six seconds for the shoe to hit the water. That was not so good, either. The sound of the splash was masked by the sounds of the wind and the beating of the wings of the Yders. She was only moderately certain that the splash was a deep water sound rather than a shallow one. She wondered, though, if her level of certainty was just wishful thinking.

She decided she would just have to take the chance. She concentrated on one more message to Solveig, not even sure that the first one had gotten through. She focused all her energy on the statement: the southern seas of the Viridian Ocean. If she survived the drop, she hoped her friends would be able to find her – or at least her body. She prepared herself mentally for the worst. Once she had resigned herself to whatever would happen, in one quick and fluid motion, she arched her back, lifted her head skyward and pushed with her knees away from the side of the beast she was riding.

It felt like she was suspended in mid-air. The sensation lasted for less than a second, but felt like an eternity, and then she began to drop. She could feel her body slide effortlessly and unimpeded past the metallic-like scales on the body of the Yder. She felt the air rush upward as gravity pulled her in the opposite direction. She felt the wind blow her hair straight above her head. A charge of exhilaration ran through her body. And then she felt a sharp pain as Bacham reached down at the last second and caught his fingers in the streaming strands of her hair.

Her descent jerked to a stop; her head snapped up; and pain shot down her body. She was dangling at the end of his arm, her face pressed against the side of the Yder. Bacham let her hang there for a few seconds before he gave a quick jerk and flipped her body back up across the neck of the Yder.

"You weren't planning on leaving me, now, were you, Princess," he asked with no humor in his voice at all. "I have a much more interesting plan in store for you. But not until your Enchantress comes to try to rescue you. You've sent a message to her, haven't you?"

Chapter fifteen

A ll through the night Solveig had remained at the bow of the ship, staring blankly ahead. Her expression never changed. Liam had stopped periodically to rest, in spite of Solveig's repeated insistence to the contrary. Each time he stopped or even slowed down, she would say in a mechanical voice, "No. We have to hurry. There's trouble." After that, even if Liam simply ignored her – which he eventually did out of necessity – she would remain silent.

Throughout the night, Summer remained at Solveig's shoulder, watching her vigilantly. Although Solveig seemed to be fully awake, Summer wasn't sure, if they hit a rough wave, that Solveig would be aware of being washed overboard again. By morning she and Liam were exhausted, but the island of the Sea Sprites was finally in sight. Not long after that, several small boats and swimmers came out to meet them. The leader was a Dryad named Ayn. Summer flew out to meet her.

"We were hoping the Princess would be with you," said Ayn, somewhat disappointed.

"With us? Why would she be with us? We thought Natalie would be here on the island. In fact, we were coming to see her. You mean she's not there?" asked Summer.

Ayn told her about the tidal wave and Natalie's sudden departure from the island to alert the faeries and the forest creatures. She was interrupted by Summer's questions about the faeries' village.

"There was no one there," Ayn informed her. "I was part of the search and rescue party that went to find the Princess. We went to the faerie village first. It was completely empty. The same thing with the Lodge of the forest creatures."

Summer was puzzled. "Do you mean they were washed away?"

"No," Ayn said. "Not that we could tell. Both places were just...empty. There's no other way to describe it."

Ayn explained how Stella had blocked the wave with a force field of some kind and converted it into rain. After the danger had passed, search parties had been dispatched from the island to see if any help was needed in both the faerie village and the forest creatures' lodge, as well as to search for the Princess. There were no signs of anyone in either location, and there was no indication that they had been washed away. It seemed as though both locations had been evacuated before the flood. There was no indication of where they had gone or that anyone had been left behind.

"So where did Natalie go?" asked Summer.

"We don't know," answered Ayn. "Actually, none of us saw her leave the island. It was the Enchantress who directed us to the mainland to search for her. She was very insistent about finding the Princess."

Summer was confused. "But if Stella knew that Natalie went to the villages, how is it that she doesn't know where she is now?"

Ayn looked uncomfortable at the mention of the Enchantress' name. She was clearly at a loss as to how to describe her current condition.

"Our Enchantress is...distraught," Ayn finally answered.

"Distraught?" asked Summer. "What do you mean, exactly?"

Ayn considered the question before replying.

"She is emotionally devastated. She has lost all contact with the Princess. No one is sure when that happened, or why. Or how, for that matter. During the aftermath of the tidal wave, she ordered search parties to the mainland. She was unable to make the journey herself. She had collapsed on the shore near the harbor in extreme pain. When she was carried back to the palace, she refused any medical attention and ordered that she be taken to her Sanctorum. Once there, she insisted on being left alone. When much time had passed, her attendant went in search of her. She was found on the floor of the Sanctorum in uncontrollable grief. She is unable to tell anyone what has happened to the Princess. We all fear the worst. The Enchantress has since been moved to a private room, but her condition has remained unchanged."

This was horrible news, thought Summer. By now the small fleet of Sea Sprite ships had come alongside the *West Wind*, which had stopped. For some reason, Solveig was silent. Summer brought Ayn on board the *West Wind* and had her repeat what she had said to Liam. Ayn was somewhat distracted by Solveig, who was standing at the front and staring off into space. She knew that Solveig and her Princess were friends. She couldn't understand how, when hearing of the disappearance of the Princess, she could remain so – detached was the only way she could describe it. When she had shared all she knew, she asked Summer and Liam what had happened to Solveig.

"We don't know," said Liam. He described the events of the last day and how Solveig had become more and more unresponsive. "It appears to be some kind of spell, rather than a physical condition. We were hoping that Natalie would be here and could find a cure or that Stella could cast a counter spell to fix whatever happened to her."

Ayn shook her head in dismay. "The Enchantress is unable to help herself. I don't think it's possible for her to help anyone else."

Once Ayn had completed the recounting of the recent events, Solveig started to become slightly agitated. It was as if she had waited patiently for the discussion to end and now needed to take action. She began walking from one side of the ship to the other, mumbling, "Can't stop. Must help." Although her physical demeanor was one of anxiety, her voice remained flat, lifeless and mechanical.

Summer and Liam had gotten so used to her talking to herself, that they had fairly well blocked her out. They were oblivious to her renewed pleas. This behavior though was new to Ayn. She found Solveig's repeated pleas to be disconcerting. She was further mystified by the lack of concern that Liam and Summer displayed. She looked from them to Solveig and back. This time, however, Solveig seemed to have tolerated being ignored long enough.

"Can't stop," she said even louder. "Must help. Must find Princess."

She was shouting more loudly, but that was the only change in her voice. The reference to finding the Princess, though, caused Summer and Liam to finally notice her. They were too stunned to react immediately, and only looked at her in silence. That changed when her impatience became unbearable and she climbed over the edge of the boat and stepped off into the water. She disappeared from their view and was replaced by a splash of water. They all ran to the side as she bobbed to the surface and began swimming awkwardly towards the island – it was almost as if she were trying to run.

"Grab her," shouted Ayn.

One of the Sea Sprites in a boat nearby tried to reach out and pull her back to safety. She got her fingers on the edge of Solveig's collar and was nearly pulled in herself. Then Solveig jerked her arm, pulled her head away from the Sprite and the boat, and continued to swim, all the while repeating, "Can't stop. Must help."

"Throw a line around her," shouted Ayn. "Use a rope."

Another of the Sprites tossed a rope in Solveig's direction. Even though the throw had come from behind her, it was as though she could see it coming. She ducked under the water far enough to make the attempt miss and kept swimming. One of the other Sprites maneuvered her boat in front of Solveig and tossed a rope from the stern.

"Grab hold and we'll pull you to the island," she shouted.

That seemed to do the trick. Solveig's expression remained unchanged, but it looked as if she were processing the statement. She hesitated for only a second or two, and then reached up for the rope, waiting to be pulled behind, rather than into, the boat. The Sprite looked to Ayn for further instructions.

"Tow her to shore," she shouted and then returned to her own boat, leaving Summer and Liam to sail the *West Wind* to shore.

As soon as the water was shallow enough, Solveig didn't wait for any assistance. She stood up and marched to land. The boats all pulled into shore and the *West Wind* was anchored at a nearby dock. Everyone got out and scurried after Solveig who was making a beeline to the palace, still repeating the words, "Must find the Princess. Must help." And she was trailing a path of water behind her.

She marched into the palace, still dripping wet and followed by an entourage. She had never been in this palace, since the Sea Sprites had moved from their bubble on the floor of the Cerulean Sea. Regardless, she moved with confidence as if she was following some invisible beacon. She bypassed the Sanctorum, where her followers were certain she was headed, and made her way directly to Stella's private room, with Summer, Liam and a growing crowd of Sea Sprites following close behind. She pushed open the door without knocking and marched right up to the bed on which Stella had been placed. Exhausted by her grief, and heavily sedated, Stella was in a half sleep. Solveig reached down and shook her.

"No," interjected a nurse who had been looking over Stella since she had been found weeping on the floor of the Sanctorum. "She's exhausted and needs to rest."

Solveig ignored the nurse and placed her hands on each of Stella's shoulders and shook her violently. Water from her hair and clothing dropped into Stella's face.

"Must find the Princess," she shouted at Stella. "Must help."

As the water splattered on her face, Stella's eyes fluttered open and she pushed Solveig's hands from her shoulders. Solveig stood upright, staring blankly into space, and Stella sat up and faced her. She fought through the grief and the sedatives. Her confusion quickly gave way to understanding and resolution.

"What are you doing here?" she mumbled, still deep in a fog of grief and depression.

"Must help. Must find the Princess. Must hurry," Solveig replied in the same flat monotone.

The odd response caused Stella to fight to clear her mind. She looked up into Solveig's eyes, which were staring blankly ahead. She ran her eyes down to Solveig's feet, which were standing in the pooling water, and then her gaze shot back up to her eyes. "Of course," Stella said to no one in particular.

She was instantly alert. She jumped up off the bed and hugged Solveig fiercely, getting soaked in the process.

"You're all wet," she said, stating the obvious.

She held Solveig by her shoulders at arm's length and looked her square in the face. She took in the blank, glassy-eyed stare and the soaked clothing. Her grief and her state of helplessness seemed to evaporate instantly.

"Find Princess Solveig some dry clothing," she ordered.

One of the Sprites ran off as directed, but the others were immobile. It was then that she saw the small group that had followed Solveig, Summer and Liam into her room. She greeted her friends warmly as the Sea Sprites looked on perplexed. They were at a loss in understanding the nearly instantaneous transformation of their Enchantress.

"Just now, when Solveig woke you up," said Summer, "you said, 'Of course.' What did you mean?"

Stella explained everything that had recently transpired, and then told them about the bonds between an Enchantress and her Princess, and how hers had been broken with Natalie. She had assumed the worst had happened, that Natalie most likely had been lost in the tidal wave, trying to save the faeries or the forest creatures. However, when she saw and heard Solveig, she realized that Natalie must have broken the bond herself and on purpose, and established some kind of link with her.

"And you came to this conclusion how?" asked Liam.

"By the look in Solveig's eyes," said Stella. "It is clear to me that Natalie transmitted a telepathic distress call to Solveig. She must have encountered some kind of threat and needs help, but she knows that if she had sent it to me, I would have responded immediately and by myself. Whatever it is, it's something that requires more than my help alone."

"So, what happened to Natalie, and where is she?" asked Summer.

"I don't know the answers to either of those questions," said Stella. "Only Solveig has that information. As soon as I touched her, I could sense that she can lead us to Natalie."

"Can't you get an image in your Sanctorum?" asked Liam.

"No. Natalie has blocked all communication with me. That must have something to do with what happened to her and where she is."

"Can't we just ask Solveig?" asked Summer.

Although, when she looked at Solveig, it was obvious to her that Solveig wasn't going to be telling them much of anything. Stella and Liam quickly came to the same conclusion. Solveig just stood there, staring blankly.

"I'm not sure she even knows herself. She seems to be in some kind of trance. Is that why you brought her here?"

"No," answered Liam. "We barely avoided the northern edge of that tidal wave. We saw what it did to the shore up there and could see it was running all the way down here. We came to see if we could help. But I have to admit, along the way, Solveig became really insistent about not stopping."

"How did she get all wet?"

"When we met up with your scouts," answered Summer, "We stopped. I think we had stopped too long, because, she just jumped in the water and began swimming. One of your scouts was able to get a rope around her by telling her that she'd tow Solveig to the island. She refused to get back in the boat."

"And she's been like this since the trance started?" asked Stella. "Like she's obsessed with getting some place?"

"Yes," said Liam. "Exactly. It's like she knows where we have to go, but she can't tell us."

"Then we just need to follow her direction."

As if taking a cue from Stella, Solveig again began to repeat, "Must find the Princess. Must help."

"We need to rest," said Liam. "Otherwise we won't be of help to anyone."

"Is there any way to keep her from going off on her own?" Summer asked, recalling how she jumped off the ship and into the water when they had stopped.

Stella walked up to Solveig and placed her hand over Solveig's forehead and eyes.

"Sleep," she commanded, and Solveig began to sag. Liam caught her before she fell to the floor and put her on Stella's bed.

"That should give us a little bit of time to plan our next steps," Stella said, "but that spell won't last long, so we'll have to hurry."

- - - - - - - - - - - - - - - - *** - - - - - - - - - - - - - - - - -

The three small kayaks that Quinn tied together had been racing blindly through the night at a breakneck speed. Lochen maintained the pace and, since he required little sleep, he stayed awake through the night listening carefully for any signs of danger. The night sky was overcast, blocking out any light from the moon, so it was impossible to see much more than a few feet in front of the craft. Lochen tried casting a spell to transmit a globe of light out in front of the boats, but a fog set in and the light merely bounced back in his face. It made things worse, so he immediately extinguished it. He didn't have a spell that would make the fog vanish.

Before Sean ducked his head under the top of the center kayak, he mumbled about running into another ship or something worse. Lochen said he wasn't too worried about running into other ships, since they hadn't seen any signs of life all day. However, to Sean's dismay, Quinn warned that there was still a lot of debris even this far out from the backwash of the tidal wave. Sean moaned something incomprehensible and kept his head buried down as far as he could get.

Not long after the suns set, Quinn stretched his legs forward into the shell of the kayak, stuffed a backpack under his head and fell asleep. Within minutes he was snoring gently. Sean complained that between the bouncing of the ship on the waves and Quinn's snoring, he would never be able to sleep. He curled up into a ball and tried to get comfortable, but was unsuccessful. Each time their makeshift catamaran hit a wave, which was all too often for Sean's liking, the shock startled him from whatever level of sleep he was able to drift into. Aroused so suddenly from a fitful sleep, he would pop his head up and then immediately remember where he was, even though he couldn't see more than a few feet in front of him. He'd let out another moan and duck down again. By dawn he was so exhausted that he could fight off sleep no longer, and finally drifted into a deep, if not restful, slumber.

Lochen was able to remain fully alert. At least so he thought. Every once in a while he would go blank and mutter, "Must not stop. Must help." He was as unaware of doing this during the night as he had been during the daytime when he had been observed by Sean and Quinn. These episodes lasted only a few seconds, but when they struck, he was completely oblivious to his surroundings. When the brief seizure ended, he was also completely unaware that it had happened.

As dawn approached, the layer of fog over the water grew even thicker. The kayaks were cutting through it at a perilous speed. Visibility was barely a few feet ahead. And anything beyond that range was entirely hidden. The first sun had just risen, generating a golden glow that poked through the shallowest parts of the fog. The heat was not yet enough to burn the fog off or to improve visibility. Not far ahead of the kayaks a large log that had been carried by the tide floated directly in line with the boats. The log was turning, caught by a wave, and was almost perfectly perpendicular to the path of the boats.

Just before it came through the fog to a point of visibility, where Lochen would have detected it and would have easily cast a spell moving it aside, he was struck with another seizure. His eyes glazed over, everything in his field of vision went black and he muttered, "Must find the Princess," just as the log struck the bow of each of the kayaks simultaneously. He muttered, "Must help," just as the front of the kayaks rose into the air and began to soar above the wave. He muttered, "Must hurry," just as the broken edge of a limb sliced through the fabric of the center kayak like a razor.

As the kayaks crashed back to the sea, Lochen came out of his mini-trance. The jolt barely disturbed Quinn who rolled over and began to snore again. Sean popped his head up and looked around bleary-eyed. Seeing no change on the horizon, he grumbled incoherently and burrowed further down into the kayak. At first nothing happened with the rip in the bottom of the center boat, and Sean shifted his position trying without success to get comfortable. And then water began to seep in. The beating from the waves and the high rate of speed of the ships began to wear against the large slit. As the water started to fill the shell, Sean began to notice that he was getting wet. At first he just thought it was spray from the top side. He had complained about that ever since Lochen had cast the spell propelling the boats forward.

He wrapped himself more tightly in his blanket and ducked as low as he could, turning his head toward the back of the kayak. Then he heard a muted ripping sound. He came fully awake and listened more closely. It sounded nearby, and he could feel the vibrations below him changing. He started to unwind the blanket from around his arms and legs. As he kicked to free his legs, he noticed that his feet were wet. They weren't just damp from spray; they were soaked. He began to be alarmed and wrestled harder to get his arms free. The small tear that he had heard at the top of the rip quickly gave way, and half of the skin covering the bottom of his pod tore wide open. The water gushed in, shoving him back, forcing him past the opening on the top and deep into the back of the shell.

The sea filled the back half of the center kayak like a water balloon, pinning Sean inside, still wrapped in the blanket, kicking his legs and struggling with his arms to get free. It wasn't until the water spouted out the top of the opening that Lochen noticed something was wrong. He immediately stopped the craft. The sail, which was on a mast lashed to the center kayak, immediately sagged and swung listlessly in time with the waves, now that it was no longer filled with the wind. The cross pieces to which the top and the bottom of the sail were attached, swayed wildly.

Seeing the center pod filled with water, Lochen reacted instinctively. He stood up immediately to climb out of his kayak and move over to the center boat to help Sean. With one foot in and the other out of his pod, the boom jerked around and struck him across the back. His imbalance and the force of the blow drove him headfirst into the sea. His robes quickly absorbed the water and began to drag him deeper below the surface. He rolled over and looked up at the fading shadows of the three kayaks as they started drifting away from him. Through the water he could faintly make out the gash in the center pod and could see something or someone struggling in the end point. He had never cast a spell underwater, but wasting no time debating the efficiency of such a spell, he thrust his arm forward.

The cut in the skin opened like a zipper and Sean, still wrapped in the blanket, eased out of the kayak. The water soaked the blankets and his clothing and dragged him gently down towards Lochen as the boats drifted out of sight. Lochen swam to the bundle before it was lost from sight. He grabbed a corner of the blanket and kicked to the surface. By the time his head reached the air, Sean had stopped moving, and the boats were lost in the fog. Lochen treaded water and carefully unwrapped Sean. Once he was free, Lochen raised his head out of the water and ran his hand over Sean's face. Sean coughed and spit out a lungful of sea water, but he was not fully conscious. Lochen looked around as far as he could see in every direction, which wasn't far at all. His gaze shifted from Sean, whose face he was patting with his free hand, to the fog surrounding them in every direction.

"Quinn," he called out.

The fog swallowed his voice, as if he were shouting into a giant wad of cotton. By now the tide had separated Lochen and Sean from Quinn and the boats by several hundred feet. Lochen waved his arm, trying to part the fog, but it was like trying to separate the air or the water. It divided for only a second and then merged together again. He thrust his arm into the air to create a flash of light, but the weight of his robe pulled at his arm and he wasn't able to generate enough light to penetrate the fog. It was difficult to move and to hold on to Sean at the same time.

"Quinn," he shouted again.

The sound echoed off the mist, bouncing back to him. Lochen strained, but couldn't hear anything that would tell him where the boats were. Sean was getting heavy, so Lochen tried another spell on the blanket, making it airtight and filling it so it floated like an air mattress. Then he pushed Sean up onto it. He was tiring quickly, and the exertion needed to keep Sean afloat while he did all this was wearing him out. It took him several minutes before Sean was secured, and he was able to hang on to the side of the improvised air mattress and could stop treading water.

"Quinn," he shouted once more.

His voice was weak and breathless. All he could hear were the waves falling in on themselves. There was no other sound. As it was, the waves and the tide were slowly moving him and Sean west towards the distant shore. The kayaks, still with the sail attached and raised, caught the slight and intermittent wind. In spite of the useless and ruined center pod, the craft was carried by the two outer pods, and was steadily moving south towards the island of the Sea Sprites. In the time between Lochen falling overboard and his creating the raft for Sean, more than a mile gap separated him from the boats and Quinn.

More than two hours passed before both of the suns rose high enough to burn off the fog. By then Sean had come around. He was glad to be alive and glad to find that he was not alone, but when the fog lifted and all that could be seen in every direction was water, all he could do was duck his head under his arm and moan. With a better field of vision and a clear sky, Lochen was able to find another passing log. He maneuvered Sean and himself in that direction, and he climbed onto and straddled it. There was no sign in any direction whatsoever of Quinn and the kayaks.

"This is not a good situation in which to be," he said to himself.

Around the same time and several miles away, as the suns were still in the morning sky, Quinn was being gently rocked in his kayak pod. As the day lightened, he pulled the blanket over his head and tucked it under the back part of the pod, out of the sunlight. He then turned to his side and continued to sleep. The gentle wind propelled the boats forward and the rocking motion of the waves only lulled him into a deeper sleep. It was well after midday when his was spotted by a scout ship of the Sea Sprites. There were two of them in a small dory. They approached the mysterious craft cautiously, not seeing Quinn who was unintentionally hidden from sight.

"What is it?" one asked the other.

"I have no idea," she responded. "I've never seen anything like it. Do you think it's dangerous, or maybe a trap?"

"I don't know. It doesn't look dangerous, but you might be right about it being a trap. How do you suppose it got here?"

"I suppose the tidal wave washed it up from some place. What do you think we should do with it?"

They circled the strange collection of kayaks, and decided to tow it to the island. Still unsure of what exactly it was, they slowly and cautiously got close enough to secure a rope to the front of the center pod. There were no signs of life on board. All they could see of Quinn was wrapped in a blanket and looked like simple cargo. To their eyes, the ship was abandoned. Once it was tied to their dory, one of them slipped into the water and swam beneath the structure to see if there were any hidden dangers.

"It looks like what it seems to be: three boats tied together," she reported. "The middle one is ripped open, though. Whatever was in that pod is long gone. It doesn't look like a trap, but I think we need to be careful just the same."

They kept a close watch on it, just in case it was hexed and slowly pulled it back to their island. They had just docked and were tying it off when Quinn finally awoke. He was still wrapped from head to toe in blankets when he sat up, stretched, and yawned loudly, startling the Sprites who immediately ran off, screaming for help.

The sudden noise startled Quinn, who, forgetting where he was, stood up. The blanket slid off his body and gathered around his feet. The rocking of the boat caused by his sudden movement made him immediately lose his balance. Because the blankets were wrapped around his feet, he couldn't move them to regain his balance, and he fell into the water. He fell flat on his back and began flailing his arms and legs, and shouting for help. He managed to kick the blankets off of his feet, and he was still splashing and screaming that he was going to drown when a Dryad reached the dock. She studied him for a few seconds, and determined that he was not a threat, in spite of the fact that he looked like a giant.

"Stand up," she shouted to him.

"Help!" he yelled, "I'm drowning. Throw me a line or a rope or a pole. Pull me out. I can't keep my head out of water much longer."

"Stand up," she shouted again.

"What?" he yelled back, still waving his arms, trying to stay afloat.

"Stand up," she repeated once more. "The water where you are is not over your head. It probably doesn't even reach your waist."

He stopped yelling for help and waving his arms and stood up to find the water was just a few inches above his knees.

"Oh," he said, "Boy, do I feel foolish."

He looked up to see the Dryad and a small crowd of Sea Sprites staring at him. He waded to shore, taking off his soaking clothing as he did. The crowd backed away from him, keeping a safe distance. They were still not sure who he was or where he came from. Once he was on land, he looked back at his kayaks. He could see clearly over the top of the pod from which he had fallen that the center one was empty and had been torn apart. The covering hung to the frame in tatters.

He ran along the dock to the other side of the boats. The pod on the other side was empty, too. He turned and looked back at the Dryad. Assuming that he was the victim of some kind of joke, he smiled at her and nodded his head up and down.

"All right," he said with a sheepish grin, "the joke's on me. Where are Lochen and Sean?"

"Who?" asked the Dryad.

"Yeah, right. You know who. Lochen and Sean. The two guys who are with me."

"There was no one with you," she told him. "You were quite alone."

"What?" he shouted.

It was beginning to sink in that no joke was being played. He ran towards the Dryad and the small crowd behind her quickly backed away. She stood her ground, but assumed a defensive fighting position. As soon as Quinn saw her reaction, he slowed down. The color drained from his face.

"Please," he pleaded. "This is not a time for playing tricks. Enough is enough, now. Where are they?"

"We are playing no tricks," answered the Dryad. "Your ship was empty except for you. No one was with you; not even when you were found out at sea."

"That's not possible," he shouted, panic creeping into his voice. "Where are they?"

Chapter sixteen

nce Quinn fully understood the possibility that Lochen and Sean had been lost somewhere at sea, he was frantic. The Dryad who had discovered him took him to the palace and debated about what to do next. Her Princess was nowhere to be found and the Enchantress was paralyzed with grief. She decided to take Quinn to the Commander of the Guards. It was then that she was informed of the Enchantress' miraculous recovery and the arrival of two other strangers. The Commander directed the Dryad to take Quinn to the Enchantress.

By the time she found Stella, Quinn was in a high state of agitation. He had been frustrated by being shuffled from one person to another. All the while Sean and Lochen were still lost and no one had started looking for them. As soon as he saw Stella, he strode up to her, waving his arms and shouting.

"We need to go look for them," he demanded, without explaining who they needed to go look for.

Stella let him rant for a few seconds, and then finally got him calmed down to the point where she could get a better idea of what had happened. He explained how he and Sean had found Lochen and then how they ended up at sea. He related his last recollection of them and what he had discovered when he woke up at the docks. He repeated his demand about going off to look for Sean and Lochen.

"No," she told him, "we can't go look for them."

"We can't...what...How can you say that?" he stammered, dumbfounded by her rejection. "They're my friends. They're OUR friends. We <u>have</u> to go look for them. I can't believe you'd just do nothing."

"When did they get lost?" she asked as she stared starkly up at him. Her voice was calm and rational.

"Uh – I don't know exactly," he stammered. "I was asleep. It was sometime after dark. I think. What difference does it make?"

"Where exactly did they get lost?" she continued.

"At sea!" he shouted even louder. Her matter-of-fact attitude was infuriating him. "I already told you that. You know? That big bunch of water that's all around this island? The same place you found me. Out there."

"I know you told me they were lost at sea. Where exactly at sea? It's an enormous sea. Where should we start, aside from "just north of here?" Which way was the wind blowing when they were lost? Which way was the tide moving? How close to shore were you?" She hammered him with questions.

"I don't know! I don't know! I don't know!"

He shouted as he grabbed his head and shook it from side to side, stomping around in a circle. Summer and Liam looked on in shock. It was evident that he could take no more questions. He needed to act.

Summer finally interjected, "He already told you that it must have happened at night. That's why he doesn't know exactly where or when. What do you expect him to say?"

Stella swiped her hand across the air in front of Quinn's face and said, "Sit."

At first nothing happened. Quinn just looked at her blankly, his face sagging. She swiped her hand again, this time closer to his face and repeated her command. He slowly calmed down. He looked around the room for a few seconds and then sat in a nearby chair, remaining quiet and subdued. Stella looked from him to her hand and muttered, "It's leaving me." Then, before anyone could ask what she meant, she turned to Summer and Liam.

"I know they are our friends and I understand that he's told us as much as he knows. I would like as much as either of you to find them, but where do we start and how long do we search? The truth is that we may never find them."

"You can't know that," said Liam. "And even so, that doesn't mean we shouldn't at least try. They were on their way here to help. We can't turn our backs on them."

"I would never turn my back on them. But I am bound to my Princess. I must find her first. My powers are fading and may be lost forever, unless I find Natalie. I am unable to make any connection with her, even in my Sanctorum. If I can't connect with her, I'll never be able to conjure an image of Sean and Lochen."

She gestured to Quinn as an example of her diminishing strength. Her first spell had limited effect, requiring that she cast it again.

"I can do nothing to help find Sean and Lochen, even if I knew where to start," she continued. "Right now, I believe Solveig can lead me to Natalie. I don't like the thought of having to choose whom to search for first, but I have to go where I think there's at least a chance of finding one of them. If I try to lead a search in that expanse of ocean, I'll be wasting time that would be better spent searching for Natalie. As painful as this is, I must find the Princess before I can do anything else."

She was met with silence for several seconds.

"Us," said Summer, finally.

"What?" asked Stella.

"You said Solveig can lead you to Natalie. She can lead _us_ to Natalie."

It hurt her to the core to admit that searching for Sean and Lochen would have to wait, but she knew Stella was right. She trusted that Solveig had some kind of link with Natalie and they had a good chance of finding her. Sean and Lochen, on the other hand, could be anywhere. She turned to Liam who had said nothing during all of this. She wasn't sure how he felt. She knew how hard this must be for him, too.

"We need you, too," she said to Liam. "Stella is right. Solveig brought us here for a reason. She must know how to find Natalie. If we can do that quickly, then we can get back here and search for Sean and Lochen. If we wait too long, Solveig might lose her connection to Natalie and we might end up losing all three of them. This is a horrible decision to make. And if we split up, who goes with whom and where?"

Liam knew he could find just about anything – on land. Two people lost at sea – who knew where – were another matter. Besides, he could find his way if he had a destination. Maybe they were right. If Stella was, in fact, losing her powers, she would not likely be much help in a search for Sean and Lochen. On the other hand, if she could rebuild her powers, they might stand a better chance at a later search.

"You're right," he finally said. "It will be tough to convince Quinn, but let me handle that. I think I can get through to him."

"It's settled, then," said Stella. "Let's not waste any more time. We need to get Solveig and see what we have to do next."

"We still need to rest," objected Liam.

"You can rest on the way; for now come with me," Stella said to him over her shoulder as she hurried to get Solveig.

When they entered the room where Solveig had been sleeping, she was already awake and sitting up. But she was still in a trance-like state. As soon as they walked in she stood up. Without a word she walked out of the room and out of the palace. The others followed her. Liam ran back and got Quinn, pulling him by the arm in his semi-conscious state, struggling to catch up to the others.

Great, he thought. Two of us in a trance and the only other one of us with any real powers is losing them. And no one knows where we're going. At least we'll be on our way before Quinn wakes up. That will make convincing him a little easier.

Solveig led them silently back to the *West Wind* and climbed aboard. The others piled in. Liam guided Quinn over the bulkhead and seated him near the stern. He then untied the moorings and set the sail. Solveig resumed her post at the front of the ship and simply pointed to the south, repeating her mantra of "Must hurry; must find the Princess." Liam set course and then Stella came to the tiller and relieved him, telling him to get the rest he needed. Totally confused and too tired to argue, he went below and was asleep within seconds.

Summer, still torn by having to make a choice that abandoned her closest friend, flew back up to the crow's nest for no other reason but to be by herself. She sat with her back to the wall of the nest and began to second-guess her decision. Her eyes filled with tears at the possibility that she may never see Sean again. Eventually, the exhaustion of the last few days overcame her, and she, too was asleep.

Quinn sat in the stern with Stella, slowly coming out of his stupor. Stella used this opportunity, while he was still groggy and less likely to argue with her, to convince him that they needed to save Natalie before they could rescue Sean and Lochen. In doing so, she saved Liam this daunting task. As she spelled things out, and because he was too numb to disagree, the wisdom of this difficult choice sunk in.

By midday, everyone had rested and come to terms with the decision that had been made. Solveig had not changed her position as the *West Wind* followed the coast line heading due south. Liam had never been in this direction or this far before, but he had a sense that they would come to a cape before long and reach the point where the Cerulean Sea met the Viridian Ocean. He had traveled far enough in the Swamp to know that the two bodies of water bordered the land. It only made sense that at some point they would meet. At that point a course change of some kind would be necessary. Maybe then, depending on which way they went, he'd have an idea of where they were headed.

------------------ *** ------------------

They had flown all through the night, and as dawn broke all Natalie could see was ocean. She couldn't see behind her, but she doubted the view was any different. She was unaware of any large bodies of land this far south. Where were they going, she wondered. Her body ached from being hauled like a sack of potatoes over the neck of the Yder, and her head hurt where Bacham had grabbed a handful of her hair to keep her from escaping. Finally, off in the distance she could see an island. That seemed to be their destination. It certainly didn't look like it was a place to rest.

She had noticed that several times during this trip, Bacham had taken something out of a pocket inside his cloak and examined it. He pulled it from the pocket and held it behind her head so she couldn't see what he was doing with it. She was only able to get a glimpse of what he was doing, but every time he did that, they made a slight change in direction. And every time he did that, she felt a wave of energy pass through her.

What she couldn't see was that he had the shattered piece of stone from Meri's pendant hung by a string. He would dangle it from his hand and watch where the pointed end faced. He now was certain that the stone pointed the way to Tebaga and that his long journey was coming to an end. The time it took for the stone to stop spinning and point the way was less and less the further they traveled. Now it seemed riveted on its target.

He looked at the small team that was flying with him in a loose formation. There were only six with him; only six remained after the demolition of the cavern and the tidal wave. He had lost many of his trusted soldiers on this journey, but he was convinced it would be a worthy sacrifice. The remainder of his amassed army waited for him back at their base. He had brought only those who he trusted most on this mission; those that would understand the sacrifices that needed to be made. He was also convinced the sacrifices were not yet over.

As they approached the island, he could see that it was completely isolated. There were no other landmasses of any size or description visible in any direction. The atoll was shaped like a large elongated teardrop – about a mile wide and less than two miles long. The tip stretched northward and was long, narrow and flat, gradually sloping upward toward a single mountain. The rounded part of the island was barren and rocky. There was no shore on three quarters of the island, and, instead, featured a sheer cliff of over three hundred feet above the water. The top of the cliff tapered off into the crest of the mountain.

The mountain itself, like the island, was devoid of any vegetation. Nothing grew anywhere on this island. The sandy shore of the north tip blended into volcanic rock that glistened in the sunlight. The giant cone rose up into the sky nearly nine hundred feet, tapering off at the top. In the center of the mountain was a large caldera, nearly a half-mile wide.

As Bacham and his men circled the island and flew over the opening, it was clear that this had been a volcano. It remained to be seen if it was still active. Bacham thought not. He pulled the stone from his pocket and this time, instead of pointing in a single direction, as they hovered over the caldera, the stone spun around and around.

Bacham was positive that Tebaga was deep inside that opening and the easiest way to get there was the most direct. He turned his Yder to the opening. However, once the Yder approached the opening, even flying several hundred feet above it, it began to screech and jerked away, almost throwing Bacham off its back. Frustrated, he pulled on the reins and forced the animal back towards the opening. Try as he might, he could not get the Yder to enter it. He made several passes; each time he was unsuccessful. The others were circling at a greater distance, waiting to follow his lead. Reluctantly, he gave up on the idea of flying into the caldera, and attempted to land on the shore.

He circled the island, gradually descending. When he was about thirty feet from the surface, he turned towards the strip of beach. The Yders fought this direction as well. They got within a few feet of setting down on the sand, but would then pull away and veer off over the water or upwards back to the sky. Not to be denied his quest, Bacham forced the Yders back to the shore. He used both hands, pulling with all his strength on the reins.

Natalie took this opportunity to make a move. When Bacham's Yder rebelled and jerked away, requiring Bacham to focus his attention on holding the reins and forcing the Yder towards the sand, she pushed and kicked and narrowly slipped under his arms. Remembering how he stopped her the last time, she yanked her head to one side as he swung his arm down and reached for her hair. This time he only grabbed air.

Bacham was furious. He watched as Natalie dropped nearly thirty feet to the sand below. He could not let her escape, even though she really had no place to go. She was critical to his plans to free Tebaga. He was furious to have come this close only to have his plans foiled. His rage overcame him. He pulled on the reins, forcing the Yder back towards the shore. When the Yder pulled away again, in one swift motion, he unsheathed his double headed axe from his back and swung it in a wide arc, severing the head from the Yder's body.

The head dropped to the ground, bouncing and rolling to a stop not far from where Natalie had landed. She was struggling to her feet. The fall had been much further than she had expected and her landing had not been so soft. Her arms were still bound to her side, but she was confident that she would still be able to swim. She only hoped that once underwater, she would be able to find some coral or a clamshell with which she could cut the bindings. After that, she could only guess what to do. She had no real idea of where she was or how far from her home she was.

She was finally on her feet. She looked at the mountain ahead of her and at the sand around her. She glanced up just in time to see this large dark object hurtling down towards her. She side stepped it and was struck numb when she saw that it was the head of one of the Yders. The reins were still in its mouth. She looked back up to see it had come from the one on which she had been riding. The remains of the Yder were above her, as was Bacham and the other Rebbercands.

Headless, the Yder's body remained aloft for several seconds. The wings flapped erratically as the body spasmed. Bacham slid down the neck and over the missing head, plummeting to the ground. The body of the Yder eventually stopped moving and dropped into the sea. Bacham landed several feet from Natalie, who had gotten over the shock of nearly being crushed by a falling head and the horror that had immediately preceded that, and was tripping as she ran through the sand towards the water. He strode over to her quickly but somewhat casually and pushed her from behind, throwing her to the ground. Before she could move, he took one more quick step and held her there pinned to the ground with his large boot in the middle of her back. He called up to the others who were circling. He motioned for them to join him. One by one, the next three each slid off their mount and landed in the sand. As they did, their beasts screeched and flew off.

The remaining three tried to force their Yders closer to the sand to allow for an easier landing. In each case, the Yder rebelled. The head on the beach only added to whatever fears they had of the island. Meeting with the same resistance as their leader, they followed his example. With a rapid slash each of them destroyed the beast he had been riding. Like the first one, two more heads joined the first to litter the beach as the bodies dropped into the sea.

The last rider tried one more time to get closer before he lopped off the head of his animal. As he started to make the jump he swung his axe as his leader and comrades had done, but this Yder had seen what had happened to its sisters. At the last minute she dropped her head and dove for the ground, turning in a somersault in mid air, throwing her rider and escaping unharmed. The rider was not so fortunate. Turned completely upside down, he failed to straighten in time. He released his grip on his axe in an attempt to avoid landing on it and tossed it away from him. However, he failed to throw his axe a safe enough distance away or in the right direction. He landed flat on his back with a thud. He opened his eyes in time to see that his axe followed immediately after him. He was unable to move fast enough and could only watch as it landed, centered in his chest, splitting him nearly in half.

"Not a good omen," commented one of the remaining five to Bacham, as they all stared uneasily at their fallen comrade.

"Neither carelessness nor stupidity is an omen," barked Bacham, attempting to diffuse the superstitious murmurings.

Bacham dismissed any further discussion, and surveyed his surroundings. Slightly more than a third of the mountain was reachable from the shore. The rest quickly rose into a sheer wall of rock. There was no apparent way in. He reached down in his anger and frustration, and jerked Natalie to her feet.

262

"Thank you, Princess, by the way, for showing us how to dismount," he said to her sarcastically, as he ripped the gag from her mouth. "I guess you won't be needing this anymore."

"You're welcome, you filthy butcher," she spat at him. "And how exactly do you expect to get back, genius?"

He brought the back of his hand in a wide arc, smacking the side of her face. The blow knocked her off her feet. He reached down and jerked her into the air, pulling her within inches of his face.

"Don't make me regret taking your gag off," he hissed between clenched teeth.

"She's got a point, my lord," said the one who had commented about the omen. "How are we getting back?"

Bacham turned on him and glared at him. The soldier took a step backwards and lowered his head, deciding not to press for an answer. Once the rest of his group had gathered around him, he looked each of them over and then turned his attention to the mountain. He saw no opening in the rocks that faced them.

"N'ald," he ordered the one who had spoken up, "since you're so eager to find a way off of this island, go and search the eastern side of the mountain. See if there is any entrance or opening that's hidden from view; or if you can see a pathway to the top."

Glad to be away from Bacham's withering glare, he ran off without a word along the shoreline towards the east side of the volcano. He hadn't gone more than about twenty yards when the sand turned soft and he began to sink. At first he thought he had just run into a dip in the earth. He kept running forward, but he also continued to sink. It was like he was running in shallow water. Within seconds, though, the sand was up to his mid thigh.

He was unable to go any further. He looked back at his leader, who was paying him no heed. Too embarrassed or afraid to call out, he twisted his body and tried to turn back the way he had come. When he only sunk deeper, he struggled in every direction to reach more solid ground. He pulled his axe from the sling on his back and lunged forward with it, hoping to sink it into solid ground and pull himself free. It sliced into the sand without resistance. He let it go before it cut into his leg, and it sunk deep into the sand – lost.

It felt like his feet were weighted in lead. He was able to turn them with great difficulty, but he couldn't lift them. He fell forward with his arms outstretched trying to swim or to reach ground his axe might have missed. Instead of touching anything he could grasp to pull himself free, he sunk even further. His fear soon overcame his pride and he shouted for help. Bacham and the others looked to where the shouts had come only to find their comrade nearly chest deep in sand and disappearing fast. Two ran towards him in an effort to free him.

"Stop, you fools," shouted Bacham. "You don't know where the safe land ends. Do you want to end up like him?"

They stopped as suddenly as they started and inched their way back. One of the others snapped his whip to its full length. The tip landed within N'ald's reach. He wrapped it around his hands and tried to pull himself free. He started to pull the whip's owner in with him. The rest of the men grabbed on to the handle to help, but even with four of them pulling, they could not extricate him. It was as if a stronger force was sucking him downward.

"Kick," they shouted.

"I can't," he answered.

The fear in his voice was thick. They pulled harder as the end of the whip held by the four men slowly began to slide through their hands until it sprung free. As it did, N'ald vanished beneath the sand, the handle of the whip trailing after him.

Bacham thought for a minute, and then concluded that the western side of the shore was just as likely to be a trap. If there was a safe way to the mountain, he guessed it would be straight forward, but he wasn't about to risk himself. To risk another one of his men might weaken the resolve of the rest of them. He tore another whip from the belt of one of his other soldiers and tied the end around Natalie's waist. Then he pushed her forward down the center of the strip of sand towards the mountain.

"This should give us some insurance," he announced to his remaining men.

"Another example of your bravery?" asked Natalie sarcastically.

She didn't wait for an answer – or another slap. She turned abruptly and marched across the expanse to the mountain. She displayed much more courage than she felt, keeping her eyes focused on the mountain ahead of her. One step after another, it seemed like she walked for miles, but it was less than thirty feet. She breathed a sigh of relief when she reached the rocks at the base without as much as a hint of any other quicksand. The others quickly began to follow.

"How do you know I wasn't small enough to cross without sinking?" she shouted to them.

They all froze in their steps until Bacham led the way, holding tightly onto his end of the whip. If she was right, he was going to be certain he pulled her in with him. He made it across without incident.

Once they all crossed the expanse of sand, Bacham again studied the sheer rock face before him. This close he was able to see that the sparkling that he had seen from the air was hardened volcanic ash. The glistening wasn't pockets of water as he had suspected. Instead, it was caused by crystallized lava that formed razor sharp edges all over the surfaces. He reached a gloved hand out and rubbed it gently across a nearby boulder. The glove came away sliced to ribbons. Some of the cuts had gone through the leather into the flesh. Bacham hadn't even felt them. He watched as drops of his blood seeped through the gashes in the glove. He looked again at the side of the mountain, searching for alternatives, but seeing none. He turned to the man nearest him.

"Ranaul, climb up to see if you can find any openings or other footholds." Sensing hesitation on Ranaul's part, he cautioned, "Be very careful. These rocks can cut like knives."

Ranaul put his gloves on and then took a pair from one of the others and put them on over his own. He adjusted his armor and carefully began to climb. He proceeded slowly, making sure not to slip or slide his hands across the rocks. Even so, he spotted nicks and scrapes that he never felt. The blood coming from these small cuts made his hands slippery. The going was slow, but he managed to avoid being severely cut, or worse - falling. He had gone nearly a third of the way up when he discovered that the volcanic rock ended. There were even niches that could be used to assist in climbing. As far as he could see towards the top, it appeared that the most treacherous part of the climb was over. A wave of relief flooded over him. He turned to look down at his leader.

"My lord," he shouted. "Once past this point the way is much easier. The sharp rock ends here and the way is clearer."

As he spoke, a low rumbling sound began and faint tremors could be felt beneath their feet. It seemed to come from deep below the island. The wind began to blow, coming from nowhere, although the sky remained clear. Bacham looked back along the shore and could see the water beginning to swirl around the atoll. At first it looked like a simple storm except for the unchanged sky, but as he watched he could see the level of the water rising, creeping across the sand and covering it. The entire island began to shudder. The reverberations were slowly becoming more violent.

Ranaul hugged the side of the mountain. His earlier elation quickly evaporated. He was too far from the top to keep climbing and he was worried that if the tremors continued, or worse, increased, his hold would be shaken loose. He started to climb down, moving faster than he should have. Another spasm shook the island and one of his hands slipped. The edge of the rock sliced through both gloves and deep into his hand as he reached to steady himself. He tried to move faster. In his haste he stepped on a loose crag that gave way. His body spun sideways and the rocks cut deeply into his knee, thigh and side. He stopped moving, hanging by one hand until he could get a better footing.

The double glove on his uninjured hand was making it difficult to maintain a strong grip and his hand was tiring. It was difficult to hold on safely. Just as he released his grip with this hand, the island shook again. He lost his balance as well as his footing and began to slide downward. His chin struck the side of the mountain and was quickly cut away. Within seconds the razor-like rocks shredded his leather armor and began to strip away at his skin. He dropped faster and faster, all the while the crystallized lava rocks kept slicing at him. He tried to grasp the rocks as he plummeted downward, but his hands were both instantly cut down to the bone. His comrades watched in horror as he was literally shredded to nothing before he reached the bottom. It happened so fast he wasn't even able to cry out.

Even Bacham was in shock. With great difficulty he forced himself to look away and back at the shore, which was disappearing under the water. The ocean was churning in a counterclockwise motion around the mountain and sweeping the long narrow strip of sand under its wake.

"Any more bright ideas," Natalie taunted him. "This one has worked out so well for you and the rest of these fools."

In his fury and frustration he grabbed her by the throat and lifted her in the air above his head.

"Don't try my patience," he shouted at her.

"My lord," interjected one of the remaining soldiers, "we must act quickly and wisely. There is little time."

Bacham forced himself to regain control. She had been irritating him far too long, but he still needed her. He lowered Natalie to the ground, looked back at the advancing sea and then up at the apparently insurmountable mountain. That witch has made a fierce stronghold, he thought about Meri's spell.

"Stay close together," he ordered. "We will ride the ocean above this cursed rock to the top of the mountain. Lock arms so that none of us is washed away."

"What about the Sprite?" asked one of the soldiers.

"She can do what she likes," he snarled.

He didn't bother to hold on to Natalie or pay any more attention to her. What good would it do to save her if he was lost in the process? Besides, there was no place for her to go. He locked arms with his remaining three men as the water swirled around their feet and then slowly rose higher and higher. Soon they were floating and were being washed around the volcano. The eddy sometimes drove them perilously close to the razor edges of rock. They kicked in unison any time the water pushed them in that direction, propelling them to a safe distance, but not too far. Out of desperation, Natalie held on to the soldier furthest away from Bacham. She hoped that at some point she might be able to swim away from them, but for now, she needed their help to avoid the same fate as Ranaul.

Before long the water had risen past the point of the razor rock and Bacham directed his team to kick towards the mountain. As they reached the edge of the slowly disappearing land, they released their grip on one another. Somehow, Bacham and managed to position himself next to Natalie and grabbed her before she could escape. They crashed into the side of the mountain with the crush of the water, but managed to hold on.

They all found niches and footholds, and started climbing to stay ahead of the rising ocean. They scrambled towards the top. Bacham shouted to them to head for the highest point of the caldera rim. He released Natalie from his grip and made sure she was immediately in front of him. He goaded her whenever she appeared to slow down. Their leather armor, their gloves and boots were all soaked and heavy with the salt water. The weight pulled at them as they climbed. Bacham was in the lead, followed closely by two of the remaining three.

The last one in the group was lagging too far behind. He was gasping for breath. He had the wind knocked out of him when he collided with the mountainside and he had fought ever since to stay about the water. His hands kept slipping. The water was lapping at his heels when it wasn't flooding over his head. Finally, the muscles in his hands, arms and legs failed him as they grew numb. The water washed over him and swept him under, driving him deep below the surface. Bacham and the two remaining soldiers were unaware until they reached the crest of the caldera.

Natalie reached the top first, climbing to the highest point of the rim circling the volcano opening. She staggered to a halt, staring into the gaping mouth of the chasm. The three Rebbercands came up immediately behind her, too focused on the whirlpool racing around the mouth of the opening to notice their companion had disappeared. The water was flooding into the opening. It cascaded over the edge and continued its swirling motion down the sides of the shaft to the bottom. Only the crag on which the four were standing was still above water. Natalie had lived all her life in and around water. For her, this was almost like returning home. Without a second thought she dove headfirst into the rushing water and was drawn down deep inside the volcano's central shaft.

Chapter seventeen

It took most of the day for the *West Wind* to reach the cape that marked the point where the Cerulean Sea met the Viridian Ocean. They had not yet arrived at the port town, but they had started to see other ships of all kinds passing in both directions. Almost all of them dwarfed the West Wind, and Liam gave them all a wide berth. He had suggested putting in to the port city on the southernmost tip of land. Not certain where they were headed, he had suggested that another boat might be more appropriate – something bigger and more durable than what they were currently using.

"No," said Stella. "We are nearing the town of Nohkmar Cambin. Not everyone here is friendly towards Sea Sprites, faeries in particular, or other strangers in general. There are many visitors whose trustworthiness and honesty are questionable. I am sure you are quite capable of defending yourself, as may be Quinn. However, the rest of us would be of little help should a larger party decide to take advantage of us. In fact, some of us may be more of a burden. It's just too much of a risk."

Liam thought about her concerns. He wasn't convinced things were as dangerous here as Stella believed.

"I don't understand. You mean to say between the powers you and Solveig have, and the hexes Summer can put on just about anyone, you don't think we could take care of ourselves?" he asked.

"I don't doubt everyone's bravery," answered Stella, "but you forget. Solveig has fallen deeper and deeper into some kind of trance as time has passed. I'm not confident that her senses or her powers would return to her if we were faced with a threat. As for myself, I can feel my power draining from me. It started when my connection with Princess Natalie was broken. It will continue to fade the longer we are separated. It also diminishes any time I try to use it, so I can't be of much help. That leaves Summer. I am sure she would be valiant, but alone she would be no match for the treachery that exists in this village. Faerie dust and a hex here or there won't be enough protection."

Liam had to admit that she made a strong argument. Since he had never been here before, he had no choice but to defer to her. He was still concerned whether his small boat would stand up to whatever they may encounter if they remained at sea for much longer. It was made for the Swamp, not the ocean. It had performed better than he expected, but it was beginning to show the stress of a long trip.

He looked over at Quinn, who hadn't moved from his spot on the side of the boat since he boarded, except to relieve Liam. He did this only when asked and then complied without comment. Other than that, he just sat around moping. It was clear that he felt responsible for the disappearance of Sean and Lochen and still was not convinced that their current journey was the right thing to do.

He looked up to the crow's nest and could see only the edges of Summer's wings. Like Quinn, she had found a place of solitude and had

271

remained there out of contact with everyone. He hadn't seen or talked to her since they left the Sea Sprite's island. She was dealing not only with their inability to search for and rescue their two lost friends, but with the disappearance of everyone in her village as well.

His gaze shifted to Solveig, who had taken position at the bow of the boat and stood like a statue staring straight ahead. The only time she spoke or made any movement was when they slowed down or needed to change direction. She hadn't eaten or slept since she first went into this trance. She hadn't even moved when they hit a wave and the water sprayed over the bulkhead and hit her in the face. Over the course of their trip so far, she had gotten soaked several times and had been dried off by the wind.

He finally concluded that Stella was right. Solveig would be an added liability in the town, and would have to be left on the boat, which meant someone would have to stay with her – probably Stella. Summer might attract too much unwanted attention and would have to stay out of sight. That left him and Quinn. If there was any trouble on shore, they would likely be doomed. He approached her with another idea.

"Look, I agree that we might be hard pressed in a fight, and it might not be a good idea for all of us to go ashore; but we don't know exactly where we're going or how long it's going to take. We've been lucky so far in that the weather has been good and the sea has been calm. Can you know for certain that won't change?"

"Of course not," admitted Stella.

"The sail is starting to tear. That needs to be repaired or it's not going to hold much longer. We've got a small leak below deck – it's not serious," he said as soon as he saw a look of panic on her face, "but it needs to be resealed. We stocked enough food before we left – at least I hope we did, but it seems for now we're all right. Still, I need to get stuff to repair the ship, and we could use some more fresh water."

"What do you suggest?" Stella asked.

"Something simple. Let's pass the port and pull ashore a few miles on the other side. Quinn and I can go ashore and get what we need. It won't take long, and we'll attract less attention than any one of you three."

Stella looked at Quinn. He was slumped at the back of the ship with a forlorn look on his face, still dressed in clothing from the Ice Kingdom, including a fur-lined hood. Stella turned back to Liam and gave him a quizzical look.

"I said less attention. I didn't say we wouldn't attract any attention. Besides, if this port is the center for as many different places as you think, then we won't stand out any more than anyone else."

"And what do you suggest the rest of us do in the meantime?"

"Drop us off on shore with Summer, and then take the boat out a safe distance and set anchor. You don't have to sail it. You can just pedal it, to make it easier. Summer can hide in the brush until we return, and then fly out to let you know we're back. You come back to shore to pick us up; I make the needed repairs; and we're back on track. We can probably do all this in just a couple of hours."

Stella thought about his proposal, trying to find the flaws. She looked up at the sail and could see several small tears near the top and some fraying along the side. He was right, she thought. We have no idea how much further we have to travel or under what conditions. It would be wise to be as prepared as possible. She looked at Solveig, back at Quinn and then up to where Summer had secluded herself. We also need to have a purpose, she thought. Our depression is destroying us.

"All right," she agreed. "But be careful and keep a close eye on Quinn. I'm worried that he still feels responsible for Sean and Lochen."

A few hours later they had changed course to round the cape of Nohkmar Cambin, passing well out of the range of the nearby ships. They followed the coastline to the northwest, in spite of Solveig's repeated pointing further to the south and her chanting of "Turn this way. Must find the Princess. Turn around."

Stella did her best to calm her, holding her hand. It seemed that her touch was enough. She was reluctant to cast a spell. She was concerned about what effect it might have on Solveig in light of whatever had caused the trance; and she was worried about losing her powers completely. Solveig sat down, lowered her head and seemed to sleep, even though her eyes never closed. She remained in this position as Liam maneuvered the boat to the shore. Once they were in shallow water, he lowered the wheels and rode it up on land. Quinn and Summer got out and waited as Liam showed Stella how to return the boat to the sea, retract the wheels and pedal it out a short way.

Summer perched on a rock near the edge of the forest. Even the chance to be on solid ground for a short while did nothing to lift her spirits. She sat with her chin propped up in her hands and her elbows on her knees. She was a picture of misery.

"I hope you know what you're doing," she said to them as they headed back towards Nohkmar Cambin.

She watched them walk off and kept watching them until they disappeared from sight. She had a very uncomfortable feeling, but couldn't identify what was unsettling her. It was more than the recent troubles that was nagging at her. She couldn't identify it and before long, she gave up trying.

"I might as well get comfortable," she said to herself, looking around at the low-lying plants that lined the shore.

She saw large leafy plant with a large, bright yellow flower. That looks just about the right size, she thought, and flew over to it. The flower was large enough for her to crawl into. The petals felt like silk and the aroma of the plant was mild and sweet. It reminded her a lot of her home. Instead of making her sad, though, the thought seemed to warm her up inside. She stretched out on the large, soft petal just under the stamen dangling over her head. She looked at the layers of pollen that covered the filament. She had never seen so much pollen in one flower before. She loved pollen. She reached up and grabbed a handful. It tasted wonderful. This wasn't such a bad idea after all, she thought.

She was resting comfortably, lying on her back with her head propped up on a fold in one of the petals. She was enjoying her snack when she heard a low rumbling sound. She looked up at the sky and saw nothing but bright blue. It's not thunder, she said to herself. The rumbling stopped and she gave it no more thought. Then a few seconds later it started again. This time it was a little louder, a little higher pitched, and sounded a little closer.

"What is that?" she asked out loud.

She sat upright and covered her ears with her hands, but couldn't block out the sound. It was growing even louder, and was starting to hurt her ears. Before she knew it, a large shadow fell over her and the flower. She looked up into the eyes of a giant honeybee. It was moving its enormous head right into the flower where she was sitting.

"Whoa," she shouted. "What the...?"

She scrambled to her knees. It was too late for her to escape. The bee was several times her size and was almost completely blocking her exit. She backed further into the flower, trying to hide behind the stamen, but it was too thin and spindly to offer any protection. The bee was inching itself further and further into the flower. In a last desperate effort, she pulled some faerie dust from her pocket and blew it into the bee's face.

It backed out immediately and the buzzing sound intensified. Its antenna raised and it looked ready to attack. It was clearly irritated and looking for something to sting. Summer focused hard and changed her coloring to blend with the flower, and then shot past the bee. It seemed not to have seen her and she looked for another hiding place, as the bee turned towards her searching for its attacker.

Summer darted one way and then the next, trying to change her coloring to hide from the bee. The bee was not fooled. It matched her move for move. It didn't exactly see her, but could sense her motion. She needed to stop moving, she realized when she saw that it was imitating her every movement. She zipped down towards a long narrow purple flower. Hovering over it, she quickly peeked inside and saw no stamen and no pollen. Good, she thought as she shot inside and flattened herself against one of the rather fuzzy petals. Her wings folded down and faded into the background, making her nearly invisible.

After a few seconds, she peeked over the edge and saw the bee turning back and forth, and circling around the yellow flower. It hadn't noticed her move to her hiding place and eventually gave up, flying off to find another flower. Summer sank back deeper into the petals and gave a sigh of relief. That was too close for comfort. She had never seen a bee so big before. What a nightmare.

She flopped her head down and caught her breath and tried to slow her heartbeat down. She had been so worn out fretting over the disappearance of Sean and Lochen and what had happened to her village that her encounter with the bee wore her out. She folded her arms up under her head and closed her eyes for a few seconds, trying to recompose herself. She failed to notice the petals surrounding her slowly begin to close in. Her eyelids were growing heavy. The thick warm air and her exhaustion were making her drowsy. She was on the verge of falling asleep when she thought she felt a slight movement. At first she didn't pay much attention to it, thinking it was just the wind, but when it happened again, she was afraid the bee had returned and discovered her. She slowly opened her eyes to see that the petals around her had closed almost completely. She felt a pressure against her legs and looked down to see the base of the petals closing in on her legs.

"What now?" she shouted. "I don't believe this. I think I'm being swallowed! By a plant!"

She kicked at the petals and clawed her way to the opening. The pressure increased, pushing against her from the front to the back. The petals were moving more quickly and small tendrils that hadn't been apparent before were now wrapping themselves around her legs and pulling her in further. She kicked harder and twisted herself free. She scrambled with all her strength and finally freed herself. She pushed open the petals with all her strength and squeezed out between them.

"What kind of place is this?" she nearly screamed once she was in the open air again, hovering over the innocent looking purple flower.

She surveyed the vegetation in every direction and assumed that none of it was safe, in spite of how appealing it all looked. She flew over to the shore and thought about sitting on the rocks, and then told herself she wasn't going to be fooled again. She spun around looking for something safer and found an open stretch of sand, far enough away from the plants and the tide. She flew over, looked at it closely and then sat there and shifted her head from the plants to the rocks to the water and back again.

For several minutes her head swiveled from one object to the next and back, eyeing everything on the shore. Just as she was able to finally relax, she felt the sand beneath her bottom begin to shift slightly. She spun her head around and looked over her shoulder at the tide, thinking maybe the water level had come this far up and was moving the sand. No. The water was still some distance off. Maybe it was just her imagination.

She tried to relax, but the sand moved again. What now, she asked. She looked at the ground around her and started to see a large oval begin to appear around her. At first it was a slight indentation in the sand, almost as if someone had dug a shallow, narrow trench around her. Then she saw what looked like small sticks start to emerge from the sand outside the oval. They looked like thin stalks of some kind of plant. There were about eight of them – four towards the front of the oval and four behind her at the back of the oval. They rose into the air and then bent at about the midpoint downward to the sand.

"This is not good," she decided.

She slowly got to her feet and then with a surge of her wings, she sprung upward just as the jaws of a large sand Brachus snapped shut. She hovered mere inches above it as it continued to snap blindly at her. She looked at the other plants along the shore, then at the water and back down at the snapping Brachus.

"This is nuts. It can't be any worse where they're going," she said.

She looked up the pathway to where Liam and Quinn had walked to the city. She looked back down at the sand Brachus and shot a blast of faerie dust at it, as a parting shot. The jaws went slack and the entire creature dropped back to the sand. Then she rose higher into the air and darted off in the direction she had last seen them.

"Hey! Guys!" she shouted. "Wait for me."

------------------ *** ------------------

While Summer was settling in on the petals of a large yellow flower, just prior to experiencing her encounter with the giant bee, Quinn and Liam were quickly making their way to the outskirts of the city.

"Let's just get in real quick and get out," said Liam. "We don't need to spend any more time here than necessary. We also don't need to talk to anyone unless it's absolutely necessary. Stay close to me and don't touch anything."

"I'm not stupid, you know," Quinn answered, a bit offended. "I <u>have</u> been to some pretty big cities. I've traveled to different places and I'm still here, aren't I? I think I can take care of myself."

"I didn't say you were stupid," Liam responded. "Or that you couldn't take care of yourself. But remember when I told you not to touch that dragon spadix, and you did. I also told you not to get it wet, and you did."

"I didn't touch it. I just sniffed the flower."

"Yeah? Well don't sniff any flowers and don't touch anything."

Just about then they came around the corner of the edge of the waterfront. The scenery changed from a simple shoreline to the chaos of an enormous central market place. It was filled with all sorts of vendors selling everything imaginable. Booths and stands lined both sides of the streets. Passersby were accosted by hucksters offering "special deals" and "one of a kind" offers. The number and variety of people was mind-boggling. Quinn's mouth dropped open. He had never seen so many people – ever, not in one place.

"Holy blubber on a biscuit," he shouted.

"Not so loud," admonished Liam. "Remember? We're not supposed to attract attention. And stop staring at everyone."

"I know," said Quinn whose head was spinning from one side to the other, trying to take in all the sights. "But I've never seen so many people before - anywhere. Who are they? Where did they all come from?"

A short creature with short, spiky green hair and yellow skin approached them. He was wearing sand colored clothing that looked like a toga with baggy pants. His feet, which looked more like hairy hands, were bare. His face was round and flat with a wide nose separating two tiny close set eyes the same shade of green as his hair.

"Good day, gentlemen, to you, " he said with an odd accent that was hard to understand. "You are looking like two people very intelligent. You have a question for me."

"We're not interested," said Liam, brushing past him.

"There's no need to be rude," said Quinn to Liam.

He turned to the strange looking person and said, "Thank you. We are pretty intelligent. What's your question?"

The stranger reached up and took Quinn by the elbow. He gently steered him out of the main flow of traffic and away from Liam. He pushed through a small group of people towards a small booth selling potions.

"Well, sirree," said the stranger, "the ladies don't they must find you irresistible, yes or not, do you thinks?"

Quinn blushed, "I don't know about that."

"Let me a potion show you that would ensure they do that. And a special deal I am giving me to you because you are being a courteous person as such. I am giving me to you two vials of special love potion this for twenty markers only. Is a price cheap if at more than double this, yes or not?"

"I don't know," said Quinn, "we don't really need two love potions – or even one, really. We're looking for..."

He felt his arm jerked before he could finish the sentence. He was being pulled unceremoniously away from the vendor and his stall and his love potions and his special deal, which was cheap at twice the price. Liam had turned around and saw that Quinn was no longer with him. He quickly doubled back to find him. Seeing him with the little stranger with the green hair and the yellow skin about to be swindled or talked into something, he grabbed Quinn's arm and pulled him away without explanation.

"What did I tell you about attracting attention?" Liam asked, clearly annoyed that Quinn had been distracted at the first opportunity.

"I didn't touch anything," Quinn complained. "We were just talking. I wasn't going to buy anything."

"Don't talk to anyone, OK?"

"What if they talk..."

"Don't talk to ANYONE!" Liam cut him off.

"All right!" Quinn answered in a huff, folding his arms over his chest.

They continued through the market place with Liam looking from one stall to the next until he found a small shop set slightly off the main path between a saloon and a knife shop, which sold sailing materials. There were fishing nets in the two windows that bordered the narrow door to the shop. The nets served as a backdrop to an assortment of sailing needs, which Liam recognized and had included on his shopping list.

"Just stand here and don't move, and don't talk to anyone" he told Quinn, who clamped his mouth shut tightly and refolded his arms.

Liam left Quinn standing at the entrance to the shop as he went in and selected the items he needed. He gathered them up in his arms and took them to the shopkeeper. The vendor told him the cost of the materials and he said he didn't have any money to pay.

"Do you think I run a charity," asked the vendor, as he began to take the items from Liam's hands. "What is it with you young people? I suppose you want to take what you need and pay me later?"

"No," said Liam, "of course not. I have something to trade instead."

"And what would that be?" the vendor asked suspiciously as he moved the items Liam had selected back behind his counter.

Liam unclasped one of the long daggers he carried from his belt, and presented it to the seller.

"This is made from the finest steel, crafted by gargoyles. It is perfectly balanced and the blade is exceedingly sharp. It can cut through just about anything and will never dull. It is worth twice the cost of these materials."

The vendor took the dagger and looked it over. While he was examining it on the inside of his shop, Quinn was being approached by another stranger outside the shop. This one was much older than anyone Quinn had seen before. He was slightly bent over and walked with a cane that he swept back and forth in front of him as he walked. He was only about half of Quinn's height, although that was hard for Quinn to actually tell since the stranger was so bent over.

He had long grey-white hair and a beard to match. He was dressed in dirty grey clothing that hung from his body and looked like it hadn't been washed since the old man was young. He was   walking from one side of the street to the other, swinging his cane back and forth. The cane tapped against Quinn's legs as the man came to the entryway of the shop. When it hit Quinn's legs, he stopped and reached out. His gnarly old hand touched Quinn's arm and ran up to Quinn's shoulder. That was as far as he could reach.

"Oh, my! What a giant you are," said the stranger. "Tall and wide. Where do you come from, my friend?"

Quinn started to answer, his mouth hanging open, the words poised on the tip of his tongue. Then looked over his shoulder at Liam, snapped his head back in the direction of the old man and clamped his mouth shut even tighter.

The stranger was puzzled at Quinn's reaction. He could feel Quinn's movement, and waited patiently for an answer to his question.

"Can you at least tell me if this is the shop of the ship's goods vendor?" he asked, when no answer to his original question was forthcoming.

Again Quinn started to answer, looked over his shoulder at Liam, then turned back to the stranger and kept silent. The stranger began to get offended.

"Are you incapable of speech?" asked the stranger. "Of course. You must be a mute. I mean, if you are, then it's quite understandable that you wouldn't respond to an old man. Are you deaf, too? Oh, how silly of me. If you're a mute you can't answer that question and if you're deaf, you can't hear it."

"I..." Quinn started to answer. He looked back at Liam again and snapped his mouth shut.

"Aha! So you can speak. You what?" asked the man, waiting eagerly for any kind of answer. But Quinn kept silent.

"Do you mock me, sir?" asked the stranger. "Are you having fun at my expense? When one person speaks to another, it's common courtesy for the other person to respond."

When Quinn still didn't answer, the man became angry and smacked his cane against Quinn's foot.

"Can you answer a simple question? I know you can speak," the man said, his voice raising. "And it's obvious you can hear, too. What kind of person pretends to be a deaf mute to an old blind man?"

He was attracting the attention of others passing by. He was only inches away from Quinn, who was trying to reach down and massage the toe the old man had driven his cane into. At the same time he kept looking back in the shop at Liam, who was engaged in conversation with the shop owner.

"What's going on, old man?" asked a burly seaman who happened to be passing by at the same time the old man was giving Quinn a piece of his mind.

"I am seeking the shop of the ship's goods vendor and this man will not answer my questions. I know he speaks, but I believe he is mocking me."

"Is that so?" asked the sailor.

By now the sailor had been joined by two of his friends. The three formed a half circle behind the old man; each of them staring hostilely at Quinn.

"So, stranger, can you answer the old man?" the first one asked.

Quinn started to answer, but remembered Liam's instruction, so stood there silently instead, sneaking peeks over his shoulder into the shop. Within seconds, several others had sensed that something was going on and a small crowd was beginning to form. Some of the less savory individuals in the crowd were hoping a fight would break out and were shouting taunts at both Quinn and the sailors. Quinn was trying to back away, trying to creep into the shop and out of the center of attention.

"Where do you think you're going?" shouted one of the sailors.

Quinn froze and edged back to where he had been standing, trying with all his might not to bump into the old man and make things worse. The crowd started shouting even louder that he was trying to escape, and it began moving in closer. Just before things got out of hand, Liam exited the shop with his supplies.

"What's the problem?" he asked when he saw the angry crowd.

He turned to Quinn and hissed, "What did you do now? NO! Don't answer."

"Your friend here was being rude to the blind man," the sailor shouted over the rumbling of the crowd. "He refused to help him out when the old man asked him a simple question. What's wrong with him?"

Quinn's eyebrows shot up in surprise. His mouth popped open, as he was about to reply. Before he could speak Liam turned to him and motioned for him to remain quiet, swiping his hand across his throat. Quinn wasn't sure if that meant for him not to speak or that someone would cut his throat if he tried to answer. In either case, he got the message and he shut his mouth with an audible snap. Liam then turned back to the sailors and the old man.

"My sincere apologies to you all. My friend here is simple-minded – a fall on his head as a child."

He made a circling motion with the finger of one hand around his ear, implying that Quinn was crazy.

"He has never been quite right and is incapable of normal social graces," he added. "Please be assured, he will be dealt with most severely by...by...his ...ah...Sage."

It was the only thing Liam could think of.

"Let me remove him from your sight immediately, and thank you for your patience."

Before Quinn could say anything or the sailors or the old man could react, Liam hustled Quinn away. Liam was walking as fast as he could, pulling Quinn along by his shirtsleeve. Quinn was stumbling behind him, shifting his head from Liam back to the crowd and back to Liam until they were out of the village.

Once it was clear they were out of earshot, Quinn said, "simple-minded? You told me not to talk to anyone. I was just doing what you said."

Liam was about to respond when he suddenly saw a flutter in the air a few feet ahead of him. It was Summer. What now, he wondered.

"What are you doing here?" he asked. "You were supposed to wait for us back at the shore."

"You wouldn't believe me, even if I told you," she said. "Let's just get out of this place. It's a nightmare. It's worse than a nightmare."

Chapter eighteen

It was several hours after sunrise before the fog had finally cleared and Lochen was able to see that Quinn was nowhere to be found. Sean had curled up into a ball with his head buried in his arms, and hadn't raised his head once. Lochen studied the waves and the motion of the makeshift raft that Sean was on and the log he was straddling. They were barely changing position. For a while they would be pushed westward towards the shore that was still far out of sight, but then the tide would shift and they'd float further out to sea. Without a sail or some other means of propulsion, they were at the whims of the sea, the tide and the winds. They could remain like this for a very long time.

"We have to do something to alter our course," he finally announced to Sean. "I'm afraid you're going to have to get into the water."

With his head still buried, he responded, "I'm already in the water. Look around you. Do you see anything BUT water?"

"That's not what I meant," he said.

He calmly swung his leg over, climbed off the log and dropped into the sea. At the sound of the slight splash, Sean raised his head.

"What are you doing?" he asked and then immediately lowered his head again. "Are you totally whacko? This isn't time to go for a swim."

Lochen moved to the edge of the buoy on which Sean was perched, placed his hands on the side and began to kick.

"We're not changing our position enough," he explained. "In fact we're moving very little. At this rate we'll never reach land. Without a sail, we have to propel ourselves. You can stay up there for a while, but I can't do this indefinitely and will need to rest. We can take turns kicking."

Sean's head popped up again and his eyes widened. "I have to get IN the water? You mean, like, I have to get off this thing and get my body in the water? Where it's wet? You have no idea what you're asking."

"Oh, yes," said Lochen. "As a matter of fact, I'm afraid I do. I wouldn't ask if there was another alternative. Try not to think about it. In fact until I need you to relieve me, forget I even mentioned it."

"Forget you even mentioned it? How do you expect me to do that? You already mentioned it. Was I not supposed to hear you? I'm less than two feet away from you. I'd have to be stone deaf to not have heard you. And if I was stone deaf, I'd probably be able to read lips. In that case, I'd still know what you said. If you wanted me to forget you mentioned it, you shouldn't have mentioned it in the first place." Sean was rambling.

"It's really not that bad," Lochen tried to calm him down. "It's not like you'll be swimming without any support. You'll be holding on to this air pod. Besides that, it's beautiful out today. The sky is clear; the sea is calm – well, relatively calm; there probably aren't any predators in the water below us."

"What?" shouted Sean.

"I guess I shouldn't have said that last part," Lochen reflected. "I'm sure there's no danger. Given the time of year and the water temperature, the likelihood of any predators that would be a threat to us is less than thirty percent, which is why I've volunteered to go first."

"Less than thirty percent?" Sean shouted in disbelief. "Seriously? Then you can go second, too," he shot back.

"As you wish. It will only take us longer to get to safety. It's also possible that any advancement made while I'm in the water may be lost when no one is in the water. But that's up to you."

"Oooh – why me?" wailed Sean, burying his head again. "All right. All right. But I'm not getting in until I absolutely have to."

"Agreed," pronounced Lochen. "I shall swim for as long as I can and only call upon you when absolutely necessary. Once nightfall comes, and I can see the stars, I should have a better idea of exactly where we are."

"Nightfall?" Sean's head popped up again. "You mean we're still going to be doing this after dark?"

"Hmmm," said Lochen, "I suppose I shouldn't have mentioned that either. But, yes, we'll still need to propel ourselves after nightfall. I promise though, there will be far fewer nights if we are both engaged."

"Nights?" Sean moaned. "You mean we'll be out here more than one night?"

Lochen decided not to say anything more. It seemed the more he said, the more he raised Sean's level of anxiety. He turned his attention to the sky and watched the path of the lead sun to determine the way west. He reasoned that this would be the surest direction to find land. The island of the Sea Sprites might be closer, but until he could get a fix from the stars, that was only a guess. The sea's current was carrying them in a southerly direction, so they were headed in the general direction of the island anyway. By paddling westward Lochen calculated that their chances of reaching land one way or the other were greatly enhanced.

After nearly two hours his legs were aching and he had to switch places with Sean. To Sean's credit, he didn't whine too much about having to make the switch. Lochen helped him get into the water and then took Sean's place on the raft. He stretched out and propped his arms behind his head to study the sky.

"You're not going to take a nap, are you?" asked Sean.

"Oh, no," said Lochen dismissively. "I won't need to sleep for several more days. Besides, I don't take naps. When I sleep it's for nearly a week. I suppose if I fell asleep, that would really make things difficult, wouldn't it," he laughed. "Well, difficult for you, I suppose, but not for me. I'd be asleep."

Sean didn't see the humor. The thought of Lochen closing his eyes for even a few seconds made his level of apprehension skyrocket.

"I'll keep my eye on you, just the same," he told Lochen.

They switched back and forth a half-dozen times before night descended on the water. Fortunately, the fog of the previous night didn't return and the stars were sparkling. The moon rose shortly before midnight, which gave Lochen a better constant against which to measure. Sean was paddling while Lochen was on his back staring up at them and making mental calculations.

"There are so many of them," Sean marveled, his eyes riveted to the stars. "How can you tell from them where we are?"

Lochen pointed out key planets and constellations and their positions in the sky compared to the horizon, which was still just barely visible, and the trajectory of the moon.

"Without the right equipment I can only make an estimate," he cautioned, "but it should be fairly accurate."

He spotted Capurnica and pointed it out to Sean. He began to reminisce about their trip to the rings. He had been talking for hours and the dawn was beginning to break. Sean had been leisurely kicking as he listened to Lochen's descriptions and recollections, oblivious to how long he had been swimming.

"Yeah," said Sean, "that was fun, but remember you got us lost."

"Yes," responded Lochen, "but that wasn't entirely my fault. And don't forget, I also got us found."

"I'm not sure that counts," answered Sean. "Besides, let's keep focused on here and now. Where are we and how…"

Something had rubbed across Sean's feet, interrupting him. He froze in place with his mouth open and his sentence unfinished.

"Where are we and how… what?" asked Lochen. "You didn't finish what you were saying. I can't offer any rebuttal or information in response to your query without knowing the entirety of your statement."

"Uh…I think there's something in the water here."

"Well, of course," said Lochen. "Aside from you, there are all sorts of sea creatures in the water. And many that are nocturnal."

"Nocturnal?" asked Sean. "What does that mean?"

"It means they're active at night. They usually sleep during the daylight hours. At night they roam around, most likely looking for food."

"FOOD?" shouted Sean. "I'm food? They're looking for ME? I knew something like this was going to happen."

He started kicking furiously, trying to put some distance between him and whatever was beneath the water checking him out.

"Stop kicking," Lochen told him.

"That's easy for you to say. You're not about to be something's dinner." Sean responded, kicking even more wildly than before.

"Your kicking is imitating a fish or bird in distress and is likely to attract more predators – the kind you would not like to encounter," Lochen said to him. "Give me your hand and get up here."

Sean reached his hand up, but then pulled it back before Lochen could grab it. He froze as he felt another brush against his feet.

"Oh, no! I'm doomed," he declared. "Save yourself. I've been tasted twice. It's only a matter of time before dinner is served. You don't need to be at risk. Move away from me. I'll sacrifice myself."

He pushed the raft away from him and resigned himself to being eaten. He tried to roll onto his back and float away from Lochen, but went too far and only managed to flip completely over and take in a mouthful of water before bobbing upright. The raft in the meantime, however, floated right back to him. Sean wiped the water from his face while he sputtered and gasped for air. Lochen still had his hand outstretched to pull Sean up. It was enough of a sign to make Sean reevaluate his situation. Just as Sean reconsidered his idea of sacrifice and lifted his arm to grasp Lochen's, Lochen knelt back on his heels and lifted his hands to shield his eyes from the breaking dawn. Having decided not to sacrifice himself, Sean reacted to Lochen withdrawing his hand.

"Hey. Wait," he shouted. "I've changed my mind. Give me your hand. Come on! Get me out of here."

Lochen peered closely at the surface of the water.

"I don't think that's a predator," he said.

He had spotted movement just inches under the water. He was certain he recognized the shape and size of whatever it was that had come in contact with Sean's legs.

"You don't <u>think</u> it's a predator? What if you're wrong? If you only think it's not a predator, then change places with me. Otherwise, get me out of here," shouted Sean.

"Hold on," Lochen told him. "There's no need to act rashly. I think I can see what it is. If it makes one more pass, I should be more certain."

Sean was beginning to panic. "Hold on? Another pass? Get certain on your own time. I'm not holding on! You hold on."

He started flailing his arms and kicking wildly again, trying to pull himself up onto the raft. His hands were too wet and the exterior of the raft was too slick. All he could do was paw at it and bounce up and down in the water. All of a sudden, he felt a large, slick body nudge against him. He screamed in terror.

"Oh Momma! I've been eaten. I'm only half of what I was. Please tell everyone I loved them. Except for my uncle Edgar. I never cared much for him. But everyone else…"

"Relax," Lochen shouted over Sean's ranting. "It's only a Tiger Grampus. It won't hurt you. They're not carnivores."

"Oh, no," wailed Sean. "I'm being eaten by some fish's grandfather. And what do I care if it doesn't go to carnivals?"

"It's not a fish," corrected Lochen.

"This is not a time to quibble. I'm being devoured by a vicious beast."

"They're mammals. And I said they're not carnivores. I said nothing about carnivals. They don't eat meat – they don't even eat whatever you are."

Sean stopped moving. He wasn't sure what to be angrier about – the fact that Lochen just now informed him that what he saw didn't eat meat, or his comment about whatever Sean was.

"You couldn't say that sooner?" he asked.

"Well, I suppose I could have," Lochen answered. "But it would have been merely speculation on my part. I wasn't sure until I saw the dorsal fin break the surface."

"So I could have been eaten while you were deciding what that thing was? Somehow I don't find that comforting. I think it's time for you to paddle."

Sean reached up for Lochen's hand as he climbed onto the raft. When he was settled, Lochen slid into the water. He was immediately greeted by a pair of Tiger Grampus. He stroked their sides and began talking to them. They were very responsive, jumping out of the water, spinning and splashing.

"Good morning to you both," he said to them. "I would offer introductions, but I doubt you could remember our names or tell us yours."

"I don't think they care what our names are," grumbled Sean.

"Of course they don't," answered Lochen. "I didn't expect that they would. They are responding to the tone and inflections in my voice. They can sense that I mean them no harm. By speaking to them in a soothing tone, I'm communicating to them in a way they can understand."

"Are you having fun?" asked Sean after several minutes of watching Lochen and the Grampus cavort.

"Actually, yes," he answered. "I studied these fine animals several years ago, and was able to establish a very basic form of communication with them. I've tried to make that connection with these fine creatures. I think it's working. I think they can lead us to the island of the Sea Sprites."

And that they did, but not directly. They enjoyed the company of their two new friends and tended to frolic. Lochen had to admit he was having fun being carried around – pulled by their fins or riding behind them.

They would lift him into the air and then dive beneath the surface. Sean was content to stay on the raft and watch, until he had to remind Lochen that they were on a mission.

"Yes, you're quite right," Lochen agreed.

Even while he had been playing with the Grampus, he had also been watching the horizon. He had noticed a darkening in the distant sky, mixed with flashes of light. A storm was approaching. It was close to sunset, so it was hard to tell for certain, but it seemed to be further south. Lochen hoped it would miss them, but it would be wise not to be on the water on a simple raft just in case. They had been lucky so far. There was no need to tempt fate. He ran his hands along the side of one of the Grampus and spoke softly to it. It seemed to understand. Lochen held on to its dorsal fin, while the other one moved behind the raft and started pushing it with its forehead. Sean had been kneeling on the small pod at the time. The sudden movement pushed him onto his back and he nearly slid off. He struggled to turn over and around and get a firm grip on the front to the raft.

"You could have told me that was going to happen," he shouted to Lochen.

"You didn't ask," Lochen responded.

They skimmed along the water almost as fast as Lochen's spell had propelled their kayaks, and were traveling almost due south. Lochen considered that they must have been closer to the island of the Sea Sprites than he had initially calculated. They maintained their pace through the night and as dawn the next morning broke across the water, the island of the Sea Sprites was visible immediately before them. A small scouting ship had spotted them and sailed out to meet them.

Lochen reluctantly bid farewell to the Tiger Grampus as he and Sean were helped on board the scouting ship. Sean was thrilled to be off the tiny raft and was looking forward to having solid ground under his feet. As they were making their way to the island, Lochen asked if there had been any sign of Quinn. He provided a description and was relieved when the Dryad indicated that a stranger had, in fact, arrived in a very odd looking vessel.

"Is he still here?" Sean asked. "I intend to give him a piece of my mind for leaving us stranded out there."

"I don't think that's necessary," said Lochen.

"No," answered the Dryad, cutting off their discussion. "He left with the Enchantress and three others who had arrived shortly before the giant."

"Three others? Was one of the three a faerie?" asked Sean.

"Yes. It was the faerie Princess Summer. We know who she is. There was someone else with her that I didn't recognize - a noblewoman who seemed to be..." the Dryad was not sure how to describe Solveig's condition. "I mean no offense, but I can only think she was...simple-minded."

"Simple-minded?" Lochen asked.

That didn't sound like Solveig; but who else would have been with Summer? Had she been injured, he wondered. He would have sensed something like that; he was sure. He recalled Sean and Quinn telling him that he had been going off into short mental lapses and making unusual comments. Could that have been connected in some way to Solveig?

"What about the other one?" asked Sean. "Who was that?"

"A hunter of some kind," said the Dryad. "He was dressed oddly and had several weapons attached to his clothing."

"Liam," Lochen said to Sean, both smiling at each other.

"And aside from one of them appearing simple-minded, they were all in good health?" asked Sean.

"Yes," she answered. "They all seemed to be fine."

"Did the simple-minded one have long red hair?" asked Lochen, still worried about the identification of the other member of the group and wondering what had happened to Solveig.

"Yes, she did,"

Sean said back to Lochen, a grin widening across his face. "The other one must be Solveig. They're all together."

"Wonderful," said Lochen. "Everyone is here safe and sound. But I still don't understand why Solveig would appear simple-minded. Please, then, when we make landfall, take us to your Princess. She will certainly be able to explain."

The expression on the Dryad's face fell.

"I'm sorry. I can't do that. Our Princess is gone," she said.

"Oh," said Lochen. "That's unfortunate. I assume she left before the arrival of our friends. Well, then, can you take us to your Enchantress?"

"She's gone, too."

Lochen detected something in the way the Dryad looked and in the tone of her voice.

"I would think it's safe to assume from your expression that the Princess and the Enchantress have not gone on some kind of vacation."

"No. Your assumption is correct."

"I see. Where exactly have they gone, if I might ask?"

The Dryad took a deep breath and tried to control her feelings, but her eyes became misty.

"The Princess has disappeared. No one saw her leave the island, but it appears she did so prior to the sudden storm that covered the island. The Enchantress was devastated by her disappearance. We assumed the worst had happened. The loss of the Princess was bad enough, but the Enchantress was so distraught that she was nearly lost to us as well until the others arrived. She came back to life at that point and then they all left suddenly and without explanation."

"I don't understand," said Sean.

"Nor do I," said Lochen. "Princess Natalie disappeared? Where was she when this happened? Did she disappear from the island?"

"We don't know for certain. Shortly after the giant wall of water was averted by the Enchantress, she collapsed as if she had been mortally wounded. Her connection to the Princess was broken. Such a break almost always happens when a princess dies. Our Princess it seems had gone to the land to save the faeries and the forest creatures from the floods and hadn't returned. We believe that is where she disappeared, although there were no signs discovered by the search parties. The Enchantress was mourning until the three arrived – the hunter, the faerie and the simple-minded one. The simple-minded one – I mean the one in the trance," she corrected herself, "seemed to have cured her. And then they left. All of them, including the giant who had arrived by himself."

"Are the forest creatures safe," Sean asked, realizing for the first time the threat his Lodge has faced.

"We don't know," the Dryad answered.

"You don't know?" Sean asked. "Has no one gone to see?" He was infuriated by the thought that no one seemed to care.

"Of course," answered the Dryad immediately. "Once the wall of water had been diverted, we sent rescuers to both villages immediately. No one was there. It seems they had evacuated long before the danger approached. There was no sign of anyone or of where they might have gone. We searched for days."

Sure, thought Sean. That made sense. They would have known something was coming and gone to higher ground. He returned his attention to Natalie, Stella and the others.

"Where did Stella and the others go?" he asked.

"They didn't say," answered the Dryad. "They only said that the Princess was in some kind of danger and they needed to hurry to save her. In fact the simple-minded one kept repeating this over and over."

"Must hurry; don't stop; must find the Princess," said Sean.

"Exactly," said the Dryad, stunned. "Those were her words exactly. How did you know?"

"I've been listening to the same thing for the last few days."

Lochen recalled that Sean and Quinn claimed he had been saying that, although he had no such recollection. He began to figure out what might have happened.

"I think I understand, now. If Natalie was in some kind of danger, wouldn't she normally make some kind of connection or send a message to Stella?"

"Yes," said the Dryad. "It would have been only normal. They were joined mystically immediately after the birth of the Enchantress. That is their bond. She would not even have to think about it. Such a signal would have happened by itself."

"But no such signal was sent to Stella. Natalie purposely must have sent some kind of distress message to Solveig, instead" he said. "I have to conclude that Natalie was aware of the danger. Could she break the connection herself?"

"Yes. But why would she. It would be extremely painful to the Enchantress."

"Because, for whatever reason, she didn't want Stella to follow her. However, she wanted to warn the rest of us of something, or of the danger she was in. She must have sent the signal to Solveig."

"But why were you saying the same thing that Solveig was?" asked Sean.

"As Solveig's sorcerer, I have a bond with her similar to that shared by Princess Natalie and her Enchantress, Stella. We often feel the sensations of one another. It's not as strong or as clear as what is passed between Natalie and Stella, though. Solveig probably was not the least bit aware of what happened to her or that she was serving as a conduit of sorts, passing the messages from Natalie on to me."

"Why do you think she was unaware?"

"The signals would have been much stronger and much clearer if they were intentional. Oh, and by the way," he said to the Dryad, "she's not really simple-minded, regardless of how she seemed. It appears she was under some kind of spell or trance. Everything is starting to fall into place now, and make sense."

"I'm glad you think so," said Sean.

"It's perfectly clear. The Princess is in danger. The others have gone after her to save her. We must join them to help find her. They can't be too far ahead," said Lochen. "When did they leave?"

"Two days ago."

"Two days?" Sean said, nearly frantic. "Two days! How are we going to find them? They could be anywhere."

By now they had reached the docks. Once they were off the small ship, Lochen asked the Dryad to escort them to the palace and to take them to the Sanctorum. She was more than happy to take them to the palace, but she was uncertain about entering the Sanctorum.

"That's the domain of the Enchantress. Although she's never forbidden anyone from entering when she's not there, we just don't. We never have, in fact – even when she's here, unless we've been invited."

"You must overcome your hesitance," said Lochen. "Now is not the time to stand on arcane traditions. We must act boldly. The life of your Princess, and probably your Enchantress, depends on it."

Sean was just as eager to help, but he didn't share Lochen's impression that the situation was so dire.

"What makes you think their lives are in danger?" he asked. "Isn't all of this just a guess on your part?"

"A guess? Of course not. Think about it," he said. "Something significant happened with Princess Natalie. She went to warn or rescue the members of your Lodge and inexplicably disappeared. There is no sign of her whatsoever or of your villagers. It is logical to conclude that she has either been seriously harmed or is in grave danger. Her connection with Stella was broken. That would happen only if Natalie had been fatally injured, unless she did it intentionally. If she did it intentionally, knowing the effect it would have on Stella, I have to assume that she was faced with such a danger that she didn't want Stella to come to her aid alone. That means whatever danger she is in is also a direct threat to Stella.

Stella appeared to have recovered - at least somewhat - upon the arrival of Solveig, who for some unknown reason seemed to have been entranced – giving the impression of being simple-minded, which I don't believe she is. Although there have been times I have found her to be exceedingly trying, simple-minded is not a term that would ever be used to describe her. Consequently, I believe Natalie was not fatally injured, and, instead, cast some kind of spell on Solveig, which would result in her bringing others to help. Because of my connection with Solveig, that signal was also passed to me."

Sean thought this all over. He couldn't find fault with Lochen's reasoning, as much as he tried.

"What kind of danger could Natalie be in, do you think?" he asked.

"I'm not sure," answered Lochen. "The fact that your Lodge was evacuated is not unusual. It is certainly reasonable given their strong bond with nature that they would know some kind of natural disaster was imminent. They are easily mobile and quite self-sufficient. Evacuation would have made perfect sense. But then I began to think. The Sea Sprites sent several search parties and they hunted for days, but found no sign of the forest creatures. Once the disaster had passed, why didn't they return to the Lodge? The same thing was true of the faerie village. They, too, would have evacuated in anticipation of a disaster, but they haven't returned, either. What could possibly make them stay away? That's the key to the puzzle. It may also be the answer to where our friends went."

Sean searched his memory until a sense of alarm caught him short.

"Rebbercands," he said.

Lochen looked closely at him, and considered his reaction. He weighed the possibilities against the facts that he knew.

"Yes," he finally said. "This may be worse than I thought."

Chapter nineteen

The Dryad led them to the Sanctorum as Lochen had asked, and had summoned the Commander of the Guard. When she arrived she saw Lochen studying the walls and ceiling. She was somewhat taken aback by the presence of these two strangers and the Dryad in the Sanctorum without the Enchantress.

"What are you looking for?" she asked, deciding not to press the issue of their presence – at least not yet.

"I don't really know," he said. "I was hoping for some kind of sign or indication of where they may be heading and why – other than just to find the Princess, of course. I didn't expect to see a large sign on the wall. I was hoping, though, for some sort of inspiration. Nothing seems to be forthcoming."

"I don't believe the Enchantress had conjured any images. However, there was a heated discussion about whether to go looking for you and your friend or try to find the Princess," she told him.

"I expect neither decision would have been an easy one to make, but it was a wiser course to search for the Princess," Lochen acknowledged. "Even we didn't know where we were – other than out to sea, of course. It would have been impossible for them to find us, and any possibility of locating the Princess would diminish almost exponentially each day they wasted trying to find us. If Solveig was receiving messages of some kind from Natalie, it's logical to assume that finding her would have been easier. Rescuing her, however, may be another matter. What else can you tell me?"

"Once they decided on the course of action, they wasted no time. They left immediately in the odd looking ship – the one that brought the hunter and his two companions to us," she went on. "They rested for almost no time at all, resupplied his ship and left."

"In which direction did they go?"

"South," she said. "They appeared to be running parallel to the coast. At least that's where they started out."

"That seems a good place for us to start as well, I would think. Where are your archives? I must see a map."

"I will bring you what you need," she told him.

A few minutes later she returned with a small stack of scrolls and smaller parchments. They were the most recent maps of the known world. Lochen took the maps and looked around the room for a table. There was a large desk on one side of the Sanctorum. It had been Stella's personal work area. Lochen walked across the room and spread the maps out on the desk, moving the various personal items to one side and stacking them in no particular order, but being careful not to knock over anything.

"Please be careful," said the Commander. "Many of those items have spells of their own. It wouldn't do to disturb things."

Lochen looked at the items he had begun to clear away. He picked up several of them to look at more closely. There were a number of small vials, obviously potions of some sort. They had no labels and he was not familiar with their appearance. There was a luminescent piece of rock he recognized as a transporter stone. That might come in useful, he thought to himself. There were a few other unusual objects he had never seen before. He started to study them, and caught himself.

"Yes, you're right of course," he said returning his attention to the maps.

He carefully placed the unknown objects in one of the drawers, along with the vials to keep them safe. He started to put the transporter stone in one of the drawers, but stopped, looked at it once again, and then decided to use it to hold down the side of one of the curled maps. In examining one particular map, he noted that there were several rivers and streams that crossed the land between the Cerulean Sea on the east and the Viridian Ocean on the west. Sean walked to the desk and peered around Lochen's arm.

"Oh, poop," Sean said. "There's a whole bunch of ways they could have gone. How do we know which one they took?"

"Yes, you're right," Lochen said distractedly, lost in thought. "There are several ways to cross the land. But if that was their goal, why would they head due south?"

Sean examined the various waterways and then, realizing the answer to the question, turned to Lochen and said, "Because they weren't going to the other side."

"Exactly. They're going to some point either in the southern area of the Cerulean Sea or the Viridian Ocean."

He turned back to the map and could find no other land mass or island of any kind past the southern tip of the cape, either due south, or to the east or west.

"There must be some destination – an island of some kind - to which they are headed that is either too small to appear on this map or hidden in some manner, unless they're headed for the cape."

"How could it be hidden," asked Sean. "How could someone hide an island?"

"By a spell," answered Lochen. "It would have to be a very powerful spell. A spell of that nature is certainly well beyond the scope of any of our powers. However, I recall ancient stories about an Enchantress – a very powerful Enchantress - who had fought and banished two sorcerers."

"Don't tell me. Ena Ray was one of them. Right?" asked Sean. "Please don't think you're going to get me to go back to the Crystal Cave."

"No. That's far to the north. Our friends have headed south. I wonder if this has anything to do with the other one, if he truly exists," said Lochen. "I thought these were only myths, but someone must believe the stories were real."

"Could they be going to the cape instead?" Sean asked.

"I suppose that's a possibility, but why?" Lochen answered, still studying the map.

He turned to Sean, but it was clear he wasn't really looking at him. The wheels were turning; that was plain to see.

"So, what do we do?"

Lochen looked back at the map and then stabbed the southern tip with his finger.

"We must get to this port town - Nohkmar Cambin."

"Why there?" asked Sean.

"They will have to pass it one way or another, regardless of their final destination, which I believe to be south or west of that cape."

"How do you know they aren't going someplace else? I know — you already told me why they wouldn't be going north around the cape, but maybe they turned east."

"No. If they were going east, they wouldn't have followed the coastline. We need to get to Nohkmar Cambin."

Sean looked at the map, studying all the land routes to the small town.

"We can go cross country, although I'm not sure what we'll run into once we leave the forest. I've never traveled that far south. We could follow the shore line, if you'd rather not go through the forest."

"No. Cross country would take too long," Lochen answered him. "Regardless of whether we follow the shore or go through the forest."

"Oh, no," said Sean, as the option of traveling by water slowly sunk in. "I'm not getting back on a raft with you and I'm not getting into those tiny Sea Sprite boats. Forget it. You'll have to go without me."

Lochen reached across the map and picked up the transporter stone. He spun around to face Sean, holding it in the air.

"No, not by boat, either. We have this," Lochen announced proudly. "We need to make up for a considerable amount of lost time. This will get us there instantly. With a bit of luck, we may be able to catch up to the others. It's possible that, if they stopped in Nohkmar Cambin, they may still be there."

Sean took a step back. There was a look of abject fear on his face.

"Oh, poop. I'd almost rather go by boat. I've had enough of being discombobulated in one place and recombobulated in another place who knows where. Those things are dangerous and unreliable."

"How can you say that? These are perfectly safe. Didn't I take you to the rings of Capurnica using a transporter stone?"

"Yes, you did," said Sean. "And you got us lost. Or have you already forgotten? And didn't we already have this conversation?"

"Yes, you're correct." Lochen responded. "We most certainly did get lost. But I also got you back in one piece, completely safe."

"Safe? You took us through a couple of worm nests along the way and then landed us in the water. I could have drowned."

"Worm holes," Lochen corrected. "I don't believe worms make nests, and besides, there were no worms in the worm hole through which we traveled."

"Whatever. You nearly got us killed. And like I said before, getting us unlost after you got us lost doesn't count. It's dangerous traveling with you. I've lost count of how many times you've nearly gotten me killed. Haven't the last three days convinced you of that?"

"But I have always saved you, haven't I? I saved your life when you were pulled into the sea; that should count for something."

"No. No. No. It doesn't count. I wouldn't have nearly drown if you hadn't put us in that quacky thing in the first place."

"Kayak," Lochen corrected again. "It's a kayak. I'm not sure what a quacky thing..."

"Kayak, shmyak. Same thing," Sean cut him off. "You can't count it as saving my life when you put me in the danger my life needed saving from. Didn't we already have this discussion, too? Or am I just imagining that?

It's probably a result of all those near death experiences I get to experience with you."

Lochen stepped closer to Sean.

"Hold it," Sean shouted, raising his hand in a stopping motion. "Don't come any closer with that lousy stone. You're not getting me to pop into thin air and reappear somewhere else like…I don't know…maybe in the middle of a mountain?"

Lochen paused and appeared to be thinking something over. He turned back to the desk and placed the transporter stone back on the map. He nodded a few times, took a deep breath and then turned back to Sean, seemingly acquiescing to Sean's concerns about the modes of transportation Lochen had been considering.

"You're right. I have put you in danger, and unnecessarily so."

He lowered his head and took a slow step in Sean's direction. He looked contrite with his head down and his hands behind his back.

"I took you without explanation or even any consideration for your objections into deep space. I was far too cavalier about entering the path between the rings of Capurnica. I should have thoroughly tested that device before making a journey of that kind, and even after testing, I should have shared with you all the potential dangers. I failed to do that, and I'm sorry."

He stepped closer to Sean, who was eyeing him warily. He couldn't recall Lochen ever apologizing for his actions. Hearing him do so now sent warning signals up and down Sean's spine. What was he up to, Sean wondered.

"And more recently, I forced you into a very small improvised boat that was clearly not designed to sail on seas as rough as the ones we ventured out on. And that was not enough. To compound the dilemma in which I placed you, I cast a spell to drive that boat much faster and much harder than it was meant to travel. And I maintained this pace during the darkest of the night. Once again, I failed you, and I'm sorry."

He moved right next to Sean. He put an arm around his shoulder and looked him straight in the eyes. Sean returned the gaze, waiting for who knew what.

"And through all this, I have ignored your protests, I've dismissed your fears, and I've discounted the danger in which I've placed you. My behavior has been unquestionably inexcusable."

He pulled Sean close to him, hugging him tightly with his arm. He raised his head and looked upward. In the brief silence that followed, Sean, too raised his head and looked up, wondering what Lochen was looking at.

"In spite of all that, you have remained a true and loyal friend; an ally that one can count on at any time to put the safety of others before his own; a true role model of heroism. I am proud that you are my friend, which is why it really pains me to do this."

Before Sean could react, or even grasp what was happening, Lochen held the transporter stone up in the other hand, having only pretended to leave it on the desk. With a loud pop and a flash of light, they were gone.

Within seconds they arrived in Nohkmar Cambin. Fortunately, they did not arrive in the middle of a mountain; but unfortunately they landed in the middle of a large animal pen. The pen was filled with pigs, which they had also been fortunate enough to miss landing on. The pigs all scattered, snorting and grunting at the sudden and unexpected intrusion.

Lochen and Sean landed flat on their backs surrounded by and covered in mud. Lochen released Sean from his grip. Sean pushed himself away from Lochen and tried to stand up, but only slipped and fell again on the slick ground. It splashed up and spattered across his face. He struggled to his knees, wiping the grime from his cheeks.

"You tricked me!" Sean shouted as he fumbled, slipped, skidded and fell over and over again.

"Yes, I did," answered Lochen, "and I'm really sorry. Seriously. I can't apologize enough, and I would quite understand if you never forgave me. But we had to come here in order to find the others, and we didn't have time to waste traveling here in traditional manners. This was truly our only option."

"We had to come to a...what is this?"

He looked around at the pen and the pigs that had scattered to the far edges of the pen, which weren't all that far. They were only a few feet away from Sean and Lochen, still snorting and grunting as they stared at the interlopers.

"A pig pen?" Sean kept shouting. "A pig pen? You couldn't aim us to a place better than this? This place stinks like...I don't know what it stinks like. I've never smelled anything so bad. How can mud smell so bad? In fact, why does mud smell at all?"

"Yes, I admit the odor is rather pungent," replied Lochen. "I believe the pigs actually live in this pen, which might account for the odor."

"So what if they live here," Sean continued to shout. "It doesn't smell this bad where I live. And I'm willing to bet where you live doesn't smell this bad either. I don't understand. This mud really stinks, and it's really wet. Why?"

"When I said they live here," Lochen attempted to explain. "I meant they're in this pen all the time – day and night. I imagine they... well...you know...this isn't JUST mud. It is probably mostly..."

"POOP?" shouted Sean as he jumped to his feet, and then slipped and fell back on his butt. "I'm sitting in poop. I can't believe this. You've done some really goofy things, but this is the worst."

"You're absolutely right," Lochen told him as he offered his hand to help Sean up. "But look on the bright side. We didn't land inside a mountain."

Sean smacked Lochen's proffered hand and got up on his own. He looked around the pen until he found the gate. Then he stomped through the mud (and the other stuff), splashing across the yard to the gate. He threw it open, not caring if Lochen was following or not and headed for the town. Sean was storming down the street without regard to where he was going, with Lochen following closely behind.

"The fresh air will help," Lochen offered in a feeble attempt to calm Sean down. "Can't you already tell the difference?"

"There isn't enough fresh air to get rid of this stink," said Sean, still shouting and waving his arms.

"Yes, yes, you're right again," said Lochen, dodging clumps of slime that were flinging off Sean's waving arms. "Fresh air alone will not really dull the smell. Actually, the longer we are exposed to it, our olfactory senses will become somewhat immune and the stench will seem less invasive."

Sean stopped in his tracks, turned and glared at Lochen. He opened his mouth to say something, and then shut it, shook his head and continued walking.

"I probably shouldn't have said that last part," Lochen muttered. "You have every right to be mad at me, and I will suffer that consequence. But we're safe and we're closer to helping our friends. If we can at least help them, then I will accept your indignation as the cost of coming to their aid."

That last comment slowed Sean down. He still refused to turn and face Lochen, but he had to admit, if only to himself, that Lochen was right about being closer to helping the others, and that this was the most important thing.

"Fine," he eventually said over his shoulder to Lochen. "Whatever. What now?"

"We continue into the heart of the town, make a few inquiries and then decide what comes next."

Lochen smiled and then quickened his pace until he caught up with Sean and put his arm around Sean's shoulder. Sean stiffened up and looked angrily at him, but didn't pull away.

"No more tricks. I promise," Lochen said, as they walked towards the center of the town.

They entered the market area from the end opposite the docks and from the opposite direction in which Liam and Quinn had entered. As they approached the stalls and shops only Sean was aware of the reaction they were getting to the odor that hung on them like a blanket. Lochen was completely oblivious.

"Excuse me," Lochen would ask, "we're searching for some friends of ours. Perhaps you've seen them? A Pathfinder, a faerie, a Princess, an Enchantress, and a rather large individual who was probably overdressed for this climate?"

Sean just rolled his eyes as Lochen was met with either silent stares or brusque responses. They moved from one side of the street to the other, parting the crowd as if by magic. Potential buyers dispersed with considerable speed as the overpowering reek that enveloped them wafted through the air. Shop vendors who attempted to intervene were nearly blown back as the smell filled their nostrils. The only creatures that seemed not to be repelled by their fragrance were an ever-increasing entourage of dogs.

Their demeanor was also attracting the attention of some of the less friendly residents of the port town. It was clear to all that neither Sean nor Lochen were regular visitors and certainly not residents. A number of rough looking individuals had taken notice of them. They were mercenaries recently from a large vessel that had been attacking smaller ships along the western coast. For the time being, they just followed and watched, trying to determine if the two travelers might have something worth stealing.

As the day wore on with no success at all, Lochen maintained a positive attitude and continued to approach anyone and everyone. He gave no thought to the looks or reactions he received. Not long after midday, he came upon an older gentleman standing near a ship's goods store. He was stooped over a cane and seemed to be daydreaming.

"Excuse me, kind sir," said Lochen. "I'm wondering if you've seen some friends of ours."

Before he could describe them, the old man cut him off. He raised his cane and pressed it against Lochen's midsection.

"That's close enough," said the old man. "I could smell you almost as soon as you turned down this street."

"Oh, yes," answered Lochen. "We had somewhat of a mishap as you can plainly see. But I was wondering..."

"Are you mocking me?" he said abruptly, poking at him again with his cane.

"No, of course not," replied Lochen, a bit confused. "I only want to know if you've seen some strangers in town. They are friends of ours. One looks like a..."

"Lochen," said Sean, pulling on the sleeve of his robe, and at the same time turning his head away from the stench that rose with the motion.

"Just a minute, Sean," he said, "I just need to know if this gentleman has seen our friends. I was just describing them to him."

"Are you mocking me?" the old man repeated more loudly.

"No," Lochen said a little more sharply than he intended as he turned back to the old man. "I'm just looking for my friends and I want to know if you've seen them. It's a simple question. And a simple answer will suffice."

"He's blind," interjected Sean.

"What?" asked Lochen, as the old man swung his cane and cracked it across Lochen's shins.

"Twice in one day," said the old man. "Is there a sign on me? Am I a target for mockery?"

"Ow!" shouted Lochen. "That was completely unnecessary. Your visual limitations are not my fault. I have done nothing to warrant your hostility."

"I've had enough ridicule," the old man shouted. "Did one of those other strangers put a sign on me? I didn't believe for a minute that the giant was simple-minded."

"Please, sir, what do you mean twice in one day," asked Sean. "You said one of them claimed to be simple-minded?"

Hearing a different, and probably a more compassionate voice, he calmed down a bit and answered.

"Earlier today. I was blocked from entering this very store by some giant. He refused to speak to me, although I know he was able. His friend claimed that he was dropped on his head; that he was simple-minded. I didn't believe it for a minute, but then they ran off."

A clue at last, thought Lochen excitedly. "What did he look like," he blurted out without thinking.

Crack, went the cane against Lochen's shins once more. As Lochen reached down to guard his battered ankles, the old man struck again, whacking Lochen's knuckles.

"Enough," shouted the old man. "You must be in league with them. And you smell bad, too. I will not be mocked. Get away from me."

At that the mercenaries who had been following close behind, approached. They decided to use the sudden disturbance as a distraction.

"Are these two strangers bothering you?" they asked the old man.

Sensing danger, Sean grabbed Lochen's sleeve and pulled him away, saying over his shoulder, as they left, "No It was just a misunderstanding. We're leaving."

Rubbing his shin, Lochen pulled himself free of Sean's grip and stopped in the street. He turned back towards the old man and shouted to the group of mercenaries.

"That man is a danger to society and should be locked up. I have a mind to report him to the proper authorities. If you would be so kind as to direct me to the nearest constabulary, I would be in your debt."

That was enough to draw more attention than Sean and Lochen wanted or needed. The mercenaries were joined by other townspeople and as a mob began to run after Lochen.

"Come on," shouted Sean. "We need to get out of here. Can you do something to stop them?"

Lochen quickly realized that the advancing multitude were not coming to his aid, but more likely meant to do him harm. He waved his hand and a cloud of smoke appeared immediately in front of the approaching mob. A few of them started coughing and stopped their chase, but most of them walked right through it.

Not enough, thought Lochen as Sean kept tugging at this sleeve. He waived his hand again and moved a fruit cart into the road. The crowd pushed it over – some running around it; others jumping over it; only a few tripping on the cart or the spilled fruit. Sean started running.

"Come on," he shouted.

He reached back and grabbed Lochen's robe again. This time he made sure he had a tighter grip, before he dragged him down the street. As he pulled Lochen along, he jerked the arm being used to cast the spells. The next one missed its mark and instead of putting up a wall between them and the crowd, it tore down the front gate of a pen holding a herd of ostriches. The giant birds joined the mob, which was immediately followed by the ostrich herders.

"Oh, my! That wasn't supposed to happen," announced Lochen as he stumbled along behind Sean. "I think it's time to run."

He and Sean turned down a side street and then turned down another, winding in and out of narrow lanes and alleys. Along the way, Lochen waved his hand at one item or another to add to the obstacles. He was not adept at doing this while on the run, and more often than not his actions only aggravated innocent by-standers. The crowd chasing them seemed to be gaining on them, and gaining members as it went. The additions came from the formerly innocent by-standers, as well as the pack of dogs attracted to their scent, and a number of other animals who were caught up in the stampede.

"You're not helping things," shouted Sean, as they dodged in and out of a narrow alley way. "Stop with the spells."

"If I could just stop for a second," he answered breathlessly. "I could better direct the spell and it would prove more effective."

He barely finished the sentence when a piece of rotten fruit sailed within a hair's width of his nose. There were far too many now and they were moving too fast for Lochen to stop and cast another spell or for Sean to fire shots with his slingshot.

"We need to get some distance between us and them or we're going to be in big trouble," Sean shouted as they made another turn. "We're losing ground fast."

This turn, however, was a mistake. They had arrived at the docks and had entered onto a long pier with no other twists or turns. At the end of the pier was a ship, resting at anchor.

"Head for the boat," shouted Lochen.

"Oh, no, not more water," wailed Sean. "What good is that going to do us?" he asked breathlessly. "We'll just be trapped."

"Not if I can help it," answered Lochen.

He focused his attention with all his might and then waved his hand. The large sail on the center mast unfurled, and the ropes on the moorings all attached themselves.

"Keep running," he shouted triumphantly to Sean as he waved his hand again.

The anchor pulled itself up out of the water and secured itself to the side of the ship. Just as they were reaching the end of the pier with the crowd much to close for comfort, the ship began to slowly take the wind in its sails and pull away from the dock.

"This is going to be close," shouted Sean.

"When we get to the end of the pier, jump," replied Lochen, panting. "I'll cast one more spell before we land to get the ship fully underway."

As they reached the end of the dock, the ship had pulled about six feet away. The two jumped at the last minute. As they floated through the air, Sean glanced at the name of the boat, painted on the transom: *The Hedgehog*. What kind of name was that for a ship, wondered Sean as they flew over the stern and landed in the hold.

As they hit, the smell rose up to meet them. This one was much different than the one coming from them. It rose from the cargo on which they had landed.

"A garbage ship," shouted Sean. "Of all the boats in the marina, you lead us to a garbage scow."

Lochen sat up and looked around. He was covered in trash and was pulling peelings, wrappings and other waste away from his face.

"Look at the bright side," he said. "At least now you don't notice the smell from the pig sty so much."

Chapter twenty

Bacham stood on the small crest that was still above water, watching the ocean swirl into the mouth of the volcano. Natalie had eluded his grasp and gone headfirst, disappearing into the maelstrom. He was torn between following her and ensuring his two remaining henchmen came with him. There was no other place for them to go, but he sensed their reluctance to jump into the gaping hole. Without waiting for them to have second thoughts, he grabbed them both and threw them, one after the other, into the vortex, and then dove in after them.

Not far below them, Natalie was rocketing downward. She tucked her arms in next to her body and skimmed across the top of the water like a surfer, circling repeatedly all the way down to the bottom of the long shaft. It opened up to a large bell shaped cave, the water cascading through the large hole at the top of the bell. In the center of the cave was a deep pool. The water crashed into the pool and splashed up against the walls and floor of the cavern. She was thrown into the pool , but instead of dropping deep into the water, the cascading falls swirled her around the surface and threw her across the moss covered rocks, up the side of one wall and back down to the ground.

She spun around as she skidded across the slick stone floor, dodging piles of debris that had been sucked in with the water and lay scattered about. She pulled her legs up and hugged them close to her body with her arms to avoid the bits and pieces of wreckage. She came to a stop and sat on the edge of the pool as her equilibrium returned. The spinning all the way down had made her somewhat dizzy and the large room seemed to be in motion around her.

As she was clearing her head, she looked around her. The cavern was enormous - much larger than she had first assumed when she broke through the ceiling. She looked around for some way to escape from Bacham or at least to hide from him. What she saw was a graveyard of ships. There were wrecks of all kinds; dozens of them – large vessels, slave galleys, fishing boats and cargo ships.

Each one had been crushed and broken as it was drawn into the giant whirlpool and crashed at the bottom and along the sides of the cavern. Masts and spars jutted out among piles of planks from broken hulls. Some were so old that the wood had rotted completely through and was barely more than dust. Others were fresh. It was evident that the mountain island rose and sank regularly over the centuries, often trapping unsuspecting passing ships.

She had been stunned by the number and the age of the ships, which had distracted her from her search for an escape. Before she could refocus her efforts, she heard shouting. She looked up to see the first of the Rebbercands coming down the water channel. Because he had been pushed he had flipped over and was tumbling head over heels as he was drawn down the shaft by the swirling rush of ocean.

Every time his head broke the surface, he gasped in a breath and shouted incoherently. He was fighting the current rather than flowing with it. He was thrashing wildly out of terror and careening from one side of the torrent to the other. As soon as he reached the pool, he slammed into a rock along the edge instead of skidding across the surface as Natalie had done. He was thrown up along the far wall. He rose up into the air where he hung nearly motionless for a second and then dropped downward towards the ground. Because of his size and the way he had fought the current rather than flowed with it, he had been flung high into the air. Before he knew what happened or could correct his fall, he plummeted down and was impaled on the spar of an ancient whaling ship. He hung there like a rag doll with the shaft piercing him from his back out through his chest.

A few brief seconds later, the second Rebbercand came down in a more controlled fashion and was immediately followed by Bacham. They both landed in much the same manner as Natalie had – safe and sound, if not seriously shaken – at the edge of the pool, not far from where she stood. Bacham rose unsteadily, looking around furtively until he spotted Natalie. He staggered over to her and jerked her by her arm.

"Did you think you could escape me with that foolish plunge?" he demanded, holding her roughly.

"Where did you think I could go?" she shot back, trying unsuccessfully to free her arm from his grip. "We didn't seem to have much choice. Was I supposed to wait for you to find your courage first?"

He glared at her and tightened his grip on her arms. "You will soon pay the price for taunting me, Princess."

He looked down at the henchman who had immediately preceded him. He was on his hands and knees, still a bit too wobbly to stand.

"Get up, Torcan!" he shouted. "Where is Perrek? He was just ahead of you."

Torcan, the last remaining soldier shook his head, trying to clear his mind. He staggered to his feet and answered.

"I don't know, my lord. I lost sight of him."

"I think he got stuck," said Natalie, pointing at the man pinned on the spar.

"Lord," shouted Torcan, "this place is cursed. This venture is cursed. How are we to get out of here?"

"Control yourself," ordered Bacham through his clenched jaw. "When we reach our goal, which is close, you will have everything you ever dreamed of. In the meantime, bind her arms and tie a leash around her throat. We can't have her doing anything foolish again."

The Rebbercand found some ropes from one of the shipwrecks and tied Natalie's arms and then ran a line around her neck to serve as a leash. As he was doing this, Bacham walked along the walls that encircled the cavern. He found no openings. There must be a way out, he thought. Or a way further in. He looked up at the shaft through which the water was tumbling like a waterfall. He looked at the pool into which it was emptying. Something seemed inconsistent.

He studied the water for a while and then realized that the level of the pool was not rising. The water had to be going someplace, he concluded. He walked along the edge of the pool and back, looking at the rocks on the perimeter. Finally, at the far side he saw a small, low opening. The water flowed through this opening into an underground stream.

"This way," he shouted.

He led the way into the shallow water along the edge of the pool, wading through it and into the tunnel. Bacham and Torcan both crouched down low and nearly crawled through the tunnel. Even Natalie had to bend down slightly. They were all feeling their way along through the growing darkness. Before long the ceiling of the tunnel rose and they could stand upright. There seemed to be a ledge that ran parallel to the stream just a few inches below the surface of the stream.

The three made their way along the narrow ledge through the tunnel. The further they went, the darker it got. After about a hundred more yards, the tunnel opened up to a larger vault. The walls of the vault were covered with crystals of some kind that seemed to light up the entire area. Torcan moved closer to the source and saw that the objects were not crystals, but some kind of luminous slug-like sea creatures. There were thousands of them inching slowly along. He reached out to touch one.

"Leave it, fool!" ordered Bacham. "This place is guarded by spells on top of other spells. You have no idea what may be protecting those things. Do you want to ever get out of here, or do you want to end up like your comrades?"

"No, my lord," Torcan answered as he jerked his hand away. "I mean, yes, my lord, I want to get out of here, and no, my lord, I don't want to..."

"Enough," Bacham cut him off.

The water continued a short way past the opening to the vault and then dropped over the edge of an immense waterfall. The path continued in a circle around the fall to the other side where it widened out. At various points on the path and along the circle around the falls, there were five large fissures in the walls.

Bacham stopped at the first opening and peered inside without stepping through. He could see that beyond the entryway, the path twisted and turned. However, he saw no indication that this was the passage to take. He moved to the next one. As the trio walked past the first fissure to the next, they heard a grinding sound. Looking back they saw the rock wall moving, closing the fissure and opening another right next to the one that had just closed. The grinding sound echoed down through the new opening.

"Trap doors," said Natalie in a stunned voice.

"More than that, Princess," said Bacham. "Each one is a door that leads to a different maze. Only one maze leads to the treasure we're seeking, and even that maze can take a lifetime to solve."

Torcan stared in disbelief. He looked at Natalie and then back to Bacham. He thought better of expressing his concerns, in spite of his growing anxiety. Natalie saw the look in his eye, and then turned to look at Bacham.

"And I suppose you expect that I can lead you through the correct maze? Is that what you think? I'm sorry to disappoint you, but I have no idea which path to take. I have no clue where you're even going or what you're seeking. If you think I can cast some spell to solve these riddles, you're sadly mistaken. I don't have that kind of power. Even if I could figure all this out, what makes you think I would?"

Bacham had only been half listening until her last comment. He stopped walking and turned his head to look at her, a half smile creeping across his face.

"I don't need you to solve this mystery, nor did I expect you would help."

"Then what do you want with me?" she shouted.

He turned to face her and patted her cheek condescendingly.

"You're merely the bait, Princess," and he walked to the next fissure.

He walked to each of the openings, stepped up to, but not into each one and examined the pattern of the maze. As soon as he passed them, he then watched as the walls moved, sealing the initial opening and creating a new one. He walked back to the starting point and started over again, with the same result. When he was done, he studied each opening, and then reached into his cloak and pulled the stone from an inside pocket. He held it closely in his hand, out of sight of the others and watched the changing colors and the light flashing deep inside. He dangled it from the strings by which it was held, but the direction of the stone didn't change. He had to rely on the shifting colors and light.

He stepped to the first fissure and looked at the stone. There was no obvious change. The colors churned slightly, almost as if there were a cloud inside that was moving. He moved to the next one as the first wall shifted, covering the opening and creating another new one. Standing before the second opening he peered at the stone. Again, there was no significant change in the color and no flashing of the light from within, so he moved on to the next opening. As before, the second opening disappeared as the walls shifted and created a new crack. When he came to the third opening, the stone faded from gold to a brownish red and was illuminated by minute lightning flashes beneath the cloudy coloring.

Uncertain if this was the sign he was looking for, Bacham moved to the fourth and then the fifth opening. The subtle shift in the color of the stone and the flashing of the light were not repeated. He returned to the third fissure. The stone clouded over, changed from gold to the brownish red as it had before and small bursts of light sparked behind the clouds. He grabbed Natalie and pushed her first through the opening.

"This one," he declared. He turned back to his soldier and said, "Follow us and don't stray into any of the other openings. If you expect to live you would be wise to stay close. Do I need to be any clearer than that?"

"No, my lord," Torcan answered as he eyed the entrance.

Bacham stepped through the opening. Torcan hesitated for a second, in spite of Bacham's admonition to stay close. The wall started to move and he quickly made up his mind, jumping into the opening after his leader. The opening through which he had jumped disappeared completely, sealed as if it had never existed. He reached back and placed his hand where the opening had been only a few seconds before. The rock was solid and immovable. Once the initial twist in the path changed with the sealing of the opening, the labyrinth ahead took on a much different look.

Before them was a long, narrow passage – as far as they could see, until it faded away to nothingness off into the darkness. Natalie was stunned, wondering how far all these tunnels went, and if each of them was illuminated by the strange luminescent creatures scattered all across the stone. On each side of the central passage were dozens of openings. Bacham slowly walked forward, one step at a time, keeping one eye on the stone and the other on the openings. All the while behind them the walls shifted, cutting off the way they had come, as well as the side passages they had passed.

"I hope you know what you're doing," murmured Natalie. "It looks like our options are being eliminated along the way."

Bacham only ignored her, but the soldier was clearly worried. Finally, the stone in Bacham's hand shifted color. There was an opening on both sides of the passage. Which one to take, wondered Bacham. He turned to the right and the stone faded back to gold. He turned to the left and the colors swirled to the brownish red and the stone sparkled. He took the left opening without hesitation.

Again, as soon as they passed into the next hallway, the walls behind them closed, sealing off any retreat. The further they went, the narrower the tunnels became. Fewer and fewer creatures were on the walls and ceiling lighting the way, making each turn more unsettling. Each time a wall closed and the passage got darker, Torcan's level of panic and fear increased. They twisted and turned to the right and to the left in no apparent pattern. Torcan had lost all sense of direction. Natalie was just as lost. All the time Bacham said nothing, only looking at one entry after another and deciding their fate.

The passageway grew narrower and darker. They were now only able to walk in a single file. With each turn, the walls behind them ground closed. They were closing at a faster rate – almost immediately after they went through. The noise echoed down the passage and grated on their nerves. Finally, Torcan could take no more. At the next turn he lagged slightly behind Bacham as he looked back down the way he had come, the walls constricted.

As the wall began to close off the opening, he gave in to his panic and shouted, "I am sorry, my Lord. I can't go further."

He stood, frozen by fear, unable to go back and afraid to go forward. Before Bacham could reach back and pull him through the opening, the wall began to move, cutting the two of them off from one another. Torcan turned around to look back down the hall when he discovered that it wasn't just a door that was closing and sealing the exit. It was the entire passageway that was collapsing. The walls were moving together, sealing the entire opening. Panic overtook him and he turned back towards the others. He had barely enough room to turn around and try to rejoin Bacham and Natalie.

He sidestepped his way back towards his leader. The walls kept getting closer and closer. He pushed futilely against the walls, unable to stop their movement. He could see the end of the path just inches in front of him. The walls were pressing against his chest. They were so close now that he could only hold his head sideways. He was almost out. He reached his arm out. His fingers were barely able to grasp the edge of the opening. He pulled himself with all his strength, but the walls had pinned him inside.

"Help me, my lord. Please. I beg your forgiveness. Save me!"

Bacham looked on in horror. There was nothing he could do. He turned to Natalie, and said, "Help him. Make this stop!"

"I can't help him," she said. "I don't know what's making this happen. You got us into this. You make it stop!"

Bacham turned back to hear muffled screams and then silence. By now the wall had closed completely and had sealed the opening shut. There was no indication an opening had ever existed, except for the tips of Torcan's fingers, which extended from the vanishing crack until it disappeared completely, and they fell to the ground. Shaken, Bacham turned back and roughly pushed Natalie ahead. They continued in silence through several more turns until they finally came through the last opening into an antechamber.

As soon as they stepped into the room, Natalie could feel a thickness in the air that made it difficult to breathe. It was stale and dead. If felt like all the life had been sucked out of the room, and it left her with a feeling of dread. Evil lives here, was all she could think. The temperature had dropped noticeably, causing goose pimples to form on her arms. She hadn't noticed how much light the luminescent creatures had provided until they entered this place. It took several minutes for her eyes to adjust to the low light. Once they did, she could see the shape and configuration of the cave.

It was a near perfect circle, about twenty or thirty feet in diameter. The walls curved up into a domed ceiling nearly forty feet high. She looked behind her to see that the passage through which they had come was no longer there. However, there were several shadows at various intervals around the room. They looked like passages to separate exits or tunnels. She slowly began to think that this reminded her a lot of Stella's Sanctorum, but on a much larger scale, and with a very different – more ominous – feel to it.

In the center of the chamber was some kind of object. It appeared to be a large rectangular shape and was generating a pulsing glow. She looked again at the walls and then back at the box. This seemed to be the source of light in the cave. She took a tentative step closer and could see that the box was man-made rather than natural. She could see some strange markings on it. No longer worried about Natalie trying to escape, Bacham dropped the rope that was tied around her neck and ran over to the box.

It was smooth on the sides and had an engraving on the top that was obscured by layers of dust. There didn't appear to be any seams or lid or any way to open the box. Bacham was struck with a momentary feeling of uncertainty. Had the legends been wrong? Had this been a fool's errand? He ran his hands over the top and along the side. He could see no way to open it and it was far too large to move.

"So this is what you've been after? A box? We came all this way for that lousy box? And how do you expect to get that thing out of here? It won't fit through those tunnels. Can you even lift it?"

Natalie was furious and confused and was ranting at him, shouting anything that came into her mind. The fear and anxiety that had been weighing on her since her capture erupted. She ran up to Bacham and struck him ineffectively on the back with her bound fists. She kept striking at him until he swatted at her as one would swat at a pesky fly. He pushed her away with the back of his hand, and she gave up in despair, as she was knocked backwards and slid across the floor.

He seemed unaffected by her tirade, lost in his own thoughts, filled with doubts. He realized he not only was unsure if he had found the right place, but that he wasn't even sure of what exactly he was looking for. And then he opened his hand and looked at the stone. It had turned a crimson red. Deep inside there were brilliant flashes of white.

He looked down at the surface and ran his hand across the top, clearing off the dust. He blew it out of the lines of the engraving. In the center was a large impression of a hideous face peering back at him. He wondered if this was the image of the creature within or the person who had cast the spell. He put the stone down on the top of the box to better brush out the dust. As soon as he did this, the stone began to turn a bright yellow and the dust vanished from the engraving, blown out as if by magic. The eyes in the image glowed red, and writing appeared from nowhere surrounding the image.

"Beware the treachery of Tebaga the Betrayer, placed in this sarcophagus by the Enchantress, Meri Hocto."

A feeling of exhilaration swept through his body. He had found Tebaga. The legends had been true. He had discovered the sorcerer. All of his efforts had not been in vain. He turned and looked down at Natalie.

There was no reason now to withhold anything. He pulled a knife from his belt and moved to where she was seated on the floor. As he bent towards her, she raised her arms to defend herself. To her surprise, he cut through the ropes from her arms and hands, removed the rope from her neck, and freed her.

"Relax, Princess. I'm not going to harm you. Well, maybe not yet, anyway. There's no place for you to go," he told her, "and as long as we have some time to wait, I'll entertain myself by answering your questions. This box, as you call it, is a sarcophagus. It is the resting place of a great and powerful sorcerer. And you're going to help me free him."

He proceeded to tell her of the legend surrounding Meri Hocto, Ena Ray and Tebaga. It was, of course, inaccurate. The account he knew had been handed down by generations of Rebbercands and twisted, modified, and revised to suit their needs and reflected their distorted version of history. It contained justification for their lives and put responsibility and blame on all but themselves. As Natalie listened, she realized that as ridiculous and incredible as this story was, Bacham truly believed it.

"Only an Enchantress can break the spell that imprisons the master," he said. That much he had correct. "I knew that if I merely captured an Enchantress, she could refuse to free the master, even if she was threatened with her life. And then where would I be? I realized I needed a bargaining chip – something that would ensure that she did as I demanded. So instead of capturing an Enchantress, I captured her princess. Your Enchantress will do whatever it takes to find you and once she arrives, she will do whatever I demand to ensure your safety. At that point it will no longer matter."

"But there are other Enchantresses and Princesses. Why us?" asked Natalie. "Was it our bad luck or was there some other reason?"

"I suppose I could say it was because you and your friends killed my brother."

"Your brother," she asked. "I don't understand."

"In the mining operation with the Trepans. The Rebbercand that was the leader of the operation – B'nair – was my brother. Your friends dropped him into a river of lava. I'm sure you recall that incident."

Natalie looked up in surprise. A look of remorse quickly replaced the surprise. In spite of all the evil B'nair and the Rebbercands had done, and the fact that B'nair's death had been for the most part his own fault, she felt badly about what had happened.

"Oh please, spare me your sorrow, and you needn't bother to feel guilty, Princess," said Bacham. "Actually, you have my gratitude. I'm glad you got him out of my way. It certainly allowed me to advance in the ranks. It also allowed me to pursue my search for the master, which my brother dismissed as childish. When you and your friends interfered with our mining program and our control of the Trepans, your presence was observed. We knew the Trepans had been aided. They could never have launched a successful revolt on their own. However, we had no information as to who helped them.

"Until, of course, we discovered that we had taken one of the Trepans prisoner. Needless to say, he wasn't immediately forthcoming. We had to apply a bit of what you might call – pressure. I won't bore you with the unpleasantries. Let's just say that in the end he was a fountain of information. After that, it was a simple matter of developing a plan to find and capture you. The first part of that plan called for creating the tidal wave that served as a diversion. Your presence in the village of the forest creatures was a pleasant surprise. We had expected to invade your island and take you by force. Thank you for making that part so much easier. "

Natalie couldn't believe what she was hearing. She couldn't understand how she could feel more upset about what had happened to B'nair than his own brother did. He was his brother, after all! Bacham apparently had been planning all this for quite some time. Had he shared his plans with B'nair? Obviously B'nair had dismissed them. How many people had suffered due to his blind ambition? What did he hope to gain? To make matters worse, she had been duped by their treachery and fallen right into their hands. Had they harmed the forest creatures and the faeries? What had become of them? She was afraid to ask. The Rebbercands must have captured them or worse. There were dozens of questions running through her mind. She debated about what to ask and what to keep to herself. The villainy of all this was astonishing. What was wrong with these people? What was wrong with him?

"Our people had been wasting time mining that foolish ore and making that ridiculous statue," Bacham continued. "B'nair and his kind were stuck in the old ways. Your disposing of him was the best thing you could have done for us. I represent the new leadership. It is my goal to return the Rebbercands to their former glory; to free their ancient master and have him lead us once again."

"You must be delusional," answered Natalie.

Bacham looked at her a while before responding.

"Delusional?" he asked. "I prefer to think of myself as a visionary."

"Really? You don't even know for certain that this master of yours is inside that box or if he's alive. What does your vision have to say about that?"

"You are not the only one with mystical powers, your Highness," he answered with a sneer in his voice. "I have been searching for years. Finding this place was not an accident and the inscription on the sarcophagus proves that."

Natalie had to admit he was right about that. She went on with her challenge, "Maybe so, but it's obvious that you can't get him out of here and you expect someone to come in after us. You saw how difficult it was for us to get in here. It also seems that there's no way out. Please enlighten me. How do you expect my Enchantress to find me and how do you plan to leave here? With that box?"

Natalie knew she had broken contact with Stella, and she was certain that Bacham didn't know this. By doing that, she was sure she had saved Stella from this fate, but wondered if at the same time, she had sealed her own. The uneasy feeling she had since entering this antechamber increased when she saw the sly smile creep across his face.

"There is always a way out. I have no intention of trying to remove the sarcophagus. Once the master is free from that prison, he will lead us out. As to how your Enchantress will find us, let me just say that I am aware of the connection that exists between Princesses and their Enchantresses, including the one between you and yours. I'm assuming you broke it in order to ensure yours did not follow us."

Natalie's head jerked up and her mouth flew open. He noticed the look of surprise on Natalie's face and his smile widened.

"I can see by your reaction that I've guessed correctly," he said to her. "It must have caused her tremendous pain. You should be ashamed of yourself."

She was angry with herself for her reaction. She would need to be more careful. She had underestimated him. He was much more clever than she had given him credit. This was a mistake she would not make again.

"Cutting your connection would have been your first instinct. Since you didn't know where you were being taken or for what reason, you probably thought there might be a chance that you could escape, or perhaps, be rescued. Since you didn't want to jeopardize your Enchantress, I'm also assuming that you were able to send some kind of message to one of your friends. They would need to find you if you escaped or come to your rescue if your escape attempt failed. How am I doing so far?"

She remained impassive at this comment and his question. She wasn't about to betray her emotions again. No matter how right he was, he'd not find out from her. Not again. Bacham studied her before he continued.

"I'm guessing that I'm right on target," he continued. "They, of course, would seek to find you. They would be desperate to ensure that you were safe, only to find that you've disappeared. They would then reach out to your Enchantress. Who would know best where you were but your Enchantress? They would discover her grieving your loss, but would convince her that you were still very much alive. She would put her grief aside and would join in the search – maybe even lead it. I'm sure your friends are very resourceful. They'll find this place, and probably much more easily than I did. Once they do, your Enchantress will be able to bypass the spells that guard it and here we are waiting for her."

He walked over to the stone box and ran his hands across the top and along the sides, as if he were searching again for some way to open it. Natalie wondered how much of his narrative was based on knowledge as opposed to what was only hope on his part. She was struck by how much he had correctly surmised. She only hoped that when and if her friends showed up, they would be able to contend with him more effectively than she had been able to.

"As I'm sure you're aware," he continued. "I have no powers. I can't cast spells or break spells. Your Enchantress' ancestor – the witch, Meri Hocto - is the one who cast the spell over this prison, and only an Enchantress can break it. I suppose any Enchantress would do, but there's a certain irony in it being your Enchantress, don't you think?"

He picked up the piece of the stone from the top of the sarcophagus. It was barely an inch long and not quite that wide. It glistened as he turned it between his finger and thumb. He had usually kept the stone well hidden from the view of others, but now he no longer seemed to care. Natalie saw the stone glimmer and could feel a wave of energy emanate from it. She had no idea what it was, but thought it looked familiar. Her thoughts were interrupted by Bacham's further commentary.

"Your Enchantress will make her way through the maze in the same manner as we did," he continued.

He shifted his gaze from the stone to Natalie. Then he looked up at the sealed passageway as if he was looking at the spot where Torcan had disappeared.

"Probably with fewer losses than we suffered," he added. "But who knows? Maybe in their rush to save you, they'll be careless and they'll meet the same misfortunes. One can only hope."

Natalie shivered at the thought of the dangers that awaited her friends. She hoped that if anyone were coming after her, they exercised more caution than Bacham's men had. She was beginning to regret having sent the telepathic message to Solveig. She had no doubts that she and the others would do everything in their power to come to Natalie's rescue.

"Even if you're right," she said defiantly, "what makes you think my Enchantress will release your master?"

Bacham smiled. "Well, because I will assure her that if she doesn't I will most certainly separate your head from your body."

The color drained from Natalie's face.

"Why don't we just sit and relax until they show up?" he said as he sat next to the sarcophagus.

Chapter twenty-one

With the repairs to the sail completed, and everybody safely back on board, the *West Wind* was heading deep into uncharted waters. Liam, Quinn and Summer had returned to the boat without further incident and only minimal discussion of their adventures as they made their way back to the pickup point. Liam was able to quickly effect repairs, and had followed Solveig's simple direction of "this way" for a heading. Summer had returned to her perch in the crow's nest and Quinn had volunteered to do the pedaling to propel the craft while Liam had patched up the sail. He had continued after the sails had been raised and taken wind.

"You need a rest," he told Liam. "Besides this will help get us there faster – wherever 'there' is."

As unsettling as their visit to the port town had been, it seemed to at least get Quinn past his feelings of guilt for having left Sean and Lochen to their own devices. They both looked towards the bow at Solveig who stood motionless facing straight ahead. The town of Nohkmar Cambin and all the land surrounding it gradually disappeared below the horizon and all that could be seen in any direction was dark blue water. Liam, even with his Pathfinder skills, had no idea where they were or where they were heading. This was nothing like the Swamp, and he was uncertain if they would ever find Natalie, in spite of Solveig's insistent directions.

For most of the voyage, Stella had maintained a vigil at Solveig's side. She wasn't worried about her friend – at least not too much; but she hoped that Solveig might be able to provide her some clue as to Natalie's whereabouts and well-being. Unfortunately the only words she uttered indicated a change of course or a need to hurry. A few hours after they lost sight of the port, Stella left Solveig's side and approached Liam. He had been standing mid-ship checking the repairs on the sail.

"The air seems to have gotten cooler," she said, rubbing her arms for warmth. "Much cooler than just from the sea itself."

"Yes, you're right," he answered, looking to the east. "The sky is darkening. There's a storm to our east, and it seems to be moving fast. If we stay on this course, we're going to run right into it. This boat was not made for the open ocean, let alone an ocean in a storm. I don't think we'll be able to ride it out. Is there anything you can do – a spell or something – to move the storm or get us to our destination sooner?"

Stella looked troubled.

"I don't think so. My powers are fading faster and faster and I don't know why. If we don't find Natalie, I'm almost certain that I'll lose them completely. I'm afraid there's nothing I can do to help."

"Will your powers return if – when, I mean – when we find Natalie," Liam tried to quickly recover from the slip.

"I don't know. This has never happened to me. I know this kind of thing can happen – has happened, but I never knew what the impact would be. I have no frame of reference to predict what may happen."

Quinn could hear the conversation, and couldn't help but interrupt.

"Everything's going to be just fine," he declared. "We're going to find Natalie and your powers will be even stronger, so you can kick the butt of whoever did this. And then we're going to find Sean and Lochen. They're probably on a beach somewhere arguing about being in the water or traveling to the stars or something like that. Trust me. Everyone's going to be fine. I just know it."

His certainty was infectious. Stella and Liam smiled and nodded in agreement, trying to share his positive attitude. For a while it worked. They could actually feel the tension in their bodies begin to ease up. Their sense of relief was short-lived, however. In less than an hour, the storm had changed course radically and was moving in on them.

The previously calm sea slowly started churning, gathering momentum as the winds began to increase. At first the waves were mild, but their intensity steadily rose. Summer was the first to really feel the severity of the sea's movement. Aloft in the crow's nest she started experiencing brief moments of weightlessness as the boat rose to the top of a large wave and then dropped to the valley. She was lifted nearly off her feet. And then a big one hit.

She was tossed into the air nearly to the top of the crow's nest, and then dropped downward, following the boat as it sank between mountainous waves. Before she could flap her wings and take flight, the boat was lifted into the air on the crest of another enormous swell and the ship shot up to meet her, causing her to crash into the floor of the crow's nest.

The rough seas were almost immediately followed by a burst of torrential rain, flashes of lightening, booming thunder, and ferocious winds. All of it seemed to appear instantaneously. The boat was buffeted in every direction – front to back and side-to-side. At one point the wind spun the tiny craft completely around in the opposite direction, and it rose up going backwards to the top of a wave more than forty feet high. Summer grabbed the railing around the crow's nest and hung on for dear life. She was afraid to fly. The winds would blow her up and away and in a few short seconds she would be lost from the ship. The winds had come up so quickly, she didn't have time to get down to the deck. Now it was too late.

Quinn stopped pedaling. It no longer served any purpose. Half the time the paddles near the back of the ship were lifted out of the water. Liam took hold of the tiller and tried to keep the boat headed in one direction while Quinn attempted to secure the sail, pulling it up to the cross piece and tying it off. Stella staggered from side to side as she made her way to the front where she found Solveig still standing there, facing ahead. Each time the wind or the seas tossed the boat off course, she pointed forward and said, "No, this way." Stella held her tightly to keep her from being washed overboard. She wished she had brought a rope to tie them both to the bulkhead.

"Help," she called back to Liam and Quinn.

Another wave hit the boat across the side and water splashed over the bulwark nearly sweeping them both overboard. The pounding rain was also making the deck slippery, so it was difficult just to stay in one place. Quinn was slipping and sliding, falling, getting back up and falling again.

He eventually reached one of the storage compartments along the side of the ship and found some rope. He ran forward, staggering from left to right and back several times as the boat was pummeled by the rain and the sea. He tied one end around the slender mast to which the lone sail was attached and then looped the other end around Stella and then around Solveig. Once they were secure, he looked up to the crow's nest. All he could see were Summer's tiny hands gripping the narrow railing and the tips of her wings as the wind shook them.

"Oh, poop," he muttered to himself. "What's she still doing up there? She's going to get blown away."

He started shimmying up the mast to the crow's nest. The water crashing over the side made the mast slippery, and beat down on him, pushing him back to the deck. It seemed for every two feet he climbed up, he slid down one. Inch by inch he forced his way to the top, where he held on by wrapping one arm tightly around the mast and reached into the nest blindly with his free hand. He felt around as gently as he could and when he thought he found her, he wrapped her in his hand and started back down.

The mast wasn't made for seas quite this rough or winds quite this strong, and it definitely wasn't made to carry the weight of someone as large as Quinn.   It bent perilously to the side as the boat shifted with the movement of the waves. Quinn was afraid to loosen his grip enough to slide down the mast. He thought if he did, he might be blown away from the mast and into the sea. Instead, he held on tightly with one arm while he held Summer in the hand of his other arm, all the while mumbling to himself, "Must not crush, must not crush."

As the boat righted itself the mast returned to an upright position, only to spring in the opposite direction with the change in the waves. The mast swayed back and forth like a metronome. The sail that Quinn had raised started to come loose and began to unfurl. It was flapping in the wind and every once in a while caught a gust full on and ballooned out. Quinn was getting sea sick with all the back and forth motion until a strong gust of wind caught the sails and put more pressure on the mast than it could handle. Quinn could feel it cracking even before he heard the noise over the howling wind and roaring water.

As soon as he did, he knew he had to take his chances. He released his grip around the mast and tried to slide down to the deck. He almost succeeded. He had just cleared the cross piece to which the top of the sail was attached. The mast snapped when he was only about halfway down, but didn't break completely through. The crow's nest slammed into the ocean, further twisting the mast, the pieces of which were hanging together by a few slender strips. Quinn hit the bulwark railing just below his hip and was thrown into the ocean. He held on to the splintering mast with his hand, holding the other with Summer above the water.

"Must not crush," he repeated to himself through gasps of air. "Must not crush."

As the boat rose on the next swell, Quinn used the momentum to lift himself up and he flipped in a complete circle, landing on the deck. He spun around on his butt several times before sliding into the back of the ship and grabbing one of the pedals next to Liam's foot. Once he stopped moving he opened his hand slowly, hoping he didn't see squashed faerie. Summer, soaked to the skin, eyes wide open in shock looked up at him.

"Next time," she gasped, "let me know you're going to do that."

"Deal," he said, breathing a sigh of relief.

He put her in one of the storage bins to keep her out of the wind, making sure there were no loose items in the bin that might crush her. When he secured the clasp to the bin, he checked the rope that was tied to what remained of the mast and saw that it was still tied securely and that Solveig and Stella were still at the bow. Then he struggled to his feet and staggered back to the stern to help Liam.

"Sorry about the mast," he shouted.

"Don't worry about it. I'm surprised it lasted that long," Liam answered. "If we don't get out of this storm soon, that will be the least of our worries. We're taking on way too much water and this thing is getting hard to steer."

Liam struggled with the keel, but wasn't sure how far off course they had been driven. Solveig hadn't said anything for quite a while. Even in the worst parts of the storm she had shouted course corrections. He was worried about her silence. He looked towards the bow and saw Stella and her huddled together. As the boat rose to the top of the next wave and started down into the next valley, Liam saw a large rock in the water almost dead ahead. He turned the keel in a futile attempt to avoid it.

He put all his weight and strength into pushing the tiller to the starboard, but the wind and the sea were much too powerful. He managed to avoid the head on collision, but the rock struck the side of the ship and ground into it all the way to the stern. Liam could tell by the sound and the vibration that his boat was mortally wounded. The rock hadn't broken completely through the hull, but it had done enough damage that the ship would be taking in water from the sea as well as from the rain and the swells.

"No," shouted Solveig once she detected the course change Liam had effected in his effort to avoid the rock. "Keep going. We're almost there."

Almost there? Liam asked himself. Almost where? What does she see that the rest of us are missing? And then he saw the giant whirlpool just past the rock he had tried so hard to steer clear of. Before he could react and pull the ship out of the whirlpool's powerful tow, the boat was trapped in the current, drawn in and down. The boat was turned nearly on its side as it swirled down the shaft of the same volcano Natalie had dove down not too long before. It was moving so fast that the water that poured into the cracks made by the rock flew out the hatchway and into the air behind them. As they moved into the funnel, the rain finally stopped, but no one even knew.

Solveig, still in a trance, looked on unchanged and unaffected by the dangers they were racing towards. She was unaware or oblivious to the tiny ship rocketing down the giant channel of water, sucking in water as it went. Stella clenched her jaw tightly, held Solveig closely and resigned herself to whatever was coming. She hoped that wherever Natalie was that she was safe. Summer, tucked away in the storage bin, couldn't see what was happening, but could feel the change from bounding up and down to dropping in a steady spiral. She grabbed the frame of the bin and held on for dear life.

Liam had gripped the tiller so fiercely, his hands were frozen in place and the muscles of his arms and wrists were screaming. He knew that he no longer had to hold on, that the rudder was no longer steering the ship, but he was unable to let go. Quinn sat next to him, holding on to the transom. His eyes were wide open and he was holding his breath. All he could think about was who would take care of Rover and Kelsey.

The boat corkscrewed down the shaft and plowed into the pool at the bottom, and then skidded across the stone floor, finally crashing into the wall. Stella had seen the wall coming at them through the spray of water when the boat shot through the pool. At the last minute, she pulled Solveig down to the deck and braced for the impact. The boat rumbled over the wreckage of its predecessors coming to a stop as it slammed into the edge of the wall, cracking into several pieces. Stella and Solveig toppled over the side as far as the rope that secured them to the mast would allow, which was a foot or two above the ground. Stella managed to undo the knots and they both dropped unceremoniously onto the stone floor.

Summer was thrown to the front of the storage bin and buried in ropes and sail material, but otherwise had a soft landing. She pushed and kicked at the items under which she was buried and then pushed at the bin door. The clasp that Quinn had used to secure it had broken off, but the door to the bin was wedged shut due to the crash. She looked behind her and saw that the side of the ship had broken open enough that she could wiggle through the crack and out into the open.

Liam had braced himself with his feet pressed up against the base of the pedal mechanism, which snapped in half when the boat hit the wall, throwing him forward. His grip on the keel never lessened and he ended up flipping head over heels and landing flat on his back on the deck. Quinn's hands never left the transom, but the transom was wrenched free of the frame of the ship. As he flew over Liam, and was about to fly over Stella and Solveig, directly into the wall, his foot caught in a hole in the tattered sail. The sail miraculously kept from ripping even further and stopped him sort. He landed with a grunt nearly on top of Stella and Solveig. The transom flew out of his hand and shattered against the wall.

"Is everyone all right?" Liam asked as he pried his fingers from the tiller and staggered to his feet.

"We're all right," Stella answered for Solveig and her.

She stood up and pulled Solveig to her feet, looking them both over for any cuts or indications of broken bones.

"Blubber on a biscuit," was all Quinn could say.

"I'll take that as a yes," said Liam. He opened the storage bin and pulled out the ropes and material, looking for Summer.

"I'm OK," she sputtered as she flew up from the outside of the ship.

Liam climbed out of the boat and crawled over to the edge of the pool to join the others. In silence they surveyed the damage to the boat. It had been totally destroyed. The frame had been shattered; the mast was in several pieces; the sail had been shredded by the storm, the transom, after being pulled from the frame when Quinn had been tossed forward, had rocketed over his head and smashed into the wall. It was in several pieces.

Each of them stared in shock and dismay. Although they were all glad to be alive, each one of them was asking themselves what they were supposed to do now, and how they would ever be able to return home. Their silence was suddenly broken.

"What a disasterpiece," said Solveig.

She looked around at the wreck of the *West Wind*, as well as the other broken ships, the water cascading down the long volcano shaft, the large pool of water and four of her friends, standing soaking wet on a water covered stone floor, all staring at her.

"So, where exactly are we, and how did we get here?" she asked.

- - - - - - - - - - - - - - - - *** - - - - - - - - - - - - - - - - - -

Sean had not been able to stop complaining about the smell.

"Which smell are you referring to?" asked Lochen, "the smell of the pig sty or the smell of the garbage?"

"The garbage," snapped Sean. "No. The pig poop. Both. What difference can it possibly make? It all stinks."

In addition to having to put up with the stench, Sean had been shooting his sling shot at the ever-present buzzards. They had been residents on the garbage scow and tons of trash, which consisted mostly of dead fish. Now they seemed to be even more attracted to the oddly interesting aroma that covered Sean and Lochen. In spite of Sean's deadly accuracy with the slingshot, they were not deterred. There were far too many of them.

"Yes," said Lochen amiably, "it all stinks, and it hardly makes a difference which odor is more offensive, but look on the bright side."

"If you tell me about one more bright side, I'm going to throw you overboard. And then I'm going to watch as you get swallowed whole by some giant fish or something."

Lochen smiled, "And fend off these vultures all by yourself?" He waved a hand and they disappeared.

"You couldn't have done that sooner?" railed Sean. "Those things have been flying over our heads for hours. And you just now decide to make them disappear?"

"Well, they weren't bothering me."

Sean rolled his eyes and plopped down on a pile of trash, only to jump up as something wet seeped through his clothing and something else moved under his weight.

"Ewwwe, yuck," he whined. "There's no place safe to sit," he complained to Lochen who was perched near the front of the scow on a mound of something unidentifiable.

"Look. That's a pile of fish guts. It's not even wrapped in anything," he continued to complain. "And over there is a bunch of rotting fruit. And next to that is some stuff covered in mold. It seems to be growing as we speak. And there's some stuff I can't even tell what it is, but it smells the most. And then...what was that? Did you see that?"

"See what?" asked Lochen, barely paying any attention to Sean at all.

"Something moved in that pile over there."

"Probably a rat or two," offered Lochen.

"No. It looked like a black squirrel. Those things are really dangerous. I hate black squirrels – even more than rats."

"I would suggest that you might be more concerned about that approaching storm," Lochen said as he pointed to the east. "If it continues on the course it seems to be taking, and we are unable to avoid it, then rats – or even those dreaded black squirrels you're so fond of – will be of little importance."

Sean turned around and carefully tiptoed through the piles of waste, making his way towards where Lochen was sitting.

"Wonderful," he said. "Maybe a little rain will help get rid of the stench. At least it will clean this pig poop off of us."

"I think that storm is quite possibly going to provide us with more than a little rain."

They both watched as the black clouds raced across the sky. The spell that Lochen had cast on the garbage scow required it to follow the direction of the telepathic messages from Solveig. He still wasn't aware that he would lapse into a trance-like state every once in a while, but after hearing about Solveig from the Dryad, he reasoned that what Sean had been observing, and what he was completely unaware of, were messages conveyed from Natalie through Solveig to him. Those messages served as a homing beacon for the *Hedgehog*. Unfortunately, the beacon was taking them much too close to the heart of the storm.

Before long, the unavoidable had occurred. The sky had turned black and the rain was coming down in sheets. The mounds of garbage became soaked. Soggy globs formed all over the scow, blending together in a toxic soup. The boat was tossed on mountainous waves and the garbage flipped, turned, sloshed and oozed. With every roller coaster drop from the crest of an enormous wave to the bottom of the valley, Sean and Lochen were smeared, covered, and awash in trash. There was no "below decks" where they could find shelter from the storm or the garbage, nor was there any shelter on the deck itself. They were instantly soaked and then coated with grime and slime.

"Hold on," shouted Lochen, grabbing at the side of the ship. "Here comes another wave,"

"Hold on to what?" Sean shouted back. "A slab of rotted meat? There's nothing to hold on to! I think I'm going to be sick."

He fell back onto a pile of something unrecognizable and that smelled even worse than he thought possible. The more he flailed his arms to regain his balance and his footing, the more he burrowed himself into the mass of oozing sludge.

"Well, look on the bright side," said Lochen as he clawed his way out from under a pile of fish heads. "If you throw up, the smell will most likely go unnoticed."

"If I could reach you," answered Sean, sputtering through the goo that was running down his face, "I'd strangle you."

Lochen crawled to the bow of the ship and held on with both hands to the bulwark railing. His body stretched out behind him as if he were flying when the ship was pushed up one of the massive waves, and then flopped onto a pile of waste when the ship dropped into a valley. Through the surge of rain a flash of lightning lit up the horizon immediately before them.

"Sean," he shouted. "Can you make your way up here?"

Sean rolled, crawled and scrambled forward as the nose of the boat rocketed down the receding wave. Then he started tumbling. Lochen reached out with one arm, holding tightly to the railing with the other, and caught Sean just in time to keep him from rolling overboard.

"What was so important?" he asked once he caught his breath. "Did you see something worse than this ship?"

"Look straight ahead, but wait for the next flash of lightning. Then tell me what you see."

They didn't have to wait long. A crack of electricity stabbed at the sea, illuminating the horizon.

"Oh, poop," said Sean. "Tell me I didn't see what I saw. That looked like a...a...a hole in the water. Was that some kind of whirlpool?"

"Yes. That's what I was afraid of," answered Lochen. "Along the near edge of that whirlpool, did you see a large rock? It appeared to bob up and down in the water"

"I saw something, but I couldn't tell what it was. Are we going to hit it? That's all we need – a bobbing rock."

"Well it's not really the rock that's bobbing. I'm sure the rock is stable. It's the undulation of the waves..." he stopped and looked at Sean who was staring at him with a look of disbelief.

"Of course. You know that. Well, regardless. This does not look good. We need to make our way to the back of the boat and see if we can find some kind of protection."

"Of course," said Sean. "We can go below to the captain's cabin and sit on his nice sofa. I'm sure he won't mind."

"I don't recall any captain's cabin," said Lochen as he began to climb over pile after pile of refuse.

"There isn't one," shouted Sean over the roar of the storm. "That was sarcasm."

They inched their way to the back just as the scow scraped past the rocky tip of the volcano's mouth. The rock cut into the side of the *Hedgehog* as quickly and easily as it had cut into the side of the *West Wind*. They burrowed beneath mounds of trash, since this was the only protection available, as the boat swayed to the side and started its spiral descent into the whirlpool.

"Can't you cast some kind of spell?" mumbled Sean through layers of rubbish, his head buried under garbage and his arms, his butt precariously in the air.

"I don't think so," answered Lochen. "My powers seemed to be blocked. It must have something to do with this particular location."

The scow spun round and round down the shaft until it splashed into the pool at the bottom, where is skidded across the surface, over the stone floor, crashing against the wall. Garbage flew in every direction, splattering everywhere as the boat broke into pieces. Sean and Lochen tumbled across the floor, spinning wildly and came to a halt in a pile of rotted vegetables, bruised and smelly, but unharmed.

Once the dizziness wore off, they stood up and surveyed their surroundings. They spotted the remains of the *West Wind* in the debris. "Oh, no," said Sean. "Look. That looks like the ship the Dryad described. That's probably Liam's ship. It sure looks like something he would build. Quick! We need to see if any of them are here and if anyone's hurt."

They ran over to the debris and scoured the wreckage for any signs of their friends. There was nothing. Most of the ship was in pieces all piled pretty much in one spot. The exception was the pieces of the transom that had shattered against the wall.

"How did this one piece get all the way over here?" asked Sean. "How could they survive this? Do you think any of them did?" "I'm sure of it," answered Lochen. "There are no bodies around, except for that one," as he pointed to the impaled Rebbercand. "And he looks rather fresh. I would judge that they encountered the same storm that we did – perhaps the front end instead of the back end as we did. They can't be too far ahead of us."

"Where did they go?" Sean asked.

They both examined the cavern, walking around it in opposite directions, looking for clues. Sean eventually found the tunnel through which the stream ran.

"This looks like the only way out of here," he said to Lochen. "Can't you tell for sure? Aren't you getting any signals from Solveig?"

"No," answered Lochen. "No, I can't tell for sure, although I believe you are correct. And, no, I'm not getting any signals from Solveig. I have to assume that for whatever reason, she is no longer serving as the conduit from Natalie."

"That would be a good thing, wouldn't it?" asked Sean. "No. I can see from the look on your face that you don't think that's a good thing."

"Let's not get hasty," said Lochen, cautiously.

"You think one of them is hurt or dead, don't you?" Sean persisted.

"I don't know what to think," answered Lochen. "The best thing we can do now it to keep going."

They followed the tunnel and the stream and exited in the same vault as their friends. They walked all around the cavern and quickly discovered the same fissures with the same moving walls.

"Very interesting," said Lochen. "Each of these seems to be a separate maze. How ingenious. It seems to be one more layer of security. It's obvious that whatever has brought all of us here is at the end of one of these mazes."

"I'm glad you're impressed. How do we figure out which way they went? Can't we just pick one?"

"No. We have to pick the right one."

"Why? Do you know where any of them lead?"

"No, I don't," Lochen answered, trying to focus his attention on choosing the right opening.

"If we don't know where we're going, what difference does it matter which path we take?" Sean asked, anxious to make a decision and to get moving.

Lochen turned his head to look at Sean, considering his question and trying to make a reasoned response.

"Normally I'd agree with you," he finally said. "But in this case, choosing unwisely could be very hazardous to our health. I have a feeling that only one option is the correct one and the others are merely traps."

Lochen thought a few minutes before answering. He walked back and forth, watching the walls move, closing off one opening and creating another.

"Let's take this one," he said after a while. "It's as good as any of the others."

Chapter twenty-two

Stella, Summer, Quinn, and Liam were all staring at Solveig. Their mouths were wide open and she was looking back at them with a look of complete confusion. It was clear to them that she had no idea of what had transpired over the last several days.

"What's wrong?" she asked, a little embarrassed by their attention.

"Don't you remember?" asked Summer.

"Remember what? I don't understand. What am I supposed to remember?" she asked, clearly puzzled.

"I guess that answers that question," said Liam as he turned away and looked back at his broken ship.

"Wait!" said Solveig, looking around at the strange surroundings. "Somebody tell me. What happened? Where are we and how did we get here?"

Stella explained what had transpired over the last few days, with Liam and Summer filling in the time between when Solveig fell into the water and when they arrived at the island of the Sea Sprites. Solveig remained quiet for the entire explanation, not asking a single question. Throughout the narrative, Quinn had also remained quiet, waiting for the one question she would inevitably ask – where was her brother?

"Where are Lochen and Sean?" she asked, looking around and noticing their absence, surprising no one with the question.

Quinn almost winced when he heard the concern in her voice. The others all looked at one another, before Quinn spoke up. He explained his part of the puzzle, trying to put a positive spin on it, but failing miserably. He explained how they had become separated at sea, and that this was the last time he – or anyone – had seen either one of them. Even Stella had not been able to conjure an image of them. To his credit, he did not go into details about the discussion they had about not searching for Sean and Lochen, nor did he place the blame on or accuse anyone. He had agreed with the group's decision about finding Natalie first, albeit reluctantly, and he took full responsibility. Solveig's eyes started to water and her chin quivered only slightly. She swallowed hard.

"I'm sure they'll be all right," she said, with her voice cracking. "They're both very resourceful."

She smoothed her clothing, brushing off imagined but unseen dust. Then, wiping a single tear from her cheek, she cleared her throat and asked, "So, what do we do next?"

Quinn started to apologize for losing them, but she cut him off. Now was not the time to focus on them, she agreed. They needed to carry on with what they came here for. The sooner they found and rescued Natalie, the sooner they could focus their efforts on finding and rescuing Sean and Lochen. None of them had any idea or clue that the two missing friends were not far behind them.

Liam had been scouting the area while the explanations were being provided to Solveig. He reported back that he had located the tunnel that seemed to be the only way out other than the way they had come in. He led them through the narrow channel and to the vault with the five openings and the moving walls. As they made the same exploratory walk that Bacham did before them and Lochen would do shortly after them, Quinn noticed and pointed out to the others the changes in the color of the stone in Stella's headband.

"I didn't need the stone to tell me which way to go," said Stella. "I just seem to be able to sense it. This is really freaky. I almost feel like I've been here before. I know I haven't but it sure feels familiar."

"OK, then let's get going," said Solveig. "We don't need to waste time talking about stones and old familiar feelings."

She pushed her way to the front of the group, right behind Stella and gave her a nudge to get moving. It was evident that she wanted to move quickly. The others were hesitant to caution her about making a wrong choice. They all knew she was anxious to begin a search for Lochen and Sean.

"I think I liked it better when she didn't say very much," muttered Quinn, a little uneasy about stepping into the maze.

Stella led the way, at first taking tentative steps. Soon, she was more certain of which turns to take and was moving through the labyrinth at a quickened pace. As they made their way through one turn after the other, no one even bothered looking at the shifting color of the stone. It was as if Stella had lived here all her life. She approached each opening with confidence and marched through without a second thought, making one turn after the other.

As the walls moved behind them, sealing the openings off, Liam grew as uncomfortable as Quinn. He turned back and watched closely as the sides of the rock almost seemed to melt together as it closed the passages behind them.

"I sure hope she's right," he said. "It looks like there's no going back. I'm just wondering how we're going to get out of here."

Summer flew immediately over everyone's head. She was fluttering back and forth above Stella in the lead and all the way to the end where Quinn was. In one hallway she had lingered, trying to see what was making the wall move, and was almost caught as it sealed the opening. After that, she kept to the front of the line as close to Stella as she could. As the passageways grew narrower, everyone had to move in a single file. The tunnels were getting lower and narrower. Quinn began to have difficulty keeping up. He had to turn sideways and crouch at the same time. His head was scraping the top and his knees were scraping the sides. He was beginning to feel a bit claustrophobic.

"Hey," he shouted with an edge of panic in his voice. "Slow down. You're getting too far ahead of me. Don't leave me behind."

Stella stopped short before making the next turn and looked back at him and the others to make sure everyone was keeping up. Quinn was tightly wedged in between the sides, the floor and the ceiling. She was surprised he could move at all.

"Oh my," she said, "I hadn't realized how difficult this was getting for you."

Without even thinking about it, she waved her hand in an arc, pointing from the bottom of the wall on the left, up and across the ceiling and down to the bottom of the wall on the right. The stone in her headband flashed yellow and the walls started to rumble. Everyone looked about them in apprehension as the scraping of the rocks echoed through the tunnel. In a few seconds, the opening had widened just enough to allow Quinn a bit more breathing room.

"You couldn't have done that sooner?" Quinn asked, turning fully forward and shaking his arms and shoulders.

"If you can move these wall in this section of the tunnel," asked Summer, "then why don't you just move them all out of the way and get us to where we need to go?"

"This whole place is a matrix of spells," explained Stella. "There are spells within spells and spells over spells. I don't know how they all got here, or who put them here, or how I even know that. I can't disrupt things – at least not too much – or the spells could be broken or changed to something entirely different. I have a feeling that would not be a good thing to do. I probably shouldn't have done what I just did. I hope it doesn't upset the balance or something."

No one questioned her and only looked at the walls all around them. As they proceeded, the tunnel section she had widened shrunk back to its original size behind them almost immediately as they move forward, and the tunnel section through which they were headed opened just enough to allow easy passage.

"Weird," declared Quinn, who looked back only for a second and then scooted to catch up again with the others.

Eventually they were so completely twisted around, that none of them – not even Stella, or Liam with his exceptional path finding skills – could tell exactly where they were or how far they had come. And then, suddenly, they walked through the final piece of the labyrinth and out into the central cavern where Natalie and Bacham were waiting for them. They had entered the cavern through a different portal than the one their predecessors had come through.

As they stepped into the room, Stella was instantly struck by the size and the shape. In spite of the ominous surroundings and the hazards they faced in getting here, she felt that this place was familiar. It looks like a Sanctorum, she thought subconsciously. Her thoughts were interrupted by the stranger's voice.

"Well," he said to Stella, "what a pleasant, but I must admit not completely unexpected, surprise. And I see you've brought company. How nice of you. You all should make a fine gift to the master."

In an instant, Stella's attention was diverted from the configuration of the cavern, and she immediately grasped what had happened. She was filled with rage at the person who had threatened her Princess. With total disregard for the impact her actions may have had on the spells, her fury overcame her rational thought and she moved to cast a spell on him. As quickly as Stella raised her hand, Bacham unsheathed his double headed axe, stepped behind Natalie and placed the blade under her chin.

"Not so fast, if you please," he said.

His tone was challenging and there was a sneer on his lips. He pulled Natalie's head back with his free hand, exposing more of her throat. The blade of the axe glistened in the dim light.

"It's your move, Enchantress," he said. "So, tell me. Who's going to blink first?"

Stella hesitated. She looked at Natalie, then quickly glanced around the room, and finally back at Bacham. Then she slowly began to lower her arm.

"No," shouted Natalie, struggling against Bacham's grip. "Blast him to the other side of the moon."

"I can't take that chance, your Highness," Stella answered as she dropped her arm to her side.

"A wise choice, Enchantress."

Bacham scanned the faces of everyone. The sneer on his face twitched slightly. Liam, who had been watching him intently, wondered if the faint movement he detected in Bacham's expression was a sign of his nervousness or fear.

"You're probably wondering why I called you all together," he said, making a feeble attempt at a joke.

"No one's laughing?" he asked. "Well then, I'll be more than happy to explain it to you anyway. We're here to celebrate the release from an unjust prison of the master sorcerer and leader of the Rebbercands, Tebaga."

"What are you talking about?" demanded Solveig. "Who is this Teabag person, and what do we have to do with him?"

"Tebaga," shouted Bacham. "You will NOT mock him!"

In his agitation, he had jerked his axe against the skin of Natalie's throat. A small trickle of blood ran down from the cut it made in her neck. Liam kept his eyes riveted on Bacham. The reaction to Solveig's question told him that what he had seen in Bacham's face had been fear. He hadn't expected this many of us, Liam thought. Or maybe he's worried that all he's done won't get him what he hoped would be here. Whatever it is, something has him spooked.

"Your Highness," shouted Stella as she took a tentative step forward. She glared up at Bacham.

"What do you want?" she demanded. "Why have you brought my Princess here? What do you want with her?"

"I don't want anything from her," he answered. "I only took her to convince you to do something for me. It's as simple as that."

"I will do whatever you ask. Just let her go."

Bacham regained his composure and lowered the axe, but he held on to her to keep her from getting out of his reach.

"A wise decision," he said. "Now, all you have to do is to simply break the spell and open that sarcophagus."

"I'm not sure I know..." started Stella.

"Of course you do," he cut her off. "Quite wasting my time and do as you've been told. Open it now!"

She was about to object again, as she took a few tentative steps towards the sarcophagus. She was looking back at Natalie and Bacham with her hand outstretched towards the box, uncertain about what she would do or say next. She was afraid that if she didn't at least try, Bacham would harm Natalie. She crept sideways up to the tomb. Bacham moved, pulling Natalie with him, keeping an even distance between the two of them and Stella.

As soon as Stella's hand came in contact with the box, everything was completely clear to her. A look of surprise came over her face, stunning her for a second or two. She knew what this place was; she knew what was in the sarcophagus and how it got there; and she knew what to do to release it. She turned to the box and placed both hands on the top. She lowered her head and began an incantation in a soft whisper, speaking words none of the others recognized or could understand. The box emitted a low rumble and began to vibrate.

The engraved top separated and the front and the sides slowly dropped towards the floor, falling in front of and to the sides of the base. Stella backed away, raised her hands in the air and continued the incantation. In the center was a mound of what looked like finely crushed gravel. Once the sides of the box dropped away, pieces of the gravel fell to the floor. The mound had filled nearly a third of the interior of the sarcophagus.

Everyone was staring at it waiting for something to happen.

"Where is he?" demanded Bacham. "What did she do to him? Put him back together," he shouted at Stella.

"I don't know what else to do," Stella pleaded.

"I don't believe you!" he screamed.

For a second he forgot about Natalie and released his grip on her. She was too stunned, though, to move. Bacham's grip on his axe tightened and he lifted it in the air as he turned to face Stella full on. He was shouting at her and she was pleading. Their argument was interrupted by a low scraping sound, and a blur of movement across the floor. All eyes turned to the pile of cinders. It was moving. The entire mound slid off the base of the tomb onto the floor. Gradually the pieces began to take shape from the ground upward. The stones that had scattered on the floor looked like they were being sucked back to the mound. They rose up into the air and joined the larger pile of cinders. After a few seconds, a pair of hoofed feet appeared, followed by legs that looked like those of a mountain goat.

"What trickery is this?" shouted Bacham, but he was unable to look away.

As the rubble continued to take shape, the legs became more definitive, and were followed by a distended abdomen, bulging forward. At the same time, a tail started growing in the back in the form of a snake where the legs came together. The trunk of the body followed, hunched forward like a question mark, the back covered with barbed spikes. Muscular arms appeared, cocked towards the back like chicken wings, but far more powerful. The huge shoulders led to powerfully built upper arms and then to large forearms, and ended in three talons with razor sharp claws. Bit by bit the pile of ashes became more solid, delineating a large and grotesque creature.

Finally the head took shape. It seemed too large for the body, even as it was first taking shape. The chin was long and pointed, extending outward like a bird's beak. Thick lips gave the face a snarling look. Deep-set eyes under a heavy brow made it look sinister. A large hooked nose sprouted from the center of the face and curved down almost touching the chin. The top of the head widened and was marked by extremely large ears the size and shape of conch shells on either side. Aside from the goat-like legs, there was no hair on the body whatsoever and the skin as well as the hair on its legs was a dull grey color.

Everyone, even Bacham, looked on with repulsion at the creature that took shape before them. When the reassembly had finished the gravel consolidated, filling the spider-web seams and gaps, and the entire body turned from the dull grey to blood red in color, except for the eyes, which glowed a deep and burning yellow. And then the creature sucked in a deep breath, shook its massive head, and let out a bellow. It took a staggering step forward and then turned its gaze on everyone who was looking at him.

"Who has set me free?" he asked.

The voice that resounded from the creature sounded like fingernails scratching on a chalkboard. The stench of his breath made everyone take a step backward. He lowered his head and scanned his surroundings, turning his face from right to left and back.

"Who has set me free?" he bellowed again when no one answered the first time.

Bacham overcame his shock and took a step forward. He dropped to one knee and lowered his head in supplication.

"I did, master."

"You are no Enchantress," the creature exclaimed.

He took one staggering step forward towards Bachman, who didn't change his position, but cowered back slightly.

"No, master," Bacham answered, his voice quavering slightly. "I brought that Enchantress here to break the spells that bound and imprisoned you."

He pointed at Stella. Tebaga turned to Stella and looked her over. Then he shifted his stare to her friends and then down at Natalie.

"Then you shall be rewarded," he finally said to Bacham. "Who has helped you? Was it these here in this room?"

"Those who assisted me have all been lost," Bacham answered, still not daring to look up. "They were killed by traps and curses set by the witch who imprisoned you."

Tebaga shifted his head back towards Stella and the others.

"Then these others are not your allies?" he asked, his voice booming in the large chamber; the stench of his breath fouling the air.

"No, master. They would be allies of your enemies, including this one."

He reached out and pushed Natalie forward and then he inched his way on one knee a little bit further back. Natalie took the opportunity to move further away from Bacham and joined her friends. Tebaga watched her move haltingly across the expanse, his eyes following her every move.

"Then they shall all pay the price," Tebaga said.

He took two or three jerky steps towards Stella and the others. He was still several feet away from them. He looked at the group and then waved one arm in the air in a swiping motion. Stella was pushed invisibly across the stone floor to one side.

"I'll save you for last, Enchantress."

He looked around the cavern and then finally up at the ceiling. He paused for a second, looked back at the small group and then raised one arm and waved his talons at the long, pointed stalactites that hung down. Several of them broke free and while they were dropping, he changed them into spears with jagged steel tips. As they descended, he waived his other arm at Summer, Solveig, Liam and Quinn, changing them into pigs. The four pigs began running in circles to avoid the falling shafts. The spears shifted direction, following every move of the little pigs and headed straight for their targets.

Stella reacted just in time. She quickly waved her hands. Her left hand changed her friends back to normal and her right hand converted the spears to flowers. The trajectory of the flowers stopped in mid air and they floated gently to the ground. Tebaga eyed her.

"So," he growled, "You want to play games."

He flicked his talons again without taking his eyes off Stella. The flowers began to writhe and twist as the landed on the ground. They skidded across the floor and intertwined, coming together into several large snakes. He flicked his talons again, and Stella's friends were immediately transformed into mice.

The snakes untangled themselves from one another and quickly slithered towards the mice. The mice twitched their noses and immediately sensed the danger. Stella thrust both arms forward, changing the mice back to normal and the snakes into butterflies. The butterflies flitted upward and spiraled through the air. Tebaga made a jerking motion as if irritated by this change. He looked at Stella and then back at the former mice.

He took a half step backwards and raised his head to look up as the butterflies fluttered towards the ceiling. He swept his arm in a back-handed motion and the butterflies turned into hawks, with steely eyes, their enormous wings spread wide. Their razor sharp beaks and talons glistened in the low light. Tebaga pointed a single needle-like talon at the four who had just been transformed from mice and changed them into chipmunks.

The hawks spotted the prey and began their attack dives. Just before they pounced on the unsuspecting chipmunks, Stella made a stopping motion and with a flash, the hawks turned into kittens, which landed gently on the ground. She waived her hand at the chipmunks and turned them all back to her friends.

"What's happening?" asked Quinn. "I feel very strange. I have this incredible hunger for cheese and nuts."

The magical battle between Tebaga and Stella raged on. It had focused everyone's attention on the various changes they each made to the predators and the prey. No one noticed a section of wall on the far side of the cavern as it opened up and Sean and Lochen stepped through. They had entered through a different portal than the others, and were out of the line of sight of all of them. Sean took in the situation immediately and, reaching for his slingshot, boldly stepped forward to join his friends. Lochen reached out and pulled him back, motioning for him to keep quiet as he moved silently behind a small niche in the wall.

"We may be at a better advantage here and as yet undiscovered," he whispered to Sean, "Let's take a moment to assess the situation, but keep your slingshot at the ready."

He nodded his understanding and they crouched down, peering over the edge to watch in silence. Stella and the others were to their left. A Rebbercand was on one knee and partially hidden by some kind of flattened box on a small pedestal. Between them was a strange and monstrous creature.

Tebaga growled at Stella's last spell, and with a more forceful gesture changed the kittens into two large and rabid dogs. He looked at Quinn and the others and with a flick of his wrist, changed them into rabbits. The dogs began snarling and headed for the rabbits. Sean gasped and stood up, ready to fire, but Lochen pulled him back down, again motioning to do nothing, yet.

"Trust in Stella," he told him. "She seems to be keeping the creature occupied."

Stella quickly snapped her fingers and the dogs changed into a pair of small sheep and with another snap of her fingers, she again undid the spell on her friends. She could feel her powers growing with each spell. She knew Natalie had not re-established their connection, but there was something about this room that was enhancing her abilities.

"Enough," shouted Tebaga and he threw his arm towards Stella.

A blast of light shot out from the taloned hand, lifting her in the air and slamming her against the wall. She hadn't expected a direct attack from him and she was unprepared. She heard a snap as her right arm struck the rough edge of the rock, breaking the bone in her arm just above the elbow. The pain shot through her arm, numbing it as it dropped uselessly to her side. She could feel her heightened powers start to fade.

Bacham, sensing the end was in sight and that his master would destroy this enemy, quickly decided it would not be wise for him to have withheld the mystical stone he was now holding in his hand. Unaware that he had even done it, during the exchange of spells, he had removed the stone from his pocket. He was holding it tightly in his hand and he could feel a surge of energy pulsating each time a spell was cast or broken.

As Stella labored to her feet, cradling her damaged arm, Bacham stood and took a step forward, holding the stone out as an offering.

"Master," he shouted.

Tebaga was still infuriated at being challenged so successfully by this small Enchantress. His rage was burning. He jerked his massive head, shifting his view from Stella to the voice that had dared to interrupt him. The intense glaring stare frightened Bacham to his very core. He lowered his head and raised the stone even higher. He had his arm fully extended and the stone held between his thumb and forefinger for Tebaga to clearly see. The colors of the stone were swirling radically and the light beneath the colors was sparkling.

Lochen recognized it immediately. He bent closer to Sean and whispered, "Can you hit that stone out of his hand? It's essential that it not get in the hands of that monster."

Sean nodded, stood and took careful aim.

"A piece of the pendant," Tebaga said.

His voice had changed from the threatening growl to being filled with awe. He emitted a guttural laugh that had no humor in it at all.

"A piece of the witch's pendant," he repeated. "That's what he was after."

His last comment meant nothing to those who heard it, but it was the sudden realization of all that had happened that caused him to begin laughing. When he stopped, he cocked his head slightly to one side and then jerked it back towards Stella and her friends. He thrust his arm forward at the sheep and changed them into one large black timber wolf. He looked at the others who had been changed back and forth and flicked his talons, changing them into baby fur seals.

"Enjoy your dinner," he said to the wolf.

He turned his misshapen head back to Bacham. "Give it to me," he ordered.

Bacham, too frightened to approach his master, actually stepped back a few feet. Realizing what he had done and the order he had been given, he tossed the stone to him with an erratic jerk of his arm. The stone rose in the air and was at the highpoint of its arch, in a direct line towards Tebaga. Sean let loose with his slingshot. His missile shot across the wide expanse, intersecting the path of the magical stone. The missile just barely struck the bottom of the stone, flipping it higher in the air, and changing its direction drastically.

Everyone watched as Tebaga lunged forward in a futile attempt to intercept the stone, at the same moment as its course was altered. All heads turned towards Lochen, still not seeing him, their eyes glued instead to the stone. Lochen stood up, never losing sight of the piece of the pendant as it flew into his hand. As soon as he had it he waved his other arm at the giant timber wolf.

The wolf was a few short steps away from the seals, its giant head lowered; its teeth bared. The wave of energy sent by Lochen washed over it, stopping the beast in its tracks. It slowly turned its head, spotting Lochen standing on the other side of the cavern and began moving towards him. It started slowly but its muscles rippled as it sprang into a run. As it moved, it grew even larger in size, and its fur began to change from black to white. It was as if it was walking through an invisible wall. The change in color moved from the tip of his muzzle, over his head, across his body, and to the end of his tail.

Once the transformation was complete, the wolf stopped coming at Lochen, who had remained standing, watching as the change took place. The wolf looked around, momentarily confused. It moved its eyes from Lochen to Stella, to the fur seals and then to Tebaga and Bacham. It looked back at Lochen and seemed to recognize him. Then, as if given a silent instruction, it turned and headed towards Tebaga and Bacham in a slow, easy gate, a low, threatening growl rumbling from deep inside.

Bacham looked from the wolf to Tebaga and back again. As frightened as he was of his master, the giant white wolf seemed even more ominous. With every step it took it grew in size. It never changed its pace and never deviated from its path. In a few short seconds it was towering over the both of them. Tebaga growled back at the wolf, staring back into its eyes. He turned his head towards Lochen.

"You are nothing but a simple sorcerer," he scoffed. "You think you can defeat me with your ridiculous parlor tricks?"

He turned back to the wolf and bellowed. The wolf growled back at Tebaga, unimpressed. Tebaga thrust his arm forward. A bolt of lightning shot out, striking the wolf in the center of his chest. However, instead of entering the wolf's heart, the bolt struck a strange crystal that dangled from a rawhide cord around the wolf's neck. The crystal absorbed the bolt and reflected it back on its sender.

When the surge of power was reflected off the crystal, a crack of thunder split the air, and the lightning exploded into a burst of blue light. The force lifted Tebaga and Bacham into the air and dropped them both back to the sarcophagus, where they both dissolved into a mound of ash. The box closed up, the sides and top snapping shut, sealing the sarcophagus as before, trapping them both inside.

Everyone had shielded their eyes at the explosion. When they lowered their arms, they discovered that Bacham and Tebaga were gone, imprisoned in the tomb, and the wolf had vanished.

Lochen and Sean ran over to Stella, helping her to her feet. She managed to wave her left arm and changed the seals back to her friends.

Chapter twenty-three

Summer, Solveig, Liam and Quinn, returned to their normal condition. As they went from transformation to transformation, they had been completely unaware of what was happening, not only to them, but in the battle between the demon Tebaga and Stella. They were speechless, but for only a few seconds, as they realized that Bacham and Tebaga had disappeared and were replaced by Sean and Lochen. Once the initial shock wore off, they started spewing questions left and right.

"Where did you two come from?"

"How did you get here? What happened?"

"We flew and we floated," answered Sean. "And it really stunk. Not just the flying and the floating, but us. We stunk, too."

"No kidding," answered Summer.

She had been fluttering back and forth around the heads and shoulders of everyone. When she flew next to Sean, she got a big whiff of how badly he reeked, and she backed away almost immediately, even though she was overjoyed to see him and Lochen.

"Where's that big ugly guy?"

"What happened to that Rebbercand?"

"They had another engagement," said Lochen, amused at his wit.

"Yeah," said Sean, joining in. "They were booked for a very long time."

Snickering, Lochen added, "It was a package deal. Get it? Package? They were 'packaged' together.

Natalie called a halt to all the questions and the silly answers.

"We need to take care of Stella's arm. It looks like it was broken."

"Can't she cast a spell on it and fix it herself," asked Sean.

"No," Stella answered. "We can't cast spells on ourselves. Besides that, Sea Sprites don't have those kinds of powers. But I think Lochen can probably do something. Especially with that stone he managed to take away from the Rebbercand."

"Of course," he said.

Lochen looked at the odd shaped piece of the pendant. He had been holding it tightly in his hand since he caught it, and only now was aware that he still had it. He stepped over to Stella and waved the stone over her arm.

"Should I recite some kind of incantation?" he asked.

"I think if you hold it in one hand and place your other hand over my arm, that should be enough," she answered.

He muttered a few more "of courses" and gently placed his hand on the damaged arm, while holding the stone in his other hand. A wave of heat passed from him to Stella. In a few seconds, she was able to move it again.

"It feels a little stiff," she said, "but that should wear off."

"That's it?" he asked.

She smiled at him and answered, "Yes. That's it. Were you expecting something more?"

"I'm not sure what I expected," he told her.

He shifted his gaze from her eyes to the stone in her headband. He pointed to it and asked if he could see it.

"If I may?" he asked.

Stella removed the headband from around her forehead and handed it over to him. He compared the triskelion seated in the center of the band to the piece he held in his hand. He recalled when he had first seen the triskelion. It had been worn as a pendant by Summer. When she gave it to him to place in the indentation in Sean's armband, the tiny stone had mystically enlarged to fit the setting. When the inner band was aligned with the outer band, they both increased in size, as did the triskelion once again, to fit Stella's head.

Without asking, and without Stella objecting, he pried the triskelion from the setting and held it in the palm of one hand. He had the larger stone in his other hand. Looking closely at the shape of the edges of the triskelion, it appeared as if the larger stone matched the base of the triskelion. He laid it flat in his palm and placed the larger stone right below it. As soon as they came close to each other, the stone was pulled by some invisible force and the two pieces fit perfectly together; the larger one attaching itself to the bottom opening of the triskelion. Within seconds, the two pieces melted together and became one.

"Interesting," said Lochen. "And judging from the rough edges of the triskelion, I would assume that there are two more pieces."

He could feel energy pulsating from the combined stones, and understood the tempting power contained within them. He understood Bacham's obsession with it. He then raised the armband and saw that the indentation, which had fit the triskelion so perfectly, had changed. It now mirrored the shape of the blended stone.

"Even more interesting," he said.

He handed the stone and headband back to Stella, who studied the stone before placing the band back on her head.

"I'm sure you'll take good care of this," he said. "And will certainly make much better use of it. It's better entrusted to you, I think."

Stella took it from him and held it in her hand, looking at the new, larger and different looking stone in the center.

"I hate to interrupt all this talk of stones and headbands, but we need to get back to the volcano shaft and figure a way out of here," interrupted Liam.

"That reminds me," said Summer to Lochen and Sean. "We had Stella and the stone in her headband to guide us through the mazes. Even with that, it was a bit scary. How did you two get through without getting lost?"

"It was quite simple, really," answered Lochen. "I followed the footsteps in the dirt through each doorway."

"Yeah, that sounds simple, but how did you know you weren't following the footsteps of someone who got lost?" asked Solveig.

"That's a good point. I hadn't thought of that." Lochen thought a minute. "I guess sometimes you just get lucky."

"I didn't really need to hear that," groaned Sean. "And you can't count that as saving my life, any more than all those other times."

"Is there an easier way back?" asked Quinn.

"I think I can help with that," answered Stella.

She put the headband back on her forehead and stood in the center of the cavern, looking at the five separate openings. As she was studying them, the walls and ceiling came alive with flashes of images. Everyone turned to look, seeing a rush of motion and light. A mob of hideous creatures flew across the walls – people none of them had ever seen before, that bore a strong resemblance to the gargoyles, but were distinctly different. An image of a huge double-bladed axe swept from one part of the wall, across the ceiling and down. Wings that looked uncomfortably like Summer's fluttered in the air, unattached to a body. At that sight, Summer gasped, covered her mouth with her hands, and flew back behind Quinn as if seeking protection.

A flurry of red specks covered one part of the wall and then disappeared like smoke. The image of an old crone filled their view and kept growing larger and larger, filling the walls and ceiling until it disappeared, only to be replaced by blue giants hiding under a bridge. That image was overtaken by a flash of golden light, which then turned a reddish-brown, and then to black. Through each of these images, quick and erratic vignettes of each of the observers swirled in and around them all.

The last thing any of them saw was not as clear as any of the other images. It was more like the image left on the eye's retina by a burst of light. It was a murky glow of five towers – each one higher than one in front of it. It was surrounded by an eerie darkness. The tallest tower, however, stood out, burning with a blue and green flame. That last image slowly faded away, and the walls and ceiling gradually dimmed and returned to the black they had been before.

"Blubber on a biscuit," announced Quinn – the first one to finally speak. "What was all that? And where did it come from?"

"I don't know," answered Stella, finding her own voice with difficulty. "I've always had to concentrate on conjuring images. That one came from nowhere."

"Did you recognize any of it?" asked Natalie. "Was any of that from past events?"

"No," said Stella. "I've never seen any of it before. I have no idea what any of those images means."

"Well, look at the bright…" Lochen started.

"DON'T say it!" Sean cut him off. "I don't want to hear that any of that has a bright side. What is it with you and all those bright sides?"

"I was only going to point out that since each of us appeared in those images, and since Stella has no impression that those were past images, it's safe to assume we get out of here – eventually."

Before anyone could say anything more, the smallest of the five openings started making a grating noise. It was opening on its own, spreading wider and wider, revealing a single, straight, short passageway. Stella crept forward, peering into the opening and then, straightening her shoulders, marched ahead. The others all followed, and in less than a dozen steps, had returned to the pool at the bottom of the shaft.

"Wow," said Quinn. "We should have thought of that the first time."

"We should have had the combined stones in that headband the first time," said Summer. "That would have made things a lot easier."

"Can that thing get us out of here and back home?" asked Solveig, pointing to the headband.

"No," said Stella. "With or without this stone, I have no powers to transport even one of us that far, let alone all eight of us. I'm not sure I have an answer for that dilemma."

"Lochen," Solveig said, still pursuing options. "How did you and Sean catch up to us so fast? We had to be days ahead of you."

He looked a bit sheepishly in Sean's direction, and said, "We had the use of a transporter stone for much of the trip, but I'm afraid it slipped from my hand at the instance of our sudden arrival in Nohkmar Cambin."

"Oh, man," interjected Sean. "You mean some pig is probably flying all over the place?"

Lochen turned back to Solveig and pleaded, "Don't ask. It's not a particularly pleasant story."

Summer had flown to the top of the shaft and reported back that the sea had receded. The storm had passed and the island mountain had risen out of the sea. It was only then that any of them noticed that the cascade of water down the central shaft had ended. During that time Quinn and Liam had been examining every inch of the cavern.

"Quinn and I have gone around this entire cavern," reported Liam. "We haven't found any other openings except for the tunnel that the stream runs under. We even dug through all the wreckage looking for some way out."

"Yeah," said Quinn. "There's not a lot there except for a bunch of different ships all broken to pieces. There was this one – it was a slave galley. There must be a hundred oars. Can you believe it? Someone chained people to benches and made them row this gi-normous boat. And there's an old sailing ship with tons of rope."

"Keep looking," said Natalie. "There must be a way out of here. Can we tie the rope together and find a way to climb out?"

"I doubt it," said Liam. "Even if we could, we'd still be stuck on the island."

"Faerie dust," shouted Solveig. "Summer, couldn't you sprinkle all of us with faerie dust?"

"I could," she answered, "But it might not last long enough to get you to the top of the opening, and even if it did, it wouldn't last long enough to get us back to land."

"Could you fly back and get help?" Solveig persisted.

"Not that far," she answered, disappointed that she couldn't do anything to help. "I wish we all could fly. We could float up that shaft like balloons and fly all the way home."

At that comment, an idea sprung into Liam's head.

"That's an excellent idea," he said.

He ran over to one pile of wreckage and then to another and finally back to the group.

"I think I can make it work. Summer and Natalie, find as much sail material as you can, and bring it all here. Sean, you and Solveig find as much rope as you can and bring it over to where that old slave galley is. Lochen and Stella, see if you can find wheels and gears – anything that looks like cogs. Quinn, come with me; you may have to do some heavy lifting. We'll gather whatever railings and spars I can find, and get things started."

They all did as they were asked, without understanding in the least what it was all for, scattering to different areas of the cavern. Quinn and Liam dug around in the slave galley, with Liam directing their efforts. He had Quinn pull out three of the slave benches and move them to a central location. After moving the benches, Quinn went back to the galley and gathered up about two dozen oars that were still in usable condition, while Liam looked at remnants of railings, selecting some and discarding others.

As Quinn was bringing one of the loads of oars back to the building site, he saw a piece of the galley's name as it had been painted across the bow: *The Cataroon*. All that was left were the last four letters. Something about the name made him pause. He thought of all the people who had been forced to row the large craft and that they were all now lost. Their friends and families had no knowledge of whatever happened to them. It didn't seem right. Someone should remember them – if not individually, at least collectively. On a simple impulse, he picked it up and took it back with the oars.

While Sean and Solveig were searching for ropes, they found more than they could ever need among the wreckage of an ancient schooner called the Salamander. It was all still in excellent condition, having avoided the repeated soakings every time the water poured in from the sea above. They pulled it from the rigging and the sails, hauling huge coils of it back to where Liam was working.

When they were taking the last coil of rope from the schooner, Solveig tossed over the mostly rotted wood of the transom. A large piece broke off and landed at Sean's feet.

"Sorry," she yelled to him. "I didn't think the wood was eaten through that much. It's a good thing we got all the rope off first."

Sean bent down and ran his hand across the schooner's nameplate on the transom. Most of it crumbled at his touch. When the dust cleared all that had remained intact was the middle of the ship's name. He considered this piece for some reason to be a good luck charm, so he picked it up and brought it back with the rope.

Summer and Natalie found most of the fabric they needed from the debris made up by the West Wind. Even though the little ship had only one small sail, Liam had used the same fabric to cover the hull. A lot of it had been cut through when the ship landed, but it was all they could find. The pieces of sail that remained on all the other derelict ship had been torn to shreds or had rotted over time.

Once they had as much as they could salvage, Summer looked almost tearfully at the little boat that had served them so well and had taken them on an incredible journey. Natalie saw the expression of sadness on her face.

"What's wrong?" she asked. "You look like you've lost a good friend."

"I have," she answered. "When we – Solveig, Liam and me - started out on this little ship, we were coming from the Swamp. We had just finished adjusting these sensor things that Liam had installed. This was his latest invention and he was really proud of it. He said he hoped to take it out on the Cerulean Sea to give it a real test, so on the spur of the moment decided to take a little vacation. We headed for the open sea. We were all so excited. It was the most fun I think I've ever had.

There was something about that day that made me feel really close to the two of them – and to realize how much all of you mean to me. We had no idea what was coming in the days ahead, but it was fun while it lasted. Liam built this boat, and it kept us safe in some really bad situations. It seems wrong to cannibalize it and leave it here."

Natalie didn't know what to say. She wanted to do something to console her dear friend. She looked at the pile of junk the little boat had become. Everything was in a heap.

"What was the boat's name," she asked, looking at the broken pieces.

"The *West Wind*," answered Summer.

Natalie looked around for the ship's nameplate. There were chunks from the ship everywhere. All she could find were the first two letters of the name. She reached down and picked up the jagged hunk of wood, turned to Summer with a smile and suggested adding to the material they were assigned to gather.

"Who knows," she said. "Maybe we can use this somehow. And even if we can't, keep it as a souvenir of better times."

Lochen offered to Stella that he thought the best place to find the things Liam had asked the two of them to collect would be found in the scow in which he and Sean had traveled.

"I must prepare you, though," he advised as they were walking over to the ship, "the odor might be a bit pungent. Sean was particularly affected by the aroma, and I have to admit, it was at times even difficult for me to tolerate."

"It can't be any worse than how you smell," she answered, making sure not to get too close to him.

Lochen looked a bit shocked, stopped and sniffed his clothing. Pulling his head back sharply, he said, "I guess you're right. I hadn't realized it was lingering quite so long or so strongly."

They dug around through the garbage that had scattered over a large area due to the crash. Stella was amazed, not only by the stench, but by the numbers and types of things that people threw away. They found several wheels and a number of cogs and pulleys, some of which were apparently used to haul large and heavy objects onto and off of the scow.

As they were headed back, Lochen tripped over a random piece of rubbish. He looked down and saw a piece of the scow's nameplate that had cracked in the crash landing and had broken completely when he tripped over it. All that was left were just a couple of letters.

"As bad as this boat smelled, it did save our lives," he mused. "It would be a shame to turn our backs on such a talisman."

Stella smiled at his musings, and added, "We can never have too many good luck tokens – as long as it doesn't stink."

He picked up the remaining piece of the nameplate and sniffed it. Finding no disagreeable odor, he brought it with him.

By the time everything was delivered, Liam had already built a rough framework for a tube-like structure out of the railings he had found. They had been tied together with the smaller, thinner ropes, and Summer sprinkled a little faerie dust on the bindings to help them hold. Then Liam covered the shell with the fabric that had been rescued from the *West Wind*. He had been able to do a little bit of stitching, using some of the rope he had unraveled and a fish hook that Lochen discovered by sitting on it. He was able to cover most of the hull, but not quite all of it.

He had Quinn place the benches inside. One was placed on either side of the construction and a third one was secured near the back, perpendicular to the other two. He then assembled the cogs, gears and pulleys to a makeshift pedal system, connected to two short, but thick, masts. He attached two large wheels horizontally to the tops of the masts. Between the two short masts he erected a longer one with a wide crosspiece to which he attached a sail.

"Now I need a little magic," he said to Lochen. "Can you make holes in the outside edges of the wheels just wide enough to fit the oar handles in?"

"Gladly," answered Lochen. "How many do you want?"

Liam told him and he did as he was asked. With Quinn's help, he fit the oars into the holes, slanting the oar blades all at the exact same angle.

Sean commented, "There's no back end for this thing. Won't that present a problem?"

"There wasn't enough sail material to cover the whole thing," Liam answered. "And it shouldn't be a problem unless we end up in the water."

"I have an idea," said Stella.

She took the piece of the nameplate Lochen had brought back and added it to the piece she had seen Natalie and Summer pick up. When she asked if there were any others, two more pieces were added. She waved her arm – now that it wasn't so stiff anymore – and the various pieces of the nameplates and transoms of the ships that had been collected started moving and blended into a single piece. It formed one, solid board that fit exactly into the opening.

"Perfect," said Liam, securing it to the back of the vehicle. "It's finished."

"Well that's good to know, but what is it," Sean asked. "And what's it supposed to do?"

"I don't know exactly what it is," answered Liam, "but I'm pretty sure I can get this thing to fly and carry us out of here."

"Yeah, right," Sean laughed. "No. Seriously. What is it supposed to do?"

"I am serious," Liam answered. "Unless someone has a better idea. If not, then there's no time like the present. Anyone wishing to depart, please climb aboard."

They all looked a bit skeptical, but in spite of any doubts they might have had, they were all more than ready to leave, and they all climbed in. Liam sat at the controls and started pedaling. The gears began to move, slowly at first, until eventually the twin masts began to turn and the oars began to spin.

"Actually," he said when the craft had not yet left the ground, "I could probably use a little faerie dust."

"I don't think all the dust I can generate is going to make this thing fly," answered Summer. "It's too big and way too heavy."

"I just need enough to kick start it."

Not believing any of this was going to work, Summer flew from stem to stern and from starboard to port, covering the odd craft with as much faerie dust as she could. After a few seconds, the small structure lifted off the ground. The oar blades picked up speed and added to the lift. It drifted into the shaft of the volcano, which had previously served as a giant drain, and rose towards the top. Once the ship cleared the crater's rim, the sail caught the wind, and the craft moved forward. Liam set the direction for home. Everyone was cheering as Liam pulled the sail and turned the ship to the north as they soared over the ocean.

"I love it," shouted Solveig. "Have you decided on a name for your newest invention?"

"I never gave it any thought," Liam answered.

Quinn turned toward the back and bent over the end of the ship to read the letters that had been grafted together: *We* **dg** *ama* ROON.

"It has a name," Quinn declared. "It's the Wedgamaroon."

And so began the maiden flight of the Wedgamaroon.

ABOUT THE AUTHOR

Richard Reda spent most of his life working for various agencies and Departments in the Federal Government. He believes this gave him a solid foundation for writing fantasy and fiction, so much so that he was encouraged to return after retirement to write some more. He lives with his wife in Manassas, Virginia, where he retired – the first time.

The Quest of Eight series originated as bed time stories for his grandchildren. As the grandchildren got older and the bed time stories got longer, it was suggested to him that he write them down. So he did. One, however, was not enough. Follow the saga in Part Four: The Race to Virkio.

www.ingramcontent.com/pod-product-compliance
Lightning Source LLC
Chambersburg PA
CBHW060150260626
47160CB00001B/196